SILENCE THAT IS NOT GOLDEN

TIBBIE S. KPOSOWA, PH.D.

TABAY PUBLICATIONS
P.O. BOX 19393
CINCINNATI, OHIO 45219-0393

SILENCE THAT IS NOT GOLDEN

By Tibbie S. Kposowa, Ph.D.

Editorial Advisers: Jerry Cline-Bailey, Ph.D.
John K. Kalubi, Ph.D.

Artist: Dave Warren

TABAY PUBLICATIONS
P.O. Box 19393
Cincinnati, Ohio 45219

Library of Congress Catalog Card Number: 95-94743

ISBN 1-887935-00-2

Published by Tabay Publications
First Printing 1995
Published in the United States of America

DISCLAIMER
The story of this novel as well as the characters and their activities are fictitious. Any resemblance to persons, living or dead, or actual episodes, is purely coincidental.

DEDICATION

This book is dedicated to my mother, Selina Kposowa. My success in school was due in large part to her kindness, love and devotion. I thank her for the moral support she gave my father as he worked to provide me with the opportunity to acquire a good education.

CHAPTER ONE

Mrs. Satta Lamboi stopped work for the day at exactly half past four in the afternoon. On coming out of her office building she sat on a wooden bench by the sidewalk and waited patiently for her husband. Her sharp dark blue-and-white striped African dress made her look very beautiful. The tailor that had made the dress was reputed to be one of the best in Bassaya, the capital of the country. He had made sure that the style matched her five-foot-eight-inch well-shaped figure. This attire clearly showed that the young accountant had excellent taste in dress.

Satta normally waited in her office for the driver to notify her that her husband, Hon. Misalie Lamboi, Minister of Health, was waiting for her downstairs. But today she decided to wait in front of the building. It was never boring whenever she decided to do this because the world of that busy and colorful downtown street was always teeming with life. What she enjoyed watching most were the transactions between hawkers and clients. As she watched the haggling over prices, which normally took place before a sale is concluded, she would smile, chuckle or frown depending on the outcome of the deal. Once in a while she would laugh if the interaction was funny enough to warrant it.

This afternoon happened to be the turn of the twenty-nine-year-old accountant to do business with one of the hawkers, an older teenager, who wanted to sell her a copy of *The People's Voice*. The prices of newspapers being fixed, there was no need for any negotiation. The boy's goal was simply to convince her to buy the paper. But since she knew that a copy would be waiting for her at home, she declined. The relentless hawker then took a step further to convince her by putting down his load of newspapers at her feet and picking up a copy of the paper to display to her. The headline she saw made her to decide to buy at once and not wait till she reached home. The news dealt with an issue that was of concern to her husband.

The front-page article was about AIDS - Acquired Immune Deficiency Syndrome. AIDS was the ominous disease which the government was unwilling to deal with publicly. This disease was no doubt a threat to the nation's health care system; but the government was quite reluctant to develop a policy for controlling it. Although over fifty people were already receiving treatment for it there were no indications that the Ministry of Health was concerned about educating the public about an infectious disease that could easily spread and get out of control. Such a nonchalant attitude was unlike that of the neighboring African countries whose leaders had brought the issue to the forefront and had appropriated funds specially for the building of many AIDS clinics across their countries.

The article was written by Ali Saffa, editor of *The People's Voice* and one of the foremost critics of the government. Satta was anxious to read it because the politician that Ali and other critics had held responsible for the neglect of the AIDS threat was her husband. They claimed that the Minister of Health was reluctant to bring the AIDS issue to the forefront because that would adversely affect the tourist industry. At the heart of this promising industry was the Golden Complex - a huge ultra-modern tourist complex - standing on a sandy beach ten miles outside Bassaya. The government's concern, the critics insisted, was that a highly publicized AIDS policy would give the impression that an AIDS epidemic was imminent. That could scare away many potential tourists thereby reducing considerably the huge profits that the Golden Complex was expected to generate. In sum, Ali portrayed Hon. Lamboi as a health minister who took more interest in tourism than in health matters.

Satta's concentration was focussed on this article when her husband arrived in a Mercedes Benz, the official ministerial car. The driver got out, greeted her politely and opened the door for her to get in. Moving a bit closer to kiss Hon. Lamboi on the left cheek she greeted him warmly.

"So, darling, how are you?"

"Very well, and you?"

"Great! Just great! It was a busy but fruitful day."

"You are in such a good mood," said the wife. "What did you and your staff accomplish today?"

"Two things," he replied with a smile. "First, I concluded plans for our vacation in London. I was able to contact some relatives there by telephone. The secretary who made our reservations told me that we shall get our tickets tomorrow. Why should I not be in a good mood for a care-free vacation?"

"I am surprised that the arrangement went that fast," said Satta. "I can hardly wait to have some good time. What was your second accomplishment?"

"I was at the Ministry of Tourism to view the new set of advertisements on the Golden Complex. You know that the senior staff of my ministry had collaborated with theirs in their production. The great news is that the airing of these advertisements on radio and television will start today. Hopefully tonight you will see on television the one in which my talents as a former distinguished soccer player are featured. Darling, the country has not forgotten to honor its former national soccer captain! The advertisements will also appear in international magazines next week. These will be aimed at foreign tourists."

At this point the driver interrupted the conversation by informing his boss that the car needed fuel. Hon. Lamboi took out his wallet and gave him some money. They continued their conversation.

"Have you read what your critics are saying about your handling of the AIDS issue and your role as Minister of Health in the promotion of tourism?" asked the wife quietly.

"Oh yes, I have." he replied with a smile. "I have already read the article that Ali Saffa wrote in today's edition of his paper. Ali is a controversial journalist who misinterprets the position of the government on AIDS. Many of the advertisements including the one in which I was featured are about the excellent facilities and services that the Golden Complex has to offer. Ali is criticizing the particular one that claims that tourists who come to our country would enjoy their vacation in an almost AIDS-free country. Since I am the Minister of Health I was asked to collaborate in its production. As you will see in that advertisement tonight or tomorrow, tourists are being invited to come to vacation in a land where the fear of contracting HIV is minimal at the worst."

"But, darling, the Golden Complex is an excellent enterprise that is already making profits," said the wife with some impatience in her voice. "Since the current advertisements are attracting a lot of customers, we do not need to talk about AIDS in promoting it. In fact it sounds strange to mention AIDS in an advertisement on tourism."

"There is no doubt that the Golden Complex is a marvel of modern architectural design," said Hon. Lamboi. "Tourists who come to enjoy its facilities are most likely to remember it also for the excellence of its many services. But since our neighbors are also putting up excellent facilities, we deemed it necessary to mention AIDS because we have fewer AIDS cases than they. Many tourists are likely to avoid countries in which the disease is rampant. To win the competition for tourists we have to use anything that is in our favor."

"I do not think we need the AIDS advertisement because the Golden Complex can shine by itself like a gem," said the wife. "The tactic of the AIDS advertisement in based on fear. It gives the impression that the neighboring countries are so infested with HIV that any tourists that go there do so at their own risk. Such a tactic is repugnant to me. I hope that there is truth in your claims."

"There is absolute truth in our claims," said Mr. Lamboi. "The evidence was produced last month by *The Free Observer*, the national paper that normally says good things about this country. When we get home I will give you a copy of the edition where the editor gives a summary of the report of the World Health Organization on AIDS. I have the full report in my office but since that is a big volume, the concise and excellent summary of it given in this newspaper will suffice. This comparative study shows that our country has the lowest number of AIDS cases in this part of the African continent. That's the record that a Minister of Health should be proud of. The disease is under control."

"Who is controlling it?" asked the wife. "You do not have an AIDS policy."

"We do eagerly treat patients that have contracted HIV," said the husband. "Early treatment is one good way of controlling diseases."

"Misalie, treatment of patients does not mean that an AIDS policy exists," said the wife. "According to Ali Saffa, an AIDS policy will involve not only the opening of AIDS clinics as other countries have done but also the education of the masses of the people about the disease. Prevention should be the main goal of a good AIDS policy. The kinds of advertisements you have told me about make me believe Mr. Saffa's claim that you are ignoring the AIDS issue in order not to scare away tourists."

"I do not think that your criticism and that of Mr. Saffa are fair," said the husband in a defensive tone of voice. "If, as the WHO report has shown, there are much fewer AIDS cases in this country than in many others, why make a big deal about the disease? Is it not enough that our few patients are receiving good treatment?"

"No, it is not enough because public education is the best way to minimize the spread of HIV," said Satta. "I am surprised at your interpreting the report of the WHO to mean that our country is almost AIDS-free. In today's article Ali does make mention of that report. He claims that it is not meant to encourage or applaud African countries that have fewer AIDS cases. On the contrary, it is meant first, to inform them that a dangerous disease has penetrated their borders, and second, to make them aware of the strains it can put on their health care systems if no drastic measures are taken to deal with it. Darling, my belief is that you are actually putting into wrong use statistical reports that have been provided by a reputable world organization to help each African country deal effectively with a coming emergency."

"Trust me, darling, that AIDS will not spread as quickly as Mr. Saffa predicts," said the husband. "We should not listen to such a prophet of doom. We shall continue giving excellent treatment to those who contract HIV. But at this time the capital invested in the Golden Complex is huge. I have to help the president of the country in his appeal that everyone contribute to its success. If this giant economic project collapses, we shall be in big trouble."

When the car stopped in front of his ministerial residence which was located in one of the most affluent parts of town, the driver stepped out and opened the doors. The couple got out and went inside. After dinner they sat down on a sofa and relaxed in front of the television set. The eyes of the thirty-five year-old husband were virtually glued to the set anxiously awaiting the advertisements they had discussed. He was quite confident that his wife would love them. But as it turned out, she did not change her mind about the one dealing with AIDS even after viewing it. It was the first advertisement that appeared.

"As I had said earlier, darling, I do not like this advertisement," she said. "There is no need to link tourism with a health issue of this kind. The assumption here is that tourists have more fun in nations that are free of HIV. This is a false assumption. Although the disease exists in industrialized countries, more tourists flock to them than to ours. The number of tourists depends on the quality and kinds of tourist facilities that a country has."

"The assumption may be wrong but in this case it is good for the promotion of our tourist business," said the husband. "Let's give this advertisement a chance to see if it can help us win the competition for tourists. The slogan 'almost AIDS-free' is what we are using to beat our neighbors."

"If we do not educate the public about this disease we shall one day regret the consequences of keeping quiet about it," said the wife. "People will best protect themselves if they are well informed about the ways to avoid contracting the virus. The 'AIDS-free' slogan is pregnant with the kind of ignorance that could lead to tragedy. If you and your president were wise you would replace it with the slogan that prevention is a better alternative to healing. But how can you? Your concern is to attract tourists?"

As they debated this issue the advertisement featuring the husband appeared. The Ministry of Tourism had decided to feature Hon. Misalie Lamboi because the handsome politician was a former captain of the national soccer team. The talent he had displayed on the field had made him a national hero. Featured in the advertisement was the highest point of his athletic career when he scored the only goal in a fiercely contested international championship match against one of the neighboring countries. Of course, the Golden Complex and its excellent facilities were also vividly displayed. Like Misalie, this tourist complex was portrayed as a victor among tourist institutions.

As this advertisement was being aired, Hon. Lamboi moved forward in his chair as if he needed to get closer in order to see better. The wife watched quietly but when it was over she looked so pleased that she kissed and congratulated him.

"So, darling, what do you think of this advertisement?" he asked proudly.

"It is very nice," she replied. "It is very appropriate for the nation to honor you that way. I hope that it does some good for the tourist industry."

After this reply she became quiet pretending to be concentrating on the television program that was being aired. There was something about the advertisement just seen that made her sad. It was on the day that that famous international match was played that she met her husband who was then only a university student. The match symbolized the beginning of a relationship that cost her her happiness as time went on. She found out the hard way that winning the heart of a very handsome national star was not the best of luck. Her sweetheart became so popular that many young women fell in love with him. What made Satta's task of making a true love connection difficult was that the man also took full advantage of his popularity by fooling around with the most beautiful of these women. So although in the end she was the one that the soccer captain got married to, she had to make a great effort to control his promiscuity. It was one thing to win the prize but another to enjoy it alone.

Although Hon. Lamboi responded to the advances of many beautiful women, he was confident that when it came to deciding about marriage, fun based merely on sensual pleasure was not a criterion to be considered. Being a clever man, he knew that a good homemaker was what mattered the most. His decision to select Satta was based on his conviction that she was the loving and conscientious kind that could make him the best home.

During the course of their courtship Satta's friends had predicted that her fiance's promiscuity could result in marital infidelity in the future. In their private conversations with her they had referred to him as a womanizer in order to discourage her from continuing the relationship. However, she was so much in love that she ignored all warnings. Regarding life as a struggle for what one wants, she followed Misalie all the way to the altar hoping that one day he would settle down. But as it turned out, he did not.

Satta became sad after seeing that soccer advertisement because it triggered memories that she would rather forget. The great skills of the soccer player shown in the advertisement were definitely good for promoting tourism but for her they pointed to something else. They reminded her of a failed marriage in which she had endured a lot of suffering.

The husband, on the other hand, so much enjoyed the advertisement that he felt like waiting until it came around again. It represented the greatest moment of his career as a soccer player. In addition to this, it brought memories of good times including the ones he had spent with other women. So, unlike the wife, this advertisement put him in an elated mood.

"I am reminded about the good old days," said the husband, laughing mildly. "I wish I can recapture them. The advertisement gives me a nostalgic feeling."

"Those were terrible days for me," said the wife with irritation. "I am glad that they are gone."

At this point the wife got up and went into the bedroom. She did not want to have a conversation about a past life she had not enjoyed. She wondered sometimes whether winning the battle was worth it.

On the eve of their departure for Britain, Satta and her husband went to say goodbye to Mrs. Judith Lansana, Satta's mother. On the way they discussed their plan to have a child after their return from vacation. Since that would be their first child, Satta had yearned a lot for the day she would hold it in her hands.

"If things work out as planned, I hope to be a little under thirty-one years of age when I get my first child," she said.

"That will not be bad for a career-oriented woman who had decided to first get a good education," said the husband. "If you were destined to be strictly a housewife you would have got married at an earlier age. By now you would be busy raising two or more children."

"Darling, that is true," she said. "Since I have spent the early part of my life working on a career, I am now going to spend much of the rest raising children. My grandmother who holds our traditional belief that women should bear children at an earlier age has constantly urged that I hurry up and start having them."

"You are young enough to have as many children as you want," said the husband. "With a good education and a secure job, you can afford to handle the financial responsibility of raising them."

"I will of course never catch up with my elder sister Miriam who has several children now," said the wife. "I hear that she is very proud of that achievement."

"What's the pride for?" asked the husband. "Since your sister was bright in high school, she could have embarked on higher education after graduation. But she immediately started having children with a man who has a beautiful body but an undisciplined mind."

This comment made both of them to laugh. Satta's elder sister already had five children. Although she was brilliant she got married after completing secondary school and started having children. Unlike Satta, she was never able to make use of her potential to become successful in life. The responsibility of taking care of the children did not allow her to do well in a social system where success came mainly from academic achievement.

Miriam's decision to have children that early in life was at first lauded by Musu Lansana, their grandmother. Since Musu did not have any formal education she held the traditional belief that once girls became adults they should join the *sande* secret society, get married and have children. But their mother Judith, a well educated secretary who was more in favor of pursuing higher education before settling down to have children, was not pleased with Miriam's decision. She lamented her decision and complained bitterly after the first two children were born saying that her daughter's bright mind had gone to waste. To make matters worse Miriam's husband who had a good education and a lucrative job was completely irresponsible. He was an alcoholic. But Musu, who was quite satisfied with the two grandchildren, gradually calmed down her daughter Judith by promising to take care of Miriam's children while she studied at the university. But this plan of pursuing higher education did not work because Miriam's financial responsiblity started to increase. First, the husband was relieved of his duties for going to work drunk several times a month. Thereafter, they had three more children which displeased even the grandmother who had been thrilled about the two children. Miriam struggled terribly although the grandmother who was a farmer regularly sent food for her from Palahun, the village where she resided.

Miriam's problems eventually made both the mother and grandmother view favorably Satta's decision to have children after completing her studies. Musu of course still maintained her traditional belief in having children at an early age, but in order to please her daughter Judith she encouraged Satta to take advantage of the scholarship that was offered to her to attend a university in England. On completing her first degree, she returned home and got married to Hon. Misalie Lamboi. But even after this achievement she did not start having children immediately because the company that had sponsored her education encouraged her to undergo an extensive practical training that kept her very busy for two more years.

The plan to get a child sounded like the next logical step to take after achieving a good education and securing a good job. This plan was to be carried out after a care-free two-week vacation in England. In fact this issue of children came up during that visit to Judith's place. Musu who had come from Palahun in Tilasa District was visiting her daughter at that time.

"So, is everything ready for the flight?" asked Judith.

"Yes, mother," replied Satta. "We are leaving tomorrow."

"My granddaughter, how long is your trip?" asked Musu.

"The country we are going to is hundreds of miles away and the trip is by air," replied Satta.

"My granddaughter, may God go with you," said Musu. "I will keep on praying for you until you return safely."

"When I return I will come and see you," said Satta.

"Please do so as soon as you arrive," said the grandmother. "You may meet Miriam in Palahun. We are expecting her next week. Since this is harvest time, she is coming to get some food for the children."

"Mother, without your help Miriam cannot survive at all," said Judith. "Her husband does not really care for the children."

"I had asked her to come and live with me in the village so that she could raise her children there," said Musu. "She had declined the offer. This made me conclude that she is not impressed by the low cost of living in Palahun."

"Mother, there is no way Miriam would allow herself to be called a villager," said Judith. "She won't leave a big town for a village even if she starves."

"Well, look at what life in the city has done to her," said Musu. "Her husband's lifestyle is destroying the family."

"That is true because none of the people her husband associates with could be referred to as genuine friends," said Judith. "Instead of advising him to get a cure for his alcoholism, they keep on drinking with him. Most of the time they drink at his expense. But despite this tough life, Miriam prefers to reside here."

"I pray that someday, they will decide to end their misery by moving to an environment where they can afford to take care of their children," said the grandmother. "Fortunately, my granddaughter Satta will not have to struggle like that when she bears children. She already has the means to support them."

"That is true but she now has to start thinking seriously about having her first child," said Judith.

At this point Hon. Lamboi who had been quietly listening as he sipped his soft drink felt like saying something. He knew that his in-laws wanted to hear his view about the topic being discussed.

"We can hardly wait to have that first child," he said. "Satta has now got all the education she had dreamed about."

"How soon will you start working on such a plan?" asked the grandmother.

"Immediately we return from vacation," said the husband.

"This news makes me very happy," said Musu. "May God grant your wishes. This is what I had always yearned for. Miriam's problems made me decide to give Satta a break until she acquired the means of supporting children. I will now go to my village in happiness knowing that in a year or two I will hold a grandchild in my hands. Let's pray now that God will grant the child."

"Grandmother, I had really wanted all these years to have a child," said Satta. "My desire to have a good education had delayed that plan. But now that formal education is behind me, I am anxious to start having children."

At this point the grandmother got up and hugged Satta and her husband. She was too overjoyed to hide her feelings. She thanked them for what she referred to as the wisest decision they had made since they got married. The issue of children dominated the rest of the conversation that evening. The grandmother narrated some stories about children. It was as if she was motivating them to do something that they very much detested.

The following day Hon. Lamboi and his wife boarded the plane for London. Since the trip was uneventful they slept most of the way. When they reached their destination they were met at the airport by friends and relatives who gave a dinner party in their honor the following Saturday. The day after such a pleasurable occasion turned out to be unpleasant because Hon. Lamboi experienced a stomach ache that forced him to see a doctor.

The medication he was given immediately relieved his pain but he was asked to undergo a series of medical tests including a blood test. The doctor told them to return for the results of the tests in a few days.

The couple relaxed at home for the rest of that day but went shopping on Monday. Since they knew the city well they had no problem finding their way to the stores. Among the many items bought were toys, baby clothes and a crib. This was in preparation for the child they planned to have.

"Darling, don't you think that it is unwise to shop now since I am not yet pregnant?" asked the wife as they entered a store for children.

"Not at all, darling," replied the husband with a smile. "It is better to shop ahead of time. I am confident that we shall soon have a child."

"What about the sex of the child?" asked the wife. "It's not advisable to shop without knowing whether it will be a boy or a girl?"

"Do not worry, darling," he replied with a broad smile. "At present we shall buy items that can be used by either sex.

The rest will be bought after the birth of the child."

Although this vacation went well, it did not have a pleasant ending. When they went to the doctor's office for the results of the tests on the morning of their departure for Bassaya, they received shocking news that glued them to their seats for over twenty minutes - - the blood test indicated that the husband had contracted HIV! Seeing that the couple was shocked by the news, the doctor excused himself and left the room. He wanted to give them time to compose themselves. But they were still in shock when he returned later to talk with them. Their reaction did not surprise him since he had in the past given such terrible news to couples. He nevertheless decided to give them some psychological counseling and suggested that the wife's blood be tested too.

After the counseling session, Satta decided against having the blood test done in London. She told the doctor that since they had to leave that day, it would be more convenient to have the test done in Bassaya."

The return trip was a very sad one. Hon. Lamboi was so distracted by the terrible news that he did not pay attention to the sights on the way to the airport. He meditated quietly on a disease for which no cure was known to exist. The wife who was restless focussed on the familiar sights of London. She looked around nostalgically as she thought about those good old days when she was a carefree student there. Those promising days pointed to a happier life in the company of a handsome husband and beautiful children. She was now certain that she would not live such a life. As the plane took off she declared that they were outward bound to a homeland where their lifestyle would no longer be the same.

Unpleasant thoughts continued to dominate the thoughts of both Mr. and Mrs. Lamboi until it was announced hours later that the plane was now approaching Bassaya. Not wanting to delve into such an emotional topic before arriving home, they had said very little to each other. The husband had insisted that any verbal interaction about it would be more constructive and productive if it were done peacefully in the privacy of their home.

The couple was received at the airport by rejoicing relatives including Judith and Michael, the younger brother that followed Hon. Lamboi. Both husband and wife pretended to be happy because they did not want anyone to know about their tragedy. The husband had suggested that they first seek a second opinion about the matter before divulging the information to the public.

It was when they were left to themselves later that evening that they had the first serious conversation about the bad news they had brought with them. As they talked they were reminded about the embarrassment and hard times that lay ahead of them. One of the advertisements on the Golden Complex appeared on television. It was the one which featured the husband as a great soccer player.

"That is all over now," said Hon Lamboi, pointing at the television screen. "Everything displayed on that screen would have mattered two weeks ago. But soon HIV will steal the vigor and agility of the hero featured in that advertisement. The hardest part of all this is that this advertisement is going to be aired very many times. It will keep on reminding me of my tragedy."

"Darling, let the advertisement keep on running," said the wife who had all this time been trying to compose herself. "It displays you at your best. Since you had in the past made this nation a regional champion, it is appropriate for the public to honor you. Champions advertise products that producers are proud of. In this case the product is the Golden Complex, probably the biggest monument in the country."

"I hope that you are fully aware of what AIDS does to people," said the husband. "If I develop the disease, the strong and vibrant body displayed on that screen will start withering away very slowly."

"I know a lot about AIDS, of course," said the wife. "But the advertisement will make people to remember you as a once vibrant achiever and hero. You did not only excel on the soccer field but also in the university where you graduated with honors. You became a cabinet minister at the age of thirty-two. So, darling, do not despair. We are going to examine all the options available to us. We shall seek a second opinion and also enquire the best treatment for your problem."

"In retrospect I should have avoided talking to you about seeking a second opinion," said the husband. "Since that British doctor is very competent, there is no need for a second opinion."

"There is no harm in seeking such opinion either," said Satta. "Sometimes mistakes are made. Moreover, he had suggested that I too be tested for the virus. So we shall go together so that you can be retested."

"If I were you I would not have my blood tested," said the husband. "Why would you want to know whether you have contracted the virus. You are better off not knowing. Look at all the mental suffering that I am going to go through as a result of my having learned that I have such a dreadful virus in by body."

"I am going to have my blood tested," said the wife. "What you say implies that happiness can be derived from ignorance. It suggests that when a parent dies the small, innocent child should be regarded as happy on the grounds that it does not know about the tragedy. I am experienced enough to know that happiness originating from my not knowing that I have a deadly virus in my body is worthless. You should realize, darling, that what a person does not know can still kill him. Thus if he drinks a deadly poison without knowing it, he will meet the same fate as the person who knowingly drinks it with the intention of committing suicide. That is why I believe that it is advantageous for me to see a doctor. If my blood is tested and it is discovered that I am infected with HIV, I can start receiving the kind of treatment that can prolong my life. It is of course painful to know such a fact but it will motivate me to start fighting the virus much earlier. Therefore, I will have my blood tested."

One fortunate thing that happened to them that night was that the advertisement inviting tourists to spend their vacation in an almost AIDS-free environment was not aired during the early part of the evening. Had it aired it would have made them prolong their painful conversation about the big embarrassment that lay ahead of the husband. But tired from their trip, they retired early.

CHAPTER TWO

Satta and her husband met with Dr. David Lakka, Director of Public Health, two days after their return. The visit was in connection with the AIDS test that they wanted to undergo. Dr. Lakka who had worked as senior physician at the government hospital for eight years was appointed Director of Public Health by Hon. Misalie Lamboi three years ago. The two men knew each other very well although they were not really friends.

David Lakka was a famous doctor. Besides his impressive credentials - Doctor of Medicine and Doctor of Philosophy in Public Health, he had also done some significant research and written many articles on the health care system of the country. All these works were published by the Government Printing Press under the title *The Lakka Reports*. The Ministry of Health, regarding many of the recommendations of this document as good for developing countries, had decided to implement them in the rural areas of the country. It was the talk about *The Lakka Reports* in high places such as the House of Parliament and ministerial offices that had earned Dr. Lakka his appointment to the position of Director of Public Health. The benefits of this promotion included a big salary increase and a large, comfortable government-subsidized housing.

There were however some critics of the director who were unconvinced that he deserved all the rewards and benefits that were being showered on him. These critics included colleagues who considered him to be too ambitious and opportunistic. He was especially disliked for his relentless attempt to win the favor of people in high places. It came to them as a big surprise when he was appointed Director of Public Health because they did not think that he was the only official that deserved such award. They claimed that there were doctors and top civil servants that equally deserved to be promoted at that time.

It did not take long for these critics to realize that they were fighting a battle which they could not win. The man they were criticizing was gaining ground very rapidly. His works were put on display at the Ministry of Health, in the office of the president and in public libraries. The visit of the Minister of Health to his office this day seemed like a routine visit. But Dr. Lakka tried to make it appear special. He portrayed it as a visit to a professional whose opinion counted a lot on very important health matters.

The government was more than happy to promote Dr. Lakka because there was something in his *Reports* that was very good for tourism. Before the result of his research was published, there were rumors going around that HIV was spreading at a significant rate across the entire country. It was the statistics supplied by Dr. Lakka on the disease that put most of the rumors to rest. The figures given in his *Reports* on AIDS patients under the categories of sex, geographical location, occupation, age, etc. were very insignificant. This finding enabled the government to claim that AIDS was not a threat to the nation's health care system. It was the result of this study, which was also in part considered by the World

Health Organization in the compilation of its AIDS data on African countries, that made the government not to take the disease seriously. After receiving an award for this work from the Ministry of Health, Dr. Lakka approached the Minister of Tourism about including the slogan "AIDS-free" in the advertisement on the Golden Complex. Since he had earned the admiration of both the Ministers of Health and Tourism, he succeeded in convincing them to adopt the slogan. In fact the Minister of Tourism recommended him for a second award which he received during the inauguration of the Golden Complex. This notoriety even made him dare to request to be featured in one of the advertisements on the Golden Complex; but later on the Minister of Tourism decided to feature instead Hon. Lamboi, the former captain of the national soccer team.

The adoption of this slogan effectively quelled the critics. Dr. Lakka considered himself to be so well ahead of them that he no longer cared about their complaints and gossip. As time went on he even became a bit arrogant in the way he interacted with those he considered to be his foremost critics. He told a news reporter in an interview that his critics should realize that he was the knowledgeable scientist that provided the evidence for the use of the "Aids-free" slogan. At the conclusion of this interview he declared that he was somebody to be reckoned with. This attitude hurt his critics all the more by making them feel humiliated. But since the doctor was dealing with them from a position of strength, he could afford to treat them that way.

Dr. David Lakka chatted with the minister and his wife for quite a while before coming to the purpose of their visit. He had deliberately prolonged this preliminary discussion so that he could talk about his achievements since he became Director of Public Health. Normally Hon. Lamboi would not have allowed him to take that much of his time; but, being in a subdued mood, he was willing to exercise a lot of patience.

When they at last got to the purpose of Hon. Lamboi's visit, Dr. Lakka was anxious to comply with their request. After thoroughly examining them he had their blood taken by a laboratory technician. He told them that they would know the results of the tests by Friday of that week.

Mr. and Mrs. Lamboi left without telling Dr. Lakka anything about the AIDS test that was done in London. They did not want that information to influence in any way the findings of the doctor. "The best second opinion," the husband had told his wife, "was the one given with no prior knowledge about what other professionals had said about the patient's condition."

On Friday Hon. Lamboi and his wife, who had had a rough week thinking over and discussing the possible outcomes of their tests, hurried to Dr. Lakka's office. As the driver drove up the driveway leading to the parking space at the back, Hon Lamboi felt that they were at the threshold of a center in which lay information that could throw the family into utter sadness. This reflection caused him to clasp his wife's hands. She responded instantly by gently leaning against him. They were in this position when the car stopped and the driver got out to open the door. They got out and headed hand-in-hand for the doctor's office.

Dr. Lakka received them with handshakes and a broad smile. As they were trying to figure out what the warm reception meant he gave them a piece of news that they did not expect.

"The results of your blood tests are ready," he said, after offering them two comfortable seats. "Both of you tested negative. Congratulations!"

Although this was the kind of news that people worried about their health would want to hear, the husband and the wife did not rejoice over it. They were shocked because they did not expect to hear any good news and were confused because the finding contradicted that of another famous doctor.

"Are you really saying that both of us tested negative?" asked Satta in a depressed tone of voice.

"Yes, I am," replied Dr. Lakka. "Ibrahim Jalloh, one of my lab technicians, did the testing but I confirmed it personally. Both of you are free of HIV."

"This is news to us," said the husband.

"Why would it be news to you?" asked the doctor. "Are you expecting to be sick? The physical examination also shows that you are in excellent health."

The Lambois did not tell him what the doctor in London had told them. Since they had not yet had the chance to reflect on the results of the medical tests in their true perspective, they could not rejoice with the doctor. They just thanked him politely with a forced smile and left the office. They were both unhappy and thoroughly confused.

"This is the worst time of my life," said the husband. "Why would two professionals give me contradictory test results? It means that one of them must be lying to me. But I must find out."

"Darling, I do not know what to say," said the wife. "Someone is playing games with your life."

"But why would anyone want to play such a despicable and deadly game," said the husband. "I deserve to know the truth about my condition. I care about the truth. It may make me sad if the news is bad; but at least it does not leave me confused and guessing about my fate. The sooner I know the better for me."

"On Monday we shall find out which of these two doctors is lying," said Satta.

"At present I have two facts to find out," said the husband. "Instead of simply trying to know whether or not I am infected with HIV, I also have to struggle to find out if some well-respected and greatly trusted doctor is failing to tell his patient the truth. Thinking over the way to find out these two facts over a whole weekend can even drive a sane man crazy. My God! Why is this happening to me?"

When the Mercedes Benz stopped in front of the ministerial residence, the driver opened the doors for them and took their things inside. The couple stepped out and walked into the living room. But they found it impossible to discuss their problems there because the advertisements on the Golden Complex kept on reminding the husband about the big problems ahead of him. He got up and walked pensively upstairs to the bedroom. Before he reached the top of the stairs he returned to tell the wife that he wanted to postpone his dinner until later on in the evening. He then walked up the stairs again.

Satta ate alone very thoughtfully and slowly. When she finished she telephoned Alice Lavalie, her best friend, and invited her over. Since the latter did not have a car, Satta ordered the driver to go and pick her up. When she arrived the houseboy took two lawn chairs and side tables to the backyard for them. After serving them drinks he retreated from the scene leaving the two women alone. They talked in private for about two hours.

Satta and Alice had been friends since elementary school days. They attended educational institutions in Britain and had shared good and bad times together. Satta who was careful about any premature leak of information about the tragedy knew that it was alright to talk to her friend in confidence. One thing she had always liked about Alice was her sense of fairness and decency. This had made her to trust her more than all her other girl friends. Thus when that evening she found herself in urgent need of a good and reliable advice, Alice was the one she invited over."

This was the first time the two friends were meeting since Satta's return from England although they had talked several times on the telephone. Alice who did not know that her friend had a big problem on hand was in a very happy mood.

"I am pleased that you had such a good time in London," said Alice after both of them had settled in their lawn chairs.

"Alice, we did have a good time but the visit ended on a terrible note," said Satta. "We have a family tragedy in the making."

Alice who was wearing a multicolored floral dress sat up in her chair and shook her head. She then displayed a frown that indicated a helpless concern. It was as if she had already heard the bad news but decided that there was nothing she could do about it. In any case, she remained quiet and listened attentively.

"My husband has contracted HIV," continued Satta. "We learned this during our visit to a doctor in London. "You are the only person I have so far told this secret. We are concerned about its leak to the public."

"I am sorry to hear this news," said Alice. "But I find it very difficult to believe you because AIDS is not very common in this country."

"It really is not but my husband has contracted the virus," said Satta. "I believe the doctor that said it."

"Satta, don't you suspect some mistake in the testing?"

asked Alice. "Mistakes such as the wrong labelling of test tubes are not common but they are a possibility."

"I doubt if such a mistake was made in this case," said Satta.

"Why don't you try a second opinion?" asked Alice. "This will clear any doubt about whether your husband is infected with HIV."

Satta paused to wipe the tears from her eyes. She felt a bit emotional about what she wanted to reveal next. She knew that it would sound even more incredible to her friend.

"Alice, we have already sought and received a second opinion," said Satta. "We have been to see Dr. David Lakka. He told us that my husband does has not have the virus. The result also showed that I do not have it either.

"Thank goodness!" Oh what a relief!" exclaimed Alice. "Dr. David Lakka is a reputable doctor whom the whole nation has come to trust. He surely would not be wrong in this matter. If I were you, I would believe him and have peace of mind. Know that if you had not gone to Britain you would have remained content with what he has told you. That in effect would have been the end of the matter. Remember that he was promoted by your husband who has great confidence in him."

"But the testing was done in a very reputable London hospital," said Satta. "The doctor is very credible. Being in charge of an entire AIDS program, there is no way he can afford to make mistakes. If his credibility is crushed, down goes his career."

"Satta we have a very difficult case here," said Alice. "I believe someone is lying to you."

"That's exactly what my husband thinks," said Satta. "We are now absolutely confused. Only God at this time knows which of the two doctors is to be believed"

The two women were quiet for a while. It was obvious that the conversation had reached a point where neither of them could make sense of the riddle being dealt with. Although Alice trusted Dr. Lakka, she also knew that the British doctor was very trustworthy. The London hospital where the test was done was one of the medical facilities in which she had done her practical training in nursing. She knew that it had very reputable doctors. Such knowledge dumbfounded her. Since she could not tell her friend which of the two doctors should be doubted, she sat there watching her tears drop wishing she were able to stop them. After thinking over the problem for five minutes, she noticed that her thoughts were going in circles. She would begin with the London hospital in question trying to figure out which doctor had done the testing. Since she had been away for some years she could not figure this out. But finding it hard to believe that any doctor working there could lie to his patients, she would travel back mentally to Dr. Lakka. Here she would encounter a similar problem. This reputable doctor had such an outstanding record that she dared not cast the slightest doubt on his character. When she got tired of puzzling over this problem she decided to give up the search for a solution and suggested that the husband be retested.

"Let's seek a third opinion at the World Health Organization clinic where I work as a nurse," said Alice Lavalie. "Dr. Mary Cole can handle your case. I will make an appointment for you for Friday at ten o'clock."

The Lambois and Alice turned up in Dr. Cole's office as scheduled. This was the second time that the doctor was meeting the minister. The first time they met was two years ago when she was brought to his office and introduced as the doctor sent by the World Health Organization to deal with infectious diseases in the country. Although Dr. Cole had been anxious to launch an effective AIDS program, the Ministry of Health had not cooperated very much. Not believing that AIDS was a big concern, the government had not given her work any priority. Dr. Cole had however continued to inform Hon. Lamboi's office of all AIDS cases she had diagnosed. Although the minister never denied the existence of the disease, he had never made an effort to cooperate with the clinic in the launching of an AIDS campaign. He had maintained a silence about something that was now personally affecting him."

The doctor was very surprised to learn that the minister and his wife wanted to be tested for AIDS. She saw an irony in the request because of the minister's past reluctance to seriously deal with the disease. But being a caring professional she tried not to show her surprise. After a thorough physical exam, she ordered her laboratory technicians to take the blood samples for the testing. They were told that the result would be ready in a week.

The Lambois had another restless week as they waited impatiently for the results of their blood tests. Since this wait was painful and unbearable they heaved a sigh of relief when that great day finally came. Since Fridays were Dr. Cole's busiest days, she had given them the last appointment for the day so that she could take some time to discuss her AIDS program with the minister. It had been difficult making an appointment for such a discussion because the minister had not shown any interest in some of the activities of the WHO clinic.

Mr. and Mrs. Lamboi were very quiet when the doctor entered the office with the results of the blood tests. There had been many anxious moments in the life of the couple but this seemed to be the most anxious. They were now about to know which doctor was telling the truth.

"The test results are ready," said Dr. Cole, after greeting them and taking her seat. "Hon. Lamboi, you have been infected with HIV. Since the results of your physical examination indicate that you are relatively healthy, it is too early to tell whether you will develop AIDS. In any case, you shall start undergoing treatment. Your wife is free of the virus."

The Lambois were quiet for a while. Like the doctor in London, this reaction did not surprise Dr. Cole who had in the past delivered such heart-breaking news to many patients. While some people had expressed no overt reaction on receiving the bad news others had reacted by either weeping or asking very many questions. The most common questions were whether they were going to die. But the Lambois who had had counseling in London and had already grieved a lot, reacted differently. They remained quiet and well composed. After about three minutes of silence Hon. Lamboi told Dr. Cole about the test results given by the other doctors.

"There is no doubt that you have contracted the AIDS virus," said Dr. Cole after listening quietly to the couple's account. "It is the doctor in London who had told you the truth. I do not, however, know why Dr. Lakka decided to lie to you about your condition; but if he had been lying to his patients, then his data on the disease are questionable. This does have consequences for the statistical data we compile because we do accept information from the Office of Public Health. The chances are that the number of AIDS cases on record are much less than the actual number of AIDS cases in the country."

"What a fraud!" said Satta. "I do not know what the government will do about this; but many people may have been hurt by him. It looks like a serious investigation should be launched."

"In order to clear all doubts about the possibility of misinterpreting the result of your blood test, I am going to telephone Dr. Lakka about it," said Dr. Cole. "I will ask him questions about the way he interprets the results of his tests. Of course, I can only do this with your permission."

"Go ahead, doctor, you have my permission to investigate this matter," said Hon. Lamboi.

The Lambois were attentive as the call was being made. Although they were no longer expecting any miracles, they were very interested in knowing why Dr. Lakka had lied to them.

"This is Ibrahim Jalloh, the senior laboratory technician," said the voice at the other end of the line.

"Ibrahim, this is Dr. Cole at the WHO clinic. How are you?"

"Very well, doctor, and you."

"Very well, thanks."

"James, I am calling about Hon. Lamboi's blood test," said Dr. Cole. "I just want a confirmation of the result. He is right here seeking another opinion. Do you know which lab technician handled his case?"

"I did. I have given the report to Dr. Lakka. He personally informs his patients about the findings."

"Is the doctor in?"

"He is gone for the weekend. I don't think that you can catch him today. He left at half past four. But I can answer any questions on the blood work that was done."

"I am just interested in knowing the result of the

minister's AIDS test."

"He tested positive," said Ibrahim. "His wife tested negative."

"Does Dr. Lakka know that the minister tested positive?"

"Yes, we gave him the result. The Hon. Minister was here in person to receive the information from him."

"That's all, Ibrahim. Thank you very much."

She hung up and turned toward the minister with a look of surprise on her face.

"Ibrahim Jalloh, Dr. Lakka's lab technician, told me that you tested positive," said Dr. Cole. "It was only your wife that tested negative. I do not know why the doctor gave you the wrong information. Ibrahim is clearly not part of any fraud that may have been committed. Since this is a confidential matter I want you to also talk to Ibrahim about it. It should go on record that you gave me permission to investigate your test results."

Dr. Cole redialed Dr. Lakka's number and handed over the receiver to Mr. Lamboi. Ibrahim Jalloh was pleased to talk with the minister although the news that he had for him was bad. After the conversation the minister hung up and leaned back in deep sadness.

"Hon. Lamboi, I am sorry about this news," said Dr. Cole. "The next few weeks or probably months are going to be difficult for both of you. But I will do all I can to make sure that your case is properly handled if you decide to be treated here. Please let me know your decision as soon as possible. As for Dr. Lakka's conduct, it needs to be thoroughly investigated. His falsifying official records does have consequences for the work we do in the area of AIDS. I am now convinced that the data that we have been supplying our head office in Europe are not accurate. Something needs to be done about this because underestimating the number of AIDS cases in any country can mean big problems for that country's health care system."

On their way home Satta and her husband dropped off Alice at her place. Satta promised to visit her the following day. Her silence during the trip was an indication that she too was very much affected by the news.

When the Lambois arrived home, Satta went straight to the bedroom, collapsed on the bed and started weeping loud. Her husband followed her and sat on the chair next to the bed, trembling. It had dawned on them that since the kind of sexual contact that could lead to conception would never take place between them again, the child they had hoped for would never be born. As she wept and rolled all over their big brass bed, she remembered what her grandmother had said about having children early in life before something unexpectedly happened to make it impossible. She wished she had followed her advice to start a family before this disaster struck.

At one point she almost fell off the bed as she writhed about in agony. Her husband lunged from his seat, grabbing her just before her head hit the floor. He pushed her all the way to the center of the bed where he believed she would be safe. But she started rolling about again. Since her movements seemed to be involuntary, he decided that it was better to put her on the floor. The carpet being plush, the chances of bruising herself were minimal.

The husband sat in great sadness. His promiscuous life had definitely hurt his wife. He wished she could calm down but a disaster of such magnitude was not easy to deal with. The woman not only had to deal with the problem of living with an AIDS patient but also with the stigma of being childless.

The houseboy and the maid normally waited for their bosses to eat before they went anywhere. But tonight the food just stood there because the bosses did not leave their bedroom. When at one point the houseboy went to remind them that the food was getting cold, he was shocked to hear the lady crying loudly. He dashed downstairs to inform the maid about it. Both of them went upstairs and listened for a while before they descended slowly. In the end they refrigerated the food and left. Neither Misalie nor Satta ate that night.

The next day Satta wept all morning. Although the husband expressed some concern about her weeping to excess, he could not stop her from doing it. During the counseling session in London, they were told that crying as an initial reaction to such an irreversible tragedy was very normal. So he let it go on while he continued to meditate in silence.

At about noon Satta called Alice Lavalie to tell her that she would visit her on Sunday instead of that Saturday evening. She wanted to sufficiently get over that initial shock before going out in public.

The couple said very little to each other that day. The husband kept on wondering what the first topic would be about if any substantial talking should take place. The one he feared most was any discussion about how he contracted HIV. If this topic came up and he failed to reveal the name of the woman from whom he had contracted the virus, jealousy would be added to the wife's present emotional state making matters even worse.

When it was time for lunch during which both of them ate very little, the husband thought that the topic of infidelity would come up. But that did not happen. When dinner came by and went without the topic being discussed, the husband concluded that the wife was following the advice of the counselor at the London hospital. "Try not to find out how your husband got the disease," the doctor had said. "Matters like this can wait. Remember that your husband's life is at stake. Attacking him over something for which he is already paying such a high price would only make matters worse. Deal with the issue of how you are going to accommodate each other and live with the disease. Do not make him feel guilty by casting blame. As you grow in your new relationship, matters of serious concern can be dealt with gradually."

The crying stopped altogether late that evening. When it had started on Friday, the husband had thought that she would lose her sanity and do something to hurt him or herself. But fortunately that did not happen. Her ability to compose herself as the hours passed by reiterated his view of her as a strong woman.

CHAPTER THREE

At about noon the following day Mrs. Satta Lamboi set out for the home of Alice Lavalie who was still single and living with her parents in a working-class neighborhood of Bassaya. It was the first time that Satta was leaving the house since the family received the bad news from Dr. Cole. She had equally shared the grief of the first stage of their family tragedy which was simply finding out whether the husband had actually contracted the virus. This stage was dominated by suspense over the outcome of the AIDS test and anger at the fact that some medical professional had lied to Hon. Lamboi. The second stage - grieving over the bad news itself - was naturally overwhelming.

Although Alice was not there to see the couple go through this second stage, she understood it well enough. All Friday evening and all day Saturday she had the urge to telephone her but she suspected that her friend's emotional state would be such that she could not talk to anybody, probably not even to her husband. Her suspicion was based on her experiences working as a nurse and counselor in an AIDS clinic. She had seen many wives express such outbursts of emotion over their spouses' tragedy. It was therefore a big relief to at last get to see her friend again. There was no doubt that a serious discussion lay ahead.

On catching sight of Satta, Alice rushed outside and hugged her. Satta responded warmly to this welcome gesture and walked inside with her. After eating the delicious lunch which Alice's mother had prepared for them they went into her bedroom to talk in private. It was the first time since the tragedy that Satta had the appetite to eat well.

"So how are you feeling now?" asked Alice quietly with no emotion on her face.

"Compared to the last two days, I am feeling much better," replied Satta.

"My friend, your case is unusual," said Alice. "Finding out whether your husband had HIV should not have been part of your tragedy because determining such a fact is not medically difficult. But for your husband, it became a nightmare since two distinguished doctors had given you conflicting results. You experienced unnecessary mental pain as you waited for a third distinguished doctor to decide which of the previous two had lied to you. What an unfair world!"

"It really is an unfair world," said Satta.

"Under normal circumstances the second stage of your grief should have been your first," said Alice. "You did not have to undergo an unnecessary grief."

"My grief was unnecessarily prolonged," said Satta. "When that bad news was finally learned I wept uncontrollably. My husband who was stunned by such a strong outpouring of emotion did his best to take care of me. I should have been the one to comfort him because he is the one that has contracted the virus. But, as it happened, I was so overcome by grief that I collapsed on the bed. I reacted to our sudden and unexpected tragedy with my whole being - wailing and rolling around vigorously as I lamented over my childlessness and my husband's tragedy."

"As a friend, Satta, I do share your grief," said Alice. "I regret that I could not be with you. If you had gone through this stage in the clinic I would have been at your side. But I had to honor your wish to go through it in the privacy of your home."

"Thank you, Alice," said Satta. "I knew you would have liked to be with me. But my reaction to my family tragedy was so strong that even my husband could not succeed in engaging in any meaningful conversation with me. He just controlled my physical movements on the bed so that I could not hurt myself. In fact I ended up on the floor. No conventional counseling technique could have helped me."

"Without doubt the toughest times are ahead," said Alice. "But I want you to know that there is something beneficial about such outpouring of emotions. Grieving to that extent strengthens your ability to better deal with any further bad news. Hopefully, instead of succumbing to further outburst of grief in the future, you will be inclined to handle matters in a more constructive way. As problems related to this tragedy arise, you will be able to see each in its proper perspective. Many patients have come out stronger from the kind of experiences you have had. Look at how relatively calm you are today!"

"Alice, I am faced with many problems at this time," said Satta. "The first thing I would like to know is how Misalie contracted the virus. I have not yet asked him because he is going through a difficult time. His life is at stake. But eventually I would like to have an answer to this."

"Do you think he will tell you without a struggle?" asked Alice. "Many men would be too embarrassed to make such a confession. You remember what happened to his friend Mr. Sefoi Juana, Commissioner of Health. He came one day from work with lipstick on his right cheek. He did not know that it was there because the woman whose lips imprinted them did not tell him about it. When Sefoi was questioned at home in front of the children, he remained silent about it. The wife secretly sent for the uncle next door. The latter rushed in with his inquisitive wife. Both were able to see the mark before Sefoi could rush into the bathroom to carefully remove it in front of the mirror. But he still refused to confess even when the wife threatened him with a divorce. I believe that he was too embarrassed to do that in front of the children and that inquisitive woman. The uncle told him that the next time an embarrassing affair like that happened she should not try to resolve the problem in the presence of the children. Even today the identity of the woman involved in that case remains unknown."

"My husband's case is a quite different," said Satta. "He is likely to face death. Being in such a critical situation he will be willing to confess. Of course, I will not be that cruel to force him to do it in public. The only problem is that Misalie may not know the woman that infected him with the virus."

"He should know her, of course." said Alice.

"It sounds logical that he should," said Satta. "But since he goes with several women at a time, he may not know exactly the one that infected him. You know how unfaithful and promiscuous Misalie is. In retrospect I should not have got married to such a man."

"Is there any particular girlfriend of his that you suspect of being infected with the virus?" asked Alice.

"It is probably Rosalyn Songa," replied Satta. "She is his main woman. She looks healthy now but she may be a healthy carrier of the virus. This is only a guess. In any case, when she hears about her sweetheart's condition, she will regret her involvement with him."

Satta laughed after making this guess. Her friend joined in briefly. This was the first time since Friday that she had expressed any other emotion beside grieving. It was understandable why she would mention Rosalyn. The bond between this particular woman and Hon. Lamboi had been so strong that nothing could break it. At one time Satta almost filed for a divorce but her parents persuaded her to abandon the idea."

"The surest way to know which of his many women gave him the virus is to have all of them tested for AIDS," said Alice. "But there is a big problem with this procedure too. What if two or more test positive?"

"In that case it will be difficult to know," said Satta. "One good thing about such a procedure is that it is likely to help me know how many women my husband has had an affair with. I suspect at least fifteen."

"That's a large number, said Alice. "Satta, you have been through a lot with this man. He has really subjected you to a lot of anguish. I believe that he may have more girlfriends than his friend Sefoi Juana."

"I believe so," said Satta. "Before I got married to Misalie, some relatives and friends, including you, had advised me against it. You all cited his promiscuity. But I ignored all warnings. Since he was a star and very handsome, every pretty woman wanted him. There is no way that I could have turned down an offer of marriage from such a man. The saying that love is blind is very applicable to my case because I did not consider other factors including my happiness. The price I am now paying for love is great."

"Do you know what my greatest joy is now?" asked Alice.

"It's hard to guess," replied Satta. "Hardly anything seems to bring joy these days."

"Well, there are some things that still bring joy," said Alice. "In this case it is your not contracting the disease. I regret that such a disaster has befallen your husband. But considering the fact that you may have very easily contracted the virus, I rejoice that you are free of it."

"Despite my family tragedy, this is one thing that I thank God for," said Satta. "I find it difficult to believe that this man almost killed me. A further secret I want to tell you, Alice, is that my relationship with this man became so bad that we rarely engaged in intercourse. Even during our vacation nothing happened between us. My frustration with the marriage was too much. So I turned down almost all his advances. But since he was getting satisfaction from many pretty women elsewhere, it did not seem to bother him much."

"I am surprised to hear this because you got along very well in public," said Alice.

"We did because I did not want to do anything that would cause a big scandal," said Satta. "What seemed to be a perfect marriage was really not. His promiscuity was not really a secret but my willingness to accommodate him enabled both of us to prevent any scandal from arising. My mother and grandmother also encouraged me to stay in the marriage. They told me that someday some benefit may be reaped from it. So, I remained faithful and devoted. Another reason why I was able to stand him was that although this man is a womanizer he was very gentle and generous. He was kind to me and my extended family and was willing to go out of the way to make sure that I get whatever I wanted. He could not however give me the love I needed. He only promised that someday he would give it to me."

"As it turned out he never gave it," said Alice. "The irony in all this is that it was your abstinence that saved you. In any case, Satta, we have to thank God that such a disaster did not strike you. Let's rejoice for this although I am very sorry that your husband is paying such a terrible price for the way he has lived."

"I am sorry too," said Satta. "Since AIDS is not rampant in this country I never really suspected that he would contract it."

"But how were you going to bear children when you refused to engage in intercourse with him?" asked Alice.

"I had decided to give up my abstinence after our return from London," said Satta. "This is a sacrifice that I would have had to make so that I could have children. But as it has turned out, I did not even get the chance to make this sacrifice. My plans were destroyed by one fell swoop. My friend, what am I going to do now? I am childless although I am young enough to have children. The problem I face is as big as Pala."

Both women became quiet at this point. Satta's reference to Pala, the huge cotton tree in Palahun, her village, indicated that she perceived her problem as insurmountable. When she was a child, many stories were told about that tree. They were about its three most important features: its size, its agelessness and its indestructibility. No matter what was done to the tree in all the stories, it survived with all three features untouched. In the olden days before the white man came and colonized the tribe, its mention at the end of any negotiation with the neighbors meant that the dispute could not be resolved and that war was the only alternative. As tribal wars ended and the white man took over the problem of governing, the usage of the word changed. When used in reference to any problem it simply meant that it was insurmountable. The word was no longer associated with the idea of conflict or war.

Alice was dumbfounded at Satta's use of this word. It was an indication of how helpless she felt. Some urgent help was needed but she did not have the means to give it.

"Satta, I think that more time is needed to consider the solution to your problem of childlessness," she said. "Since this tragedy has just occurred there are other matters that should be dealt with urgently. The first is how to help your husband with his anguish. The second is how to work out a new relationship with him; and third, how to handle the reactions of your parents. The issue of childlessness will be better dealt with when life becomes more normal. Your mention of Pala in this context came as a surprise. Since it is also an indication of how nostalgic you feel about your village, you need to go and seek the advice of your grandmother who resides there. Palahun is the home of Pala. Regardless of how much advice you get from your western-educated friends and relatives in Bassaya, you should go to that village and seek the advice of the sages there. The solution to this problem may be found in the home of Pala where your ancestors lived."

Satta left her friend's place a bit relieved because she was able to have a genuine discussion about some important implications of her husband's contracting HIV. Her aim of going there was not to get immediate answers to such a complicated problem. It was to say what she felt about her problem without being concerned about any leakage of confidential information.

That evening Satta and Hon. Lamboi had dinner together. When they finished they retired to the living room where they discussed the husband's medical treatment. They decided to make an appointment with Dr. Mary Cole for Wednesday of that week.

"Satta, this problem is going to put me through a lot of anguish," said the husband. "Since you are a caring woman it is also going to affect you seriously."

"This is a bad time for us," said Satta. "I am however encouraged by the result of your physical examination," said Satta. "Although you have contracted the virus, there is no indication that you will develop the disease. So there is some chance that medication will help you considerably. Dr. Cole said that there are infected people who have not developed the disease even after carrying the virus for ten years. Since you have none of its symptoms, darling, my hope is that you will not develop it."

"Satta, that's my hope too," said the husband quietly. "But the hope to live just for a few years is not what any human being craves for. Everyone prefers to live long and enjoy life to the fullest. It distresses me to know that I am in a situation where I can get terminally ill. I know that I am the cause of my disaster but regardless of how I had lived my life I am still very angry that I face the possibility of an early death. Oh what an unfair world! There is no way I am going to accept this fate."

He stood up as if to leave. The wife tried to hold his hand but he repulsed the approach. She bowed her head momentarily in frustration. But realizing that that repulsion may hurt her feeling he did not go away as planned. He remained standing in front of her. When she raised her head their eyes met. She looked at him attentively dwelling on the features of a face many women considered good-looking. Her eyes continued their journey downward from his face all the way to his feet. What she saw was a slim six-foot, well-built and proportioned body."

"Misalie, you are an attractive and well-built man," she said.

"That is exactly what I no longer want to hear from the lips of any woman," he said impatiently. "For years I was flattered by their saying it. That made me go after them with such an avid appetite that I ended up completely destroying myself. Whatever it is that women saw in this body that excited them is no more. Take a look at me. I am a withering man. The physical changes that will occur if I develop AIDS may be imperceptible for a while; but as time goes on they will became discernible. That means the beginning of the end of an object that had attracted those who are after good looks. Whatever emerges after the beauty of this body gives way will not be of any use to those who are after things that glitter."

Just then he was seriously distracted by the advertisement on television. It was the one that featured him as a hero. He dashed toward the set and turned it off furiously. But as he walked back to his seat he stopped suddenly in the middle of the living room and remained motionless.

"Darling, I am sorry for complaining about your admiring my body," he said. "You are in fact the woman that has the right to admire it. If you alone had admired it in the past, I would have been happy today because I would not have contracted the virus. It is some admirer out there in the city who has destroyed it. All I am going to do now, if luck does not come my way, is to sit around and wither just as I am supposed to."

At this point the husband dashed upstairs to the bedroom. The wife who was not sure why he took off so suddenly ran after him. She was afraid that he would do something terrible to himself. But as she quickly found out, all he needed was some privacy. When their eyes finally met, the face that the wife saw was horrible. It was a face pregnant with grief. As if to conceal the fact that he was actually crying, he covered it with his hands. But that did not take away all the evidence that this strong man was at last pouring out his emotions. His sobs became very audible and very frequent. He struggled to contain them but without avail. The sighs and convulsions became so strong that he could not stay on his feet. Falling backward on the bed like a huge sawn-off tree he raised his hands as if calling for help. This enabled his wife to see the face he had been trying to conceal. The tears streaming from his eyes were as uncontrollable as a heavy fall of rain. Then came the wailing which reminded Satta of the thunder and lightning that accompany a rain storm which had been brewing for a long time.

All Satta could do at that point was to sit by him and wait. Fortunately this outpouring of emotion was so strong that it quickly wore out the devastated husband. It ended in less than fifteen minutes.

"Darling, I was surprised to see you lose your patience when I praised your body," said the wife. "You rarely ever lose it in such a context. I want you however to know that it was appropriate for you to vent your feelings in that manner. Your wailing was also very appropriate. On Friday night you stood over me as I wept pretending to be a monster whose emotions are not subject to grief. You were wrong to have suppressed your emotions. It is unfortunate that men are taught during their youth that it is weakness to shed tears even when struck by a disaster of this magnitude. What you did just now does not in any way indicate weakness. This outpouring of emotions and frustration is likely to make you stronger and more able to deal with the pressing and disheartening problems ahead of us."

"Thank you, Satta, for being very understanding," said the husband. "My biggest regret is that I have no child to remember me as a loving father. I have probably enjoyed more women than my uncle in the village with three wives. Yet he has many children while I have none to show for all the great sex I had with many beautiful women."

"Darling, I do not think that you can go to work this week," said the wife. "Your grief is too strong at this point to allow you to concentrate on your job. Since Parliament in not yet in session, I will call tomorrow to tell your secretary to postpone all your appointments. You need some privacy and some counseling before you step into that office. Your appointment for Wednesday will be changed to Monday. You will also start taking your medication tomorrow."

"Thanks, darling," said Misalie. "We shall talk to Dr. Cole about this matter first thing in the morning."

"Misalie, I think that we should let some of your relatives know about this problem," said the wife. "They should know so that they will learn to accept whatever is going to be your fate. Your brother Michael will also give you good advice on how to handle matters from now on."

"Satta, I do not want anyone to know about this problem," said the husband. "If they know it will eventually leak to the press. I am too fragile at this time to be bothered by all the publicity that will follow any public revelation. So, please let us keep this a secret."

"Do you want me to deal with this problem all by myself?" asked the wife anxiously.

"Satta, you and I will handle it together," said the husband. "Have we not in the past handled many difficult marital problems? We have, of course. So, we are strong enough to handle one more problem."

"This problem is very different from the others," said the wife. "The problems of your unfaithfulness are not as tragic as this one. Here we are dealing with possible death. I cannot handle it in secret."

"Please do not bring this shame on me," pleaded the husband.

"What if it leaks before we have the chance to divulge it in confidence to those that are close to us?" asked the wife.

"Satta, I am old and matured enough to know that like all well-kept human secrets, this one is bound to leak someday," said the husband. "But in the meantime let me enjoy some peace of mind."

"I will think over your request," said the wife.

"Please do; but when deciding please consider me," said the husband.

The following day Hon. Lamboi did not go to work as suggested by his wife. He went to see Dr. Mary Cole. The three counseling sessions that week proved to be very helpful. They made Hon Lamboi put his tragedy in perspective and also calm down considerably. His wife participated in the Friday session. Overall, the meetings with Dr. Cole paid off because that weekend the couple relaxed and had some constructive conversations about the problems ahead.

CHAPTER FOUR

After a relatively peaceful weekend, the couple resumed work on Monday. Satta was a bit uneasy all week because of her concern about the leakage of her big family secret. Each day she would buy and read all the newspapers to see whether any mention would be made of it. She also listened to the conversations in her office to find out whether anyone would talk about it. The husband however was more at ease and more trusting. He expected the staff at the clinic to act professionally by not leaking the information about his condition. He suspected of course that some day the information would fall in the wrong hands. But by then they would have got used to living with AIDS. That would help them deal better with all the publicity that would ensue.

One day something happened at work that made Satta to suspect that somebody in the office had discovered her family secret. At around ten in the morning Veronica Johnson, her husband's secretary, came to their building. Since this was the first time she had seen her there she thought that Hon. Lamboi had sent her on an errand. But Satta waited in vain because Veronica did not go into her office. To her surprise she went into the office of the two secretaries. Only one of them, Sylvia Gbondo, was in that day. Satta had never really liked Sylvia because she felt that the woman was too inquisitive. When she first started working there Sylvia had asked her too many questions about her past and how she met her husband. She had therefore never appreciated her conduct and had avoided her when she could.

Veronica and Sylvia talked in low voices for about ten minutes. As Satta wondered why the husband's secretary was not at work, she heard the two of them coming in the direction of her office. Before she could guess what they were up to, they were already standing in front of her desk. She trembled slightly thinking that they were bringing to her the big news she had been expecting - - information about her secret.

"Good morning, Veronica," she greeted politely with a warm smile. "It's a long time since I saw you. How are you?"

"I am quite well," she replied cheerfully. "Yes, it's a long time since we saw each other. Since you no longer come often to our office, I decided to come and see you."

"That's very thoughtful of you. Thank you," said Satta.

"So how was your vacation?" asked Veronica.

This question made Satta to suspect very strongly that the two secretaries had already received information about what happened at the clinic in London. She felt that they were in her office for confirmation of the facts.

"The vacation was great," she replied. "We had a good time."

"I know that you did," said Veronica. "My friend wrote that she saw you and Hon. Lamboi at a party in London. I came to find out if you know her and also show you the pictures."

"I remember the friend that you are talking about," said Satta. "She was the only one taking pictures that evening. I never dreamt that I would see her pictures."

"Well, all things seem to be possible these days," said Veronica, giving the pictures to Satta. "I am glad that you do remember her. It was her fiance that took you and your husband to the hospital later that evening."

Satta's heart leapt again as she pretended to examine the pictures. Although Veronica paused to give her chance to see and make comments on them, she was in such an emotional state that she could not focus her attention on what she was looking at. To her the conversation looked like the beginning of the unfolding of all the events that had transpired in London.

The pictures themselves were very good. One of them showed Satta and her husband dancing happily. But Satta felt that the scenes presented in those pictures reminded her of an unpleasant vacation she would rather forget. Examining the pictures entailed revisiting those scenes.

"So, your husband got sick during your vacation," said Sylvia. "What happened to him?"

Satta did not reply. She pretended to be too preoccupied with the pictures to say anything.

"It was not serious," said Veronica. "Just a stomach ache."

"But stomach aches can ruin vacations," said Sylvia. "It depends on how serious they are."

"The doctor seen that night was competent," said Veronica. "A slight stomach ache like a slight head ache cannot by itself ruin an entire vacation. It takes more than a slight illness to ruin a big event."

Satta felt that this conversation was very inappropriate because these two ladies were not friends of hers. Thus it was no business of theirs discussing what happened to her husband during their vacation. As far as she was concerned they were being plainly inquisitive.

Since her return from London, Satta had avoided going to her husband's office specifically because she did not want Veronica to ask her any questions about her vacation. She knew that the latter and her friend Sylvia liked to investigate other people's misfortunes or weaknesses in order to make fun of them. Their targets were ambitious employees and progressive neighbors. It was rumored that both of them were jealous and frustrated women because, since their graduation from secondary school many years ago, they had not done anything to earn promotion on their jobs.

Not all bosses had allowed Sylvia and Veronica to get away with their obnoxious behavior. When they worked as secretaries in the Ministry of Communications five years earlier under Mrs. Judith Lansana, Satta's mother, they were forced to temporally terminate their inquisitive activities. Mrs. Lansana disciplined them by keeping them busy all the time. This made them to be afraid of her. But one day they fought back foolishly and lost.

It was just after lunch that day when Mrs. Lansana, on entering their office to give them an assignment, saw Veronica passing an empty box to Sylvia. Both were laughing as they made funny comments about it. Curious about this behavior, Mrs. Lansana rushed to Sylvia's desk to see what was in the box. It was then that she noticed that the box was the container for the brand of wig she was wearing. It was clear that they were making fun of her.

This mischief so much annoyed Judith that she decided not to let them get away with it. She embarrassed them terribly by telling them that they were behaving like very young girls anxiously looking forward to the age of maturity. This comment, which took the other employees in the office by surprise, caused much laughter. It was their first taste of what life would be like under a boss that would not tolerate nonsense in the work place. Both women were transferred to other offices shortly after that.

Satta knew of this story. Knowing her mother to be a difficult woman, she did not then approve of her insulting them the way she did. But today she felt that her mother was justified because the women were just too inquisitive. Like the mother, she also had power over the two of them and could request that they be transferred to other branches of their respective institutions. But she had decided against such action. First, she was not as strict as her mother; and second, it was not prudent to strike at people who may have information about something that she was trying to hide. They may fight back by embarrassing her. Thus her power over them seemed worthless.

As she kept on thinking over what to say after she had reluctantly examined the photographs, one of her colleagues came to get her. The meeting that was scheduled for that afternoon was about to begin. Getting up at once, she handed back the pictures to their owner and left the office in a hurry without answering any of their questions or making any comments on what she had seen.

Satta participated in that meeting with a troubled mind. She was curious about how the conversation with the two inquisitive secretaries would have ended if she had not suddenly left. She did not feel that she was prepared to handle the embarrassment that would have resulted if the conversation had touched on the issue of her husband's contracting HIV. It appeared like the meeting saved her, at least, temporally.

At the end of that frustrating day, Satta was convinced

that unless their secret was revealed to the public, an embarrassing incident like the one that occurred at the office would happen again. With the pressure on her rising steadily like a flood, she needed somebody to talk with. But there was no need discussing with her husband what happened in the office because he would not take it seriously. So, feeling that Alice could help again she visited her immediately after work and narrated the incident.

"Are you really convinced that these two ladies know your family secret?" asked Alice after listening to the story.

"Satta, since the discussion was interrupted before it got to the point when a reasonable conclusion about any leakage could be drawn, I cannot tell you whether these two ladies know my secret," replied Satta.

"I advise you to be patient and wait," said Alice. "One thing I am sure of is that if they have some important information about your husband's condition, they will soon approach you about it. When these ladies are looking for a confirmation of the veracity of a rumor, they will go all out to get it. So wait until tomorrow. But do not spend your evening worrying over it. It is possible that Veronica only came to show those pictures to you today."

"I have never been comfortable with the inquisitiveness of Sylvia Gbondo," said Satta. "Sometimes I wonder why she was hired in the first place. She has been dying all this time to know about my vacation. Veronica's visit offered a good opportunity today. But unfortunately for her, the discussion was interrupted."

"She is a hard worker," said Alice. "Since your colleagues have hitherto been comfortable with her, they had to retain her. You may consider having her transferred but if you do that, you will lose an excellent typist. Do you know that it was your mother that trained and disciplined both of them?"

"Yes, I do," replied Satta. "But she eventually kicked them out."

"They learned a good lesson from that experience," said Alice. "Both girls were sent to Mrs. Judith Lansana's office immediately after graduating from secondary school. After training them she delegated important duties to them. This gave them no time for petty gossip especially when she was around. In the end however she told them off and threw them out. Fortunately they ended up becoming good workers as a result of that training."

"You know that my mother does not tolerate nonsense and childishness," said Satta. "I asked her one day whether her letting them go had something to with the wig incident. She told me that it was not because of that. She got rid of her two hard workers because they had remained petty. They looked in nooks and crannies for small matters that they could blow out of proportion. Thus they have not been able to achieve anything worthwhile in life. Another woman in the office that day told me that she saw a big frown on my mother's face on seeing the two adults playing around with an empty wig box. She declared that that was the height of imbecility."

Satta and her friend laughed. This pleasant reaction was a lull in the continuing anguish that had been sapping the energies of the conscientious married woman.

"As I told you earlier, just wait and see what happens tomorrow," said Alice. "If it turns out that they know your secret, ignore them and inform your husband about it. Both of you will decide on when to inform friends and relatives that are important to you."

"My biggest concern at this time is that these inquisitive

people will leak our secret before we get to inform our own relatives about it," said Satta. "That will be quite an embarrassment."

"Your husband needs some time to get adjusted to his tragedy," said Alice. "That is very understandable. But three weeks of counseling is enough time for such adjustment. Try now to convince him about revealing the secret to relatives. They may help you adjust sooner. Keeping big secrets like this is like carrying a big load on one's head. You will feel much better after getting rid of this load."

Satta went home quite relieved. The discussion did her some good although she still had to interact with her secretary the following day. When she entered the house she went into the living room where the husband was watching the evening news on television. He was in a good mood.

"Darling, how are you?" he greeted her with a smile.

"I am very well," she replied. "Thank you."

"How was your day at work?" he asked.

"It was a good day," she replied. "I passed by Alice's place on my way here."

"I was at Dr. Cole's," said the husband. "The counseling sessions have ended although we can request some more from time to time. I also got a refill on my medicines. She examined me again and told me that it was unlikely that I will have any symptoms of the disease in the near future. In fact she said that my chances of living a near-normal life are very good. She only cautioned me about taking my medicines."

"Let's hope for the best, darling."

The couple then moved to the dining room for dinner.

CHAPTER FIVE

The following Wednesday information about the secret leaked! It was during lunch hour that Satta discovered the leak. As she was returning to the office after a pleasant meal with her colleagues she stopped to take a brief look at the headlines of the newspapers that a hawker was selling. On catching sight of the headline "Minister Contracts HIV" in *The People's Voice* she gestured to her colleagues, who had stopped to wait for her, to continue without her. Obviously she did not want them to see the headline and start asking questions about it. That would have made the rest of her day very miserable.

Taking the money out to buy the paper was not easy. Her heart leapt several times as she opened her purse. The newspaper boy noticed that her hands were shaking but did not ask any questions. He was more interested in the sale. After picking up a copy of the newspaper she walked across the street to the office of a friend and tried to reach her husband by telephone. She would not dare make that call from her office out of concern that Sylvia Gbondo, the inquisitive secretary, would eavesdrop on their conversation. After two unsuccessful attempts to reach the husband, she returned to work. While in the office she kept the paper in her handbag. She did not want Sylvia to see the headline and dash downstairs to buy a copy. On reaching home that evening the first thing she did was to sit down and carefully read the editorial that Ali Saffa had written on her family tragedy.

The most famous AIDS case in our country has been confirmed! Hon. Misalie Lamboi, Minister of Health, tested positive a little under two weeks ago at the Government Hospital. The testing was done by Mr. Ibrahim Jalloh, the senior laboratory technician, and his boss, Dr. David Lakka, Director of Public Health. Our informant, whose identity is being withheld, told us that it was over the telephone that Ibrahim Jalloh informed Dr. Mary Cole, Director of the World Health Organization clinic, that the minister tested positive while the wife tested negative.

This development however seems to involve an intrigue. The test results given by Dr. David Lakka and his senior lab technician are conflicting. While Mr. Ibrahim Jalloh insists that Hon. Lamboi tested positive, Dr. David Lakka says that he tested negative. Imagine how confusing this might have been for our Minister of Health. He could not figure out who was telling the truth. The editor of this paper believes that it was to clarify matters that Hon. Lamboi and his wife went to Dr. Cole at the WHO clinic for a second opinion. At present we have no information about what Dr. Cole did or told the couple. We only know that Hon. Lamboi has so far paid a total of five visits to the World Health Organization clinic since his return from London. These visits are probably in connection with contracting HIV. When the editor visited the clinic late Friday afternoon to request an interview with Dr. Cole, he saw Hon. Lamboi leaving the premises. Dr. Cole declined politely our request for an interview but confirmed the number of times the minister had been to the clinic. Her reason for declining was that all information on visitors and patients to the clinic was confidential. While this riddle remains to be solved, this paper maintains the belief that Ibrahim Jalloh is telling the truth.

The irony involved in the fact that the Minister of Health has contacted HIV is so embarrassing that the government is now more likely than ever to develop an AIDS policy. When information about the first celebrated AIDS case was publicized by the news media four years ago, the government ignored it completely because the patient was a poor man. Today Maurice Bangura, a former employee of the Golden Complex, is struggling with the disease. Although he and other patients are receiving treatment, nothing has been done to educate the public about AIDS. It is now time for our government to start telling the truth about this disease. The Minister of Health should start educating the people on the nature of the disease, its symptoms, how it is contracted and its devastating effect on the individual and his family. It should be realized that keeping people ignorant about it will do this nation more harm than good because that will not give them the opportunity to take the necessary steps to avoid contracting the virus.

The promotion of the Golden Complex seems to have hindered the development of any AIDS policy in this country. In the campaign to attract tourists the government has aired some advertisements inviting tourists to come to have a good time in a land where they stood the least chance of being infected with HIV. Implicit in this advertisement is the understanding that a significant percentage of the populations of the neighboring countries is infected with HIV. But the scandal involving Hon. Misalie Lamboi is going to show that promoting tourism this way has the potential to ruin the tourist industry itself. In order to effectively challenge or discredit these advertisements all our neighbors need to do is to point to the irony involved in the fact that our Minister of Health is infected with HIV. That personal tragedy, they would say, is an indication that our people are seriously infected with the virus.

If our government is wise and wants to be realistic, it should compete for tourists based on the strengths of our tourist facilities and programs. It should air advertisements that demonstrate the superiority of the Golden Complex over similar tourist facilities in neighboring countries. Since tourists know that there is hardly today any country that is absolutely free of AIDS they will not penalize our country for having citizens infected with the virus.

In the meantime we look forward to hearing from Hon. Lamboi and Dr. Lakka. The intrigue needs to be clarified as soon as possible.

When Hon. Misalie Lamboi arrived home he met Satta in the living room staring at the newspaper on the coffee table. He picked it up and read it quietly. The wife waited anxiously not knowing what reaction to expect. One thing she was sure of was that the husband would now be willing to deal publicly with the AIDS issue.

"Let's go to the dining room and eat," said the husband after putting down the paper.

"Is the food ready?" asked the wife, very surprised at the husband's first reaction.

"Satta, I am surprised that you ask such a question," said

the husband. "You know that the food is always ready when we come home."

After dinner the two retreated to the living room to discuss the matter. But hardly had they started talking when the telephone rang. The wife got up and picked it up. It was Michael Lamboi, the younger brother closest in age to Hon. Misalie Lamboi. Misalie was the eldest of three brothers. Michael had read about the terrible news and wanted to come to visit his brother right away. He told her that he would telephone Stephen Lamboi, a university professor, to inform him about the disaster.

"Your brother Michael on his way," said the wife. "I would not be surprised if we get more calls like this. Your many relatives and friends will be calling to express their sympathy. Moved by grief or out of concern, some may even come without first calling."

There were two calls after that. They were from Mrs. Judith Lansana, Satta's mother, and Mr. Sefoi Juana, Commissioner of Health. Sefoi was a very close friend of the minister. Both callers told the couple that they were on their way.

"Darling, we have an hour to decide which information to reveal and which to keep secret," said the husband. "What do you think we should do?"

"I want us to give only the facts that we would not be embarrassed about discussing in public," said the wife. "We can tell them about what happened in London and elaborate on everything that was touched on in the editorial. That will be enough."

"Why should I talk about the testing that was done in London when no one knows about it?" asked the husband.

"There is really nothing bad about revealing that information," said the wife. "It does not really matter whether the confirmation was done in London or at a health facility in this country. The embarrassment involved is the same. Not saying anything about London may bring problems later if that information leaks. Since you are a famous politician, the public, especially the journalists, are going to go all out to investigate this matter. These are the moments when one wishes that he or she were a private citizen. It's not easy being a politician."

"I agree with you on this," said the husband. "It makes sense to reveal the result of the test done in London. The other problem is what to say if asked by the press how I got the disease?"

"Ignore personal questions like that," said the wife.

This conversation was interrupted by the arrival of the three visitors that had called. They were served drinks as they arrived. Michael Lamboi, a successful businessman, was the first to arrive. Michael was the only one of the children that did not get a university education. Since he never liked school when he was young, he dropped out before finishing secondary school and started petty trading. That was a shock to Reverend Matthew Lamboi, a Methodist minister, who had tried to inculcate intellectual and Christian values and habits upon his three children.

When the three boys were growing up their parents used to praise Misalie saying that he would do better in life than Michael. Their assessment was based on the motivation of the two children. Misalie finished secondary school and entered the university where he got his Bachelor of Science degree. After earning a Master's Degree in Architecture in England two years later, he returned home and worked for a while as an architect before getting into politics. During this period, Michael was on the streets trying to demonstrate that he could be a businessman. What was disheartening about his dropping out of school was that he proved at an earlier age to be the most brilliant of the three boys. The parents could not figure out why such a gifted child ended up losing interest in all academic work. He was at the top of his class when he dropped out of school. A secondary school teacher, who was also disheartened by the boy's decision, informed the parents that at the time of Michael's withdrawal he could solve problems in the mathematics and science text books for final year secondary school students. His main problem was lack of motivation.

There were neighbors who were not surprised at Michael's decision to quit school. They claimed that his father, a Methodist minister who eventually became a lecturer at a Methodist Bible College, pushed him too hard to keep on performing excellently. His belief that the boy was a genius made him to push him that hard. But when the thrill over his achievements reached its highest point, Michael found himself incapable of going ahead any further. Like an edifice that had been seriously beaten and undermined by all the bad elements of nature - wind storms, heavy rains, relentless heat, etc. - to the point of ruin, he collapsed intellectually and stood up to the father he later referred to as an intellectual tyrant. But much later in life he became the most reliable child and financially the most prosperous member of the family. It was he who built for his father the modern house in which he was spending his retirement years.

Mr. Sefoi Juana and Mrs. Judith Lansana arrived shortly after Michael. After a short general conversation which looked like a warm-up for the big story ahead, they all listened very attentively to the couple's terrible experience. When the narration ended, all the listeners, except Judith Lansana, Satta's mother, were stricken with grief. They expressed in various ways the sympathy they felt for the sad husband. Judith, who said nothing, got up suddenly and went into one of the bedrooms to make a phone call. Her only goal of coming over was to find out whether her daughter was infected. Once she had learned the good news about her condition, she decided not to participate in any discussion. The attitude she portrayed clearly indicated that she did not care about the husband's fate. Feeling that his tragedy was a logical outcome of his promiscuity, she did not want to spend any time lamenting over it.

The daughter was so unhappy with his mother's attitude that she followed her into the bedroom. Her aim was to calm her down although she knew that the mother was unlikely to listen to whatever she had to say.

"Do not tell me anything, Satta," she said angrily. "This matter is between me and that womanizer. He almost infected you with HIV. If you had heeded the advice I gave you before marriage you would not have been living today with an AIDS patient that cannot give you a child."

"But, mother, we have to be merciful in the way we treat a man who is faced with certain death," said Satta. "It will be too hard on me if I deal with this problem by first blaming him for his promiscuity. That is why I have not yet bothered to ask him how he got the disease. That can wait till later."

"I am glad that I not going to talk to the womanizer," said Judith. "If I have to talk to him, that will be the first issue that I will discuss with him. Child, look at your self - - young, pretty, highly educated and also well mannered and trained to be the best housewife a man can have. What did you as a woman with all these wonderful qualities get for a husband? None other than a man who went to bed with almost any beautiful woman that came his way. Just imagine the state that I would have been in if you had contracted the virus. God is great! I have many things to be grateful for. One of them is your survival in the home of a pleasure-seeking man! It is very appropriate to use the word "survival" in your case because you faced many perils during your long stay with him. The greatest of these perils are contagious diseases. It is a miracle that you did not contract any. Let me talk now with his father."

"Mother, I understand all what you are saying," said Satta. "But now that I have survived, we should soften our criticism."

"I will not," said the mother angrily. "Let me call his father and tell him my feelings about this matter."

"Please do but try at least to be diplomatic in dealing with his parents," said the daughter.

"Hello! Is that Pastor Lamboi?" she asked.

"Yes, is that Judith?"

"Yes, pastor, how are you?"

"Praise the Lord! I am very well. Thank you."

"Pastor, have you read *The People's Voice* today?" asked Mrs. Lansana.

"No, I have not," replied the pastor.

"If you had read it you would be right here beside your son Misalie," said Mrs. Lansana.

"What has happened to him?"

"It is unfortunate that I am the one to break this news to you," said Mrs. Lansana. "Your son should have broken it to you a long time ago. I am sorry to inform you that he has contracted HIV."

There was silence. Satta who was sitting on the bed noticed the father's silence. He was too shocked to say anything.

"Are you still on the line?" asked Mrs. Lansana.

"Yes, I am. I am just in shock," said the pastor. "The occurrence of this tragedy does not however come to me as a surprise. Since my son lives a promiscuous life in a period when a deadly virus is going around, this outcome is inevitable. There is a saying that he who lives by the sword, dies by it. I have spent my entire life warning this young man about his indulgence in unrestrained sex with beautiful women. He was brought up well in my church and had learned that adultery is sin. But he did not put into practice what he learned. My threats to him that the wages of sin is death were never taken seriously. My goodness! I find it hard to believe that this son of mine is capable of causing so much unhappiness in this family. My heart goes out to your daughter. She has suffered so much on behalf of this young man. I am sorry, Judith, I am very sorry."

"Pastor, I am very angry," said Mrs. Lansana. "I also find it very difficult to believe that this highly intelligent son-in-law would knowingly follow such a path of self-destruction."

"Judith, we have here a situation that is a paradigm of the weakness of the will," said the pastor. "My son knows that being promiscuous in this age increases the risk of catching HIV. We warned him about it and you specifically vented your anger at him several times for such a lifestyle. I remember the evening we sat on the case involving Rosalyn Songa, who is only one of the very many women he is involved with. You almost hit Misalie that night. Everyone thought that your verbal attack would make him decide to change his conduct. Unfortunately he did not. His continued involvement with women demonstrates that he lacks the will to control himself. He is likely to die because of his propensity to indulge too freely in sexual intercourse."

"This donkey has learned the hard way to avoid rear ends," said Judith. "I am sorry, pastor, for being so vulgar in my use of words but that's the way I feel about him."

"That's alright, Judith, I know that the Lord will always forgive you. You are an angry and frustrated woman. I also know that you are concerned about the fate of your daughter. Any mother would naturally be very concerned."

"Pastor, I am sorry about my indiscriminate use of

language," she repeated her apology. "My daughter is today paying a price that she does not have to pay. She is a victim. Yes, an utter victim. Her devotion to such a husband was like a calling. It was a divine summons that could not be refused. Thus she served him faithfully to the very end despite all indications that the sacrifices she was making were not worth it."

"Judith, there is something that I am very afraid to ask," said the pastor. "I was expecting you to mention it but you have not yet touched on it. Now I have to ask it."

"Please ask; you will be given a response," said Judith. "The worst has already happened. What else is there in the dark that can scare me again?"

"The worst will not be over until I know the medical condition of your daughter," said the pastor.

"My daughter tested negative," she replied.

"Praise the Lord!" said the pastor. "Although I am grieving over the tragedy that has befallen my eldest son, I also have to rejoice over your daughter's deliverance by Jesus Christ. Since they are husband and wife, the chances of one catching a contagious disease from the other are great. We are, therefore, very lucky not to have a double tragedy in our hands."

"Thank you, pastor, for being understanding," said Judith. "I appreciate your empathy. My daughter is now in a very difficult position. Although she has worked for a good life, she is going to remain childless and broken-hearted. As for my son-in-law the other immediate problem is dealing with the prejudices associated with contracting HIV. This news will definitely hurt his image. You know that AIDS has been referred to as the mystery disease for three reasons. First, because there is no known cure yet for it; second, because it is easily contracted; and third, because it is contracted in many ways. So, there are many people who will avoid him. My understanding of this disease is that frequent contact with him, even if it is not sexual, can lead to infection. That is why people are afraid of getting close to the patients that have it."

"Oh yes, Judith, that is what I have also heard," said the pastor. "A member of our church was talking to us the other day about the unusual communicability of the disease. I agree with you that one of the consequences of having the disease is the problem with one's image. People are hesitant to approach you out of fear of easily contracting it. In any case, the Lord will provide the help we need. Let our faith in Him keep on glowing. I am coming over to visit. Please inform my son and his wife about my coming."

When the mother hung up she told the daughter about the father-in-law's reaction and what he thought about the son's tragedy and conduct. She also explained their concern about how people would avoid the husband because of the many ways the disease could be very easily contracted. By the time she finished the explanation, tears were dropping from Satta's eyes.

"Thank you, mother, for that good talk," she said. "When you picked up the telephone to call, I thought that you were going to start a big quarrel with my father-in-law. But you engaged in a very polite conversation. The summary you just gave of his reaction and what I myself heard you say show that you have lots of concern about my husband and about AIDS in general. I assure you that your concerns will be appropriately addressed to your satisfaction."

"I hope so," said Judith.

"Did you notice how cooperative my father-in-law was?" asked Satta. "He is a very caring man. I want you too to calm down now. There is no need for you to behave in a way that will reflect badly on me. My reputation and yours are at stake here. It is imperative that we show everyone in that living room that we are sorry about Misalie's tragedy. If we do not do so, then we will be perceived as an unkind family. So, when you return to the living room, try to portray a good attitude and participate in the conversation."

"Everyone knows that you have been a good wife," said the mother. "So do not worry about our reputation. That has been established. My concern now is about your rights and safety."

"Mother, it is true that I have been a good wife, but I would not want to appear unsympathetic at such a difficult time of Misalie's life. I may be judged and remembered more for the way I behave to him now than previously. You are right that we have the right to be angry but let us not allow our anger to tarnish my image as a good and loving wife. The attitude you displayed when you were out there may have made people very uncomfortable. Although you said nothing, your facial expression very clearly indicated that your position on this matter is likely to be uncompromising. I want you to change that attitude before you step out of this room. Try now to surprise my husband by being nice to him in front of his guests."

"My daughter, if your husband had been faithful to you and made you happy, I would not have been this angry with him," she said mildly. "But as his father himself said a little while ago, this man deliberately set out to destroy himself and almost destroyed you in that process. Your advice that I try to be nice and show some understanding is a good one. I will be. But this does not mean that I cannot look for solutions behind the scenes to your terrible situation. Let's go out and talk. This weekend we shall set eyes on Pala. Your relatives in the village, especially your grandmother Musu Lansana and your uncles Abibu and Beimba Lansana, should be informed of this tragedy. So, on Friday after work, I will be waiting for you to come and pick me up in your car. We shall return on Sunday. You can do the driving so that the driver can stay and drive your husband around in the official car."

As soon as the mother had left for the living room, Satta telephoned her friend Alice. Fortunately, she was the one that picked up the receiver.

"Alice, can you come over right away," said Satta in a tense voice.

"Is it urgent?"

"Yes, it is."

"I can come over but since I am a bit worried it will help if I am briefed about what lies ahead.

"Alice, the news about our big secret leaked today," said Satta. "But a controversy is about to begin even before we start dealing with the problem. My mother is the one that is likely to cause it."

"Where is she?"

"She is here already. Other family members are on the way. I believe that the controversy will be partly hinged on a basic misunderstanding about AIDS. My mother who just had a telephone conversation with my father-in-law expressed concerns that indicate that both of them do not understand the nature of the disease and the ways it is contracted. Since you are a nurse who works in an AIDS clinic your presence and explanation of the disease will help. So I am sending our driver to get you."

"See you soon," said Alice. "Please keep calm until I get there."

Rev. Lamboi and his wife arrived with Stephen, their youngest son. They looked sad and worried. Twenty minutes later Alice Lavalie arrived with a girlfriend who was a nurse at the Government Hospital. The first thing the pastor did after the details of the tragedy had been explained to them was to lead the group in prayer. After that a long discussion ensued. Mrs. Judith Lansana was well-behaved as she had promised. This attitude made the son-in-law feel very comfortable. Although he had earlier noticed his mother-in-law's displeasure, he was happy to see a change in attitude.

The atmosphere in the living room was somber. This was due partly to the nature of the issue that had brought them together. However, the pastor's prayer contributed to it. He prayed as if death was about to occur in the family. He ended by asking Jesus Christ to deliver the young man that was about to be removed from their midst. Alice later told Satta that that kind of prayer was not appropriate because it tended to discourage and demoralize the infected man.

"As an AIDS counselor I would not start the meeting with a prayer of that kind," she said. "Its contents are inconsistent with our goal, which is, to make the patient and his relatives believe and feel that there is hope for the afflicted individual. We will of course be realistic by explaining to him the outcome of developing full-blown AIDS; but we will stress the prospects of living a life that is almost normal for several or many years if the patient receives the appropriate treatment."

After everyone had said "Amen" at the end of the pastor's prayer the conversation centered on AIDS and the treatment that the infected man was receiving. Hon. Lamboi who already knew a lot about the disease was surprised at how ignorant most of the people in the audience were about it. It dawned on him what journalists had said about the importance of educating the public about AIDS. He now wished that he had taken them seriously. In any case, he dared not admit his mistake in front of such a gathering.

"So this is the most horrible of viruses since it invariably brings death within months," said Rev. Matthew Lamboi very thoughtfully after the husband and wife had explained the full story.

"That is not necessarily true because one can contract the virus but have no symptoms of the disease," said Alice, trying to make the parents understand the nature of the disease. "At the World Health Organization clinic where I work as a nurse and AIDS counselor, we have people who contracted the virus over four year ago but have still not developed AIDS. With good medical attention it is now possible to contract the virus and live a near-normal life for ten or more years. Early treatment is crucial to combatting the disease."

"So the key is treatment," said the pastor. "Early treatment."

"Yes, Matthew, you heard the learned lady clearly," said Dorothy, the pastor's wife, anxiously. "Treatment is the key. And Matthew, just imagine how much longer AIDS patients would continue to live if treatment continues without interruption! There is really more hope for patients these days than previously. The addition of prayers to the powerful drugs that my son is taking is likely may make him live more than the ten years that Alice has mentioned."

It was clear to everyone that as parents the pastor and his wife were very much affected by the news regardless of the way their son had lived. That is why they were trying to console themselves by talking about the possibility of a prolonged life if their son underwent the proper treatment. That kind of talk was inspired by parental instinct which drives all parents to wish for the best for their children. There were people in the audience that were perceptive enough to notice what the parents wanted to hear. One of them was Sefoi who felt that emphasizing the positive aspect of the problem was good for the morale of the parents. So he said something very consistent with the wishes of both parents.

"The biggest luck would come if AIDS patients or those infected with the virus are alive when a cure is finally found," he said. "They would live as long as people that are free of the virus."

"Sefoi, you should not refer to the finding of a cure as luck," said the pastor. "It will be a miracle. Only God will allow such a great fortune to strike our world."

"A cure would be a miracle," said Hon. Lamboi. "But I am pessimistic enough not to expect one soon. Scientists are not even close to that. They seem to be more preoccupied with treatments that would prolong our lives. If my own treatment works I may be able to live longer and enjoy a life that is a bit comfortable."

"I have an uncle who was infected with the virus four years ago but has not yet died of it," said Alice's girlfriend. "Since he takes his treatment seriously, he is expected to live for many years."

"My son, why don't you seek this uncle and get some information on the kind of treatment he is receiving?" asked Mrs. Dorothy Lamboi.

"My uncle's case is not a secret," said the girlfriend. "Many people now know Maurice Bangura, the former employee of the Golden Complex that tested positive with the disease. The newspaper report about his illness occasioned panic among the people."

"The reason for the panic was that many people were then ignorant of the disease," said Alice. "Today we know that it is transmitted mainly through sexual contact and blood transfusion."

"Is this what has been established by AIDS researchers?" asked the pastor anxiously.

"Yes, this is what has been established by scientists," replied Alice. "There are other ways of contracting the virus but in this country it is contracted in these two ways."

"Well what about ways such as handshakes, hugging, inhaling the air in a room with an AIDS patient and sharing cooking utensils and clothing items?" asked Rev. Matthew Lamboi.

"AIDS is not contracted by any of these means," said Alice. "The rumors that circulate about these means are not backed by scientific evidence."

"But this is supposed to be an infectious disease, is it not?" asked Judith, speaking for the first time.

"Yes, it is an infectious disease but is not contracted by the trivial means just mentioned."

"Mother, I am not going to contract AIDS by merely living with Misalie in this house," said Satta. "Alice who works in an AIDS clinic is qualified to give you the facts about this disease. My married life is of course ruined because I will not be able to share the same bed with him; but I will not contract AIDS by merely living in his house and sharing the same facilities with him. I will not meet such a fate because I am a careful person who understands the disease."

The smiles that came to the lips of Mrs. Judith Lansana indicated that the conversation was enlightening her. The pastor and her wife also smiled. They were quite relieved to receive such valuable information about the disease.

"So, our understanding of the virus can help us live with AIDS patients without hurting ourselves," said Mrs. Judith Lansana.

"That is correct," said Alice.

"Then what we have to do is to pray to God to grant us such understanding," said the pastor.

"It was lack of such understanding that brought most of the confusion when this disease first reached the public's attention," said Alice's girlfriend. "My uncle Maurice Bangura was not the only one that suffered as a result of the unexpected revelation that he had AIDS. I do remember very well another panic that occurred at the bus stop that same day. People refused to enter the bus because Santigie Kamara, an innocent victim that fitted the description of a person with full-blown AIDS, was in it. His civil rights were violated because he was forced to get off the bus. Everyone involved in the incident referred to him as the slim man. It turned out that he did not have the disease. Today he has recovered from whatever illness he then had and has gained weight. He was a victim of prejudice."

"I am pleased with the progress that has been so far made toward finding a cure," said Dorothy. "I came here with the belief that my son was going to die within a few weeks. This has been a very enlightening evening for me."

Although Mrs. Judith Lansana was also enlightened by the information, she did not like the way the conversation went because nothing was mentioned about the fate of her daughter. All focus was on the plight of the husband. But since she wanted to keep to the promise she had made to her daughter, she did not vent her displeasure.

By the time the company was about to leave the atmosphere had changed considerably. Not perceiving Hon. Lamboi as a person on his way out of this world, everyone was relieved and some talked a bit more freely about the disease. When the company finally broke and people started to leave, Satta asked the driver to take her mother home and drop off Alice and her friend on his way back.

"The discussion went as it should," said Alice as they moved to the car. "I am glad that no one tried at this time to criticize Hon. Lamboi. He deserves all the sympathy he can get. If emphasis is put on his faults it will affect the over-all morale of the family. That will make life difficult for everyone."

"I only wish that the conversation had also focussed on the future of my daughter," said Judith.

"Mother, remember your promise to me," said Satta, giving Judith a stern look. "The evening is not over yet."

The mother who was adjusting her head tie noticed the look. Not wanting to provoke a confrontation she smiled and extended her hand to her daughter.

"I am sorry," she said, shaking the daughter's hand gently. "The promise will be kept. Be careful and take care of yourself. I will see you on Friday."

"Alright, mother," said the daughter. "Have a good night's rest. Remember that I am a grown-up. So, I will always take care of myself. See you on Friday."

When Satta returned to the living room the husband hugged her and gave a big sigh of relief.

"The meeting went well," said the husband. "What almost ruined it is people's misunderstanding of the nature of the disease and the ways the virus is contracted. This shows that there is a big struggle ahead of us."

"I had to invite my friend Alice in order to help enlighten our guests about AIDS," said the wife. "Being a nurse who works in an AIDS clinic, I was sure that they were more likely to listen to her than to us."

"Darling, that move saved the day," said the husband. "Your mother's real concern is your contracting the virus from me. She had believed the false rumors that it could be contracted through casual contact and sharing the home together. It is interesting how ignorant our people are of the nature of this terrible disease."

"Darling, you can now see for yourself how adopting no national policy for this disease can hurt everybody," said Satta. "You do, of course, remember our debate over this issue at the time you were making those advertisements on the Golden Complex. I told you then that the people needed to be educated about AIDS. Being the Minister of Health you could have easily launched a big public education program that would have helped individuals and families to deal with the disease. Your failure to do this did hurt the public's interest. You learned during the conversation tonight that informing the public is not only the best means to prevent the spread of the disease but also the way to avoid becoming a victim of people's ignorance of it. If you think that my mother's hostile reaction made you feel uneasy, just imagine how Maurice Bangura, the first AIDS patient, felt when his identity was revealed by journalists. Since the public then knew very little about the disease, people were even afraid to get close to him. A earlier attempt by the government to educate the people would have helped to eliminate the stigma that is attached to having AIDS. As we all saw this evening, my mother was about to treat you tonight the same way Maurice Bangura and Santigie Kamara were treated by the public. She was very concerned about my sharing cooking utensils and personal items with you. I assured her as we walked to the car that I am a grown-up and so would take good care of myself. Misalie, you have become a victim of the official position that you and the president had taken on AIDS."

"Darling, in retrospect, I think that our failure to deal earlier with the disease is wrong," said the husband. "I am sorry that AIDS patients are still being victimized by people who are ignorant of the disease. I wish I had paid more attention to what you had to say before our vacation to London."

"Indeed your negligence of the issue definitely encouraged

ignorant citizens to violate the civil rights of people suspected of having AIDS," said the wife. "As Ali Saffa said in his article, the government was so preoccupied with the profits to be generated from the tourist industry that it turned its back on this disease. As people were suffering from it, the Ministries of Tourism and Health were busy airing advertisements that invited tourists to come and enjoy themselves in an AIDS-free environment."

"But, darling, are you not willing to give the government some credit for taking care of those that contracted the virus and developed the disease?" asked the husband. "All patients were treated and provided with medicine. We said little or nothing about the disease because that would have interfered with tourism; but we did help those who developed it. So, we were not all bad."

"I see that you are still trying to defend that terrible policy," said the wife. "Aggressively promoting tourism while quietly treating AIDS patients is altogether bad because it is not in the national interest in the long run. Can't you see now how your failure to launch an AIDS education program has become a source of embarrassment for you?"

"I can see that," said the husband. "I am not trying to defend the failed policy at all. I only want to say that we meant well when we mentioned our AIDS record in the advertisements."

"You may have meant well," said the wife," "but merely treating AIDS patients is not enough. Something more effective is required to combat the disease."

"Darling our plan failed completely," said the husband. "I concede that remaining silent about the disease has turned out to be a bad policy. I am not sure at this time what the president and the Minister of Tourism, who are in excellent health, would think of my present opinion."

"It was also this non-caring attitude of the government that attracted Rev. Harry Collins, that conservative preacher from the United States, to this country," said the wife. "His coming here on vacation with a large number from his congregation was of course good for tourism. But he selected the Complex because of your AIDS-free advertisements and the belief that you were doing everything you could to eliminate sin. For him AIDS is the result of sin and its absence meant that the government is doing all it could to 'purify' the country. So, in effect he was rewarding you for a job well done."

"Satta, we never endorsed the position of Rev. Collins," said Misalie. "He came here on vacation and whatever he said and preached was part of a personal agenda. The airing of his message on radio was done in collaboration with other churches and the radio station. The government had nothing to do with it. We did, of course, appreciate his business."

"Some of your critics, especially the journalists, are bound to bring his name up in any discussion of your case," said the wife. "I am mentioning it so that you will not be very surprised if you are reminded about his activities and how they inspired your policy of silence on AIDS."

"Satta, as you said earlier, there is a big struggle ahead of us," said Misalie. "Before the public revelation of our secret, I had carefully thought about my mistakes and how they would affect me. Ali Saffa's paper today pointed to the irony involved in my contracting HIV. I do not know of an irony more embarrassing than this. It stems from the fact that I am not merely a cabinet minister; I am also a symbol - a symbol of good health. When people think of our new health care system, they think about me, the person that set it up. 'How, my critics would ask, can somebody who represents such an institution contract such a deadly virus?' "

"Misalie, I know that these criticisms are bound to come up," said the wife. "I only mentioned them so that you can anticipate their coming. I am not trying to discourage you. Your referring to yourself as a symbol of health indicates that you are trying to be too hard on yourself. Please do not criticize yourself so severely. That may prevent you from getting a good night's rest."

"Darling, there is no need to talk about rest," said the husband. "It is past eleven and I am still wrestling with the possible consequences of this tragedy."

"Misalie, you have to put your role in society in its proper perspective," said the wife. "It is true that you are a symbol of good health but so are medical doctors. The latter, notwithstanding their knowledge of medicine, do get sick. It does not follow that because someone practices medicine that he cannot get sick. Likewise, the fact that you are a Minister of Health does not suggest that you cannot contract a disease. Thus you should not indulge in serious self-criticism."

"What you say is true, darling, but my situation is different from that of the medical doctor," said the husband. If a medical doctor gets sick, it is in general regarded as a private matter regardless of the kind of illness and how he caught it. But I am a public figure and a policy maker. Not all my illnesses are regarded as a private matter. My downplaying a deadly disease that is now destroying my life and that of many innocent people is not a private matter. It is a public affair because my tragedy is the result of a health policy that failed. The irony in my eventual death is very clear."

Hon. Lamboi then got up to leave but collapsed on the couch. He was in tears. The wife gave him all the words of encouragement she could.

"Don't you think you should again take some days off as

you did the other time?" asked the wife. "The press will not be kind to you tomorrow."

"I should but, darling, I will go and face the storm," said the husband. "If I face it I will feel better than stay home and agonize over facing it in the future. So by eight I will be in my office."

"Well, let's go to bed," said the wife.

"Satta, I want you to use the master bedroom from now on," he said. "I will take the adjacent bedroom. That is perfectly alright with me. I am paying the price for my past promiscuous life. I can never do anything to infect you with the virus. So, goodnight."

Satta slept soundly because she was really exhausted. The energy spent agonizing over their secret had worn her out at last. She slept as soon as her head touched the pillow. But the husband stayed awake for about two more hours. After turning on the radio, he continued thinking of the new changes in his household. He found it difficult to believe that he was a man that could never sleep again with his wife on the same bed. As a matter of fact he could never again have normal sexual relationship with any woman except if he intended to kill that woman. He shuddered at the thought that he could no longer indulge in sex, a pleasure that had occupied a paramount place in his life. Although he was not impotent he could be easily referred to as such a person by anyone that wanted to ridicule him. This thought brought to mind a businessman in his small town who was noted for his impotence. After paying the bride price and the cost of initiating a girl into the *sande* secret society, he failed to take her home. He told the parents to hold on to her while he went on a business trip. It was rumored in his absence that he had gone to get a cure for his problem. On failing to get that cure he never returned. Somebody else eventually married the girl. The chances are that Hon. Lamboi could also be thought of as impotent for failing to share the bed with his wife. This worried him for a while before his mind strayed to other issues related to the scandal ahead of him.

As he stretched out his hand to turn off his radio which was standing on the night stand, he heard the mention of Rev. Harry Collins's name. That made him to decide to listen to the cassette which contained the message of this controversial American preacher. He put it into the recorder and turned it on.

"Greetings to the people of this noble country. Yours is a country that has been declared to be almost free of AIDS! My name is Rev. Harry Collins. I am an evangelist from the United States of America. Today I am going to tell you what the Bible, God's Holy Word, says about this disease. I say to you without the slightest hesitation that AIDS is the result of God's decision to punish man for his sinful ways. It was introduced among sinners by homosexuals whom God condemned in the Bible and drug addicts who live the kind of life Jesus Christ would never tolerate. Adulterers and fornicators whose sexual activities are inconsistent with the teachings of Christ are also paying a heavy price. Likewise, people with multiple sex partners are being punished. The virus is spreading among them like wild fire.

"I appeal to all these sinners to give up their sinful way of life and turn to the Lord. Christ is waiting to save them. It should not be forgotten that the wages of sin is death.

"I commend the leaders of this nation for their decision to suppress this evil disease at any cost. Those of you out there that are criticizing their tactics to keep out this disease should bear in mind that it is spreading very fast among the residents of countries in which it is not tightly controlled. You must count yourself lucky to live in a country where so much stigma is attached to this terrible disease that no one wants to engage in homosexual and drug activities. You must count yourself lucky to live in a country where the pride of its tourist industry is based not merely on glittering physical structures but also on the absence of a disease brought about by sinful acts.

"My organization is one of the foremost opponents of communism, a godless institution brought about by the sinful acts of men. I am however in total agreement with the Cuban government's policy of mandatory quarantining of those infected with HIV. I will recommend this policy to your government. A quarantine center should be built for the very few that are infected. The existence of such a colony of invalids will serve as a lesson to all that consider engaging in a sinful lifestyle. We must also not forget that when the residents of that colony of death pass away they will condemned to burn forever in hell's everlasting fire..."

Hon Lamboi turned off the cassette angrily. "I wish this man does not come here on vacation this year," he said to himself. "If the government had adopted his policy, I would now be getting ready to become a resident of the AIDS colony that would have been built. The public disgrace to which I would have been subjected could have led to a complete nervous breakdown."

CHAPTER SIX

The discussion the Lambois had at the breakfast table the following morning was lively. There was a lot to discuss because the major newspapers, including *The Free Observer*, the number one paper in the country, had written something on their family tragedy. The basic facts were revealed but there were also false rumors which the Lambois decided should not go unchecked.

"With all the information circulating about us this definitely is not the day that we can work quietly in our offices," said the wife. "We have to do something to check the spread of the false rumors."

"I agree, darling," he said. "Something has to be done. I decided this morning that we should go and talk to the president about this problem. Why don't you make arrangements about your absence from work today and come with me to the Ministry of Health. From there I will make a appointment to see the president about this issue. He is likely to give me some valuable advice."

"One good thing about the public revelation of your tragedy is that all the cards are now on the table," said Satta. "There is a saying that he that is down need fear no fall. We are presently at our lowest point since our marriage and we cannot fall any further. Anything constructive we do now about our misfortune will only make things better for us. There is no way life can get worse than this."

"Well, here we are on the big revolving stage," said the husband. "As the revolution continues slowly the public would see and scrutinize all aspects of our disaster. Let's expect no mercy from the press or the public because a disaster like mine which entails a big irony is likely to be a source of ridicule. But after the dust settles down, we shall begin the reconstruction of our lives. This is a time of sadness but it is also a time for the rebuilding of shattered hopes and dreams. Let's go out and face the day expecting even colleagues to show us no mercy."

Before the couple left home, Satta called Sylvia Gbondo, the secretary, to tell her that she would not be in her office that day. The drive to the office of the president was a quiet one since the couple was busy reading the daily papers. That showed how preoccupied they were with the many things that were written about their lives.

When they arrived at the ministry, the husband immediately made an arrangement to see the president. The meeting which took place at ten that morning went very well. The president suggested that a news conference be held on the matter. He told Hon. Lamboi that a public statement about his personal tragedy was more likely to arouse public understanding and sympathy than trying to keep the matter a secret. The Lambois thought this was good advice. Since questions were also bound to be asked about the current position of the government on AIDS, the president told him that it was alright to promise the public that an AIDS policy would be developed and that an announcement about it would be made shortly.

Their discussion eventually touched on the activities of Dr. Lakka. The husband explained in detail the fraudulent activities of the Director of Public Health and their consequences for the nation's health care system. The president was shocked by this information and assured him that an investigation would be made into his conduct. The meeting ended with handshakes.

Hon. Lamboi and his wife were delighted about the way the meeting with the head of state went. Their concern had been that the man would refuse to accept the idea of developing a policy on AIDS on the grounds that it would adversely affect tourism and tarnish the image of the country. If this had happened, the husband would have had to defend in front of the press a governmental position that had discouraged the education of the public about the disease. He would have had to defend such a position even though he himself was a carrier of the virus. That is why he was relieved by the president's willingness to allow him to make that promise. It averted a press conference that would have been steeped in controversy and irony.

"Darling, the president is sympathetic," said the wife, as they drove back to the Ministry of Health. "But the criticism of the press is likely to be that an AIDS policy is now being developed as a result of the personal tragedy that has befallen a cabinet member. Many critics would wonder why the government waited until a top politician contracted the virus before getting serious about the disease."

"There is reason to suspect an ulterior motive in our change of position on AIDS," said the husband. "But, Satta, that does not matter now. Our fault has been uncovered and I am willing to take the blame for my share in it. What matters now is that I am able to promise the nation something. It is better for me to bear the blame for supporting a bad AIDS policy in the past than look stupid still trying to support that same policy even after it has been shown to be flawed. So I am fortunate to be in a position to tell the people that the government is going to introduce an AIDS policy. This is the silver lining in the dark clouds that are rapidly engulfing us. It indicates that matters can only get better, not worse."

"The granting of your request by the president has removed a big stumbling block in your attempt to deal with the public," said the wife. "Being an understanding man he does not want you to experience further embarrassment."

"Yes, he had proved to be understanding and I am very grateful for that," said the husband. "The news conference is at three o'clock this afternoon in the conference room at this ministry."

When Satta left her husband's office, she drove straight to her mother's office. She wanted to have lunch with her and also invite her to the news conference. The mother was pleased with the idea and agreed to go. After lunch they decided to pass by Satta's office so that she could check on her mail before returning to the Ministry of Health. As they approached the office building they saw Veronica Johnson, Hon Lamboi's secretary, entering it.

"I wonder what she is doing out here when she is supposed to be at work," said Satta. "Today is supposed to be a busy day in my husband's office."

"Veronica has probably come to see you," said the mother. "She may be bearing an important message."

"That is not possible because she knows that I will not be in my office today," said Satta. "She was here a week or so ago to see Sylvia. After both talked for a long time they came to my office to ask questions about my vacation in London."

"Well, you will soon find out what she wants," said the mother. "Have they found out about your husband's disaster?"

"I am not sure that they have," replied the daughter as she took out her key to open the office door. "But they do read the newspapers."

"In any case, she is not supposed to be coming here for

private conversations," said Judith. "She should be at the office working. You can see for yourself why I had to get rid of her when she was working for me. Both of them are a waste."

At this point both women heard the two secretaries laughing loud. Since they did not expect Satta to be in the office at that time, they were not cautious about how they talked and what they talked about. The laughing indicated that something was exciting them. Satta wanted to go in there to tell them to control themselves but the mother signalled to her to sit down and be quiet.

"My goodness! A Minister of Health with AIDS? This is the news of the year!" exclaimed Sylvia.

"Yes, it really is," said Veronica. "It is news that just will not go away. There is again something about it in today's issue of all the papers."

"That should not surprise us at all," said Sylvia. "It is, after all, the news of the year."

The two laughed again. If either of them had stepped into the hallway she could have seen Satta's door wide open with the lights on. Realizing that they were being clearly heard they would have either stopped the conversation or changed the topic.

"There is a big irony in the Lambois' tragedy," said Veronica. "The man that is supposed to warn the country about AIDS has himself contracted it. This is an indication that our health care system is in disarray. I am really sorry for Satta, you know. She is one of the sweetest women any man can marry; however, she has never had peace. The husband is too promiscuous. He is a donkey."

"I am sure that you must know a lot about the husband's promiscuous activities because you are his personal secretary," said Sylvia.

"Oh yes, that man would like to have an affair with any beautiful woman he meets, even if she is married," said Veronica. "I am not surprised at his contracting HIV. He has paid dearly for his lifestyle."

"Poor Satta! How much I pity her!" said Sylvia emphatically.

"Her mother, a very perceptive woman, advised her from the onset not to marry that man," asked Veronica. "She now wishes that she had listened to that advice."

"There is no way she could have listened," said Sylvia. "The man was a national football star and every pretty woman including me admired and wanted him at that time. Grabbing him from everyone was a victory for Satta. She got what everybody wanted."

"Now she has what no one wants," said Veronica.

Both women laughed again very delightedly. Satta wondered whether both were interested in working that day because they had talked past their lunch hours. Judith sat there angry and looking stern. She could not believe that people could have so much fun at work.

"We know from experience that Mrs. Judith Lansana is a very strict woman," said Sylvia. "She should have taken stricter measures to forbid the union. I am surprised that she merely advised her against marrying such a man."

"I heard that she eventually took stricter measures but still failed," said Veronica. "She had in fact refused to participate in the wedding. It was at the urge of Pastor Lamboi that she finally consented to participate."

"Well, Satta is an innocent victim today," said Sylvia. "She is childless and has no husband."

"But they are still married," said Veronica.

"Yes, they are, but the man is virtually useless to such a

young and pretty woman," said Sylvia. "They can only have intercourse at the risk of her life. I doubt that Satta, after going through so much suffering in her life, would be interested in taking such a risk."

"Well, if she refuses to have intercourse with him, Rosalyn Songa would step in to fill the gap," said Veronica. "She is somebody that likes to take risks. Look at the risk she takes by going with Hon. Lamboi. She knows that the wife knows about this affair but she does not seem to care."

"I doubt if she would like to get involved with a man that is infected with HIV," said Sylvia. "She may like to take risks but she is not stupid."

"Rosalyn tells me all that goes on between her and the minister," said Veronica. "She trusts me very much and through me she can have easy access to the man she loves. She is not stupid but she is capable of doing foolish things. She is capable of having intercourse with this man even though she knows that he has contracted HIV. When I discussed this AIDS issue with her yesterday in her big office, she told me that she did not take it seriously."

"So she has a big office," said Sylvia. "How did she get it?"

"Yes, she has a big office that she does not deserve," said Veronica. "Hon. Lamboi gave it to her. It was specially decorated to attract her. I will take you there sometime. She is friendly and would enjoy talking with you. She works for Mr. Sefoi Juana, the Commissioner of Health."

"This is news to me," said Sylvia. "I would be interested in going to see that office."

"What impressed me most when I went there the first time was the state-of-the-art office equipment," said Veronica. "There is a telephone, a computer, a printer and a fax machine. The furniture and the carpet looked new. Behind the large executive desk was an executive swivel chair that turns freely in any direction. It has an air-lift control for height adjustment and adjustable arms and back. The seat has extra cushioning for extra comfort. The pictures on the wall are not the types that can put the occupant of the office in a working mood. One of them is a very colorful travel poster advertising a luxury hotel in Jamaica. The activities of the tourists enjoying on a sunny beach give a feeling of not wanting to stay in the office and work."

"The atmosphere of such an office would definitely put its occupant in a play mood," said Sylvia.

"That's true," said Veronica. "The office was equipped for play anyway. In fact one day they played to excess and had an accident."

"What happened?" asked Sylvia.

"On that particular day Hon. Lamboi went to her office just to play," said Veronica. "Since both were in that mood, they immediately fell to it. Sitting in the executive swivel chair, he asked his sweetheart to sit on his lap so that they could spin around a bit. It is their merry-go-round, you know. But what happened next was a crash that brought Sefoi Juana's junior secretary to the scene. She was the one that later narrated this incident to me. She told me that the crash was quite painful. Both love birds were on the floor moaning. It's interesting how care-free adults play."

Both secretaries laughed for a while. Their audience in the adjacent office continued to listen attentively.

"Was anyone injured?" asked Sylvia.

"Fortunately no one was injured," replied Veronica. "But the crash ended the play for that day. I think that Rosalyn Songa would have been a better match for the minister than Satta. They are madly in love. That is why I believe that she would take a risk to please the minister even when she knows that he is infected with HIV."

"You want to tell me that she can sacrifice her life for him?" asked Sylvia.

"I would think so," said Veronica. "She knows about AIDS but has refused to take the report about the minister's condition seriously.

"She is stupid then," said Sylvia bluntly.

"You can say so about her if you wish," said Veronica. "Let's call it a stupid risk."

"But do you really think that Hon. Lamboi will be willing to have intercourse with her when he knows that he is infected with the virus?" asked Sylvia.

"That's a difficult question to answer," said Veronica. "If Rosalyn did not know about his condition, you would accuse the minister of deliberately trying to kill her. The thing however is that she does not take the disease seriously. Hon. Lamboi does take it seriously and may resist the temptation of having intercourse with her. But if the woman continues to tempt him, he may succumb to her advances. When that happens Rosalyn will be another loser. As you know, human passion can be controlled only to a certain extent. Do you know that they have a date this Thursday evening after work?"

"Are you joking?" asked Sylvia?"

"No joke," said Veronica. "He is coming to her house with Mr. Sefoi Juana for dinner. Some women would already have considered breaking up with this man in order not to be tempted to engage in anything that would jeopardize their lives. But this woman wants the relationship to continue like before. Who knows what will happen between them after the guests are gone?"

"Will you be there this time?" asked Sylvia.

"Of course, she told me yesterday that she would like me to

come" replied Veronica. "I accepted the invitation. The woman is an excellent cook. We shall again eat on Thursday with a hearty appetite."

"I wonder what will happen if Satta gets to know about this dinner," said Sylvia.

"She will not get to know at all," said Veronica. "He will tell his wife that Parliament will be in session that evening. That will give him the chance to go out and she will not suspect anything."

"But even if she suspects something she should not do anything about it," said Sylvia.

"Why should she not," said Veronica. "That is her husband and she loves him. It is her right to prevent any other woman from enjoying his company."

"You are right," said Sylvia. "But if Satta decides not to go to bed with a man carrying the virus, she should not prevent him from getting sexual gratification elsewhere. In fact allowing him to go out will help contain the emotional urge that the man may experience from time to time. That will prevent him from going after Satta."

"If Satta is that understanding, then she should decide never to ask any questions whenever the man goes out to seek his gratification from some stupid woman," said Veronica.

"I agree with you," said Sylvia with a restrained smile. "And she should also decide to throw all jealousy out of the window."

"Exactly so," said Veronica. "But don't you think that Satta may consider it morally wrong for someone with AIDS to go to bed with somebody that is free of the virus?" asked Veronica.

"I think that she may," replied Sylvia.

"Will she then not feel guilty for allowing her husband to involve himself with other women?" asked Veronica.

"She may not feel guilty at all because it is not a secret that her husband is infected with the virus," said Sylvia. "Those who go to bed with him do so knowing well that they can get infected. So Satta will bear no blame for failing to intervene. Her conscience is clear. Besides, she cannot control the movements of an uncontrollable grown-up."

At this point, Judith who felt that she had heard enough, wanted to go there to interfere but the daughter pleaded with her not to do so. It was after they were in the car heading for the news conference that Satta gave the reason for her decision.

"Mother, I did not want them to know that we were eavesdropping because I want to verify the information about that dinner," she said. "Interfering with their conversation would have made Veronica to alert Rosalyn about a possible clash between me and Misalie over the invitation. Suspecting that I will stop my husband from going there may lead to a cancellation."

"Your decision is not bad," said the mother. "But what precisely do you plan to do about it?"

"I do not know yet the action I will take," said Satta. "In any case, it will be drastic. If that dinner is held, it will be the turning point in my relationship with Misalie. Hitherto, I have been very mild and very cooperative because I want to help a husband in a very difficult situation. I hope that the dinner will not be held so that I can continue to give him my moral support. But if it is held as planned, that will be an indication that he is determined to continue with the same lifestyle that has not only landed him in this disaster but also made my life miserable. I am no longer going to make foolish sacrifices. Thursday night will be the turning point for me."

"Do you think that you will be able to remain calm until Thursday after all that you have heard today about the affair between your husband and Rosalyn?" asked the mother.

"Yes, mother I will be able to contain my indignation one more time," replied the daughter. "Remember that turning points are the dramatic moments that separate the past from the present. Since such moments are very important, one should be very patient in dealing with the circumstances that lead to them. Hasty actions and decisions can lead to mistakes. Knowing myself to be a conscientious person, I will feel guilty if I err. To avoid such a feeling I need evidence that is irrefutable. So I will first patiently confirm the information I have gathered today before taking action."

"My daughter, you know how I feel about Misalie," said Judith. "If matters were left to me alone your relationship with him would have ended a long time ago. As far as I am concerned, there is no need to confirm this dinner before taking action. You can simply confront him with the information you have and see what he has to say. But since I respect your views and feelings, I will not dissuade you from confirming the information otherwise. When you get the irrefutable evidence you are looking for I will be willing to advise you if you so desire."

The news media was present at the news conference which was held in a big hall at the Ministry of Health. Although there was no rush on the part of the public to go to listen to what the minister had to say about his condition, there were no unoccupied seats by the time the conference began. The empty space at the back of the hall was occupied by those that could not get seats. These did not mind standing and talking as they waited for the appearance of the Minister of Health on the stage.

Maurice Bangura, probably the most wildly known AIDS patient, occupied a seat in the last row. His case came to national attention four years ago when he was injured in an accident at the Golden Complex where he worked as a bricklayer. It was during his recuperation that it was discovered that he had HIV.

The accident itself took place on the day a big fountain was being set up in the main lobby. In order to give this lobby an attractive appearance the interior decorators had suggested that the statue of a mermaid be made a part of the structures from which the water would flow. The supervisor of the project, in a conscientious attempt to ensure that no one got injured, had instructed his workers on how to properly handle each statue in a way that it would not tilt too much in any direction. But despite all the precaution the unfortunate bricklayer got pinned under the mermaid when it unexpectedly tilted toward him. He could have avoided the injury by simply letting it fall. If that had happened the financial loss to the Complex and the embarrassment to the supervisor would have been great. But the conscientious bricklayer would not allow that disaster to happen. Like a patriot that would never allow his fatherland to be destroyed, Maurice gallantly stood his ground. One could hear his groans as he continued to push the statue upward to prevent it from hitting the ground. On seeing the tilt and hearing the groans, the supervisor rushed to the help of the unfortunate victim. But he failed miserably in that attempt. When the groans gave way to yells, everyone knew that something had gone wrong and tried to help remedy the terrible situation. But since the size of the object could not allow all the workers to see each other and there was no one to coordinate their efforts, the statue was pushed and pulled in different directions. Maurice who was now completely exhausted gave up the struggle and let go the statue. It lay across his lap. At that point the supervisor shouted: "lift the statue and move it to my left." Since everyone then knew very clearly what to do, the pushing and pulling ended. The statue was soon in the air and the poor man was moved away. Despite the pain no bones were broken. He recovered completely but left the hospital with the terrible revelation that he had contracted HIV. Since his discharge four years ago treatment had slowed down the progress of the disease. He had remained strong enough to go around but knew that he would one day be incapacitated by it.

Sitting next to Maurice was Santigie Kamara the man who was forced to get off the bus by ignorant civilians who suspected him of having AIDS. Both Maurice and Santigie attended the news conference because they felt that they were victims of the failure of the government to develop an AIDS policy. They were anxious to hear what a cabinet minister who had contracted the virus had to say about the disease.

"I think that Hon. Lamboi fully deserves this fate," said Maurice. "Since he is responsible for the tragedy that has befallen some of us, it is only fair that he too contract the virus."

"I agree with you," said Santigie. "If he had launched an effective AIDS campaign, people like you would have known about the disease and avoided doing whatever you did to make you contract the virus."

"Santigie, I am a very prudent man," said Maurice. "If anyone had told me that a deadly virus was going around threatening the lives of people, I could have instantly changed my lifestyle so that I would not contract it. It was well after the existence of AIDS was known that I contracted it. Dr. Cole is the one treating the woman that infected me. The government knew about the deadliness of the virus before I started going with that woman. So, if the Ministry of Health had educated us earlier about HIV I would never have gone with her. I do hold Hon. Lamboi responsible for my impending death. That is why I believe that he fully deserves his fate."

"But, Maurice, unlike this cabinet minister, you do not

deserve such a fate because you did not know about the existence of the disease," said Santigie. "While you can be said to be the victim of his negligence, he can be said to be the victim of his stupidity. He knew about the existence of the virus but still decided to be promiscuous. What a silly fool!"

A couple sitting next to them laughed. That made them laugh too. Santigie continued talking.

"I read in one of the papers today that he has very many girlfriends," continued Santigie. "It is hard to believe that an educated man like this could make the kind of decision that is leading him to such a tragic end?"

"Santigie, things like this do happen," said Maurice. "People who are expected to act rationally sometimes do things that destroy their lives. Their knowledge of the facts does not necessarily make them use those facts to their advantage. As Minister of Health, Hon. Lamboi has all the facts about AIDS. He has tons of the literature on AIDS sent to his ministry by the World Health Organization for distribution among citizens. Although he knew that the information is in all those documents, he never used it to protect himself. The man is just plain hopeless."

The couple laughed again. Maurice continued.

"Since his passion for beautiful women and sex is more in control of him than his reason, I hope that he does not transmit this virus to others."

"I have also heard about his indulgence in sex," said Santigie. "If this information is true, then he is likely to go around spreading the virus."

"This should be a matter of concern," said Maurice.

"You know my story, of course," said Santigie. "I do not have AIDS but I was victimized because I once looked like somebody with full-blown AIDS. If the public were given the appropriate education about the disease, I would not have suffered so much at the hands of ignorant people. I believe that the president and his Minister of Health are responsible for my suffering. I experienced a lot of discrimination because of my appearance."

"Are you still being discriminated against?" asked Maurice.

"No, of course, I have gained weight," replied Santigie holding apart his hands to indicate how much weight he had gained. This gesticulation made Maurice to laugh. The couple joined him. "The memories of the way I was treated make me very bitter. "Many people refused to shake hands with me and my landlord threw me out of the building. Those who were bold enough to visit me would not eat with me out of fear that they too would get infected. I suffered a serious humiliation at the bus stop because of the government's refusal to develop a policy on AIDS and launch an effective campaign to educate the people."

"We shall now wait to see whether such a campaign will be launched," said Maurice.

"Of course, it will now be launched because a cabinet minister has contracted the virus," said Santigie. "Politicians are like this. It is when one of their own is affected by a problem that they hurry to seek a solution."

"But this time no amount of legislation would save their colleague," said Maurice. "Not even his admission to the best AIDS hospital in the world would at this time eliminate the virus from his body. If he develops the disease he will eventually meet the same fate like all of us."

The appearance of the Minister of Health and his wife on the podium interrupted this passionate conversation. Mrs. Judith Lansana who was sitting in the front row felt uncomfortable on seeing the minister moving toward the loudspeaker. Her mind was still on the conversation between Veronica and Sylvia. She was very disappointed to learn that her son-in-law was still indulging in the kind of lifestyle that had led to his ruin. She just could not even start considering the possibility of forgiving the man that almost ruined her daughter. But unlike her, Satta who occupied the chair placed by the podium, was very calm and in full control of her feelings. Although Rosalyn's dinner was very much on her mind, she was already too used to disappointments to allow herself to be distracted at such a critical moment. She wanted the news conference to be a success. If it failed the gossip and the disappointment would be difficult for his family to deal with. Her eyes were all over the place trying to see who and who were present. She also looked several times in the direction of the journalists to see which news organizations were represented. Having been a politician's wife for years she knew most of them. Her heart leapt when her eyes fell on Ali Saffa, the man she considered to be the most critical among them. Although she had liked his articles and editorials on AIDS because they had helped bring the importance of the disease to the forefront, she was concerned about his asking the type of complicated questions that may be difficult to deal with in a news conference. If the husband made a mistake in answering such questions the goal of the news conference, which was to contain the rumors about the scandal, would not be met. But all this hard thinking came to an end when it was announced that the minister was about to begin speaking.

Hon. Lamboi had planned his short speech all day. He had also prepared answers to the kinds of questions that he believed the press would ask. He looked so relaxed that he smiled slightly before beginning to speak. At one time his eyes met those of his wife but he pretended that there was no eye contact. Her nod of approval assured him that his wife wanted him to succeed.

The first few statements were clear and to the point. Hon. Lamboi confessed outright that he had contracted HIV. The wife was very pleased with that. Some journalists may have been surprised since some politicians would not have headed straight for the truth. They would have looked for indirect ways of getting to it. After this confession the minister explained his family tragedy in a chronological manner. He started with the visit to the hospital in London where he was told that he had the virus. He then talked about the conflicting positions of the two doctors on his situation and gave reasons why he believed Dr. Cole. After the discussion of his current medical treatment, he talked about the government's plan to urgently develop a policy on AIDS. When he finished speaking, his wife smiled. All the facts were truthfully and concisely presented in about ten minutes.

The journalists then started the questioning. Satta was concerned about how her husband would deal with the personal ones. Fortunately, all the journalists were prudent enough not to ask any. They devoted their time and attention on the new AIDS policy to be developed and why it had not been developed all this time. Since Hon. Lamboi had anticipated this question, he had prepared for it. He accepted the blame for the delay in coming up with such a policy. He also acknowledged that many people were hurt by the failure of the government to initiate it earlier. Many questions were asked about Dr. David Lakka. The revelation about the conflicting results issued by the two doctors generated more curiosity than expected. Many journalists wanted to know if and when an inquiry into the scandal would be launched. Hon. Lamboi told them of the president's commitment to appointing a Commission of Inquiry to investigate the scandal. The discussion of this issue left no doubt that after the news conference many journalists would descend on Dr. Lakka's office like a combat unit.

When the news conference was over, Satta took Judith back to her office. On the way she asked the mother for her reaction to Hon. Lamboi's performance.

"Mother, tell me what you think of how he handled the conference," said Satta.

"He did very well," said Judith. "The reason for my saying this is that the journalists remained very orderly. You know what happens when journalists become critical about a politician's performance during a news conference. They will shower him with many embarrassing questions. They can be very mean."

"Can you tell me precisely why they were not as mean as expected?" asked the daughter.

"The reason is that Misalie was very honest in his narration of his tragedy," replied the mother. "He confessed that he had contracted the virus and then went on to accept some of the responsibility for the lack of an AIDS policy in the country. He even conceded that there was an ulterior motive involved in his willingness to develop an AIDS policy immediately after he had contracted the virus. Misalie did the unexpected. He was so frank that the journalists could not attack him with ardor. But if he had tried to be evasive in answering questions, Ali and others would have hit him very hard. Nothing he said eluded them. This was definitely not the kind of day journalists would dream about. A heyday for most journalists would be one on which a delicate issue unexpectedly explodes bringing to light some sensitive or scandalous information. But no explosion occurred today. Your husband was as meek as a lamb and as submissive as a person that is eager to tell the truth."

"Is there any other reason for the orderliness of things?" asked Satta.

"There is of course another important reason," replied the

mother. "When the journalists went to the news conference they expected it to deal with one scandal - the one involving the minister himself. But then they found another one that equally captured their attention. That was the one involving Dr. Lakka, the Director of Public Health. Few things can be more scandalous than the discovery that such a high-ranking public official had been lying to his patients. As we sit here the press reporters are looking for him. If the Commission of Inquiry establishes the fact that he had been falsifying documents, then all the statistics on AIDS are questionable. This very big, unexpected scandal equally attracted the attention of the press."

"Mother, I agree with you on both points," said Satta. "My husband's honesty and the second scandal did very much contribute to the success of this news conference."

When Satta dropped off her mother, she went to her office. Her colleagues, who had been concerned about her problems came in to express their sympathies. She gave some details about her husband's condition and explained what happened at the press conference that afternoon. Unlike Veronica and Sylvia, they were very sincere in their attitude and Satta knew it.

When the Lambois got home later that evening, Satta congratulated her husband on his performance.

"Darling, I was impressed with the press conference," she said. "I believe that you did the best you could."

"Well, I gave the facts but tomorrow we shall see how those facts will be analyzed in the papers," said the husband. "The reactions will vary from praise to harsh criticism."

"I would not worry too much about that," said the wife. "We have to ride the criticisms like a sailor rides a storm. What is important is that the conference was orderly and the scandal was contained to some extent."

At about eight o'clock Michael and Stephen, Misalie

younger brothers visited. They could not attend the press conference and so they wanted to find out how it went. When they learned the details they too were of the opinion that it went well. As they talked, one of the advertisements on the Golden Complex came on television. It was the one that invited tourists to come and have a good time in an almost AIDS-free country. Despite their serious involvement in the discussion of the press conference, none of them could ignore the advertisement. All of them fixed their eyes on the screen and listened to it as if this was the first time it was being aired. They all knew that continuing to air it was very embarrassing for the minister.

"Misalie, did you discuss the withdrawal of this advertisement with the president today?" asked Stephen. "It should be withdrawn because the publicity over your having contracted HIV has ruined it. It is more likely now to remind people about your catching the virus than about attracting tourists to the Golden Complex."

"I did not discuss it with the president today," said Hon. Lamboi. "Even if it occurred to me, I may not have mentioned any thing about it because I expect the Minister of Tourism to withdraw any advertisement that is obviously no longer valid."

"I wonder what is wrong with this fat tourist minister of ours," said Michael, who is well known to be a very funny man. "Does he have to be told that the contents of this advertisement are now obsolete? I assure you that he may be at home right now sitting in his over-sized chair and watching that advertisement. He may not act as quickly as we would like him to."

This comment made the others to laugh. They all knew the Minister of Tourism, a huge man weighing close to three hundred pounds.

"I believe that he may have it withdrawn by tomorrow,"

said Hon. Lamboi. "His problem is that he is too forgetful."

"If I were you, Misalie, I would call to remind him about it tomorrow," said Satta.

"This man is very disciplined and hard-working," said Hon. Lamboi. "The problem with him is his forgetfulness and his size. I may have to remind him several times tomorrow before that advertisement is removed. He is so forgetful that anytime he comes here he leaves something behind. I have to send my driver to rush it to him. His size is also a concern to us whenever he is here. The only chair he can fit in is the special one standing over there. Since it is bigger than all the others we always make sure that we offer it to him when he is here. We worry that he may forget and sit in the normal chairs. That would cause an accident. He broke a chair before."

The others laughed. They were very amused by the story.

"But why does he not sit in the chair you have bought for him?" asked Stephen." It is without doubt visibly bigger than all the other chairs in this living room."

"That is very true," said Hon. Lamboi. "But sometimes he forgets to sit in the right chair. We were very embarrassed the very first time he visited us because we had no chair that he could fit in. So we all moved into the verandah and offered him the hammock. But that became the beginning of our uneasiness. Although the hammock was strained to the point that it was squeaking, he swung comfortably in it. Our concern was that it would break; but we dared not tell him to get up. First, he would feel unwelcome if we did; second there was no other seat to give to him. Unfortunately for us he stayed for hours swinging gently from side to side and enjoying his long pipe. Although our worst fear did not come to pass, our uneasiness was terrible. All our nerves were on edge."

The narration of this incident brought enough laughter to

make everyone to temporally abandon the serious topic being dealt with.

"The squeaking was coming from the two iron hooks that attached the hammock to the wooden planks of the ceiling," said Satta. "It was the first time we ever heard the sound. When his pipe ran out of tobacco we thought that he would leave but he refilled and relit it. The swinging continued. He was inattentive to the squeaking that preoccupied us. In effect the incident ruined our evening. Thus there was no way we could have forgotten to buy that over-sized chair the following day. A repeat of that incident in the future would definitely have caused one to become a nervous wreck."

Michael made a few more humorous comments about this incident before they returned to the topic at hand. The brothers left about ten o'clock.

All evening Satta had in mind the conversation between the two secretaries. Although she was unhappy about it, she decided to be patient and not do anything that would make the husband feel suspicious and decide not to attend the dinner. So, she behaved normally. One question she kept on asking herself was whether Rosalyn would take the risk of going to bed with him. Veronica said that she would although going to bed with Misalie meant standing a good chance of contracting the virus. It was like committing suicide. Thoughts like these occupied her mind until she slept.

The following day was uneventful. Satta's colleagues continued to have polite conversations with her about the turmoil in her life. Veronica who tried to be inquisitive asked to go to lunch with her but Satta turned down her request.

The other big news that day was the appointment of the Commission of Inquiry to investigate the conduct of Dr. Lakka. The government was shocked by the extent of his fraud.

According to the final report of the Commission, which was released months later, he did falsify the records of many patients and lied to the government about the number of AIDS cases in the country. After confessing to his crime, he claimed that he committed it in order to promote tourism. He was sentenced to six months' imprisonment.

CHAPTER SEVEN

Thursday finally arrived! Satta was still more determined than ever to make the day a turning point in her relationship with her husband if the latter went to eat at Rosalyn Songa's place. Although she had informed her mother and her friend Alice of her plan to be at the dinner, she had refused to give them the details of what exactly she would do there. This was to prevent anyone from convincing her not to execute her plan. Alice and Judith, two highly trusted people who should have known the details, were surprised at her secrecy. But during her meeting with both of them during lunch that day, she invited Alice to go along with her. The latter quickly accepted the invitation to such an important event. Judith, who was also keenly interested in going, felt disappointed when Satta told her that it was inappropriate for her to go.

"Satta, I think that you should invite me too because I suspect that a conflict is very likely in such a situation," said Judith. "You need the presence of an older and more mature relative to help you deal with it. Since I am that kind of person, I am qualified to be there."

"Mother, the presence of a trusted friend like Alice will suffice," said Satta. "Since this is a matter between me and two passionate love birds, I do not want any close or important relative to be there. A mother's presence in a situation where a grown-up daughter should prove her womanhood is an indication of weakness. It implies that the daughter is so weak that she needs a backup. I simply do not want your presence because I do not want to look weak. I want to look very strong. Matters would even get worse for my image if you happen to interfere in the altercation especially when such interference is not warranted. The maternal sympathy women are endowed with is innately good; but it can be detrimental when applied in a situation like this. Alice, being only a close friend, would be better able to contain her emotions and resist any temptation to interfere on my behalf. I am confident that she would be a good witness and remain one till the very end. Her job is to observe and objectively narrate what happens. She is only going because her presence may prevent Rosalyn or any member of her household from giving a different version of the incident. So with all due respect to you, mother, your absence is what is in my best interest. To console you a bit, I have to say that if my father were alive and expressed any interest in going, I would have told him the same thing. I promise, however, that I will tell you the details when it is all over. So expect to see me very late tonight."

So strong was this appeal that the mother agreed to stay. Wishing the daughter good luck, she advised her to take strong but appropriate measures.

"Remember, my daughter, that there is a difference between doing what is appropriate and doing what is disgraceful," said Judith. "You can do to the love birds whatever you like but it should be appropriate. If it is, it will reflect well on your character and reputation. So do not do anything outrageous to them."

"Mother, please trust me," said Satta. "The measures I will take will be very appropriate."

When lunch was over they all returned to work. At about two o'clock, Hon. Lamboi called to tell Satta that he would come home late that evening because of a cabinet meeting. She politely wished him good luck with the meeting and hung up.

A righteous indignation took over Satta's entire being. Her husband's intention affected her to such an extent that she felt the room moving round and round. It was as if she had just sat down in a chair after spinning around on her heels. "Veronica is right about the dinner!" she whispered after composing herself. She started to wonder why the man with whom she had gone through such terrible times would betray her to such an extent. Finding no answers to all the difficult questions she asked, she called Alice to update her on the matter.

"Alice, the information about the dinner is true," she said angrily. "My husband just called to tell me that he would be coming home late due to a cabinet meeting."

"Have you checked whether or not there is a cabinet meeting?" asked Alice.

"Yes, I have," replied Satta. "There is nothing on his calendar for this evening. Besides, I overheard Veronica saying this morning that she would eat very little for lunch in order to save space for a big dinner to which she had been invited."

"I am sorry, Satta, that you are experiencing such a terrible betrayal," said Alice. "Your husband is as elusive as ever. I doubt if you can claim to understand him. He has big problems and needs much more help than we had thought. Satta, since this looks like the beginning of the end, just make sure that you come out of this hardship a victor. So do not do anything that would tarnish your reputation. This man has destroyed himself, not you. You will recuperate your losses some day but he will not. He is heading rapidly for an irreversible disaster. I wish you can cancel whatever plan you have made for tonight. It may not be worth the trouble interrupting that dinner. In any case, I will go there with you. Since their dinner is not until seven thirty, can we go over to my house for dinner? From my place we shall go directly to Rosalyn's."

"Thanks, Alice, I will pick you up at five after work," said Satta. "I will enjoy your good company until seven thirty."

Satta picked up Alice as planned. From the city center with its attractive sights they passed through some upper and middle class neighborhoods heading for the low-class neighborhood where Alice lived with her parents. Since Satta had driven along these same streets many times the way was very familiar. At one point she glanced at her friend and wondered why she was so devoted to her. That made her to reflect on their long friendship. It started during elementary school days and continued through secondary school. Both were fortunate to earn scholarships to go to London where Satta studied accounting while Alice Lavalie studied nursing. But although they came from homes with similar socio-economic backgrounds, fortune favored Satta when Hon. Lamboi, a wealthy politician, got interested in her. The marriage landed her in one of the best neighborhoods of Bassaya while Alice, who was still single, continued to live in a low-class neighborhood. So although Satta's marriage had been disastrous she lived a lifestyle that could be contrasted with that of Alice who had to work hard to help her father with family expenses. Since no one in her family owned a car, Satta either picked her up or sent a driver to get her whenever they planned to go to places together. Despite this contrast in fortune, the friendship had grown over the years and both women respected each other very much. Satta believed that the moral support that Alice had given her was worth all the money in the world. She lived in wealth but was unhappy enough to need a genuine friend to advise her from time to time.

The ride ended in a part of town where the houses were smaller and the streets narrower. It was a neighborhood where the joy of life depended more on the pleasant social relationships between the residents than on affluence. Although no well-to-do people lived there it was a well organized community whose residents were mostly from towns and villages in the provinces. They had come to the city for their share in what was commonly referred to as the good life. Their occupations ranged from laborers in the fishing, construction and transportation industries to petty trading. It was a stable community where everyone worked for a living. If the drive had continued two miles past Alice's house they would have entered a neighborhood with high unemployment, condemned houses, and streets that were badly in need of repair.

Saidu Lavalie, Alice's father, was sitting in the verandah when the two women arrived. The first thing they noticed was the jolly smile that characterized his personality. Saidu was one of the community leaders and a member of a local council whose goal was to address community problems and promote social cohesion among the residents in his part of town. He was well-respected for his honesty and caring attitude. Satta had come to like Saidu whom she considered one of the wise men that had managed to unite the neighborhood. Since the government did not have the means to develop all neighborhoods she felt that Saidu's low-class area of town was relatively thriving due to his contribution to it. One contribution for which he was willing to take credit was his initiation of a neighborhood-watch program that eventually drove away from the area thieves and unwanted characters that engaged in anti-social behavior. Some either returned to the provinces or moved two miles away to a place where such behavior was not dealt with very severely.

Satta was fond of Alice's parents especially the father

whose smile made people feel comfortable. Immediately he caught sight of them he sat up in his hammock.

"Here come my beautiful women," he said jokingly. "How was your day?"

"Our day has been good," they answered.

"How are you, father?" greeted Satta politely.

"I am very well," replied Satta. "And you?"

"I am quite well, thank you," replied Saidu.

"You are home early today," said Satta.

"Yes, I am," said Saidu. "Normally I arrive at about the same time as Alice. But today I did not ride the bus. My supervisor at the Golden Complex happened to be coming this way and offered me a ride."

Since the two women did not have much time, they did not want to encourage a conversation with Saidu who would have continued entertaining them with all sorts of stories about life in his small town in the provinces. They went inside and greeted Jebeh, Alice's mother, who served the delicious dish she had prepared for them. As they ate Alice's younger brothers and sisters came from the back yard, greeted and left. They were very fond of and proud of their twenty-nine year old sister who had set a high educational standard for them. The two brothers were about to finish secondary school while the three sisters were in elementary school.

Satta did not fail to notice that Alice had renovated her father's house. She had given it a complete facelift. The cracks in the verandah and living room had been repaired before the entire house was given a new coat of paint. On entering the living room, Satta was struck by what she saw. The house looked very different. Alice had finally decorated the living room and installed a brand new carpet and a new set of furniture. It took a year to save for all this. The old furniture and decorations had been sent to their small town in the provinces so that they could be used in the family house there. Saidu's younger wife lived there and took care of their farm. She visited Bassaya often to get supplies and money for the hired farm workers. It was the produce and the small supplementary income from that farm that enabled Saidu to feed his family and pay the school fees of his children. Satta felt that although this man had no western education he was very organized and relatively successful.

The air blowing from the big fan was hot but since Alice had bought a new refrigerator the drinks served were cold. Jebeh had requested the refrigerator so that she could start selling soft drinks and beer.

"You have done very well for your family," said Satta in admiration. "As our people would say, you are buying your father's blessing. I admire the way you have decorated this place and given this old house a facelift."

"Thank you," said Alice. "I want to do my best for them before I get married and start raising my own children. Life may then be a bit more difficult. So I better help while I can."

"Your parents have always had a very high opinion of you," said Satta. "It is good that you did not disappoint them."

Satta who looked remarkably relaxed ate well. During lunch Judith had expressed the concern that when the time for action got nearer her daughter would get nervous. But Alice did not notice this at all. She was surprised that Satta could even talk about topics unrelated to the task ahead. She even reacted pleasantly to some of Saidu's jokes. Both of them left the house in a good mood.

"Have you been to see the office where Rosalyn works?" asked Satta as she started the car. "I hear that it is so luxurious that it puts one in the mood for a vacation. It was Misalie that decorated it for her."

"No kidding!" exclaimed Alice. "I have not heard about it," said Alice.

"Veronica described this office in her conversation with Sylvia," said Satta. "She said that they use it for a playpen since Rosalyn herself does very little work. We shall go to see this office some day."

"More facts emerge everyday about Misalie's outrageous behavior," said Alice. "He is a terrible husband."

"I have also learned that he had hired a cook and a houseboy for her," said Satta.

"Why would Rosalyn want a domestic staff?" asked Alice. "Can't a single woman like that take care of herself?"

"Since we are on our way there we shall soon verify this information," said Satta. "If this staff exists then they should be there tonight ready to serve the guests."

"I am not surprised that Mr. Sefoi Juana was invited," said Alice. "He too is breaking his wife's heart. He is quite promiscuous."

"Since both of them are friends they live the same lifestyle," said Satta. "They are masters of the same craft - the pursuit of beautiful women. I have heard that his wife is also preparing a surprise similar to mine."

"I wish that she would carry it out," said Alice. "Similar crimes should carry similar punishments."

Satta and her friend reached Rosalyn's place a little after seven. Since there were no cars parked in front the house, Satta knew that the guests had not yet arrived. In order not to be seen by anybody, she continued for a hundred yards and parked off the road. They got out and walked slowly toward the house. The first car they saw as they waited behind a big tree was the Mercedes Benz of Hon. Lamboi. The driver got out and opened the door for him. He got out. As he climbed the steps Satta noticed that he did not have his business suit on. He was dressed informally in a plaid short-sleeved shirt and a grey pair of pants. Soon after that Mr. Sefoi Juana arrived with Veronica sitting next to him in the front. He parked and they got out. When they entered the house, Satta and Alice approached the building and stood under one of the living room windows. The conversation in the house was loud and very lively. The two women could hear it very clearly.

"I smell something nice," said Veronica. "The aroma is making me hungrier. Rosalyn, what did you prepare this time?"

"As they say, seeing is believing," said Rosalyn. "I will wait until you come and see for yourself. It should be a surprise."

"I am ready to deal with whatever is on that table," said Sefoi. "The aroma certainly makes me feel hungry. It reminds me of my mother's cooking."

"Your mother would be angry with you if she were here," said Rosalyn. "You know that traditional women are excellent cooks. They complain that we modern women do not take the time that should be taken to see that husbands eat the very best. But I know that you are only flattering me."

"There may be some flattery in what I am saying but I doubt that Misalie here will dare flatter you," said Sefoi.

"Don't you think that my darling Misalie is capable of flattering me?" asked Rosalyn.

"He cannot do that," said Sefoi, laughing loud.

"Why don't we hear directly from him," said Rosalyn. "That's one good way to find out the truth."

"O.K. Misalie, whose cooking is more delicious - the traditional dishes prepared by your mother or the one prepared by this modern lady?" asked Sefoi.

"To be frank, Sefoi, the deliciousness of the food is sometimes enhanced by one's knowledge of who cooked it," said

Hon. Lamboi. "Eating a lover's dish is always accompanied by strong emotional feelings. So, as I eat this food my heart leaps each time I think of the hands that prepared them."

Laughter erupted. It was clear to the two women outside that the group was having a good time.

"From what Misalie has said, I would have no problem deciding whose cooking is more delicious," said Sefoi.

At that point the houseboy was heard telling the guests that the dinner was ready. Everyone moved to the dining room and took their seats at the table. The houseboy stood around ready to serve anything that was needed. The driver sat in the small back verandah quietly eating whatever was given to him.

It was at this time that Satta and Alice decided to strike. When they entered the house they headed straight for the dining room where the four guests were just about to start serving the main course. Hon. Lamboi was sitting next to Rosalyn while Veronica was sitting next to Mr. Sefoi Juana. The surprise was so thorough that the four people at the table remained immobile and speechless. Satta and Alice stood over them watching their reactions. The houseboy, a young man in his early twenties, went to the back to hastily inform the maid and the driver about the development. The three of them rushed inside to become spectators of this extraordinary event.

The atmosphere was very tense. Although no one said anything all minds were at work trying to guess what would happen. But Satta, the only person that knew exactly what would happen, was not thinking about anything. She stood there with a demeanor that scared even the husband who had never seen her that angry. Any of the two men could easily have quelled Satta but the shame and embarrassment the four of them felt were too great to make anyone dare to do that. Besides, the wrong move would trigger a reaction that would cause Satta to hurt somebody. Veronica tried to raise her head and look at the women but she was too embarrassed to look at Satta in the face. It was a shame to have come to eat dinner in the home of her bosses' girlfriend. Hon. Lamboi and Sefoi Juana sat still, not knowing what to tell Satta. Both of them tried not to underestimate a woman who had already suffered a lot in her marriage to a promiscuous husband. It was reasonable to assume that she was now taking her final stand. Rosalyn was the only one in the mood to put up a fight. But concluding that she would gain nothing in such an embarrassing situation, she remained calm. She however hoped that Hon. Lamboi would do something to control his wife.

This scene seemed to have lasted a whole hour but in actual fact it lasted only three minutes. Satta maintained it just long enough to embarrass Rosalyn and her guests. When she at last made the first move to act the husband greeted her with a smile. She answered with a smile and gestured politely to everyone to remain quiet and seated. Since that looked like a friendly gesture, they obeyed instantly thinking that the wife was now in the mood to talk things out in a respectable manner. But what happened next took everyone by surprise. Satta quickly grabbed the big bowl of steaming soup, raised it in the air and dropped it on the wooden table with a big bang. The fragile dish was not spared the rage of an angry and jealous woman. When it broke the soup splashed all over the four of them. They all struggled to their feet in panic but before their ears could recover she hastily grabbed the bowl of rice and dropped it on the table with all her might. That bowl also broke.

"Let's go" she said to Alice with a smile. Both women then walked out slowly and quietly.

The scene they left behind was the funniest that the three spectators had ever seen. The loud bangs did shock and startle them but they recovered quicker than those who were sitting right at the table. These bore the brunt of Satta's rage when the bowl of steaming soup seasoned with hot pepper broke. The contents splashed in their faces causing a burning sensation in the eyes. It would have been impossible to fight back at that moment even if they had wanted to. Washing their faces did not bring relief any sooner.

For some unexplained reason Rosalyn started wailing. It was not clear if her crying was due to the burning sensation or to the feeling of remorse she was experiencing. She was crying out Satta's name pleading with her to return to the house. This appeal was heard by both Satta and Alice but they ignored it and kept going. As they approached their car, the maid caught up with them and told them that her boss wanted to talk to Satta. She ignored her but she pleaded with them.

"My Miss wants to talk with Satta," she said quietly.

"Who are you?" asked Satta politely.

"My name is Memuna," she replied. "I am the maid."

"I am too upset to talk to anybody in that house," said Satta mildly. "I am sorry."

"Why does she want to talk to her?" asked Alice.

"I do not know but she really wants to talk to her," said Memuna.

"But you heard what Satta just said," said Alice.

"My Miss is crying a lot at this time," said Memuna. "I believe that Satta can stop the tears. I have never seen her cry. It makes me worried. She urged me to convince Satta to go and talk to her."

"What if Satta does not go?" asked Alice.

"I will be very sad," said Memuna. "I know that Satta is right but I am very concerned about the way my Miss is crying. It is only Satta that can make her stop crying."

Satta and Alice observed her for a few seconds. She was about fourteen and had no formal education. What struck both women was her beauty as she stood there chewing on a bone she had picked up from the table after the four guests had withdrawn in pain. She seemed to be enjoying her free treat. Although the expression of innocence on her face disqualified her as the likely person to settle such a complicated dispute, her soft voice did make the two women to consider her plea. Telling her to go back to her boss, they drove slowly and stopped in front of the house.

"Satta, you are not in any position to go in there," said Alice. "I will go in, observe a bit and ask Rosalyn what she wants to talk to you about. Expect me back shortly."

Alice was surprised at what she saw when she entered. What she and Satta had failed to notice as they left was that besides preventing the guests and their host from eating the meal, they had actually hurt them physically and emotionally. The hot pepper in the food had caused so much pain that they were not in a position to leave. Alice moved over to Rosalyn who was sobbing in an armchair in the living room and asked her what she wanted.

"Is that Satta?" she asked with her eyes tightly closed.

"No, it is not," replied Alice. "I am Alice, her friend."

"Alice, is there any way I can talk to Satta?" she said giving her hand to Alice.

"At present Satta is too moved by this experience to come here and talk to you," said Alice.

"I understand why she cannot talk now," said Rosalyn. "Please tell her that I am not angry with her for what has happened today and that I am sorry to have ruined her marriage. Also tell her that I look forward to meeting with her, if she would let me, so that I can apologize in person for the wrong I have done to her."

"I will deliver your message but I do not think that she will come to see you," said Alice.

"If she refuses, Alice, please return and stay with me for the evening," said Rosalyn. "I would like to talk to you. Just promise me that you will come back. Do not leave me in this condition."

Alice was quiet for a while. The request had taken her by surprise and she did not know what to do. She was hesitant to make any commitments because this was the first time she was meeting Rosalyn in person. So she remained quiet.

"Alice, do you promise?" asked Rosalyn. "Remember that in this world there are times when people go out of the way to do things for strangers and enemies. This happens all the time. I am requesting that you do this favor for me. There is no way that I can ever settle matters with Satta without your help. So please give me your word."

This appeal was too strong to be turned down. It so moved Alice that she felt that she had to give a helping hand. But if she offered to settle the dispute her role in the affair would change dramatically from that of a passive observer to an active mediator. It was her awareness of this that made her reluctant to make any promise.

"Alice, I know that the role I want you to play is not an easy one," continued Rosalyn, still holding Alice's hand. "But you are acquainted enough with the case to be able to deal with it. So please help."

"Rosalyn, I promise," said Alice thoughtfully as she left the house. "I will be back later this evening. You need at least two hours to wash up and put yourself in a better frame of mind."

After the three guests had washed their faces, they sat in the living room with hand towels in their hands. They were waiting for the moment they would feel comfortable enough to leave.

Although they heard the conversation none of them tried to talk to Alice.

The domestic staff and Hon. Lamboi's driver seemed to be the lucky ones that evening. In cleaning the table they saved the portions of the scattered food that could be safely eaten. After thoroughly cleaning the dining room they moved into the back verandah where they divided the food into three large parts and ate to their satisfaction. After the meal the driver commented that he ate more meat and fish that day than he had ever eaten in any two-week period. Moving to the front verandah to enjoy the cool breeze he lit his cigarette and smoked peacefully until his boss was ready to leave.

The first destination of the two friends was Satta's place. As they went Alice described what she had seen in the living room. Satta was pleasantly surprised to learn that the hot pepper did as much damage as her destruction of the dinner. Both laughed a bit about this. She then narrated Rosalyn's request.

"Satta, I made a promise to return later because Rosalyn's appeal was very powerful and very moving," said Alice softly. "I wonder what you think about my decision and her request that you meet with her someday."

"It is alright for you to spend sometime with her," said Satta with a smile. "It is possible that you can use your counseling techniques to convert her to a decent way of life. She is morally bankrupt and needs someone like you to straighten her. I will not, however, honor her request that I meet with her sometime."

"Thanks, Satta," said Alice. "I believe that the decision for me to talk with Alice is a good one. "It will satisfy my curiosity to find out how this woman actually feels after such a dramatic incident. I would like to know why she cried and why she did not fight back."

"From what I know now I do not think she would have

been able to fight back," said Satta. "She was incapacitated by the pepper that entered her eyes. What surprised me was her wailing and friendliness. I am also surprised at her inviting me inside after all what I did to her."

"Satta, I sincerely believe that Rosalyn would not have fought back even if her eyes were spared," said Alice. "She is very remorseful. If she were in the fighting mood she would have threatened to put up a struggle at a later date."

"In any case, you can go ahead and talk to her," said Satta. "I will bring you back later to her house. Since Misalie is there his driver can take you home when you are ready to leave. Tell Rosalyn that I will never meet with her."

When they reached Satta's place she picked up enough clothes and toilet items for a week. She planned to spend that much time at her mother's before returning. They then set out for Judith's place without even leaving a note for Misalie.

Judith who had all this time been thinking of her daughter's adventure hastily got up to open the door when she heard the car approaching. Hugging Satta warmly she served them soft drinks and sat down anxiously to listen to their story.

"That was an appropriate response," she said after Satta had described the incident at Rosalyn's. "You were not violent at all and you did not insult or curse anybody. You went there to interrupt a meal prepared by an adulterer. You not only prevented it from being eaten but also broke those bowls with enough bang to tell them that getting involved romantically with someone's spouse is wrong, dead wrong. My daughter you meted out a reward they all deserved at the right time and in the right place."

When Satta narrated what Alice had seen when she returned to the house, Judith burst into laughter.

"You mean that the three guests were sitting in chairs

wiping their eyes with towels?" she asked as if she wanted the story to be repeated.

"Yes, the pain in their eyes was too much," replied Alice. "You know that your son-in-law likes spicy food. So Rosalyn added a lot of pepper. Ironically, it was this that made them shed tears in silence. Only Rosalyn wailed."

"But why would she suddenly want to apologize now after inflicting so much pain on my daughter all these years?" asked Judith. "I doubt her sincerity."

"She admitted her guilt and said that she was not bitter about the way Satta reacted tonight," said Alice. "She sounded sincere. I told her that I will convey her message."

"Satta, your account is pleasant and amusing," said Judith. "Now give me your reaction to Rosalyn's request.

"I will have nothing to do with her," said Satta. "I cannot accept her apology and I question her sincerity."

"I do not blame you for standing firm," said Judith. "Alice will hear tonight what else she has to say. Let's wait until we hear from your friend after our return from Palahun on Sunday. My advice is that you should make no deals with which you are not comfortable."

"Thanks, mother, for agreeing not to go there with me," said Satta. "Your presence might have ruined my plan."

"Satta, you have shown yourself to be a strong woman tonight," said Judith. "You were right this time."

"I wonder whether Veronica would be at work tomorrow," said Alice. "She had boasted so much about a dinner she never got to eat."

"I do not think that this incident would keep her away from work," said Judith. "What I am not sure of is whether she will go to see her friend Sylvia during lunch. If she goes there, she will have to tell an embarrassing story."

"Well she better be ready to tell it," said Alice. "She has talked a lot about this dinner. Sylvia and others would like to know how it went."

"She may have learned a lesson from this experience," said Judith. "Likewise Misalie and his friend Sefoi. The lesson is that he who consistently wrongs a patient and innocent person will one day be subject to her wrath. For a long time to come they will remember sitting in that living room lamenting their conduct while Rosalyn wailed in anguish as she confessed her guilt to Alice."

Satta dropped Alice off at Rosalyn's at ten o'clock. She thanked her for her moral support and promised to call her on Sunday night when she returned from her home town.

When Mrs. Satta Lamboi returned to Judith's place she went straight to bed. The dream she had that night was so vivid that she remembered it for a long time. In that dream she found herself sitting in an old rocking chair at the edge of the forest near her village. It was a hot humid day and since she was feeling thirsty she got up to get a drink from a nearby stream. But on standing up her necklace came off and fell to the ground. On bending over to pick it up all her hair came off suddenly and fell at her feet. She raised an alarm but there was no one around to help her. Sitting in frustration on the ground she took out a mirror from her bag and started examining her head. What she saw shook her emotionally. Her dark hair had been replaced by white hair. Covering her face with her hands she sobbed for a while. Her concern was how the public would react to the sudden change in her looks when she returned to Bassaya the following day.

In an attempt to remove the unwanted hair, she started rubbing her head vigorously. Then all of a sudden a boy about four years old appeared from behind her saying: "Let me help you, mother!" On turning around she inquired who the child was but he did not answer. As he repeated the same phrase he removed her white hair and took it to the stream. After depositing it there he returned and put her dark hair back on her head. She felt a sense of relief and thanked the boy. But as she wondered who this small savior was, he sat on her lap and leaned back on her chest. "Hold me, mother! Help me!" he said, and went to sleep.

This dream seemed so real that when she woke up she felt like looking around for the child. But her thoughts were interrupted by her mother who had entered the room telling her that it was time to get ready to go to work.

"Your husband called here after one o'clock this morning," said the mother. "I told him that you had gone to bed. He will be calling you later from his office."

"Mother, I will only talk to that man after our return on Sunday," she said angrily.

CHAPTER EIGHT

Although Alice felt that she was torn between two enemies - Satta and Rosalyn - she was relieved that her friend was willing to allow her to keep her promise to Rosalyn. On entering the latter's house, she met her and her guests still sitting in the living room. The pain in their eyes had subsided but the redness was still very visible. The guests could have left an hour ago but they had to stay around to comfort Rosalyn who was complaining of pain in her abdomen and sides.

"Thank you, Alice, for keeping your promise," said Rosalyn. "I want to make sure that Satta knows how I feel about what I have done to her marriage. To be frank, the fight I was expecting to have today was with Jane Williams, Misalie's other girlfriend. She had called here and threatened to disrupt this dinner. I had looked forward to a good fight with this very jealous woman. Unfortunately she did not show up. My revelation of this information must be a surprise to Misalie himself because he is not aware of our struggle for him."

At this point she wiped her eyes which were now pain-free and almost dry except for occasional tears that dropped from them. She called Memuna and asked her to bring her some water to drink. The driver told her that Memuna had gone to sleep and brought the water in a tall glass. Rosalyn drank and continued to talk.

"I was dumbfounded when I saw Satta standing by the table," continued Rosalyn. "The sight of this nice and patient woman almost paralyzed me. I have never been that close to her and was not expecting to get that close anytime soon. I asked myself where Jane Williams was and wondered what would happen if she too turned up. In any case, here was Satta standing by the table. The impression I got was that of a queen forcibly reentering her kingdom to reclaim her rights. I would not be surprised if any of you here admit to having a similar impression. I think that this was the reason why no one tried to put up a fight or a quarrel. Although the preparations I had made for a head-on collision with Jane were at my disposal, I felt it inappropriate to apply them on an innocent victim. It would have been alright to fight Jane because it would have been a struggle between two thieves over what is not theirs. But it would have been a moral failure on my part to fight a decent human being over what is rightfully hers. That is why I did nothing to stop her from venting a rage that was completely righteous.

"I am experiencing pains in my lower abdomen and sides because the unexpected bangs made me shudder violently and fall off my chair. I believe however that I deserve all the punishment. Alice, I want you to help me get in contact with Satta. I want to apologize and ask for forgiveness. Those loud bangs will ring in my ears for a long time to come."

"I will try my best to bring the two of you together," said Alice. "However I cannot guarantee her cooperation."

"Your task is a difficult one," said Rosalyn. "The sooner it is achieved the better. But it is alright even if it takes you a year to achieve it. I will never be at peace with myself until I meet Satta and tell her how I feel."

At this point Rosalyn got up and walked to the couch. She lay on it still complaining of intense pain in the lower part of her belly and her sides.

"Please take me to the hospital," she appealed to her audience. The two men got up at once and took her to the car. Every one followed.

On the way to the hospital, Hon. Lamboi was very quiet. He knew that he was in a very difficult and embarrassing situation. He not only had to deal with his wife in connection with what had happened that night but also with Rosalyn's unexpected illness. He was, however, not the only one that was affected by the outcome of events. Veronica and Sefoi were equally overwhelmed. Neither would be proud to narrate that night's experience to an acquaintance.

When they reached the emergency section of the hospital, Rosalyn could not walk. Complaining of increasingly intense pain, she almost collapsed. The two men had to hold tightly on to her to prevent this from happening. It was a big relief when the emergency squad finally came outside with a stretcher and put her on it. The doctor told them that Rosalyn would be admitted for further observation and testing. It was not until one o'clock in the morning that they were able to leave.

Hon. Lamboi was very surprised not to find his wife at home. He had kept on wondering what the nature of their conversation would be like when he met her face-to-face. Since he was not prepared for whatever would have happened that night, he felt relieved that she was not home. But to satisfy his curiosity about her whereabouts he called Judith's place. The latter told her that Satta was exhausted and was not likely to entertain any conversation at that time. That sounded like good news to him. Since any delay in meeting or talking to his wife was welcome news, he hung up promising to get in contact with her during office hours. He also felt good that his mother-in-law did not make any inquiries.

Sleep did not come easily to Hon. Lamboi's eyes that night. He lay awake thinking of what Rosalyn had said about Jane Williams. He wondered how Satta got to know about the dinner and why Jane never fulfilled her threat. The information about the struggle between his girlfriends came to him as a big surprise. He wondered why Jane and Rosalyn would hate each other when he was not married to them. It confirmed his prejudicial belief that women were foolish and petty. This conclusion seemed plausible to him because he saw no reason why the two should fight over what was not theirs.

As he thought over these problems he started to suspect that Jane was the one that told Satta that the dinner would be held that evening. This was to provoke his wife to take some action. The plot was to instigate somebody with better rights to do her fighting for her. Jane was so confident that such a trick would work that she did not consider it worthwhile going to the dinner.

"Ah ha! I've solved the mystery " he said aloud as if talking to someone. "I never suspected that Jane could be evil. But she has proved to be so. I will call at once to find out why she did such a terrible thing to me."

He got up and looked for a secret diary in which he kept details of all his extra-marital affairs. It was hidden in a locked file cabinet which his wife had never bothered to tamper with. Looking up Jane's telephone number he sat up on the bed and called her.

"Hello! Is that Jane?" he said calmly.

"Hello! It's me. Darling, is that you?" she replied in a tone of surprise.

"Yes, it's me. Are you still awake?" he asked with a frown.

"Yes, I am and I'm very disturbed," she replied, yawning.

"Over what?" asked Hon. Lamboi in a harsh tone.

"Over the dinner you went to eat at Rosalyn's. I have been thinking about it all evening."

"It is foolishness to be disturbed over that," said Hon. Lamboi angrily. "I am just having an affair with you. Since we are not married, there is no need to do anything that will make my wife to get angry with me. The same goes for Rosalyn. I am just having an affair with her. So it is wrong for the two of you to start a quarrel over me."

"I believe that our fight is appropriate because we have heard that you are going to divorce Satta," said Jane calmly. "I have to make sure that I win you over. I love you and I want to marry you. Rosalyn wants to do the same thing. This is how the fight got started. Before this we were all willing to share you peacefully. But when the rumor went around about your divorce, the fights started. I assure you that there are other women out there preparing themselves for a fight. The earlier you find out about them, the better. Since you do not want that many women struggling for you after your wife gets out of that beautiful ministerial residence, you have to take some concrete action to contain the situation."

"I have reason to suspect that you are the one that told Satta about Rosalyn's dinner," said Hon. Lamboi in a softer tone of voice. "Your purpose of doing this is to instigate a quarrel between my wife and Rosalyn so that if the divorce takes place I will blame Rosalyn for it. This will give you a chance to be selected by me. You are a devil."

"Please do not say that," said Jane, trying to calm down the angry man. "I was an angel when you met me. You corrupted me. In any case, I did not tell Satta about the dinner. I knew about it, of course, and had a quarrel with Rosalyn about it. I even threatened to go there to disrupt it. This is why she was expecting me. But I did not tell Satta about it. Trust me, darling,

I did not tell her about it at all. One thing I want you to know is that I have never lied to you. If I had told Satta about the dinner, I would have admitted it regardless of the consequences. Another thing I want you to know is that all your girlfriends are agreed on one thing: Satta is such an angel that we will do nothing to hurt her. We all respect her. She is a real lady. You are a lucky man to have such a woman. We expected your relationship with her to continue indefinitely because she had never cared to deal with us for disrupting her married life. But once the rumors about your divorce went around we started struggling for you."

"Well, I do not want you to struggle for me because I am not going to divorce my wife."

"I am glad that you do not plan to divorce her. Trust me, darling, that I will not fight over you anymore. I had threatened to disrupt the dinner but I decided against doing so at the last moment. I decided to make a better dinner and invite you to it. So, I gave up the idea of interrupting hers. By the way how did it go?"

"I have told you that Satta was informed about it. Do you expect such a dinner to go well?"

"Why not? Satta has been very patient so far. She can tolerate one more dinner."

"I know my wife more than you do. She is patient, nice and kind; but she is not a fool. One can drag her around for a while but there are times when she can respond appropriately. We should not interpret her kindness as weakness."

"Well, did she respond appropriately tonight in order to demonstrate that patience is not weakness? I would be surprised if she did. That woman gave up on you years ago. She is only in that home so as not to hurt her reputation."

"As I have already told you, I know my wife better than you

do. If you push her too much she will react."

"Did she then react in any way when she heard about tonight's dinner?"

"Of course, she did. Do not underestimate her. I am sure that Rosalyn will never again underestimate her. You never know how tough Satta is until you get into a direct conflict with her."

"What exactly did she do to Rosalyn?

"She acted appropriately."

"Can I know the details?"

"I don't feel comfortable telling anyone about it but I will tell you so that it will help you decide to get out of my life. Satta is not joking anymore. She dealt Rosalyn a big blow. If you do not want to suffer a similar consequence, you had better stop seeing me. I do not want her to go after you."

"What did she do to Rosalyn."

"She interrupted her dinner."

"No kidding!"

"Yes! No kidding!"

"I will not give you the details. But the interruption of that dinner serves as a warning to you and others that Satta is no longer going to tolerate my promiscuous lifestyle."

"I will not insist on knowing the details. I will know them tomorrow any way. What I am concerned about at this time is losing you. I do not want to lose you simply because Satta is now pursuing your girlfriends. I want to continue seeing you. She will not know about it. You have been very kind to me."

"I will not continue with you as before. The reason is that I want to change my ways. Since it is possible to be friends without being lovers, I suggest that we be just friends."

"I doubt if you can change your ways. I have never seen anybody pursue women as you do. I put up a strong resistance when you went after me but you still got me. I find it very difficult to understand why you would call this late in the night only to drop me from your list. Are you going to do the same to all the other women?"

"Yes, and no exceptions."

"Even to Rosalyn?"

"No exceptions."

"Please make me an exception."

"Do you know that I have contracted HIV?" asked Hon. Lamboi very softly. It was in the news. I also held a news conference about it."

"Yes, I know about your condition. I read about it in the papers. But that's not a disease that I take seriously."

"Why don't you take it seriously?"

"Because I do not believe that I will contract it. Besides the government has never taken it seriously."

"Jane, you should take it seriously. Once you get the virus there is no way you can get rid of it."

"I would like to take a risk. There is so much that I will lose if I stop going with you. To prevent my contracting the virus, we shall not engage in activities which may increase the risk of my contracting the disease."

"By the way, are you talking to me from the other bedroom?"

"Why do you ask?" inquired the husband curiously.

"Because I do not want your wife to hear us speaking."

"You should have expressed that concern at the time we started talking."

"That did not occur to me."

"She is spending the night at her mother's."

"Good. Then send your driver to get me. As I said, we can keep our contact at a minimum. Our involvement with each other once in a while will not make me contract that virus. Frequent sex is what leads to infection."

"Jane, it's too late to come here. Tomorrow get some literature on AIDS and read. I believe that you need time to think over what I have told you about it today. The more you know about it the more you will realize how tragic this disease is. Getting rid of your ignorance about it will help you. It is a disease that gives a person a one-way ticket to exit this world. Good night."

This conversation made Hon. Lamboi realize how immense his troubles were. Concerned that the fighting among his lovers would break into the open and occasion another heartache for his wife, he decided to call his two remaining girlfriends. They too confessed that they were getting ready to get involved in a struggle over him because of rumors that he was about to divorce Satta. Although he told them that the rumors were false he failed to successfully break his relationship with them. The women refused to take seriously his intention to break with him. None could believe that a womanizer like him would ever give up his promiscuous lifestyle. Not even the threat of AIDS made them to give up on him. Another problem was his kindness to them. Since he had been generous to all of them they found it hard to just suddenly break up with him because he had AIDS. The last girlfriend he spoke to lectured him about human relationships.

"Relationships that involve much kindness cannot be suddenly broken in the dead of night. Since we have neither quarreled nor wronged each other it is just very difficult to break up without notice. I advice you to get some sleep and not try to deal with such a problem in a hurry. It is night-time now. At night people tend to do things that they would not do during the daytime. It may be alright for me to break with you at this time but when daylight comes it will cast light on my ungratefulness. So I will not break with you now. I remain unconvinced that there is good reason to break with a kind person like you at such a time. So we shall meet again. Goodnight, darling."

Hon. Lamboi rolled over and slept. Despite the many problems and the hectic evening he slept like a care-free person. His exhaustion warranted such a dreamless rest. It was eleven o'clock the next morning when he jumped out of bed. He had not slept that late in a long time.

CHAPTER NINE

Friday was a busy and difficult day for Hon Lamboi. He was faced with two very difficult tasks that he had to satisfactorily perform. First, he had to talk to Satta. He wanted to call to apologize and accept responsibility for everything that had transpired at Rosalyn's dinner. The embarrassment and the pangs of guilt he was feeling were too much for him to be at peace with himself. Second, he had to check on Rosalyn at the hospital. The latter's illness took him and the other guests by surprise. The three of them had felt terrible about her unexpected admission to a medical facility. None had expected that the cheerful hostess that invited them to a pleasant dinner would spend the evening in the emergency unit of a hospital.

The biggest problem involving Rosalyn's illness was keeping secret the fact that the Minister of Health was one of the people that had taken her there at one o'clock in the morning. If this information were made public, people would wonder what a married politician was doing at that time of the night with another woman. To make matters worse it was the minister himself that had signed the admission papers. His wish, therefore, was that Rosalyn would be released that day in order to prevent rumors about the incident from circulating.

What the poor husband lacked was adequate time to prepare for the two tasks. Since he got up late and did not get to the office until almost two o'clock, he was concerned that both Satta and Rosalyn may be already angry with him for not telephoning them sooner. At a quarter after two he picked up the telephone and called Satta. Unfortunately she was in a meeting. After two further unsuccessful attempts without getting her on the telephone he left a message and decided not to call again until after work. Next he tried to reach Rosalyn who had been moved to a private room in the hospital. Nobody answered the telephone. On trying unsuccessfully three more times to get her he felt frustrated. Replacing the receiver, he leaned back in his swivel chair looking attentively at the ceiling as if expecting the solution to his problems to descend from there. Suddenly he got the feeling that getting in contact with his wife that day was not a good idea after all. Going after her aggressively for a settlement of their conflict may lead to a cancellation of her trip to her village. If that happened he would not be able to go to see Rosalyn and help her with the problem she was crying about last night. "I have to let Satta go to Palahun so that I can deal with one task at a time," he said to himself, giving a sigh of relief. Convinced that by the time Satta returned to Bassaya he would have completely solved the problem involving Rosalyn, he called Sylvia Gbondo, her secretary, to leave another message that he would be in a meeting for the rest of the afternoon.

Satta did receive all the husband's messages but had decided not to call back. She was resolved not to have anything to do with him until she returned from Palahun. Although Judith was also very upset about what happened the previous night, she had advised her daughter to contact the husband. But she refused to do so. They left Bassaya at six that evening.

The trip to Palahun was delightful. Satta did the driving all the way stopping once to take a short break. Since Judith had sent a message earlier in the week about their visit, Abibu

Lansana, Satta's uncle, and all the relatives in the village were expecting them. Although they visited this village several times a year, this particular visit would be different from the others. In addition to planning to take supplies for relatives as they normally did and returning to Bassaya with the locally-grown food produce they needed in the city, they also wanted to discuss Satta's problem with the leaders of their extended family. Despite the fact that the daughter was educated in the western world, she so much valued the traditional beliefs of her people that it would have been impossible for her to make a decision about the future of her marriage without consulting Abibu, the head of the extended family. That is why Judith Lansana who did not want to be the only adviser in such an important family matter, was taking her daughter to consult with him.

Although the Lansanas were among one of the noteworthy extended families in their chiefdom, they had their own share of the kind of problems that plagued many families. These included jealousies and petty conflicts that made cooperation among them difficult. The biggest problem that the Lansanas ever wrestled with started after the death of Satta's father twenty-five years ago. He was the revered head of the extended family. When he passed away there occurred a power vacuum that had to be filled. The unfortunate thing was that many members were not pleased with the choices that then existed. Musu Lansana, Satta's grandmother, was liked by everybody because she was patient, kind and considerate. But in a culture where the tradition was in favor of male heads, she could not be considered for leadership. A strong male was needed to lead. Two of Ann's eldest uncles, Abibu Lansana and Beimba Lansana, engaged in a fierce competition for the position. During that struggle, Musu talked in private to several members trying to know their views about the two men. Judith, her daughter, was one of these. She called her into her room two days before the selection of the leader for a secret discussion of the issue.

"Judith, you are one of the younger members of this extended family but without doubt you are one of the most responsible ones. As you know, we are about to choose somebody to replace your husband who was an excellent leader. What I want to know is your choice for the leadership of this family. Abibu Lansana and Beimba Lansana are the two men contending for the position. Abibu, as we all know, succeeds in everything he undertakes but he is very strict. He has no patience with non-achievers. Beimba Lansana is very kind but he is rash. Which of these two do you think will lead this family to prosperity?"

"It is bad luck for any extended family member to be faced with the choice between a rash and kind man on the one hand and a successful but very strict one on the other," said Judith. "So it is not easy for me to decide between these two uncles."

This comment made both of them laugh. Musu, who had already secretly interviewed other family members on this issue, was this time not surprised at the laughter. Other interviewees had also laughed at their hearing her description of the two men struggling for the leadership of the extended family.

"Can you tell me precisely why you think it is difficult to choose?" asked Musu.

"I believe that the rash man will make hasty decisions without carefully considering the consequences," said Judith. "So, Beimba is likely to ruin us."

"But since he is kind, is he likely to help your daughter Satta and other children in the family?" asked Musu.

"Yes, he is likely to help them," replied Judith. "But I want us to carefully consider the nature of the kindness of a rash man," said Musu. "The problem is that he may carry the virtue of kindness to extreme because he is unable to limit or restrain himself. His uncontrollable spending may lead to bankruptcy. He acts fast but thinks little. That is tragic."

The two laughed again. Musu got up to adjust her long traditional wrapper and sat down again.

"If rashness is his vice, and kindness, which is a desirable, is likely to be carried out to excess, then Beimba cannot be an effective leader," said Judith. "We then have to decide whether Abibu Lansana should lead us."

"Abibu is of course always successful but, as I said earlier, he is very strict," said Musu. "Consider some of his achievements. He is the best farmer among the adult males. His yearly yield is almost double that of the male that is second in rank to him. He is also an excellent fisherman. Each year he brings from the towns along the coast lots of fish for sale. His greatest achievement is the building of our nice extended family compound in Palahun."

"This man has never failed in anything," Judith added. "Once he puts his mind on some goal he will achieve it."

"That is true," said Musu. "But in fairness to Beimba we also have to discuss Abibu's weak point. It lies in the way he achieves his goals. Let us take the building of this beautiful compound. I still tremble when I reflect on the way he worked almost everybody to death in order to meet his deadline and also save money in labor costs. The women carried many buckets of water and building materials each day while the men made the bricks and put the structures together. The result was a brand new compound. Although nobody today disputes the quality of the work, it is an indisputable fact that people groaned under the heavy task. The money contributed by the family was wisely and economically used in such a way that nothing went to waste."

"After listening to your analysis of Abibu's weak point, I am left with no choice but to go back to my former conclusion that we are faced with two difficult alternatives," said Judith.

"Come on, Judith, let me know your decision," said Musu. "With all your education and experience you should be able to know the difference between walking on a path that leads to bankruptcy and the one that leads to profits."

"The decision that I am going to make is based on the wise use of family resources," said Judith. "Since profits are preferred to bankruptcy, I would choose Abibu. He is more capable of restraining himself. If Beimba had been put in charge of the building of the compound, we would never have finished it. The available resources would never have been sufficient to pay for hastily-made plans. Thus we would have ended up with an unfinished compound. At present he has two unfinished houses in Tilasa. Being rash, he made grandiose plans without making good estimates of the resources available to him. He ended up quickly running out of money. I have heard that his kindness led him to overpay his workers. For these reasons I prefer Abibu."

"I knew that you would be able to make a wise decision," said Musu with a smile. "When we meet to select our leader make sure that you express this view."

It was through this kind of discussion that Musu was able to convince many family members to back Abibu. After carefully analyzing the problem together with each interviewee, she helped them draw the inevitable conclusion that rashness is more dangerous than severity when it came to the wise use of resources. The word "bankruptcy" was intimidating enough to scare people away from Beimba. Although some family members in the end blamed Musu for Beimba's loss of the struggle, Musu's wisdom became evident as the years went by. While Abibu mellowed with time and did things that made all family members appreciate him, Beimba remained rash.

Judith was one of those family members that never regretted her decision to back Abibu Lansana. It was the latter that eventually took over her daughter's higher education expenses. Satta's father, who was a school teacher, died when she was only ten. Two years after his death, Judith, who had a secondary school education and lots of secretarial experience got a promotion in the civil service and was transferred to Bassaya. She remarried but when her second husband died she devoted her time to raising her two daughters. When Satta finished secondary school she expressed the desire to go and study accounting in England. It was then that the mother asked Abibu, a prosperous farmer and fisherman, to help her. He agreed although he admitted that he did not have all the money needed to support someone in London for five years. Fortunately he got a small fortune by diving for pearls during one of his fishing expeditions. Many fishermen in the community engaged in this dangerous business but none of them was lucky to find enough pearls to finance an undertaking as big as that of sponsoring a relative to study overseas.

The way Abibu came up with the funds to educate his niece in London became the subject of much gossip. Some said that a water spirit that protected him when he worked as a fisherman directed him to the oysters that bore the most precious pearls. Others said that it was a mermaid that had directed him to those pearls. Still others said that an amulet prepared for him by a famous medicine man in one of the neighboring countries directed him to his fortune. What the gossips were unwilling to do was to simply acknowledge the fact that Abibu risked his life to dive for those pearls. It was true that he had an amulet that he wore on his arm for protection. It was however not prepared in another country. It was locally made. The medicine man that made it claimed that it had supernatural powers and Abibu fervently believed him. But despite the possession of this charm, eyewitnesses to his last dive attested to the fact that a combination of hard work and luck were responsible for his fortune.

That last dive took place on a beautiful day in the afternoon. It occurred on a spot along a stretch of shore that many divers avoided because of rumors that it had a strong undercurrent that could disorient a diver making him to fail to resurface. It was Abibu's determination to dive at that particular spot that had made him to consult the medicine man that prepared his amulet. As he prepared for the plunge, friends on the shore told him to choose a different spot but he refused saying that if no one ever dived at that particular spot then it must contain lots of oysters with good quality pearls. Thus with his amulet attached to his arm and his basket in hand he made his first successful plunge bringing to the surface a large number of oysters. After going down three more times his son seized the basket and told him not to dive anymore. But he argued and snatched the bag. A noisy splash that sent the flying water several feet into the air was all that was heard in the next minute and a half. When the father did not reappear, the son wailed and other fishermen came to the spot and rescued the poor, unconscious man. He lay helpless on the shore throwing out all the water that he had swallowed during the course of his struggle below the surface.

Abibu's explanation of what happened below after he had regained consciousness made him to be considered a lucky man. He said that he was attacked by a large fish that looked like a shark. It was during the attack that he got disoriented and could not quickly get to the surface. His belief was that the presence of his rescuers made the fish to retreat from its malicious activity. Although none of the rescuers saw the shark they believed that the cuts on his legs and right arm must have been the result of an attack by some creature in the water. He was treated in the hospital and released the same day. It was the money from the sale of the pearls found that day that was used to send Satta to England.

Judith's mention of this adventure to Satta as they headed for Palahun that Friday made her daughter to talk about her special affection for Abibu who had sacrificed his life so that she could get her higher education in London. The mother reacted by expressing her concern about what this uncle would say on learning that Satta would not have children to benefit from the fruits of that education.

"My daughter, the family meeting over your plight is not going to be a mild one," said Judith. "After such a sacrifice on your behalf, your uncle Abibu is not going to have kind words for a husband whose marital infidelity has made it impossible for you to have children. If you think that my reaction to your problem has been harsh, wait until you hear his."

"I agree that the meeting will not be mild," said Satta. "It will be very difficult for in-laws to feel any sympathy for a son-in-law whose promiscuous lifestyle almost made him to infect their daughter with a deadly disease. My wish, however, is that this meeting will be orderly. Any advice given and any decision made should reflect the fact that I am fragile at this time. I am still married to Misalie and as long as I am living with him I should not create an atmosphere that breeds animosity. For our survival through difficult times as these my husband and I have to avoid anything that will lead to misery and mental anguish. I realize that it is good to fight sometimes, but it is not good for me to fight at this time. I want this transition period in our relationship to be smooth. I am not sure exactly where we are headed but let this stage be smooth."

"Do not worry about fighting, my daughter," said Judith. "You know how to fight. You did so successfully last night."

"That is true, mother," said the daughter. "But I do not want another fight during this transition stage."

"I respect your view," said the mother. "I have never known you as a fighter. But from the way things are developing you may find yourself fighting more often. The rumors about what you did last night will reach Misalie's other women. The big bang on that dinner table should serve as a warning to them to keep away although I don't think that they will. So you may have to strike again."

"That's possible but let the fight be restricted to Bassaya," said Satta. "I do not want my relatives in Palahun to be involved in it. I want them to help me in my attempt to find a solution to my present problems."

This conversation continued until they reached the junction where the small, unpaved road leading to the village branched off the main road leading to Tilasa, the district headquarters. As soon as they passed a few houses, Pala, the village's famous and legendary cotton tree, came into view. It was a dark night but the bright headlights of the car brought it to the attention of the two women. Pala was not as tall as many other cotton trees in the area but its huge size gave it a look of grandeur. The oldest woman in the village once told Satta that witches had fought in the tree when it was young making it to experience a distorted growth.

When the car stopped in front of the compound of the Lansanas, many relatives came out hastily to greet them. As usual, everyone tried to make them feel welcome. Although it was late in the evening, Abibu who had looked forward all day to seeing the two relatives, still wanted to chat with them. He briefed them about new developments in family affairs. Just before he bade them good night Satta asked him to make arrangements for a meeting for Saturday evening. As head of the extended family it was Abibu's job to bring family members together whenever such a request was made. The notice was too short but since this was not a general family meeting which normally involved the pouring of libation to the ancestors and a feast, Abibu could easily arrange it. Only a few important family members were usually summoned to meetings requested by a particular family member.

As Abibu stepped out of the house he wondered why Satta was requesting a meeting and hoped that it was not about something bad. However, he decided against returning to request that he be briefed on the matter. He felt that if it were a complicated case the discussion may extend too late into the night.

Satta's relationship with Abibu was special and had grown since her return from London. In gratefulness for the uncle's kindness, she had bought him two years ago a new medium-sized truck for use in transporting his farm produce to the market. She had saved that money during the year she worked in London after her education and from her salary. Abibu was taken by surprise when one evening he came from a business trip from Tilasa and met the truck standing in front of the compound. When he learned that it was a present from Satta he danced before going inside to thank her. But despite this cordial relationship Satta wondered how this uncle would react at the meeting on learning that she would not have children as a result of the nature of her husband's disease. One thing that she was sure about was that Abibu did not like the minister because of the way he had treated her in the past. When two years ago the relationship between her and her husband got so bad that the mother brought the two of them to Palahun so that Abibu could settle the dispute, the latter almost quarreled with Hon. Lamboi. The main complaint was about Rosalyn Songa with whom Hon. Lamboi was spending too much time. Satta also complained about other women on whom her husband had spent a fortune. The hard evidence she produced in support of her claim included receipts made out to Hon. Lamboi for the rent which he paid for some of the women. It was unfortunate to have invited Beimba to that hearing. He almost did the unexpected by threatening to lay hands on the minister. Two strong men were immediately summoned to take him away. When calm was restored Musu who had remained very calm all this time took over the matter. Since both Satta and Hon. Lamboi were very cooperative she settled it to their satisfaction and that of the others including Abibu. Before the meeting ended Abibu even shook hands with Hon. Lamboi. Judith suggested that they bring back Beimba to shake hands with the guilty husband but Musu refused promising to talk to the angry man at a later time. "My concern is that in the process of shaking hands he may injure our in-law. Do you remember what happened three years ago when he shook hands with an old enemy? He almost broke his hand."

The meeting ended on this light note. Everyone including Hon. Lamboi laughed. The memory of this incident made both Satta and Judith expect a difficult meeting the following day. Fortunately the guilty husband was in Bassaya. So matters may not get out of hand.

Early on Saturday morning Beimba Lansana came to visit Judith and her daughter. When Satta caught sight of him approaching the house she wondered how this kind but rash man would behave at the meeting that was to be held later that day. She whispered this concern to her mother. Both of them smiled and waited for the uncle to enter the verandah. He greeted them warmly and presented a chicken and a bag of rice as a welcome present. As they sat in the verandah talking, he called Abibu's youngest wife and handed over the items to her. She was the one that always did the cooking for Satta and Judith whenever they came to Palahun.

"Thanks for the present," said Satta. "That's a big chicken. We are going to have a delicious lunch. As for the rice, we shall take most of it with us to Bassaya."

"Beimba, you really know how to make us feel welcome," said Judith. "We are grateful. Thanks. May God bless you. How is farming this year?"

"The rice farming is going well," replied Beimba. "I expect a bigger yield this year than last. Chasing birds away from the seeds and animals from the stems is an enormous task but everything is expected to go well. Since the rains are more than adequate, my coffee and cacao plantations are also doing fine. I should do better in the market this year. I plan to use a good portion of my earnings to sue my contractor in Tilasa."

"Beimba, you like litigation," said Judith. "What did the poor man do this time?"

"I am upset because my two houses are still incomplete although he has been paid in full for the job. A big court case is on my agenda after the harvest."

This statement made Satta and her daughter laugh. Beimba joined them. But he soon became serious again.

"After the harvest much of the money would go toward my court fight," said Beimba. "I want to finish up this crook."

The laughter continued for a minute. When it died down Satta expressed the view that the way Beimba handled the deal was not prudent.

"Uncle, you should not have paid the contractor in full before the completion of the job," she said. "It is always advisable to withhold a portion of the payment until the job is complete. Many of these contractors would either slow down the job or stop working altogether on projects once they have got their full pay. Holding back a portion of the agreed amount is advisable. It serves as an incentive."

"That's the problem with generosity these modern times," said Beimba. "Not many recognize it. Since I saw no reason to delay full payment, I readily handed the money to him. But not being appreciative of my generosity, he neglected my houses. I will show him that being kind and generous is not a weakness. The contractor will have his day in court."

"Beimba, try first to see if the threat of a lawsuit will help before actually filing your case," said Judith. "Since many crooks yield in the face of such a threat, you should not rush to pour money into a suit. The problem is that if he loses the case and cannot pay the fine, you will not recover your expenses. So threaten him first with a law suit and see what will happen."

"Threats mean nothing to hardened crooks," said Beimba as he got up to leave. "If he cannot pay the fine and my expenses, he will live on the prisoner's diet for a while. A punishment of this kind will be gratifying. As our people say, he who does evil in society will land in a tight corner. By the way, I am heading for my farm. I will send some palm wine later for you. When you come to our village we entertain you with our own local produce. When you go back to Bassaya you drink champaign."

Satta and her mother laughed as he left. After they had eaten the lunch prepared by Abibu's wife, they walked across the courtyard to Musu's house. Since the latter was already asleep when they arrived the previous night they were not able to see her. They met her sitting in her living room spinning. Standing next to her was a basketful of the fibers of cotton she was using.

She hoped to give the thread she was making to a weaver in the village to make cotton cloth for Judith. That would be her Christmas present. On seeing her two visitors she got up and gave each a hug.

"Grandmother, you look healthier now than before," said Satta after warmly greeting Musu.

"I was sick when I was with you in Bassaya but I am better now," said Musu. "Thanks to God, the chief, who made us. I thank you for the medicine you gave me. It got to where the illness is and did a good job getting rid of it. The next time you come back please get me some more of it."

"I brought some with me," said Satta. "I will give it to you before leaving tomorrow."

"Thank you," said Musu. "May God reward you for your kindness. May whoever plans evil for you be struck down by our ancestors. Please sit down."

"We want to talk to you about an urgent matter," said Judith after they had talked for a while about what Musu had been doing lately.

"Then let's go into my room," said Musu. "The traffic in and out of this living room can interrupt any serious talk."

They entered the room and sat down on the bed. Musu left briefly to get her cola nuts and offered them some. They declined.

"I know that both of you do not eat cola nuts," she said. "They keep me going all day. So how are things in Bassaya? Satta, how is Misalie?"

"Misalie is not doing well at all," said Judith. "The meeting we have called is about him. But we want to consult you about the matter before the family meeting later today. We need your advice."

"What is wrong with him?" asked Musu.

"He has contracted HIV," said Judith. "If he develops AIDS he will die. The doctors say that there is no cure for it."

"We have never heard about such a disease," said Musu. "Are you sure that there is no cure for it?"

"Yes, there is none," said Judith. "He may or may not develop the disease but since the virus is communicable Satta will contract it if she engages in sexual intercourse with him. Our worry now is that Satta will never bear children. This is the problem we have come to put before the family. I do not know what to do about it."

At this point tears came to the eyes of Musu who was very deeply moved by the news. Judith and Satta waited until she could speak.

"How did Misalie contract the virus?" asked Musu.

"He may have got it from one of his many women," replied Satta.

"I doubt if your uncles will be sympathetic," said Musu. "You saw how angry they were the last time Satta brought a complaint here about marital infidelity on the part of Misalie. We had expected him to change but clearly he has not. I expect the discussion tonight to be focussed strictly on the future of Satta instead of on the husband's terrible fate."

"What do you think that I should do?" asked Satta.

"My advise is that you stay by your husband and give him all the moral support he needs," said Musu. "I know that he has wronged you but if you have tolerated his bad treatment of you all this time, it makes sense for you to continue supporting him till it is all over for him. He is so vulnerable now that he cannot even engage in the acts that landed him in this terrible situation. As for children, they are God's gift to people. If God says that you will get one, no matter what you do, you will get it. So, after your initial panic, try and relax. We shall consult a diviner before you leave. He will determine whether or not you will have children in the future."

At this point Musu got up and called one of the younger grandchildren she was raising. He came rushing in. She told her to go to the next village and summon the famous diviner and medicine man that lived there.

"I wonder what our uncles will think about your suggestion that Satta exercise some more patience in dealing with this matter," said Judith. "Don't you think that they may advise her to exercise less patience?"

"That is possible because some of her uncles are themselves impatient men," said Musu. "But just as one should not be surprised to see a drunken man give alcohol to someone who does drink, likewise, we should not be surprised to hear an impatient person telling a patient person to take hasty steps in dealing with a complicated problem. The drunken man and the impatient person would like others to act as they do. But we shall wait and see what tougher measures they would suggest to Satta. My concentration this evening will be devoted to persuading them from making unreasonable suggestions. It should be realized that my granddaughter's mental health is likely to be damaged by rash measures."

"Thanks, grandmother," said Satta. "Let God give you the wisdom to mediate this matter effectively."

The meeting that evening was held in the living room of Abibu Lansana, the head of the extended family. Abibu and Bunduka, his eldest son, were in there chatting when Satta and Judith entered. They greeted the two men and occupied two of the six armchairs bought from the local carpenter four years ago. Shortly after that Musu arrived with Jami, Satta's aunt. Last to arrive were Beimba and Ngele, Musu's brother. Beimba's loud laughter could be heard outside as he approached the house. It looked like Ngele, a very funny man, was entertaining him. It was said that the latter was the only man that could control Beimba even in a fit of rage. As soon as the two were in their seats, Satta started narrating her case. She explained everything that had transpired in her life since the day the doctor in London informed Hon. Lamboi that he had contracted HIV. As her narration continued, Beimba's indignation became very apparent. Since Satta suspected that he was likely the one to first vent his anger she kept on looking in his direction. The expected interruption came when she reached the part about Rosalyn's dinner.

"I almost struck this womanizer the last time we met on a case concerning his infidelity," he said, banging violently on the stool next to him. "Next time I will first deal with the relative that tries to dissuade me from taking such a drastic measure before getting hold of Misalie himself. So anyone thinking about restraining me when he is here should think twice."

This interruption occurred before the narration of the incident was complete. Out of concern that a second bang would destroy the stool, Musu moved it away. Beimba who was now on his feet excused himself and stepped out. In addition to his being indignant about the way his niece had been treated by a promiscuous husband, he was also annoyed with by six men spinning tops outside. Their passionate involvement in the game had forced them to raise their voices to the extent that it started to bother the family members at the meeting. In fact the joyous atmosphere they had created was in sharp contrast to the gloomy mood that pervaded the meeting.

"Move your game out of here," he said sternly, pointing his index finger menacingly at the loudest among them. "The next time I am forced to come out to control your obnoxious behavior, I will show the big man among you that I am a man."

The players involved in the contest knew him well enough to dare disregard his warning that they be quiet. To avoid provoking him any further they picked up their equipment consisting of a big truck tire and a mat and moved to a verandah far away from the compound of the Lansanas.

Satta, who had also felt that the top players were too loud, was relieved when quiet was restored. She did not have to raise her voice in order to be heard. When her uncle returned she explained what she did when she surprised Rosalyn and her guests. Nothing had ever pleased Beimba more than the narration of the way the entire food was destroyed and the reaction of everyone at the table when the pepper got in their eyes. The explanation of this episode momentarily became a source of distraction because Beimba wanted her niece to dwell on it. He laughed loud and clapped once.

"Oh! How I love those big bangs!" he shouted out, laughing pleasantly. "That was their last meal together. Very well done, niece!"

"Satta, your reaction was appropriate," said Abibu, leaning back in his chair. "As the saying goes, it is something that brings about something else. The correct punishment was meted out to the evil group. They all got what they deserved."

The laughter that erupted was an indication that Beimba and Abibu were not the only ones that believed that the group got what it deserved. Satta's undisputed victory gave everyone a good feeling.

The fault with Satta's explanation was that she had assumed that everyone in the audience knew about the nature of the virus that her husband had contracted. She did not realize that only her mother and her grandmother, who had only been told about the virus earlier that day, knew about it. This fault had made the audience to direct its indignation only at the marital infidelity of

Hon. Lamboi. But when Judith vividly explained the devastating consequences of the disease in response to a question asked by Ngele, the audience became momentarily speechless. This information changed the climate that had been created after the explanation of the dinner episode. No one now dared to laugh. The silence that ensued gave Judith the chance to summarize some painful facts about the virus in such a way that everyone was overwhelmed by sadness.

"I have to let you know at once that first, Hon. Lamboi will not recover if he develops AIDS; second, that the disease is incurable; and third, that since it can be sexually transmitted, Satta can no longer share the same bed with him. Thus my only daughter will never have children. We shall never have a grandchild from her."

"Was Satta tested for the virus?" asked Abibu quietly. "I am asking because she may already have contracted it without knowing."

"Yes, she tested negative," said Judith. "She is completely free of the virus."

"Alleluia!" exclaimed Beimba, laughing louder than before. "God has spared my niece. Her safety and well-being are all that I care about."

"What about her husband who stands a chance of developing a disease that will sooner or later make him die in a slow and very painful way?" asked Musu quietly.

"What about the warning we gave him against his involvement in marital infidelity and promiscuity?" asked Beimba. "Why did he not listen to us? Why did he expose our daughter to such a big danger?"

"Despite his conduct he still deserves our sympathy," said Musu. "Does he not?"

"I am not so sure about that," said Beimba. "This man had

a choice not to engage in activities that could ruin his life. He decided not to take good care of his life. Is that the way to deserve someone's sympathy?"

"Regardless of the way he had lived his life he still deserves our sympathy," said Bunduka. "When a man finds himself in the worst of conditions, we humans should be moved to sympathize with him unless he had been evil. Although Hon. Lamboi has wronged our daughter, he is not an evil man. So he deserves our sympathy."

"I agree with you," said Musu.

"I agree too," said Beimba. "I only expressed that opinion because I am upset with the man. I am angry not only because of his consciously embarking on a path of self-destruction but also because he exposed my niece to the greatest of dangers. He does, of course, deserve my sympathy. However I am so overjoyed that my niece is free of the virus that I can't sympathize with him at this time. Let me rejoice now and sympathize later."

"I am surprised and disappointed that Hon. Lamboi did not listen to our advice," said Abibu. "I am not going to waste my time convincing people like Beimba to be sympathetic with a man that senselessly exposed himself to such a deadly virus. I am, however, concerned about finding solutions to my niece's problems. The minister is now incapable of giving my niece what she wants and deserves - a child. What can she do? My sympathies are with my niece. This is such a big problem that I am not going to waste my time thinking of what Hon. Lamboi should do now with what little time is left for him in this world. It's an irony that a Minister of Health does not know how to keep himself healthy."

"Abibu, we have to consider Hon. Lamboi in our discussion because Satta is still living with him," said Musu. "If their relationship is bad, she will be sad. We have to realize that Satta is such a caring person that she is not likely to abandon her husband that soon. From my earlier discussion with her I gathered that there are two things that she needs our help in accomplishing. The first is that she is childless and needs advice on how to deal with this problem. Second, she needs our moral support in her struggle to adjust to her new way of life with her husband."

"Uncle Abibu, these are the two things that I came to consult the family about," said Satta. "At this time I do not want to do anything that may reflect badly on my reputation. I want to continue living with Hon. Lamboi and give him all the moral support I can. I will feel happy if all of you can give me some moral support in doing this. In our tradition individualism has no place. I want to leave here knowing that my extended family is firmly behind me. The next time you pour libation to the ancestors remember me too. It is difficult to forgive a man like Misalie but I now declare that he is forgiven for his past marital infidelity. I need your support as I stand by him until his fate becomes clear to me."

"Abibu, you have heard Satta's appeal," said Musu. "I think that we should grant her wish. It is really difficult for Satta to abandon a person on whose behalf she had already suffered. At present no one knows the fate of the husband. But Satta would like to be regarded as the faithful wife who remained by her husband till the very end. After that she will be free to do whatever she likes."

"I would do the same if I were in her shoes," said Jami. "Satta needs us now more than ever. The only way we can help her and make her happy is to accept and support her wish. Abibu, let this young lady not leave Palahun in tears."

When Abibu noticed that the family members were almost

at an impasse because some favored forgiveness while others were against it, he requested a private talk in his bedroom with Beimba and Musu. Satta liked her uncle's move because she knew that these were the two to talk to if a compromise could be achieved. Musu clearly represented those that were for forgiveness, while Beimba represented those against such an idea. She knew that such side talks were normally helpful in resolving sharp disagreements among family members.

When the three got inside and shut the door to ensure privacy, Beimba at once presented a radical solution he had planned to eventually put before the family members. He expected it to be accepted since he was convinced that it was very reasonable.

"Abibu, I have a solution to this problem of childlessness," he said hastily. "Since Hon. Lamboi can no longer give her a healthy child, she should get another husband that is capable of doing that. Any arrangement short of this would make my niece to remain childless. Why should she pay such a price? Is it not after all the husband who decided to ruin himself?"

"Are you suggesting that she divorce Misalie?" asked Abibu looking straight into Beimba's eyes.

"Yes, he deserves to be divorced," said Beimba. "He is very compatible with Rosalyn Songa on whom he has spent a fortune and more romantic time than Satta. I see no reason why anybody would think it cruel or inconsiderate for an innocent woman to get rid of an unfair burden placed on her head by a promiscuous and uncaring husband in order to legally enter a new situation in which she can experience happiness. The benefit to be derived from such a pleasant situation is a child - the fulfillment of an innate desire in women. Yes, my solution looks radical but it inspires a sense of fairness and also allows this young woman to satisfy a basic craving in women. Any suggestion that she sit down and allow her reproductive years to glide by without producing an offspring of her own is tantamount to the gravest of punishments."

"Abibu, I am glad that Satta is not in here to hear this suggestion," said Musu. "If you had made it when we were out there she would have collapsed at once. I do not know what we would have done to revive her. This young lady is too fragile to embrace such a radical solution. Your suggestion may sound logical to many but the problem is that it falls far short of what she wants. As an educated woman she knows that such an alternative is available to her. But since she does not want to pursue it, your solution may be regarded by her as arbitrary. Thus what looks fitting to you may be injurious to her. The issue is not what is best and appropriate for us; it is what is best and convenient for an innocent lady who is caring and honest by nature. Let's not make her feel abandoned and betrayed. All she needs is our moral support."

Abibu Lansana was the first of the two men to agree to give Satta his moral support. His taking sides with Musu against Beimba made the battle easier to win. In the end they prevailed over him. They however tried not to make him feel bad. Before they returned to the living room he promised to stop verbally attacking Hon. Lamboi and allow the extended family to grant Satta her wish.

"Satta, we shall back you all the way in your struggle to deal with your problem," said Abibu after they had taken their seats among the others. "One thing that is good about our traditional democracy is that it allows us to keep on negotiating till in the end everybody agrees with the most reasonable view. So when we were in that room we did not do anything to make any of us here feel isolated. Since we all trust Satta's good judgment, we came to the conclusion that she knows what she wants and so the best we can do in this case is to give her our moral support. As Musu had said the issue is not about what is fitting for us but what is best and appropriate for Satta. I am glad that we could come to an agreement on this issue."

After Abibu had spoken, everybody in the meeting expressed views in favor of Satta's appeal.

"I wish to congratulate this gathering for doing something positive for my granddaughter," said Musu. "Nobody doubts that the smile on Satta's face serves as evidence that we have succeeded in making her happy."

"I want to thank all of you for your decision to support me," said Satta. "As grandmother has said, you have truly made me happy."

"Of the two requests that Satta made, the second, which is her need of our moral support, has now been granted," said Abibu. We now have to turn to the first, which deals with the issue of childlessness. At this point suggestions can be made about how best to handle it."

"I have hired and invited a medicine man in our area to deal with this problem," said Musu. "Being an excellent diviner he will predict whether Satta will have children."

The diviner who had arrived an hour earlier had been sitting all this time in Musu's living room waiting to be invited to perform his task. When he was at last summoned to Abibu's house, he did the divining in full view of the gathering. After unfolding his well decorated and colorful mat he sat on it and took out of the chest pocket of his embroidered traditional robe a small bottle filled with clear liquid. Rubbing some on his face he returned it and took his divining mirror out of his bag. Placing it between his legs he meditated for a few minutes before addressing Satta.

"Satta, are you hearing me," he asked looking keenly into

the mirror.

"Yes, I can hear you," said Satta.

"I see two stars in this mirror," said the diviner without raising his head. "One belongs to you and the other to Misalie, your husband. The problem I am having is that both stars are too far off. If they were close enough I would readily have made the prediction. To bring them closer I have to fall into a trance but that will be possible only if the rest of you here cooperate. I am in need of absolute silence. Someone please close the door and make sure that no one interrupts me."

The diviner's wish was granted. Beimba took the seat by the door making sure that no one coming from outside interrupted the divining. All eyes turned toward the man on the mat. As he looked into the mirror, everyone wondered what he would say. Although Abibu and Musu had confidence in this diviner, Jami and Bunduka would have selected someone else. Their choice would have been another diviner in a village further away from Palahun. There was no reason why they would not have selected the present diviner other than the fact that they had never done business with him. In any case, they had to be patient and await the outcome of the divination in progress.

After seven minutes of incredible concentration the diviner started speaking to Satta without raising his head.

"Satta, one star is dull and seems to be descending toward earth," he said. "Since it has masculine characteristics, it represents Hon. Lamboi. He has a bad future. I am sorry Satta but there is not much even I can do for him. Look at how fast that star is falling. I know the kind of sacrifice that should be made to the ancestors to prevent it from hitting the earth but I am afraid that even such appropriate step will not prevent its descent. Even if you give me a handsome fee now to prevent its descent, I will not take it. I am too honest to take that money knowing well that I cannot stabilize this star. It will hit the earth. Oh no, Satta, I am sorry. This star is so unstable that I cannot bring it into focus. Satta, are you hearing me?"

"Yes, I am."

"Listen carefully because I am now bringing the other star into focus. It is very bright and has feminine characteristics. So, it is yours. It is a very stable star with no defects. I see a child in there. In the near future a child is coming your way. A child is coming into your life. It is your child. Congratulations, Satta! Now let me tell you more about this child. It is...."

"Wake him up from that trance!" came the voice of Beimba as he stood up to open the door."

Beimba interrupted the divining because he felt that the diviner was lying. He reasoned that if Satta's husband had a virus that made it impossible for them to have intercourse, there is no way a child would enter Satta's life in the near future. Although everyone knew that this was the reason for his interruption of the divining, they felt that out of politeness the man should have been allowed to finish his job and get his pay. Musu was the first relative that tried to repair the damage.

"Beimba, you should not have spoken," she said. "I am not sure if the divining is over. But we got the message."

"We know the rest of the story," said Judith, also trying to prevent the diviner from feeling bad. "We are glad that Satta will have a good future but sad that her husband will not. Since I am responsible for paying the amount that the diviner had charged for his services when he was hired, I am going to double it. I am very pleased with his prediction of my daughter's future."

"I will add something to that amount," said Satta, also trying to please the diviner and prevent his leaving in embarrassment.

"He will also get from me the same amount that Satta will

give him," said Abibu.

"Musu how much did he ask for his services when you hired him?" asked Judith

When Musu disclosed the amount Judith doubled it and asked Satta and Abibu the exact amounts they were going to give. The total looked impressive but the diviner refused to accept it at that time.

"I thank you for inviting me to do the divining for you," he said. "I assure you that you will hire me again some day. The liquid I rub on my face before looking into the mirror is not an ordinary liquid. It makes me see through problems. It has never let me down. My policy however is that I do not accept any fee until what I predict comes to pass. So Abibu, collect that money and hold on to it. I will come for it some day. But before I leave I would like to know whether anyone would like to add anything to the amount. These are hard times and I do not mind enjoying some more generosity."

"I will double the total of the amount that Abibu will collect," said Beimba, getting up with a smile and shaking the diviner's hand.

"Thanks, Beimba, he said. "May God bless you. Abibu, do not forget the grand total of all this. I will return someday to collect it. Just make sure that everything is collected today."

When the diviner put together his equipment and left, Beimba laughed. Since nobody actually believed the diviner, nobody blamed him for his conduct. Some even laughed along with him. All were pleased that they did something to avoid embarrassing the man any further.

"Beimba, thank you for offering that large amount of money," said Musu. "Your offer contributed a lot to our ability to please him."

"I will give you my own amount later," said Beimba. "I am

as confident as anyone here that that prediction will not come to pass. That is why I offered such a big amount. He will not get a penny."

Satta and her mother returned to Bassaya the following day. The daughter was feeling much better after such a pleasant weekend. She knew that she could now count on the moral support of the entire extended family.

CHAPTER TEN

Satta's departure for Palahun was a big relief for Hon. Lamboi who felt that he had all the time in the world to deal effectively with Rosalyn Songa's case. His goal was to get rid of her and all his other women as soon as possible and turn his life around. He had so much disappointed his wife during their marriage that the guilt was pushing him to demonstrate that he could be a decent husband and a caring human being. But he could not do that with the Rosalyns and Janes still hanging on him. He had to get rid of them.

There was no doubt in Hon. Lamboi's mind that many critics were ready to question his sincerity. They could accuse him of bad faith on the grounds that his motivation to please his wife was not due to a genuine interest in her. It was due rather to his need for some caring and understanding human being to be by his side during such a very difficult period of his life. But after thinking over this accusation for a while, he was comforted by the fact that Satta had the choice to abandon him at any time. Since she had failed to do so, he had no choice but to find ways of pleasing her regardless of what his critics thought.

The first concrete step in the fulfillment of his new resolution was taken on Thursday night when he called Jane and others to tell them that he had finished with them. Although it was a unilateral decision, he had stood firm and even told them of the tragic consequences of their continuing with him. Their pleas and opposition did not matter. As far as he was concerned they were the building blocks of the world of infidelity that he had built. Once they are out of his life, that world would fall in ruin.

The second step was to get rid of Rosalyn who was the most beloved of his girlfriends. Her case had become complicated because of her illness and Satta's personal involvement in it. Unlike the others whom he easily got rid of on the telephone, he needed more time to get rid of her. Fortunately he had the weekend which he felt was enough time to handle her case. She deserved a bit of sympathy not only because she was sick but also because of her painful and dramatic encounter with Satta.

Immediately after work on Friday he set out to accomplish a mission he felt was vital to building a new relationship with his wife. He went to the hospital with Veronica Johnson who had earlier called Rosalyn to tell her of their visit. Since the sick woman had requested Alice's presence they passed by the WHO clinic and picked her up. They reached their destination at exactly six o'clock.

Hon. Lamboi who had been worried all night about Rosalyn's condition was happy to set eyes on her. She looked completely relaxed despite her terrible experience the previous night. Her looks pleased the minister who shook her hand warmly. After the three of them had taken their seats she showed them the medicines that had relieved her pain. She then told them about the series of tests that the doctor had ordered. The results would be available Saturday afternoon and, if everything went well, she would be discharged on Sunday by noon. Everybody was very pleased to hear this. For Hon. Lamboi who was hard pressed for time this was great news. The only test of concern which Rosalyn felt was premature to discuss with Hon. Lamboi was the pregnancy test that was to be done on Sunday morning. Since she had failed to experience her menstrual flow which should have started the day before, she suspected that she may be pregnant. But the doctor told her to wait for two or three days in case there was a delay that month due to her abdominal illness. He, therefore, postponed that testing till Sunday morning when it could be done with greater certainty.

The conversation between Rosalyn and her visitors was very pleasant. Hon. Lamboi who had expected some bad news was pleased that so far everything was going well. When it was time for them to leave Rosalyn told Alice that she would like her to come back with the others on Saturday. She was convinced that so long as she remained in contact with Alice, the chances of eventually meeting Satta remained good.

After dropping off Veronica and Alice, Hon. Lamboi passed by the home of Sefoi Juana, the Commissioner of Health. The latter had wanted to go to the hospital with them but he was not in at the time the others were leaving. He expressed his disappointment immediately after offering a seat to his friend and ordering the houseboy to get them beer and soft drinks.

"I feel bad that I could not go," he said. "Please make sure that you let me know tomorrow when you are going there. I had very much wanted to see Rosalyn."

"I will make sure that you know the exact time," said Hon. Lamboi.

"So, how is she?" asked Sefoi anxiously.

"She is doing very well," replied Hon. Lamboi. "Her pains are gone and she is ready to be discharged. The doctor will give most of the test results tomorrow but since she is feeling well, these will not matter much. If any further medical treatment is necessary, it will be done during normal visits."

"Misalie, I will be very relieved when she gets out of the hospital," said Sefoi. "If she stays there until the return of Satta from the provinces, you will have problems going to see her."

"I am glad that by the time Satta returns this problem will have been behind me," said Hon. Lamboi. "I do not think that I will ever run into such a problem again. Sefoi, I am going to leave the field of marital infidelity in your hands."

"Why would you leave such a vast field in my hands," said Sefoi. "I cannot handle all those women by myself. You know that they never stop running after us. One of them called even today asking me to get her a bed for her new apartment. I told her jokingly that there are no beds for sale in town."

"But Sefoi, if you do not buy the bed what would you sleep on with her? Besides, very few men will consider turning down a request by a pretty lady for a bed. It is the household object that unites both of you."

This comment made the two friends to laugh. Both men were from the same village. Their friendship which had grown over the years started in their childhood days.

"Since I have contracted HIV, I am now very restricted in what I can do with women," said Hon. Lamboi seriously. "Sexual involvement with them entails my giving them the virus. On Thursday night after we had left Rosalyn's place I called to tell all of them that I am no longer interested in continuing with them. I told them that their involvement with me sexually entails their contracting the virus."

"What was their reaction?"

"They are reluctant to break with me," replied Hon. Lamboi. "I did not find any that was hesitant about going to bed with me. Can you believe that Jane wanted me to send my driver to pick her up on learning that Satta was spending the night at my mother-in-law's place?"

"This is a big surprise to me," said Sefoi. "The truth is that not many people take this disease seriously. So how are you going to deal with them?"

"I will no longer continue with them," said Hon. Lamboi. "I am completely finished with them. As for Rosalyn, I am only waiting for her to recover. As soon as she gets well and becomes strong enough to stand some bad news, I will tell her that I am finished with her. Sefoi, I have to change my life around. There is nothing that a helpless man like me can do for Satta at this time. I cannot give her children and I cannot pay her enough for all the sacrifices that she has made on my behalf. What I can show her at this time is that I am a decent human being that deserves her devotion. I have to demonstrate that I deserve any favor that she can do for me. To continue encouraging other women is to prove to Satta that I am the most ungrateful of men. So, Sefoi, I have finally withdrawn from the world of women."

"Misalie, that's an excellent decision," said Sefoi. "You should let Satta know that you are grateful. These women may tend to resist but they will soon decide to leave you alone. They are all gainfully employed and can now take care of themselves. Rosalyn needs some attention now but she also will be willing to go her own way as soon as she is discharged."

"I think that she will be the easiest to deal with," said Hon. Lamboi. "Last night she apologized for having ruined Satta's marriage. We all heard that apology although Satta had by then left the house. I believe that she was sincere."

"What happened last night took me by surprise," said Sefoi.

"Do you have any idea who gave Satta information about the dinner?"

"I do not at all," said Hon Lamboi. "After I returned home I called to ask Jane Williams but she told me that she did not do it. I have however realized that finding out cannot in any way help me with my marital problems. Satta's conduct last night and Rosalyn's confession were both surprises to me too. Anyone familiar with my relationship with both women would have expected some conflict; but I did not however expect that it would be that dramatic. Satta struck a blow incapacitating all of us at once. What could be more dramatic than that. Don't you think that she scored a big victory?"

"Her victory was total and we deserved the punishment," said Sefoi. "Who would have dreamt that a lady whose patience the four of us had taken for granted would one day belittle all of us at the same time in the same place. Do you know that she could have further harmed us if she wanted to?"

"Yes, of course," said Hon. Lamboi. "I was really afraid that she would hit us. We were defenseless."

"So you too got that feeling," said Sefoi. "When she made the move to leave I thought that she was about to land the blows. It was a relief when she passed by quietly. It would have been the first time in my life to be beaten by a woman. Thank God that that did not happen."

The two men laughed. This comment showed that the incident, although serious, had its funny aspects.

"As for me it would not have been the first time that a woman would have hit me," said Hon. Lamboi. "Do you remember when I got involved in a fight with a tomboy in elementary school? That was my first time. This would have been my second."

The two laughed again. Sefoi remembered that incident very well. It happened when they were in Class Three. They had gone to visit Sefoi's uncle in the village. Coming from Tilasa, the second largest town in the country, they tried to make fun of the village children of their age group. They felt confident doing that because they had on city clothes and were wearing shoes. But they took their taunting too far when they happened to confront a tomboy who publicly challenged them. The girl was barefooted and did not like being referred to as an illiterate country girl. During the fight Misalie tried to display his boxing skills. The girl, who was much bigger than he, managed to grab him without being hit and dropped him to the ground. She held on to him, dragged him and then let him go. Sefoi would have been a better match for her but was powerless to intervene because the village boys were standing there ready to defend their own.

"Satta did really achieve her purpose last night," said Sefoi. "The woman whom she went to challenge was so humiliated that she apologized to her."

"Sefoi, I am glad that that apology was made," said Hon. Lamboi. "It was good for Rosalyn who felt that the admission of guilt could win Satta's's forgiveness. It was also good for Satta because it made her realize that there are people who are willing to admit their guilt and take responsibility for their conduct. We would have had a chaotic situation in our hands if Rosalyn had tried to challenge her. I am not, however, sure if Satta will ever accept her apology."

"I am not sure either if she will," said Hon. Lamboi. "But we shall wait and see what will happen in the near future."

It was about four on Saturday that Hon. Lamboi and Alice Lavalie arrived at the hospital. They met Sefoi Juana and Veronica Johnson in the lobby. Rosalyn who was expecting all of them greeted them with a smile and told them that she would be discharged on Sunday. As they were talking the doctor entered and examined her. He told her that since the laboratory was closed on Sundays, the results of her tests would not be available until around noon on Monday. So her discharge would be delayed by a day. The doctor's only concern was the abdominal pain which was likely to recur. But he promised to give medicines that would take care of the problem at home. This good news made everyone including the patient very happy. It made Hon. Lamboi to feel that everything he had planned would go as expected.

When the visitors were about to leave, Rosalyn asked Veronica and Alice to stay and spend the rest of the evening by her bedside. Her intention was to seek their advice about the nature of her relationship with Hon. Lamboi.

"I guess that it is all over now between me and Misalie," she said.

"Why do you say that, Rosalyn?" asked Veronica with some curiosity in her face. Being an inquisitive woman, she wanted Rosalyn to tell them everything she thought and felt about all the new developments in her relationship with Hon. Lamboi. In fact she had been waiting for a moment like this. Hitherto Rosalyn could not say much due to her anguish and pain.

"Veronica, you know me very well," said Rosalyn. "I am the out-going and optimistic type of person. But the disgraceful incident that occurred on Thursday night shook me to the extent that my outlook on life is no longer pleasant. I had a nightmare about the incident last night. I believe that the nightmare is the result of my constantly conjuring up mental images of Satta standing at that dinner table. In this terrible dream I saw her again pick up the bowl of soup and raise it in the air. But this time she held the bowl much longer in the air as if trying to warn us of what lay ahead. Then came the first big bang crashing to pieces an expensive dish that was reputed for its durability. The action was repeated with the rice bowl. These deafening sounds made my nightmare very uncomfortable. My eyes were burning again. This terrible dream was so real that I wept when I woke up. The question I now ask myself is whether going with Hon.

Lamboi is worth the humiliation that I have undergone. The answer is that it's not worth it at all. The man himself is very unreliable when it comes to women. Thus it's not worth the trouble struggling to possess such a person as a husband. As I said on the night of the incident, I am not upset with Satta. I am sorry that I have caused her such sadness. What I am going to tell Hon. Lamboi on Monday after my discharge is that I no longer want him. I will advise him to apologize to his wife for his marital infidelity. I want Alice to tell Satta how sorry I am for the wrong I have done to her."

"Rosalyn, I think that your decision is honorable," said Veronica. "From now on you should avoid the kind of situation that is regarded by society as morally wrong. To continue with Hon. Lamboi will make you feel that you are a slave to your passions. To be free and happy, try to get involved in a relationship that is genuine and non-disruptive to somebody else's life or yours. Something else I want you to know is that the incident was a rude awakening for me too. I had failed to realize that my job is that of a secretary and not a messenger. Arranging my boss' dates and conveying messages to his many women in return for favors became so routine that it looked as if he was doing the right thing. I share your guilt as well as his. Like you, I owe Satta an apology. I will make it soon. My hope is that Hon. Lamboi will not continue with his promiscuous lifestyle. But if he does I will no longer be the one to convey his messages. We went to your home to enjoy another meal but those deafening sounds and the burning sensation so effectively killed my appetite that did I not eat till late the following day. I will never put myself in such a situation again."

"I doubt that Hon. Lamboi would ever put himself in such a situation," said Alice. "His contracting HIV is the great price he has paid for his marital infidelity. So, like both of you, he is trying to change his life. I believe that he will readily accept Rosalyn's decision to end the relationship. There is no way both of them can possibly continue after his wife's actions."

"Do you know how he got the virus?" asked Veronica.

"No, I do not," replied Alice.

"It is difficult to tell," said Rosalyn. "The man has so many women that he himself may not even know who gave it to him. Fortunately I am now out of his life. Alice, the request I now make of you is to get me in contact with Satta. Please keep on talking to her. As I told you on Thursday night I will never be a happy woman until I meet her in person and apologize for my role in the destruction of her marriage."

Hon. Lamboi spent Saturday evening at Sefoi's place. Both men had a more relaxing evening because of the good news they had received at the hospital. Their conversation dealt with the hopes and new plans of Hon. Lamboi. It was during this discussion that Sefoi advised his friend about to the kind of conduct that would help him build a new and lasting relationship with his wife.

"Misalie, despite all your problems, I believe that your relationship with your wife will soon get on track," he said. "It is now up to you to work hard to get things moving. To demonstrate to her that you are serious about changing your ways, you have to avoid doing anything that will make her to even suspect that you are still fooling around with women."

"This is good advice, Sefoi," said Hon. Lamboi. "I am prudent enough to realize that this is my last chance to prove to Satta that I deserve her love. So, I am going to show that I am worthy of her."

"Misalie, you have broken many resolutions in the past," said Sefoi. "It is one thing to say that you are going to do something and another to actually do it. If you do not demonstrate to her this time that you are serious about changing your behavior, you will find yourself in very big trouble. As far as I know, this is the only woman that will be willing to stand by you till the end. The others are after you for your wealth. They will abandon you the day you stop supporting them."

"Sefoi, I am trying to change," said Hon. Lamboi. "As I told you yesterday, I have already telephoned all the other women and ended my relationship with them. The only woman I have not talked to about my decision is Rosalyn. I cannot now because she is sick. But as soon as she is discharged, I will tell her that I am through with her."

"That is a good idea," said Sefoi. "That will set you completely free to devote yourself to your wife and prove that you can be a decent and honest husband."

Hon. Lamboi was so exhausted when he arrived home that he went straightaway to bed. Not having slept well the last two nights he could not stay up to make plans for Sunday. It was when he got up at noon the following day that he started debating whether he had enough time to visit his sick girlfriend. His concern was that his wife may return home from Palahun while he was away at the hospital and inquire his whereabouts. But not wanting Rosalyn to feel abandoned by him, he decided to pay her a quick visit. He was happy that Monday was the last day of a relationship he did not care about anymore. All he planned to do that day was to go to the hospital to hear what the doctor had to say about the discharge and then bid her farewell for good. Instead of taking her home himself, he intended to send her away in a taxi. That would be the end of the sweetest affair that he had ever been involved in. Letting her go in a taxi is a reflection of the way he now felt about the woman. To get the message across the parting had to be that unceremonious.

Hon. Lamboi's decision to leave the home that Sunday was

unfortunate because Satta arrived in his absence. Although she did not get angry, she decided not to stay there. Unloading her share of the food supplies brought from Palahun and packing a few belongings in a traveling bag, she went to spend the night at her mother's.

During their stay in Palahun, they had thought a lot about Alice's meeting with Rosalyn on Thursday night. Since they were anxious to know what happened at that meeting, the first thing they did after they had eaten was to call Alice to tell her that they were on their way to see her. But just before they stepped out of the house at four o'clock, Michael Lamboi, Misalie's immediate younger brother, came to visit them. It was the houseboy at Satta's house that had told him that Satta was at Judith's place. Since they were in a hurry to leave, they asked him to go along with them.

Both Judith and Satta liked and trusted Michael very much. Unlike Hon. Lamboi, he was very caring and lived a harmonious life with his wife. The narration of what happened on Thursday night made him laugh excessively all the way to their destination. He declared that his brother fully deserved the punishment.

When they reached Alice's house, she gave them a warm welcome and led them to the living room. They were very attentive as she told them everything that happened from the time she returned to the scene of the incident on Thursday through their second visit to the hospital on Saturday. Her audience was overwhelmed by the account.

"Misalie had a very busy weekend," said Judith. "Satta, I would not be angry with his effort to seek medical care for Rosalyn. He acted out of necessity. There is no doubt that the relationship itself is dead."

"Yes, it is dead," said Alice. "Satta, I assure you that Rosalyn herself is no longer interested in it. As I had told you, she wants to meet you and apologize for her wrongdoing. She is really anxious to meet you. I believe that she is genuine although you may think otherwise. Your husband has also lost interest in the relationship. He was in and out of the hospital all weekend because he feels morally obliged to do so. He could not unexpectedly abandon her while she was on a sick bed."

"I will never go out of my way to meet Rosalyn," said Satta. "The longer she feels remorseful for her bad treatment of me the better it is for her."

"Since Satta is going to be too busy dealing with her own problems, she is not going to have time to consider Rosalyn's request," said Judith. "She should have to work on her problem by herself. Her apology would not mean anything to anybody."

"Mother, I agree with you," said Satta. "There is nothing that I can do with her apology. So let her deal with her problem by herself."

"I find it very difficult to believe that Satta could stand up to aggression the way she did," said Michael, laughing aloud. Being a funny man he was so fascinated with the way the dinner was disrupted that he did not want that topic to be discarded. He was determined to dwell on it for a while.

"Well, it came to a point when I had to take a firm stand and I did," said Satta. "I wanted to show Rosalyn that she cannot win all the time."

"Satta, you look very mild mannered but you are really a woman of great strength," said Michael, still laughing. "Look at the way you totally incapacitated four people. It's hard to believe that a proud woman like Rosalyn could be so quickly brought to her knees. As for Sefoi and Veronica, they got what they deserved. I know that they had eaten many such meals in the past at Rosalyn's and at other women's. They experienced the pangs of hunger that night."

"That's true, Michael," said Alice. "They did not look like people who cared about food that night. The incident was too dramatic for them to feel hungry. I felt sorry to see them using hand towels to wipe their burning eyes."

Their laughter was loud. Michael fell back in his chair and let his hands hang freely on the sides as if in complete resignation to an uncertain fate. He laughed in a care-free manner. After a while he took off his glasses, wiped them and put them on again.

"This is an incredible incident," he said. "If both Rev. Lamboi and Stephen, our youngest brother, hear about this, they too would say that all the guests got what they deserved."

The conversation then moved to the issue of childlessness. Judith told Michael that this was the problem that was bothering Satta.

"When we were in Palahun, a diviner told us that Satta would get a child," she said. "But we still cannot figure out how this would happen. There is no way my daughter will ever share the same bed with that sick man."

The narration of this prediction made Michael to express his skepticism in divination.

"The diviner's prediction is clearly false," said Michael. "This confirms my view that divination is based on superstition and should not be seriously considered when solutions are being sought to important problems."

At this time Saidu Lavalie, Alice's father, who had been sitting in a hammock in the backyard entered the living room. On hearing Judith's concern about Satta's problem, he joined the discussion without quite understanding what it was all about.

"Satta, you are young enough to have a child," he said. "Please be optimistic about it."

"Let's hope that my prayers will be answered," said Satta.

"I will pray for you too and for Michael, your brother-in-law here," said Saidu. "He had done a great kindness to my wife. The money he gave covered her hospital bill. I have come to say thanks to him and also to you because it was through you we came to know him. May God bless both of you. Satta, may God grant you that baby."

"May God grant your prayers," said Michael with a smile.

"If you people had not acquired the kind of education that made you skeptical in some of our traditional beliefs, I would have got you a diviner that would tell whether or not Satta would bear a child." said Saidu. "I would guarantee absolutely his prediction."

Everybody was astonished to hear this but remained quiet, not knowing how to react. The problem was that nobody thought it appropriate to reveal to him the fact that Satta could not get a child because she could not have normal intercourse with a husband who had contracted HIV. Besides, Satta, who did not take Saidu Lavalie's statement seriously, did not want to get involved in any fruitless search into whether she would bear a child for her husband. But Michael was thrilled by the suggestion. Although he was a skeptic he very much wanted that diviner to be hired. He thought it would be fun to hear what he had to say.

"Father, they will need some time to think over your suggestion," said Alice quietly. She did not want her father to give such a guarantee without first learning the fact of the matter. So, she wished that the father did not insist.

"I understand of course that they need time to consider my proposal," said the father. "I am going to the backyard to eat. If they decide to get the information they need, simply let me know. I will immediately invite over a very powerful diviner. He has just come from our village to pay his brother a short visit and will be returning early tomorrow morning. This man will tell Satta with certainty whatever she wants to know."

When Alice's father went back to the backyard, Michael suggested that they invite the diviner over.

"Michael, since you know very well what will be outcome of this search, why would you want to employ the services of this diviner?"

"I have heard of his powers," said Michael. "He is said to be more powerful than the one you had hired in Palahun. This is a unique opportunity for me to see him at work. Although I do not believe in divination, I may start believing if his predictions come true. You see, there are two possibilities here. If he predicts that Satta cannot in the near future bear children, then his prediction is consistent with what happens when a woman abstains from having an intimate relationship with her husband. Since there is no intimacy, there will be no conception and so no offspring is expected. And since such prediction is consistent with the facts of the matter at hand, it will not make me believe in divination. But if he predicts that Satta will have a baby soon, then his prediction contradicts the facts. There is room for excitement as we wait to see whether what is predicted will come to pass. If the child is actually born, then I will henceforth believe in divination. In fact who would fail to believe such a miracle? I really think that we should make the best of this unique opportunity by hiring the man."

"So, Alice, what do you think?" asked Satta. "I know that you are concerned about your father's promise to give an absolute guarantee of the outcome."

"I am of course concerned but he is very confident," replied Alice.

"Then let's give him a chance," said Michael.

The diviner was then summoned to perform his task in

Alice's room in the presence of everyone including Saidu. He used cowries and some other charms in the process. Upon finishing, he told them what he found.

"A baby boy will enter Satta's life in the near future," he said. "She will enjoy motherhood."

The skepticism expressed over this prediction could be perceived in the faces of everyone except Alice's father.

"Congratulations, Satta," said Saidu who got up to shake her hand. "You can sleep peacefully tonight. I do share your joy. In a few months time we shall be celebrating the arrival of the new boy."

The laughter that ensued was started by Michael who was surprised by the prediction. It was joined by Satta and Judith. This reaction could have embarrassed the diviner who might have thought that they were laughing at his prediction. But when Alice got up and hugged Satta congratulating her at the same time, the diviner interpreted the reaction as an expression of their joy. Alice gestured to Michael to also get up and join the hugging. Since he got that non-verbal message, he got up and hugged Satta. Judith did likewise.

"How soon will this child arrive?" asked Michael.

"In less than a year," said the diviner.

"Well, Satta, you will soon conceive," said Michael, turning toward Satta.

"I did not say that she would conceive," said the diviner firmly. "Pregnancy is out of the question here. We have to be careful about the way we interpret the prediction."

This statement seemed to confuse everyone. Michael was now more excited than before. Although he did not believe in divination there is something about interacting with diviners that had always fascinated him. In this case it is what everyone sees as a contradiction: the diviner says that Satta would have a child but without conceiving.

"Can you predict the way the child will come?" asked Alice's father. "These people look confused."

"Yes, I will very gladly," said the diviner, setting up again his equipment for more divination.

Everyone waited anxiously. They expected the second round to get rid of any doubt or confusion that his first interpretation might have caused.

"Satta will have a child but I see nothing about conception in the set-up before me," he said quietly. "I am only describing what I am seeing. I see her with a baby in her hands. That is what I want to talk about. As intelligent people you can draw the appropriate inferences. But I will not draw any. If we have another excellent diviner here he would examine this set-up and make a similar prediction. By the way, I accept no fees or payment for my services. When this prediction comes to pass in less than a year, and I believe it will, Michael will voluntarily give me something. I am confident that he will be so impressed that his generosity will overflow."

Everyone laughed. Alice's father saw that the second round did not clarify matters but he told them to wait for a year.

"Satta, does the content of this prediction remind you of anything you have seen or any experience you have had lately?" asked the diviner.

"Well, a dream I had lately involved a small boy that kept on referring to me as mother."

"Please narrate that dream to me," said the diviner calmly.

Satta took time to narrate the dream as objectively as possible. She tried not to give any opinion about it. When she finished the diviner made his comments.

"If you had told me this dream earlier, I would not have even bothered to do the divination. Its contents would have enabled me to make a similar prediction. My interpretation of it is that you are going to have a child. I still cannot talk about conception because you were not pregnant in the dream. Like in the case of the divination, I cannot talk about what I do not see. Again, you can draw your own inferences about the way the child would come. This dream clearly confirms my earlier prediction. Michael, I look forward to your generosity in less than a year. For now I want nothing from anyone."

"Congratulations again, Satta," said Saidu, getting up. "By the way, if you want a confirmation of what this man has said, I will get you another diviner. Let me know your decision when I return."

Saidu then walked outside with the diviner. He had other matters that he wanted to discuss with him in private. The rest took advantage of his absence by discussing the two predictions.

"The predictions of these two diviners are identical," said Judith. "What gives credence to their predictions is the fact that they used different divining techniques to arrive at the same conclusion. The man in Palahun used a mirror in his divination while the one we just met used cowries. Moreover, both diviners do not know each other. But even if they knew each other, they could not have possibly communicated with each other. Palahun does not even have a telephone system. So, Michael, what do you think of the fact that their predictions are the same?"

"Judith, you like to know my opinion on difficult matters," he replied with a smile. "The problem is that this one seems to be the most difficult ever!"

The three of them laughed loud at Michael's statement. They all knew that Judith had directed the question at him because he was the skeptic among them."

"You have to be asked such a question because you do not believe in divination," said Judith.

"It is true that I do not," said Michael quietly. "But these two have baffled me. I do not have an explanation of why both men made identical predictions. I want to believe that it is a coincidence."

"Michael, you are a true skeptic," said Judith with a smile. "I expected you to at last believe."

"But how can I believe when Satta is not now in a position to have a child?" said Michael. "The two men made the same prediction but the facts at hand do not seem to support what they have said. Their prediction is so baffling that it fails to impress any true skeptic."

"I am willing to concede that you have reason not to believe the two men," said Judith. "The confusion here is caused by the fact that Misalie has HIV and Satta has told me that sexual contact with him in any form is completely out of the question. That prediction will only come to pass if Satta has a secret plan to have a child by a means we do not know of."

"My goodness!" exclaimed Satta. "What secret plan? That's not possible at all"

This reaction of Satta brought laughter. Judith's statement pointed to the possibility of Satta's getting involved with another man.

"Well, since Satta has vehemently denied that such possibility exists, then there is no child coming into her life," said Michael. "The predictions are therefore false. The fact that they are similar is not a guarantee that they are true. We have here a case of two predictions that are identical and false. This is my view."

"Mother, what is your view about this matter?" asked Satta quietly.

"I took you to a diviner in Palahun because I believe in divination," said Judith. "Although the facts are not consistent with their predictions, I am satisfied with what the two diviners have said. I am looking at the similarity of the predictions while Michael is strictly after the facts."

"I wonder if he will believe if a third diviner makes a similar prediction," said Satta.

"He should because such coincidences are very rare," said Judith.

"It's not very easy converting a skeptic," said Michael. "However, you may succeed in arousing my curiosity if a third diviner makes a similar prediction. As you know, curiosity makes people to seriously start investigating problems they do not normally care about. Why don't we ask Saidu to invite over the other diviner. Since he is readily available, it does not hurt to hear what he has to say."

Alice who had been very quiet left to get her father. The uneasy feeling she had about the guarantee given by Saidu had made her to decide not to say much about this matter. When her father heard the decision of the guests he sent one of his sons to go and get the diviner. As they waited he took time to narrate the powers of the man being summoned.

"This man is so famous in his part of the country that people travel for miles to go to see him," he said. "Clients have testified that his predictions have saved them from disasters. Even my boss here in town admires him. He had predicted that the man would be promoted and sent to England for further training. It came to pass. My boss likes me because I was the one that introduced this man to him."

When the diviner arrived, Saidu introduced him to his guests. He then explained the problem to him saying nothing about Hon. Lamboi's condition and the prediction of the diviner that had just left. Everyone was attentive as the man prepared himself for the task. His divining technique was quite different from the other two. He used water to make his predictions. After a long prayer which involved many gesticulations he poured his water into a clean bowl and focussed his attention on it.

"Although Satta has a bright future, I find nothing to indicate that she will have a child in the near future," he said without raising his head. "No child is coming into her life in the next twelve months because her husband has a bad star."

"What about my daughter's star?" asked Judith anxiously.

"The star that represents Satta is bright and healthy. The difficulty in having a child lies with the husband. The star representing him is dull and weak."

"What about Satta's having children in the long run?" asked Saidu. "Can you please find out and tell us?"

"I cannot investigate this matter at this time," said the diviner. "The behavior of weak stars is difficult to predict. You first have to take its owner to a medicine man for cleansing. Since I am only a fortune teller, I cannot do the cleansing. When the medicine man investigates the husband's past and finds the cause of his misfortune, he will prescribe a sacrifice. This rite is part of his purification process. After the purification ceremony, you can come back so that I can predict his ability to have children with Satta. But as matters stand, I can say with certainty that Satta will not have a child in the next twelve months."

After the diviner had answered a few more questions, he demanded his fee and left. The atmosphere he left behind was subdued. His prediction was so consistent with the facts of the matter that it made sense for both skeptics and non-skeptics to believe him. Saidu who had invited the diviners over after guaranteeing the outcome of their divination knew that Satta was terribly disappointed. So he tried to encourage her a bit.

"Satta, there is no doubt that the prediction of one these

two diviners is discouraging," he said. "However, I urge you not to lose hope. Normally the diviners I consult on any particular issue do make similar predictions."

"So this is a rare case," said Michael.

"Yes, it is," said Saidu. "But despite the conflicting predictions I still believe in divination. One conflict is not enough to discourage me. Most of what I do in life is guided by what diviners tell me. That is why I do not feel comfortable embarking on any important project without consulting them. In difficult cases like this it is advisable to consult one or two more diviners."

At this point Judith thought it worthwhile to help Saidu by telling him what the diviner in Palahun had said. She definitely shared Saidu's view that the solution lay in consulting more diviners.

"Saidu, I have to mention at this time that a diviner in Palahun had predicted that Satta will have a child in the near future. He is in agreement with one of your two diviners."

This was welcome news because it made Saidu feel confident about pursuing his plan to consult more diviners.

"So we have two predictions in favor of Satta's having a child," said Saidu. "Since conflicting predictions are rare, the chances are that other diviners would make predictions similar to theirs."

"Are you sure that the solution to this problem lies in consulting more diviners?" asked Michael.

"Oh, yes, I am," replied Saidu without hesitation. "More diviners should be consulted."

"So, in the end whatever the majority of diviners say is what should be believed," said Michael with a smile.

This statement caused some laughter. Saidu was the only one who did not laugh. He was uncomfortable with the conclusion that Michael was trying to draw from his suggestion."

"Your inference indicates a basic misunderstanding of my position," he said. "What I meant is that consulting more diviners is helpful. You probably could not help drawing such inference but I do not want my suggestion to be interpreted as a quest for a majority view. I am aware of the fact that when it comes to divining, the majority may be wrong. Matters become even more complicated and ridiculous when a majority does not emerge. I made my suggestion in the hope that one more excellent diviner would make a prediction similar to the first two. That will make Satta more hopeful."

"Since I am a believer in divination I would like us to consult one more diviner," said Judith. "True believers do not give up easily. It is good for Satta to leave this place with good hopes of having a child."

"A good prediction is, of course, good for her morale," said Michael. "But in this case it seems a dangerous move to try again. Failure to come up with the expected result can be devastating. What do you think about all this, Alice?"

"I agree with Michael that trying again is dangerous," replied Alice. "Both Judith and my father feel that since the first two men are excellent diviners the next one is likely to make a prediction similar to theirs. If that happens there will be lots of rejoicing. But it would be devastating to Satta's morale if it does not. So if I were Satta I would turn down this suggestion in order to eliminate the possibility of experiencing such a devastation.

"But as anxious as Satta is to have a child, waiting for twelve months will be painful," said Judith.

"The pain involved in waiting is much less than the one involved in experiencing a serious disappointment," said Alice.

"Mother, I agree with Alice," said Satta. "I want to wait and see which of the three predictions will come true."

In the end Satta's wish was granted. On saying goodbye to Alice and Saidu, the guests returned to Judith's place. Satta planned to spend the night there. Michael who had left his car there, rode together with them.

When they arrived Hon. Lamboi who had been reading in the verandah walked to the street to meet them. He had come to visit his wife. After the three had greeted him they all went inside.

Satta did not stay in the living room where everybody sat to talk. She went upstairs at once to make a phone call to Rev. Matthew Lamboi and his wife. Stephen Lamboi who was visiting them that evening, answered the telephone. Satta told him that she had a problem and would like him to bring over his parents to Judith's house. She returned downstairs and joined the others at the dinner table.

When the meal was over they moved back to the living room. But they had hardly settled in their seats when the pastor arrived with his wife and son. Hon. Lamboi's heart leapt because he knew that it was Satta that had invited them over to complain about Thursday night's incident. Judith who was not aware that her daughter had made that call was very pleased. She felt that it was proper again to take Hon. Lamboi to task for attending that dinner. As for Michael, he was secretly excited because he looked forward to hearing another narration of an incident which he felt was very serious but funny.

The last time they all met together was when the news about Hon. Lamboi's contracting HIV appeared in the newspaper. At that meeting Satta had given her husband her full support in order not to put him in an embarrassing situation. But tonight her mood was different. She had a complaint to make and was ready to cast blame rather than support an unfaithful husband.

Rev. Lamboi first led the group in prayer. He talked about the lost sheep that had not yet been brought to the fold and asked Jesus Christ to make him into a changed man. When he finished his wife, also a devoted Christian, prayed. After this prayer, Satta narrated what happened at the dinner and what Alice Lavalie had told her about the hospital visits. She finished by clearly stating again the purpose of her complaint.

"Although I was the one that was wronged, Misalie neglected me and went to comfort Rosalyn in the hospital."

The narration shocked those who had not yet heard it. Rev. Lamboi who had lost patience with his son felt like slapping him. But the days when he could mete out corporal punishment were long gone. Since he was dealing with adults who were responsible for themselves, he had to behave differently.

"Misalie, is this what happened?" he asked angrily.

"Yes, father, that is what happened and I now apologize to Satta for it."

"But why did you do it when you knew that it was wrong?" asked Rev. Lamboi.

"I did it out of habit," said Hon. Lamboi. "I take full responsibility for what happened at the dinner. I am also sorry about my going to the hospital. I did not think that it was wrong at the time I decided to go there. I felt it was justified to go because I regarded it as part of the steps needed to put my life together."

"Misalie, why don't you tell your wife what these steps are so that she can determine whether you are serious about changing your ways?" asked Rev. Lamboi.

Hon. Lamboi then explained his plan to break up with all his women including Rosalyn. He visited Rosalyn at the hospital because he felt that he was partly responsible for her being there. He just wanted to be around until her discharge on Monday. After that he would have nothing to do with her again.

Since no one wanted to see the couple break up that suddenly, they all pleaded with Satta to forgive her husband and exercise some more patience. When everybody left, Judith encouraged her to return to her husband.

"My daughter, since you have been patient all along with this man, you have to continue with him. Was this not your plea with the family when we went to Palahun? I used to be upset with him but your pleas have softened me considerably. If you had decided to make this sacrifice, then stick to your plans to the very end. This is a helpless man trying to solve his problems as he sees fit. Just relax and watch the spectacle unfold. Since he got himself into the mess, he should take himself out of it."

CHAPTER ELEVEN

It was Monday! According to Hon. Lamboi this was supposed to be the day of liberation. With the other women out of his life and Rosalyn Songa on her way out of the hospital, he regarded the day as the beginning of his new life. It was a life in which he would be free to devote himself to Satta and demonstrate to her that he was capable of appreciating the sacrifices she had made on his behalf.

His day in the office was good. Since Rosalyn had requested the presence of Alice at the time of her discharge, he had asked Veronica to call and inform her that they would pick her up at half past four. He suspected that the three women would be spending the evening together.

When the three visitors entered Rosalyn's room at half past five, they met a nurse waiting for them. She took them at once to another room where Rosalyn had been taken for counseling. The counselor greeted them politely and led them into her office. They were very surprised to find there Henry Songa, Rosalyn's uncle, and his wife Patricia. Rosalyn who was sitting between them had a somber look on her face. Both uncle and aunt were holding her hands in a manner that clearly indicated that something had gone so terribly wrong that she needed her relatives' physical and moral support. Tears were flowing freely from her eyes.

Hon. Lamboi became instantly apprehensive of trouble but tried not to show it. After they had all taken the seats offered them, the counselor revealed the test results and explained why Rosalyn had been sent there for counseling.

"The results of the blood test are ready. They indicate that Rosalyn has contracted HIV. She has been recommended to Dr. Mary Cole's clinic for treatment. Her case is complicated by the fact that she is pregnant. We are not sure if the baby would contract the virus. But it is possible for it to be free of it. Further testing during the pregnancy and after it is born would help us determine the status of the baby's health. Rosalyn can go home tonight and start visiting Dr. Cole's clinic tomorrow for medication."

This stunning news shook the small audience. Rosalyn who had hitherto wept in silence started to cry aloud. It was as if a relative had died. The sweat and the tears rolling down her face were ruining the make-up and the lipstick she had put on that morning. But despite this, her natural beauty was still evident. It was that beautiful face that had made Hon. Lamboi to make her his number one girlfriend. But if beauty were an asset it was the least considered object of value at the moment. The counselor informed her visitors that since weeping was an integral part of the way people reacted to such a dramatic news, they should not interfere with her doing it.

"Oh no! Oh no! How did this happen to me? How did I contract such a fatal virus?" she cried out in agony as she stretched herself out as if trying to free herself of the virus that was about to destroy her young life. "God, why are you about to recall me so early? Why don't I get a break? Why am I going to die young? Oh no! Oh no! Oh no ... o ... o!"

Hon. Lamboi collapsed in his chair and wept aloud like a child that had been severely beaten by a wicked step-mother. He was overwhelmed by both grief and guilt. First, he was convinced that he had infected Rosalyn. Second, he realized that he had a child on his hands and did not know what to with it. Third, the new life he had promised himself was now only a mere wish. He wondered what Satta, who was still childless, would do to him on hearing that he was going to have a child with Rosalyn. He felt so remorseful for his past indulgence in women that if he were given a chance to start life all over again, he would prefer a monogamous lifestyle to a promiscuous one.

The visitors were also stunned by this excessive outpouring of grief. Veronica who had known her boss to be a strong man could not believe that he would be so thoroughly overcome by emotion. She and Alice were busy comforting him while Henry and Patricia devoted themselves to controlling their niece. The AIDS counselor again reminded the four of them that it was alright for the two people to express their emotions that way. She knew Hon. Lamboi and knew that he had contracted the virus. What surprised her was her seeing him at the hospital crying on behalf of a woman that was neither a spouse nor a blood relative.

Hon. Lamboi was thankful for the effort made by Veronica and Alice to help him cope with his tragedy. However, his sense of guilt was so strong that he felt that they were wasting their time.

"What's the use comforting me," he said. "Rosalyn and Satta are the ones to be comforted. Since I am the cause of their grief, all I deserve is blame. What a wasted life! If I had the chance to start life afresh, I would go around making people happy rather than causing grief. Oh! My God! Help me!"

It was around eight o'clock when they all set out for Rosalyn's place. Henry Songa, Rosalyn's uncle, took her in a taxi while Hon. Lamboi rode together with Veronica and Alice. No one talked during the ride. Hon. Lamboi, who had by then composed himself very well, looked calm but very pensive. Going to Rosalyn's place had not been part of his day's plan but if others were going there out of concern for her well-being he would be regarded as cruel if he did not go. Such an accusation would be justified since nobody doubted that he had put her in the present predicament. But although he was aware of such a criticism, he felt a big urge to go home because he knew that Satta, to whom he had made promises of a new attitude yesterday, was expecting him home at that time. Being unexpectedly caught between two overwhelming desires - - the urge to be with his wife as he should and that to fulfill a moral obligation to a person that he had placed in the worst of situations, rendered him mentally confused. As the journey continued the mental anguish became so great that he suddenly said aloud what he believed was the solution to his problem.

"To avoid my wife's wrath, I am going to stay indefinitely at Rosalyn's place."

This statement shocked both Alice and Veronica. They wondered why he would unexpectedly make a decision that would completely end the relationship with Satta and begin a new one with Rosalyn. Both felt that Hon. Lamboi had temporally gone out of his mind.

"Hon. Lamboi, are you alright?" asked Alice who was sitting beside him.

"I almost asked that same question," said Veronica, turning her head to take a look at the minister in the back seat.

"Yes, of course, I'm alright."

"But why did you make such a shocking statement?" asked Veronica.

"The reason is that I do not have a solution to my problem," said Hon. Lamboi, wiping his brow with a white handkerchief.

"Just yesterday we had a meeting at my father's house. Satta had brought relatives there to make a complaint concerning the amount of time I was devoting to Rosalyn's illness instead of paying attention to her plight. I told them that since I am instrumental in Rosalyn's being in the hospital, I feel morally obliged to give her my moral support until her discharge. To show that I was talking in good faith, I explained how I had gotten rid of all the other women in my life. I also divulged my plan to get rid of Rosalyn today. But as things have turned out, Rosalyn will always remain in my life. So at present I am deeply involved with two women. I do not want to be living with Satta when the news reaches her later that Rosalyn is pregnant with my child. Such a blow would be too much for her to withstand. It would look like a great betrayal of her trust. My decision to move in with Rosalyn is due to the fact that I cannot meet squarely with my wife on this issue."

"Hon. Lamboi, I cannot really predict what Satta would do when she hears of this development but I would advise you to continue living with her," said Alice. "You are more likely to be able to cope with her than Rosalyn whose frustration with her tragedy is so great that she would vent the worst of angers on you. I am of course not asking you to abandon Rosalyn at all. You have to continue giving her your moral support. Something else I want to point out is that when it comes to taking care of her, it is her aunt and uncle that are in a better position to do so."

"I believe that Alice has given you a good advice," said Veronica, turning in the direction of her boss. "Right now it looks like Rosalyn is so sad that the only thing she needs is someone to comfort her. You can give that comfort for a day or two. But when she starts venting her anger and frustration, you will be an appropriate target. So continue living with your wife and leave the job of taking care of her in the hands of Henry and Patricia. They will be in contact with you and will tell you when it is appropriate to see her."

"I appreciate this advice," said Hon. Lamboi. "It is naive to believe that Rosalyn will continue to be calm around me in the near future. What am I then going to tell my wife? I should tell her something."

"Since you have already gone through one emotional crisis today, another one would not be good for you tonight," said Alice. "My advice is that you should not yet reveal anything about Rosalyn and what the doctor has told you about her condition. By postponing this information you get some time to think matters over and adjust yourself to your new disaster."

"Your task tonight and in the few days ahead is to remain calm at home," said Veronica. "Your manhood is going to be demonstrated by your ability to compose yourself whenever you find yourself in difficult situations. You may be arriving home at around ten o'clock tonight. It looks late but that is not so unusual as to arouse the curiosity of your wife. Just go inside with a smile, eat well and manage to engage her in a pleasant conversation. Give whatever excuses you can for staying out late."

"Alice, since Satta is your girlfriend, I wonder what you will tell her when she suspects something and questions you about what happened tonight," said Hon. Lamboi.

"She does not know that I am with you tonight," said Alice. "I will not bring this topic up in any conversation."

"I do not expect you to voluntarily do that," said Hon. Lamboi. "However, one of these days you may find yourself in a situation where you will be forced to make a revelation of this affair. When that happens, please inform me first before you tell her. If am not aware that you have told her of this development,

I may find myself in an unexpected storm. I do not want to be terribly surprised by her. So promise me tonight to let me know when you decide or are forced to tell her."

"I promise," said Alice with a big smile that was meant to cheer up Hon. Lamboi.

Rosalyn looked calm when they all entered the house. She had been told on the way home that excessive emotional outbursts or uncontrollable reaction to her disaster would affect her health and that of the baby. This advice had made her try to contain her emotions. Alice who was an AIDS counselor went into her bedroom with her and gave her more information on the disease. She told her that she would remind Dr. Cole about her appointment.

Hon. Lamboi reached home a little before eleven. Although his wife asked how the day went she did not seem to suspect how difficult a day her husband had experienced. Misalie who dared not divulge his secret about that day told her that it went very well. Both then ate dinner and watched television for a while before retiring for the night.

Although he was obviously exhausted, he had too much on his mind to easily fall asleep. The first thing he did when he lay down was to take out his five-year diary to record what had transpired that day. Since he now slept by himself, he did not have to check whether his wife was watching him. Recording most of the things that he did or happened to him was a habit that he picked up since his final year in secondary school. It had become a hobby. He enjoyed reading that diary whenever he had time.

Most of what Hon. Lamboi had recorded in the past had been pleasant. They were about his carefree lifestyle. He described the women he had gone with, the good times he had had and the delicious dinners he had eaten at their places. But what he had entered since his return from London had not been pleasant. It was all related to his contracting HIV and his attempt to get rid of his women and develop a new relationship with his wife. As he turned over the leaves to find the page to record the day's episode his eyes fell on the descriptions of some amusing episodes and some very good times he had had. Unfortunately what he wrote that evening when he finally got to the right page was not amusing. He described Rosalyn's tragedy and how he wept over it like a child who had lost his mother. When he finished writing he did not put the diary back in the small safe where he normally hid it. Instead he put it under the pillow hoping to add a few more things in the morning. He then lay on his back thinking over his current problem. Since nothing unusual happened between him and Satta that day he focussed his attention on Rosalyn. The feeling of guilt soon descended on him again. To minimize his guilt he tried to console himself by nurturing the idea that he too had been infected by someone else. Thus he was equally a victim. This comforted him momentarily. But then it occurred to him that if he had not lived a promiscuous lifestyle he would not have transmitted the virus to Rosalyn. This thought brought back the feelings of guilt. His mind remained occupied with this issue until sleep finally came to his eyes.

The following day both husband and wife went to work. To Satta who had put the latest problems in perspective everything looked normal. Assuming that Rosalyn was now out of her husband's life, she did not bother to ask him about her. Since she had a very busy day attending meetings, she did not even notice the presence of Veronica, her husband's secretary, in the building at around four o'clock. The latter had come to seek Sylvia's advice about a problem that was seriously bothering her.

It was around ten that morning when Veronica called her

friend to inform her of her intention to meet with her after work. During that call Sylvia had asked to be briefed on the issue but Veronica, who did not want to touch on the matter while in the office, told her that it concerned her boss but would rather wait to discuss the matter after work. Expecting her friend to bring along the latest information on the promiscuous activities of Hon. Lamboi, Sylvia was thrilled and could hardly wait to meet her. Gossiping about the minister's marital infidelity was a source of joy and fun for both of them. Since the man had involved himself with about fifteen women at different times, there was always something exciting to talk about.

Sylvia had sometimes jokingly referred to Veronica as Hon. Lamboi's messenger. A closer examination of what she did for her boss qualified her for such a title. She was the one who arranged all the private encounters between him and the women he went with. She also ran most of his errands.

Veronica, who appeared comfortable with her role, told her friend one day that it was adventurous and exciting. Regarding the activities of her care-free boss as a harmless adventure, she saw nothing wrong with such a role. It never occurred to her that her attitude reflected a lack of concern for the welfare of those who were hurt by Hon. Lamboi's promiscuous behavior. It was the chaos at Rosalyn's dinner that made her start having second thoughts about the propriety of her conduct. First of all, she was now saddened by the thought that some of the minister's women may be carrying the virus without knowing it. It dawned upon her that sooner or later some of them may develop AIDS and die. Secondly, the infidelity of Hon. Lamboi had badly hurt Satta. She now felt remorseful for her insensitivity to the suffering of such an innocent victim. Thirdly, Rosalyn, the woman that she liked more than all the other women was facing certain death. Finally, her boss' life had been shattered by his extra-marital affairs. These thoughts made her finally declare that the adventures of Hon. Lamboi were after all not good for him. The pangs of guilt that were plaguing her led to the decision to urgently seek Sylvia's advice.

"So, how did that day of liberation go for your boss," asked Sylvia, as soon as they got settled in a taxi and headed for Sylvia's home. "I am sure that he was very relieved when Rosalyn finally left the hospital."

"What happened at the hospital was as disastrous as the incident at the dinner," said Veronica. "It looks like the fun days for those of us associated with my boss' carefree lifestyle are over. We are today feeling as guilty as he."

"So, what happened?" asked Sylvia anxiously with a big frown on her face.

"Sylvia, I will tell you the whole story because I need your help."

Sylvia was in shock after hearing the entire story. This reaction was completely unlike her during previous narrations of the adventures of Hon. Lamboi. Today she did not laugh. There was not even the slightest smile. She was not close to Rosalyn but she knew and liked her. The news about her contracting HIV made her feel sad.

"Veronica, you have yourself been through a lot lately," said Sylvia. "What started as fun has turned out to be tragic."

"That is very true," said Veronica. "I feel guilty because although I am faithful to my husband, I enjoyed seeing others engage in marital infidelity. I am a hypocrite who is now paying the price for my past actions. I feel partly responsible for the disaster of those that will die or get sick as a result of their personal involvement with Hon. Lamboi. I do share his guilt. Oh how terrible I feel now!"

Veronica's the tears were just starting to flow when the taxi stopped in front of Sylvia's house. As the latter was about to pay the driver, Veronica suggested that they go at once to her house because she was feeling very uncomfortable. So the journey continued to Veronica's home. As soon as they entered the bedroom, the latter continued to express her feelings about her role in Hon. Lamboi's tragedy.

"Sylvia, I tell you that my boss is finished," she said. "The way he wailed last night was incredible. It was like a child who had lost his parents. I could not believe that such a strong man would cry that way. As for Rosalyn, I expected her to react the way she did. Women are more prone to behave that way."

"Do you think that her child would contract HIV?" asked Sylvia.

"I do not know," replied Veronica. "The doctor does not yet know either. He told us that further testing would have to be done in order to find out the fate of the baby."

"Another big problem that Hon. Lamboi faces is keeping a lid on all this," said Sylvia. "He has to make sure that his wife does not know that he is going to have a child with a girlfriend. Being herself childless, Satta may not survive such a blow."

"That is my biggest concern," said Veronica. "Hitherto, this faithful and devoted wife had proved to be very resilient. She had over the years become immune to all the scandals and unfaithfulness of her spouse and had recovered her strength and spirit after each tragedy. But I doubt that she would handle the news that Rosalyn is bearing Hon. Lamboi's baby. The fact that she would never have a baby with the man she had loved dearly would tear her apart. Sylvia, my biggest concern now is her reaction when she receives this disheartening news."

"Let's hope that she will receive it when she is in the company of responsible people," said Sylvia. "These will give her good advice and help her contain her emotion."

"That's my hope too," said Veronica. "If the revelation is made in the presence of Rev. Matthew Lamboi, he will help control her outbursts. He will work together with Judith to help her. In the past they have been very successful in settling the differences of the couple."

"Veronica, your feelings of guilt will go away with time," said Sylvia. "Do not however dwell too much on the blame you believe you bear for what happened. Concentrate rather on the positive things you can do to help Rosalyn. She will need you now than ever before. Try to work closely with her uncle and aunt."

"I hope to follow this advice but it is not going to be easy," said Veronica. "After observing this man's involvement in at least fifteen extra-marital affairs there is no way I can fail to be guilty. I was the one that sometimes telephoned them, took messages and ate in their homes with him. That was quite an involvement. I enjoyed the company of each of them except one."

"Was that Mary Ann?"

"Who else could it be?"

"What finally became of her?" asked Sylvia. "I have not seen her for a long time."

"She was transferred to Alota in the north," replied Veronica. "Hon. Lamboi went after her for her beauty. She yielded but she refused to share the man with the others. She wanted to eventually get rid of everyone including Rosalyn and have Hon. Lamboi all to herself. Anything less than this was unacceptable."

"That was quite bold," said Sylvia.

"Yes, it was," said Veronica. "When she noticed that I was not in favor of her plans she disliked me. She relieved me of my duties as her messenger. But Hon. Lamboi was in love. They carried on their romantic affair without me until the day when the hot-tempered woman almost physically attacked him. I intervened and separated them before things got out of hand. She cursed the two of us thoroughly before she left."

"I believe that that was the first woman he ever readily gave up on," said Sylvia.

"Yes it was," said Veronica. "She was too ambitious and too aggressive."

"How did he get to know about her?" asked Sylvia.

"It was Sefoi Juana that brought her to his office," replied Veronica.

"By the way what is Sefoi's reaction to his friend's problems?"

"He is also really scared," said Veronica. "He finds it very hard to believe that his friend is being ruined by his excessive involvement with women. Concerned about experiencing a similar fate, he told me that he is going to abandon his promiscuous lifestyle. He was not with us yesterday but there is no doubt that his friend will narrate the incident to him. I do not yet know what he will say about it but I am sure that the news will stun him."

"So far he has been lucky," said Sylvia. "He has escaped all the problems that are plaguing his friend."

"He values his luck seriously," said Veronica. "He does not at this time want to do anything that will land him in trouble. So he too is trying to turn his life around."

"The difference between the two men is that Sefoi knows when to stop doing anything that is not in his best interest," said Sylvia. "He can contain his passions. But your boss cannot. His will is very weak. I wonder if he is aware of this weakness."

"I am not sure about that at all," said Veronica. "He has never tried to change his ways. I wish I had not got involved in his activities. Oh, how guilty I feel!"

"As I said earlier, please do not dwell on your guilt," said Sylvia. "Dwell on the positive things such as spending time with Rosalyn and apologizing to Satta who may be relieved to know that there are still conscientious and decent people around. Make sure that you have a frank talk with Hon. Lamboi about his activities. The goal is to make sure that he changes his ways. Veronica, it is never too late to help desperate people in difficult situations."

"Thank you very much, Sylvia," said Veronica thoughtfully. "I am going to need more advice from you as time goes on."

"You are very welcome," said Sylvia as she got up to leave. "I will be here again tomorrow to see you. Remember that what you have done in the past cannot be undone. But there is something you can do to help minimize the consequences of your conduct. That's the way it is in life. We should try to find ways of containing our problems and seek advice on the best way to rectify them."

Hon. Lamboi left his office for Rosalyn's place about the same time that Veronica went to meet Sylvia. On his arrival he was told that Rosalyn had moved in temporally with her uncle Henry. This was to ensure that she got the constant care and attention she needed. He left at once for Henry Songa's place still worrying about what to expect. He still had in mind the mental image of Rosalyn wailing in the counselor's office at the hospital. He hoped that she would be more composed today.

On his arrival he was disappointed to learn from Henry and Patricia that Rosalyn was still at the WHO clinic. They had dropped her off at two o'clock to see Dr. Cole. Alice Lavalie who worked there as a nurse and an AIDS counselor had called to tell them that she would bring her home after work. Hon. Lamboi was pleased with this attempt to make sure that Rosalyn got the treatment she needed. He thanked Henry and his wife Patricia for their help in comforting her. During their conversation he tried to conceal his worries and remain calm. He wanted to demonstrate to the couple that he was in a better position that day to handle the tragedy.

Henry Songa was the uncle that was closest to Rosalyn. Since her father who lived in the village could not afford to take care of all his four wives and eight children, Henry decided nine years ago to help him by educating Rosalyn. Although the salary of a lower-class civil servant was not adequate, he managed to send Alice to one of the best schools in Bassaya. She graduated and got a job in the civil service. It was when she met Hon. Lamboi that her life turned around. The politician was instrumental in her being transferred to the Ministry of Health and her later getting a scholarship to do a two-year health-related course in Britain. Since then she had lived well and had shown her gratefulness to her uncle by helping to educate his children. She was also the main stay of her poor father in the village. Her tragedy was therefore a family tragedy.

One important decision that Henry and his wife had to make was when to go to Ndoba to break this disheartening news to Rosalyn's father and mother. Since they knew that there was no best time for the task, it was up to them to do so whenever they deemed it appropriate. The irony in their relationship with Hon. Lamboi was that the man who had helped them so much financially was the one who eventually landed them in a disaster they were just beginning to comprehend. In any case, they tried to remain calm and thoughtful in their dealings with him. They also tried to demonstrate to Rosalyn that they were in control of matters. Their concern was that any expression of weakness would make her worry too much.

"So how did things go yesterday after my departure?" asked

Hon. Lamboi with some anxiety in his voice. It is this anxiety that had always betrayed his feelings whenever some problem arose between him and his wife. As soon as she heard the husband speak that way she knew at once that he was uncomfortable talking about the issue. That made her decide whether or not to pursue the matter at that time or later.

"She did much better," replied Henry quietly. "She had tried to heed the advice that she was given by Alice that her mental fitness is very important to her safety and the baby's survival. Since this is her first child she should make sure that nothing happens to it."

"Did she sleep well," asked Hon. Lamboi.

"In fact that is all what she did," replied Henry. "She went to sleep shortly after you left. Worn out and helpless, she slept until eleven this morning. She refused to eat last night and this morning."

"We are hoping that she will eat today," said the wife. "I have prepared something delicious for her."

As they were talking Rosalyn and Alice entered. Hon. Lamboi's eyes were all over Rosalyn. It was as if he was trying to get a clue to her emotional state by merely examining her physical appearance. The only clue came from her eyes. They were slightly puffed up, an indication that she had cried quite a bit.

Both women greeted them and sat down. Henry and his wife were surprised at the calmness of their niece. The anxiety with which she had left the house that afternoon was not apparent. This made them wonder about what had transpired at the clinic.

Henry who was the first to speak asked them about their visit to the clinic. Alice explained the physical examination Rosalyn had undergone and the counseling session that had followed immediately after. She also described the medicines that were prescribed.

"When is she supposed to go again to see Dr. Cole," asked Patricia.

"She is scheduled for Thursday of this week and Tuesday and Friday of next week," replied Alice.

"Alice, my wife and I want to thank you for your help," said Henry. "If you were not around yesterday to help us we would not have been able to handle matters on our own."

"I am happy that I could help," said Alice. "Rosalyn contacted me last week asking for help. She did it in a way that I could not refuse. I am glad that I had agreed because she needs all the help she can get."

"Alice, I also want to thank you for your help," said Hon. Lamboi. "I am grateful for your kindness."

"As I just told Henry and his wife, I am more than happy to help," said Alice. "I have also enjoyed being a close friend of your wife. Over the years Satta had proved to be a very reliable person."

"I want at this time to apologize to Rosalyn for my infecting her with HIV," said Hon. Lamboi quietly. "She is no doubt a victim of our relationship. I consider myself a victim too since somebody infected me. Unfortunately, unlike Satta, I do not know who infected me. My emotional outbursts when I first got my own bad news were a major concern to my wife but today I am adjusted to living with the virus. Dr. Mary Cole, my doctor, is giving me excellent treatment. I am on medication that is expected to prolong my life."

"Is Rosalyn also going to be permanently enrolled at this clinic?" asked Henry. We hear that the doctor is very good."

"Yes, she is going to be your niece's doctor," said Hon. Lamboi. "Rosalyn will get first-class treatment from a first-class

AIDS doctor. She does not have to worry about expenses."

This statement of assurance pleased Henry and his wife who did not have the means of taking care of a sick person. They felt very relieved.

"We are very pleased to hear this," said Patricia. "As you know we have so much responsibility that the cost of this medical treatment would have sent us under financially."

"No matter what I do now will not reverse your niece's condition but as long as she is living I will try to give her my moral support," said Hon. Lamboi. "Such disasters do occur in life and when they do the best people can do is to cope. When the child is born I shall make arrangements to ensure that it gets a comfortable future. I am not sure myself how long I am going to live but I shall see to it that it does not suffer because of financial difficulties."

After they had finished talking, Rosalyn and Alice went into the dining room to eat. Rosalyn who did not have any appetite ate very little. After dinner she went to her bedroom upstairs. Hon. Lamboi followed her instinctively because he was surprised at her unwillingness to talk to him. But when she noticed that he was following, she tried to quickly enter and close the door. Her pursuer, however, forced himself inside. She fell on the bed and wept for a few minutes.

"Darling, I am sorry," he said. "I never meant to hurt you. Please forgive me."

"I will not forgive you," she said. "I want you to leave and never come back here. The mere sight of you torments me seriously."

"Darling, I am sorry," said Hon. Lamboi. "I am also a victim."

"That is the lie you were telling downstairs," said Rosalyn. "Since you did not have to live such a promiscuous life, you are not what one would normally refer to as a victim. Victims get in adverse situations through no fault of theirs. So they do not share the blame for what happens to them. But in your case you went after fifteen or more women for no other reason than sex. I believe that you define life in terms of the amount of sex you get out of it. So without sex your life is meaningless."

"Rosalyn, do not be too hard on me," pleaded Hon. Lamboi. "I have apologized for what I have done to you. I remain convinced that I am a victim."

"Yes, I agree that you are a victim of your passions," said Rosalyn. "You should have told the people downstairs that this is the sense in which you are a victim. You victimized yourself because you cannot control your indulgence in sexual pleasure. Fortunately people do not normally sympathize with a person that keeps on doing the wrong thing. Since a married man like you was not forced to go and have sex with the woman that gave you the virus, you are not a victim in the sense that you got into an adverse situation through no fault of yours. You are a foolish man that deliberately set out to destroy himself. Unfortunately you have destroyed other lives in the process. Misalie, I will not forgive you and I do not want to see you again."

At this point Rosalyn went downstairs and invited Alice to join their passionate discussion. Hon. Lamboi sat quietly thinking about what he had just been told. When Alice entered Rosalyn held her hand for a few minutes before saying anything.

"Alice, I do not accept Misalie's apology because he lived the kind of lifestyle that caused him to contract a disease that is going to kill me," said Rosalyn. "I do not want to see him anymore and so I want him to leave and never come to see me again. If he comes here the very sight of him will cause me the kind of emotional distress that would have bad consequences for my life and that of my baby. This is what I want him to understand."

The three of them were silent. As a counselor Alice knew how to handle the situation but that was not the right place to talk to Hon. Lamboi. So she suggested that they leave Rosalyn alone.

"Rosalyn, I realize how important it is to respect your wish," she said. "At this stage of your grief it is important to allow you to meditate on your problem and learn to handle it. We shall leave you alone now. Please make sure you keep to your appointment. I can hardly wait to see you there."

Hon. Lamboi was very worried and disappointed as they left. When they got into the car, he informed his driver that they were going to drop off Alice on their way home.

"Misalie, do not worry too much about what Rosalyn has just told you," said Alice. "She is still at the most painful stage of her tragedy. This initial stage is characterized by anger and frustration. Since you have been through this stage yourself you can readily identity with her feelings. You have to wait for her to move to the acceptance stage of her grief before you can start having meaningful conversations with her. So it is alright for you to stay away for a while without any feeling of guilt. I will keep on talking to her. As soon as she asks for you, I will inform you. There will be a time when she will do that. So relax a bit and allow her to go successfully through this initial stage."

Hon. Lamboi was quiet for about two minutes before saying anything. His having gone through that stage made it easy for him to accept Alice's suggestion.

"I will stay away from her for a while," he said. "During this period I will make plans for the baby."

"Please do that," said Alice. "Just exercise some patience. One day she will contact you somehow."

When Hon Lamboi reached home he had dinner and sat in the living room to watch television. He did not immediately ask for Satta since he knew that she was in her room. He tried to focus on the evening news. One of the advertisements that came on was about the Golden Complex. He did not feel uncomfortable watching it because the ones in which he was featured had been taken off the air.

CHAPTER TWELVE

While Hon. Lamboi was watching television, Satta was in her bedroom reading his diary. She had come across it by accident while looking for something in the husband's bedroom. Hon. Lamboi had always locked it up in his safe and hidden the keys. But after recording the dramatic incident at the hospital yesterday he forgot to put it away. It had fallen on the floor where the wife found it.

The reading of the diary turned out not to be an interesting affair. There were events such as official trips, business and cabinet meetings that were no cause for alarm. But there were at the same time descriptions of incidents involving the husband's extra-marital affairs which shocked the wife. She had heard that her husband had many girlfriends but that evening she was able to find the exact number.

After reading several of the husband's encounters with his women, she decided that that was enough and looked at the back of the diary where he had made a complete list of all his women, their nicknames, the dates the affairs started and ended, the most memorable events in the relationships and the monies spent on each. Each brief description was followed by a few notes. There was a total of fifteen names on the list.

Satta's examination of this part of the diary, which was actually a concise summary of her husband's affairs, left her with a sad feeling. She was much disturbed to learn that her husband had secretly spent a substantial part of their income on his women. The first woman that caught her attention was Rosalyn whom he nicknamed "Milky Way". The amount of money he had spent on her was so large that Satta felt like dashing downstairs to attack him. In addition, he had rented a beautiful house for her and hired a maid, a houseboy and a watchman to take care of it. The beautiful office he had furnished for her was mentioned. Satta had already heard about this office during the conversation between Veronica and Sylvia. She had always wanted to go to see it but had had no chance to do so.

Most of the women on the list were unknown to her. She felt that she knew Jane Williams, nicknamed "Sparks", and Beatrice, nicknamed "Cool". In the notes written on them, he contrasted their attitudes and said that he preferred "Sparks" because she was very romantic. He spent about the same amount of money on each. The combined total was however much less than the amount spent on "Milky Way".

Almost all of these women seemed to have been nice to him except Mary Ann, nicknamed "Powerball". This was the girlfriend that never got along with Veronica. Hon. Lamboi wrote in the notes that "Powerball" was rude, violent, uncompromising and selfish. Although he spent a lot of money on her the relationship was so turbulent that it did not last. Just before they broke she had the audacity to engage him in a struggle in which she almost hit him. The affair was short-lived.

The affair that most astonished Satta was the one with Susan, her former girlfriend. She could not believe that the name of Susan, nicknamed "Lamb", would appear on such a list. "How could a dear friend at that time engage in an affair with my husband?" she asked herself. Although her friendship with her did not last she still felt betrayed. Susan's affair with Hon. Lamboi ended four years ago.

The most dramatic incident in the diary was a fight that took place between "Powerball" and "Sparks". It was vividly but concisely described in the notes. Powerball, whom Hon. Lamboi referred to as the most aggressive of women, confronted "Sparks" at a night club on learning that both of them were going with the same man. The two actually went into grips in the club causing some property damage. It was Sefoi Juana and his friends who separated them. Powerball was the victor. Satta was surprised to read that Hon. Lamboi was the one who voluntarily paid the cost of repairing the damage to the night club in order to prevent the two women from being sued. From what she had already read about both of them, Satta felt that the fight was inevitable. Sparks was proud and arrogant while Powerball was hot tempered and pugnacious. There was no way the two could have peacefully enjoyed themselves in the same night club without a fight.

The role of Veronica, as described by the husband, came to Satta as no surprise. She already knew that she was his messenger and the main link between Hon. Lamboi and her husband and his girlfriends. Her meeting her at Rosalyn's dinner was the hard evidence that Veronica was at the center of all his extra-marital activities. Although she was not on the list because he did not have an affair with her, he did write something of interest about her at the end of the notes. Satta was actually surprised to learn that Veronica had successfully struggled against Hon. Lamboi's attempts to date her. Because of her resistance he had nicknamed her "The Rock".

"I wanted to have an affair with the 'The Rock' the first day she stepped in my office," he wrote. "Her bright-colored dress, spotted here and there with attractive red and green flowers, made her look so charming that I yearned to have her at once. Although I admired her credentials which paralleled what I was looking for in a secretary, I said nothing about them. Instead I commented on her dress and looks and expressed an immediate interest in going out with her in the near future. But she told me right away that she would never go with any other man besides her handsome husband. I had to assure her that I would never interfere with her before she agreed to work for me. She is quite a tough woman."

Satta admired Veronica's courage but felt that she was wrong to have become a messenger for Hon. Lamboi. It looked like she did more in handling the extra-marital affairs of the minister than in doing her secretarial job.

When she had finished reading the list and the notes she decided to read what had transpired in her husband's life during the last five days. She wanted to know his feelings about developments since Rosalyn's dinner. As she was turning the pages looking for those dates, a telephone call interrupted her. It was one of her business colleagues calling to remind her of a business meeting the following day. When she hung up she decided to join her husband downstairs instead of continuing. Her decision was not to mention anything about the diary to him until she was through with it. She was of course upset but being somebody who knew how to control her emotions, she had no problem peacefully chatting with him.

When they said goodnight to each other around ten o'clock she went upstairs and continued reading. What the husband wrote about the last five days turned out to be the most heartrending information in the diary. It was about Rosalyn's test results. The discovery that Rosalyn was expecting a baby - Hon. Lamboi's baby - made her to roll over in her bed and lay still on her back. Everything in the room seemed to be moving round and round while she lay still and helpless. The idea of Rosalyn bearing Hon. Lamboi's child so much occupied her thinking that she did not even consider the news about her contracting HIV.

"So Rosalyn is the winner after all," she gasped in frustration. "My goodness! The only child Misalie will ever have is going to be with Rosalyn!" Her tears dripped freely as this thought went through her mind.

As Hon. Lamboi slept, his wife lay on her bed agonizing over her discovery. He was so tired and mentally exhausted that day that he fell asleep immediately his head hit the pillow. Fortunately, he did not try to write in the diary that night. Not finding it would have led to a restless search that would have deprived him of his sleep.

After a while Satta who could not sleep at all got up, wiped her eyes and called the colleague who had called her earlier. She pleaded that their business meeting be postponed because she would not be in the office the following day. The colleague agreed and they hung up. Her state of mind was such that she needed to stay home all day to deal with her problems. It was the first time that the possibility of a divorce entered her thinking.

When Satta's quiet sobs had subsided she decided to go and confront her husband about Rosalyn's condition. But then it occurred to her that attacking him at that time was not prudent because Hon. Lamboi would refuse to tell the full story. The information in the diary was incomplete because he had not finished writing it. Since only the main points had been jotted down, there remained many unanswered questions. One of them was about his plans for the financial security of the baby and her mother. Satta debated in her mind about returning the diary in the hope that he would finish writing the details. But this involved taking a great risk. The chances were that after writing them he would not forget to hide the diary in his safe. Remembering the saying that a bird in the hand is worth two in the forest, she decided against returning the diary. The possibility of losing such a treasure seemed too strong.

As she thought over this matter, Alice came to mind. Since the latter was present at the hospital and at all the incidents, she knew the details. It was easier and more convenient getting them from her than from Hon. Lamboi. Armed with such information she would be in a better position to confront her husband.

Getting up slowly as if in pain, she sat quietly for a few minutes before making the call. Although she had carefully assessed the advantage of getting the details from Alice, she had mixed feelings about calling her. She was more than convinced that the latter had betrayed her not only by her involvement in Rosalyn's affairs but also by failing to tell her about the baby she was expecting. So, instead of talking to her straightaway about the details she needed, she decided to first confront her with the issue of betrayal. She wanted to find out why she would do that.

"Hello, is that Alice?" she greeted.

"Yes, Satta, good evening. How are you?" replied Alice.

"Not doing very well at all, and you?"

"Life is normal although I am having some painful experiences on my job," said Alice.

"That's interesting. What new experiences are you having?" asked Satta.

"I am learning more things from my new patients," replied Alice.

"Do I happen to know any of those patients?" asked Satta.

"I definitely think that you don't; but working with them is quite a task."

"So you are absolutely sure that I do not know any of them," said Satta.

"Yes, I am," replied Alice. "Satta, are you curious about who they are?"

"Yes, I am curious. Very curious. As a friend, I want to know your new experiences,"

"It is normal for friends to share each other's painful experiences," said Alice. "But I am worried because you are talking as if you know at least one of my new patients. I, therefore, want to take back what I just told you about your acquaintance with any of them. As a matter of fact you know the patient very well."

"Alice, I am facing the worst crisis of my life," said Satta. "I am on the verge of a divorce. So I want you to tell me the patient's name and what is wrong with her."

"Satta, you can rely on me as a friend," said Alice. "You are going to be told the information you are seeking but I am curious as to how you came upon the idea that I have a new patient whose affairs are of interest to you. It is such a secret that you are not expected to know it at all. I cannot even guess who gave you the information about my new patient."

"Well, this is a small world," said Satta. "Besides, miracles do happen. I definitely know that you have a new patient whose condition should be of interest to me. As a trusted friend you should tell me whether or not I reveal the source of my information."

"I am very sorry, Satta, to have tried to deny the fact that you know this new patient," said Alice. "It was supposed to be a secret and I promised the people involved that I would keep the secret from you. The reason is that they were in such a terrible condition that if I had refused they may have done something very terrible to themselves. Understand, Satta, that we medical professionals sometimes find ourselves in situations where we have to withhold information in order to save patients or their relatives. Sooner or later you would have known the facts. But we felt that knowing them at a later date would be better for all involved. Unfortunately you found out the secret sooner than we expected. So, I am now obliged to give it to you. Please accept my apology."

"I do understand that medical professionals do sometimes find themselves in such situations," said Satta. "That is why I fully accept your apology. It will be in fact unfair to blame you for your attempt to withhold this information from me. I did put you on the spot by unexpectedly asking about the incident."

"Thank you, Satta," said Alice. "The only request I want to make is that you wait until tomorrow. I will come over immediately after work and give you more information than you had expected."

"Thank you, Alice," said Satta. I am willing to wait. Since I want to be fair to you, I will allow you to give me this information on your own time."

"Satta, you have already been through a lot," said Alice. "Let whatever information you now have not lead you to make foolish decisions. Please try to be calm and think of the future rather than the present emotional distress that you are experiencing. You will some day be able to bounce back from this disappointment just as you had bounced back from past ones. Remember that you have been a conqueror. Conquering this last obstacle entails conquering all the others ahead."

"Thanks for your advice, Alice," she said quietly. "I promise to wait patiently until I see you tomorrow."

When they hung up Alice wondered how Satta got to know about what happened to Rosalyn. She ruled out Sefoi because he was not at the hospital and ruled out Veronica because she would not dare call Satta in her home. As for Satta's husband, he was clearly beyond suspicion because he was the one that had made her promise not to divulge the information to his wife. It was due to that promise that she could not tell Satta anything that night.

The following morning Alice went to Hon. Lamboi's office before going to work. Since the latter was a little late, she sat in Veronica's office to wait for him. Veronica herself was not in. She had gone on a quick errand in another office. When the minister arrived they went into his office to deal with the problem that Alice had come to consult him about.

"Misalie, I have reason to believe that your wife knows about Rosalyn's pregnancy and illness," she said as soon as they had greeted each other.

"Are you sure?" he asked with a frown in his face. "I do not want to think so. Last night we talked peacefully about several things but she did not say anything that indicated that she knows about Rosalyn's present predicament. When I was leaving this morning she did not get up to complain about anything."

"She called me last night to tell me that she is sure that I have a new patient whose condition is of interest to her," said Alice. "I believe that she was talking about Rosalyn Songa who is one of the newest patients at the clinic."

"Why did you not ask her for the name of the patient?" asked Hon. Lamboi.

"She was unwilling to give the name but expected me to give information on the identity and illness of the patient," said Alice. "I am concerned about the consequences of lying to her."

"From what you have said, there is reason to believe that someone has told her that we were at the hospital yesterday," said Hon. Lamboi. "I do not, however, think that she knows why we were there. If she knows, then the big question is: who divulged the information to her? The people who are sharing this secret with us know that telling her will lead to an explosive reaction on her part."

Both of them were silent for a minute. It seemed that they

had a mystery in their hands. Hon. Lamboi leant back in his swivel chair rocking back and forth gently. He was thinking hard.

"I do not want to refuse to tell her because if it turns out that she knows the details of what happened yesterday it will put our friendship in jeopardy," said Alice. "The same applies to you. If you go home today and she asks you something about Rosalyn you will be forced to tell the truth. If you don't, you will be in trouble. Both of us have to come to an agreement about telling her the truth. Let's act before she surprises us with the evidence. I should have told her last night but since I had promised you not to do so, I did not."

"Alice, please let us not tell her yet," pleaded Hon. Lamboi. "If you tell her I will not know how to face her today after work. She will be very shaken by the information."

"I promised her last night that I will tell her today" said Alice quietly.

"Such a promise has put you in a very difficult situation," said Hon. Lamboi. "I do not believe that she knows why we were at the hospital. You made that promise without any concrete proof that she actually has the details."

"Yes, I did because I felt that I had no choice but to do so," said Alice. "She wanted the information from me at once. Only my promise made her to agree to wait until today."

"Well, I do not want any one to reveal this information at this time because I am not prepared to handle the consequences of her knowing it," said Hon. Lamboi. "You should not have made any promise. You have to find a way getting out of the difficult situation in which you have put yourself. Oh Alice, I am sorry that I have to tell you this. But today and the days ahead let us reveal nothing. Saying nothing can imply having a peace of mind."

"Refusing to allow me to divulge the information to Satta entails breaking my promise to her," said Alice. "This puts me in a very difficult situation. It is going to be embarrassing for me to call to tell her that I'd rather be quiet about the information I had promised her. Her mood and the tone of her voice last night indicated that she is not going to take this kindly. Our friendship may even be destroyed. Fortunately for me, I can afford to be quiet about this latest development and stay away until she finds out about it herself. I can afford to do so because I am only a friend and I live in my own home. So I do not have to come face to face with her anytime soon. All I will do later is to go and apologize to her for not telling the truth at the time she needed it. Hopefully she will accept a valid excuse from me. But Misalie, this is not so in your case. Since you live with this woman, you cannot afford to be quiet about this development and live peacefully. Telling her something now is more compatible with living with her in peace in the long run. There is an adage that says that silence is golden. But in this case silence is not golden at all. You should have learned this by now. When the problem of AIDS first came to national attention, you and the government suppressed all news about it on the grounds that the information may adversely affect the tourist business. You had in effect instituted a policy of silence that seemed to work for a while. It brought the gold that enriched your tourist industry. But as it turned out, you, the foremost politician in charge of the nation's health care system, contracted the virus. Maintaining silence about your disaster became very difficult. When the information on your tragedy was unexpectedly divulged, the silence which you had treasured turned out to be fool's gold. And here you are again trying to make a similar mistake! You are claiming that keeping silent about Rosalyn's illness and child will give you peace of mind. But like in the case of the secret kept about AIDS, you will soon again learn a similar lesson that there is silence that is not golden. You are better off taking the telephone right now and breaking this silence than waiting any further. Simply tell her the truth about Rosalyn's condition. I agreed last night that you should wait because you need some time to recover from the your emotional distress. But now that your wife has discovered the secret sooner than expected, it will be in your interest to tell her the truth before she confronts you with it. Doing so will make you look credible and will make you come out of this crisis a much stronger man."

"Thank you Alice," said Hon. Lamboi pensively. "I plan to go along with your suggestion. Instead of waiting for a month or more as I had originally planned, I will now wait only for a few days. I will tell her on Saturday. Since I have been through a lot lately, these few days will do me some good. They will give me the rest I need before receiving another blow. Thanks for the advice that she should not know about it before I tell her. I am convinced that she will not find out anything before Saturday. Her suspicions about the condition of your new patient may have some grounds; but she will have no way of verifying her information before my telling her. Fortunately, we who know the facts can be trusted not to reveal them before then. Please be assured that I will defend your credibility at the time I divulge the information to her. I will tell her that I am the one who told you to hold on to the information for a while. That will convince her not to blame you for the delay."

"What if she decides to ask you directly after failing to talk to me about it within a day or two?" asked Alice.

"I know my wife very well," said Hon. Lamboi. "Satta is not the one that can accept or act on hearsay evidence. She prefers to go after hard evidence. That is why she did not ask me about this matter last night. Not wanting to disturb me without good reason, she decided to ask you instead and may ask others also. But since those of us who know the facts have decided to keep the secret until I am comfortable about revealing it, she will never find it out. So she will have no choice but to wait until Saturday."

"Your agreement to divulge it as soon as Saturday is better than telling it at a much later time or not telling it at all," said Alice. "I will find an excuse to wait until then. I am going to tell her that I will have the information for her on Sunday."

"Thank you, Alice, for your understanding," said Hon. Lamboi. "On Monday I wept like a child in front of all of you when Rosalyn's test results were announced. On Tuesday Rosalyn attacked me verbally and refused to accept my apology. That caused me much emotional distress. I am pleading with you to wait because I want to recover a bit from these blows. I may be a bit stronger by Saturday to withstand another one."

Alice left Hon. Lamboi's office with the feeling of being caught between a couple that highly respected her integrity. On the one hand, she wanted the minister to have the peace of mind he had requested while on the other she wanted Satta to have as soon as possible the information she needed to deal effectively with her crisis. Hitherto, she had not experienced any pressure in helping them handle their problems. But she was now paying the price for the promises she had made to both of them. As she entered the taxi to leave she wondered if the arrangement with Hon. Lamboi would work. It would all depend on how his wife would react.

During lunch she called Satta and told her that she would visit her on Sunday instead of that evening. The latter was surprised by the change in her plans but since Alice was calling from the clinic and appeared to be very busy and in a hurry, they had no time to talk much. Satta was, therefore, forced to quietly accept the new day. Alice was aware of the fact that her tactic did not go well with her friend but she nevertheless felt that she was a victor. First, she had successfully convinced a reluctant husband to agree to divulge a very damaging and delicate secret to an angry wife. Second, she had succeeded in postponing the day of her visit to Satta without any overt resistance on her part. She knew that the victory was not perfect since there was reluctance on both sides but taking into consideration the delicacy of the situation, she did not hesitate to give herself credit for doing a good job. There was no way a victory of that kind could been scored without the parties involved experiencing some inconvenience. So, she worked happily for the rest of the day.

After the very brief telephone conversation between Alice and Satta the latter carefully assessed the wisdom of waiting until Sunday. Feeling that the date was too far away, she decided to immediately take her husband to task about the diary without waiting for more information from Alice. What mattered most to her at that point was Rosalyn's pregnancy. It broke her heart because the father of the child was her own husband. It was very disheartening for a woman grieving over her childlessness to hear that her husband was going to have a baby with another woman.

Satta was better composed by the time her husband had returned home from the office. She descended and greeted him as he ate dinner. Having decided to wait for about two hours to see if her husband had any intention to break the news to her, she went and sat in the living room where she expected him to settle and watch television. Around nine o'clock she told her husband goodnight and went upstairs. Surprised and disappointed that he had no intention to divulge to her any information about his baby, she picked up the diary and returned to the living room where he was still relaxing and watching his favorite program. It was a program that she too liked watching but there was no way her mood that night would have allowed her to watch it. In fact the next thing she did was to turn off the television set telling her husband that there were bigger matters to attend to. She then handed him the diary and sat down.

"Oh no! Oh no! Not again! Not so soon!" he exclaimed

Silence ensued. Satta who had at first leaned back in her armchair sat up. Hon Lamboi sat up too. Their eyes met and Satta smiled. Hon. Lamboi did not smile. He moved his head away slightly to break that eye contact. He succeeded momentarily but Satta restored it. Another smile indicated that she was waging a war of nerves. Her husband frowned slightly and stretched himself out in utter frustration. This move completely broke the eye contact in a way that it could not easily be restored. Satta leant back too. She was completely relaxed as she waited patiently for the husband's reaction.

After stretching, Hon Lamboi slumped into his armchair. Then he sat up suddenly and looked intensely at the diary. It was as if he was seeing it for the first time. A red pencil in it caught his attention. On making a move to open the diary, it opened automatically on the page where the pencil lay. Satta had planned it that way. That was the page on which he had recorded information on Rosalyn's illness and pregnancy.

He lay back again in sadness. What Alice had told him in the morning came to mind. He wished that he had divulged the information to his wife before she confronted him with it. He remembered the exact words of Alice: "Let's act before she surprises us with the evidence." He wished he had agreed to this suggestion.

"Oh! My goodness, Satta!" he said aloud in frustration.

"The evidence you have presented me is so overwhelming that the only thing I can say is that I am sorry."

"What are you sorry about?" asked Satta. "Your sorrow won't make this problem to go away."

"I am sorry that another woman is bearing my child," said Hon. Lamboi. "This is a scandal. It hurts you too because you are childless while my former girlfriend is going to have the only child that I will ever have. This is what I am sorry about. Satta, do not think that I do not know how I have hurt you. I understand the pain as much as you do."

The two of them wept quietly for a while. Satta was angry while he was simply feeling the pangs of guilt.

"Misalie, it's been tears after tears," said Satta. "Disaster after disaster and tragedy after tragedy. My God, why me! When will I have a break."

"Satta, I am sorry," said Hon. Lamboi. "Let me really tell you the nature of my mistake in life. It is the kind of mistake that has so many consequences. If it had only one consequence, it would have been rectified long ago and we would have been living a peaceful life today. But it is one big mistake with many consequences. To put matters simply, my mistake consists in my involvement in the past with fifteen women. The price I have paid for it is contracting HIV. But that is not all. There are other serious consequences. I have infected Rosalyn who is bearing my baby. I say this without hesitation because I am certain that I am the only man in her life. This same mistake has made it impossible for me to have a child with the woman I got married to. Finally, who knows how many of those women out there have contracted HIV from me? I wonder when this series of consequences will come to an end. Some time ago I told you that I am through with Rosalyn. Little did I expect that I will soon sit before you to apologize for something else concerning her. Satta, I am afraid to face each new day because I keep on wondering what new unexpected and painful consequences it will bring to my doorstep. My past deeds have made me to be afraid of tomorrow.

"What I admire so much is your strength and courage. I do not know how you are able to persevere for so long. Even I, the person who is the cause of all this suffering, can no longer withstand the pressure. You should have seen me at the hospital when Rosalyn's test results were announced. I fell back in the chair and cried like a child. I had simply gone to tell her goodbye and hire a taxi to take her home. I had no reason to suspect that that day had another tragedy in store for me. But, as it turned out, the calamity it brought buried me alive. The way I cried shocked everyone. It showed how sorry I am. But, as expected, that was only a prelude to more disasters. The following day Rosalyn refused to forgive me and drove me away in anger. She told me never to appear again at her door steps. I was not even given the chance to express my new worry, which is, whether the child will be infected with HIV. Your friend Alice who is a counselor told me to stay away because Rosalyn's state of mind was such that she could not stand the sight of the person that is responsible for her disaster.

"I am glad, Satta, that I did not infect you with the virus. If I did, I would have been in a much more terrible state than I am today. I have two wishes at this time. First, that you agree to forgive me; second, that no more disasters occur in my life. In any case, you can do with me whatever you want to. You are even justified to request a divorce."

"I know that I am justified to do that," said Satta. "As a matter of fact I could have made that request a long time ago based on all the other things you have in that diary. I had known that you have many women although it is through the diary that

I have come to know the details of your activities and the exact amount of money you have spent on them. I am going to file for a divorce. I can't live this kind of life any more."

"Satta, I am sorry to have suggested a divorce to you," said Hon. Lamboi. "Divorce is not really what is on my mind but I feel that having disappointed you so much there is no punishment that better suits my crime than divorcing me. In the case of Rosalyn, a divorce is out of the question because we are not married. But her driving me away is tantamount to a divorce. It is a divorce from my child. That's the worst punishment that can be meted out to a man who has no other children."

"I am driving you out of my life just as she did," said Satta.

"But before we start going into the details of a divorce I would like to make clear the role of Alice in this matter," said Hon. Lamboi. "She had asked my permission this morning to immediately divulge this information to you. We came to an agreement that it should be divulged on Saturday. That is why she called to postpone her visit to Sunday. I wish now that I had agreed with her suggestion that I divulge the information right away. If I did it would not now look as if I was trying to hide this information from you. The reason for postponing the revelation of this affair is that I needed a few days to recover from the previous blows I had received. In any case, Alice bears no blame. If she knows now what has happened she would say: 'You see, I told you so!' I regret for ignoring her advice."

"Tomorrow, I shall make an appointment to see a lawyer," said Satta. "I will file for a divorce before the end of this month."

After this declaration Satta went into the dining room to drink a cup of tea. As she drank there pensively, her husband entered and took a glass and a bottle of gin. He went upstairs with both items. The bottle was only half full but there was enough in it to enable him to get the sleep he needed. After a few minutes he returned to get some ice and a bottle of soda water to mix with the gin. Satta observed what was going on but pretended not to notice. Knowing that her husband did not drink, she wondered what he was doing with the gin. Although she felt that somebody drinking for the first time was better off first experimenting with beer, stout or wine, she did not give any advice. In any case, the gin was likely to knock him out if that was his goal of taking it.

Satta lay in bed as she told Alice what had transpired between her and her husband that evening. Her friend listened attentively until the long explanation ended before giving her reaction.

"Satta, I am sorry that you are going through another disaster," she said. "I had myself advised him to try to divulge the information before you found it out by yourself and surprised him with it. He was unwilling but eventually agreed to tell you this Saturday. His plan would have worked if he had not written anything in that diary. I wonder why he keeps such a document."

"My husband is quite meticulous and likes to keep a record of many things," said Satta. "So I am not surprised that he would keep a diary of this kind."

"Well, he has paid a high price for it," said Alice.

"Yes, he has," said Satta. "I think that he is going to destroy this diary and may never keep another one again."

The two women laughed. Alice was surprised to hear her friend laugh.

"So, what do you plan to do with him?" asked Alice.

"I have told him that I am going to divorce him," replied Satta. "Alice, I am not going to continue with a man that is incapable of giving me a child but capable of giving it to a girlfriend. He should have been careful not to get that woman pregnant. I doubt if I can ever recover from this blow."

"My advice to you is to talk to your mother about this problem before you come to a final decision," said Alice. "In any case, I will see you on Sunday."

The rest of the week was very quiet at the Lambois. They did talk about other matters except the divorce which Satta planned to discuss with her mother on Sunday. Convinced now that there was nothing worth staying for in the marriage, she had decided to move out and start a new life. Keenly aware of his worthlessness to Satta, Hon Lamboi resigned himself to his fate and started looking forward to the inevitable. The couple's relationship had reached its lowest point ever.

Satta and Alice spent the Sunday at Judith's. They were there at about two o'clock. Judith was very surprised to hear this latest story about the diary. She fell back in her folding chair and laughed loud on hearing the nicknames of Hon. Lamboi's women.

"There goes the donkey again," she said, laughing uncontrollably.

Alice and Satta joined the laughter. They were surprised at how excited the mother was on hearing the story.

"Once the divorce takes place the Powerballs, Sparks, Milky Ways and Galaxies will take over the universe," said Judith.

"There was no one with the nickname 'Galaxy', said Satta.

"That does not matter," said Judith. "There would have been nothing wrong in giving that name to the next woman. The next blow to Misalie after your departure is likely to be a big fight among these women. The struggle will be for him and for his money. You should not be around when Galaxy collides with Milky Way or when Powerball collides with Sparks. It will be a grand display of celestial fireworks. The bangs and brilliant lighting effects may even threaten your life. Fighting over the money of a passionate lover is not something to be taken lightly."

This explanation caused much laughter. Satta joined in and laughed for quite a while. But then Judith became very serious. Both young women were surprised to see such a sudden change in countenance.

"My daughter, your consideration of a divorce is very appropriate," she said. "I realize that it is very frustrating for you to stay in a relationship in which you keep on experiencing disappointment after disappointment. The kind of mental anguish you are experiencing has its limits. If a stop is not put to it, a mental breakdown is likely. So for your safety a divorce is appropriate. But you should not suddenly embark on a divorce because going through it is a painful process. My suggestion, therefore, is that you first separate from him informally for a while."

"Mother, I will not accept a separation," said Satta. "A divorce is the only way out of this poignant and incomprehensible situation. A complete break will make me forget altogether Misalie and his ways."

"My daughter, divorce has its advantages," said the mother. "You have just mentioned one of them. But the break you are talking about is a physical break. Since you were emotionally attached to this man, it may turn out that your physical break with him may not be accompanied by an emotional break. Thus you will be bothered by second thoughts and regrets. To avoid this mistake you should first separate from him for a while. If you feel competent during this period to handle a divorce, then go ahead with it."

"I need to think over your suggestion," said Satta. "But I will not stay in that house one more day. I am tired and fed up with Misalie."

"Satta, your mother's suggestion makes sense," said Alice. "She does not want you to make a hasty decision that you may regret later. It is advisable to be a bit cautious in making your plans."

"You can move in with me today," said Judith. "Remember, however, that moving out is a form of separation. You are coming here so that you can think over which course of action to take. That may take you about a week. But if you stay longer than that without actually filing for a divorce then an informal separation is already in effect."

"Tonight I will move in with you," said Satta. "While I am here I will decide on what to do next."

"That's alright with me," said Judith. "When you go home politely inform Misalie about your decision. I will send a message to your uncle Abibu Lansana and your grandmother Musu in Palahun inviting them to come for a discussion of your decision this weekend. As you know, I should not be the only one to advise you on this matter."

When Satta went home to get her things Hon. Lamboi pleaded with her not to move out. He refused to discuss the separation and the divorce. Satta ignored his pleas and sent the first car load of her belongings with the driver to her mother's house. When he noticed that the wife would not change her mind he decided to sit down and have a constructive discussion with her about her decision."

"Satta, what do you really want of me," asked the husband quietly.

"Ultimately, I want a divorce," said the wife. "But in the meantime, I want a separation. Just an informal one. I want us to come to an agreement about the proper way to do it."

"Since I have never separated from a woman before, I do not know how to properly do it," said the husband. "What is your suggestion?"

"To do it correctly, we have to involve our parents in it," said Satta. "You know that since I depend on my extended family for moral support I cannot take any step without informing them."

"Satta, you are comfortable involving your family in this matter but I am not with mine," said Hon. Lamboi. "You know that the Lamboi's are already upset with me for ruining this marriage. Each time we go there for mediation, they learn something about me that shocks them. The reason we are going to them this time will shock them more than ever. That is why I am reluctant to face them about another mediation."

"Misalie, you have no choice but to face your people and mine," said Satta. "There is no way you can separate from your wife without their knowing about it. Tradition dictates that they be informed. If for any reason you fail to do so, you end up isolating yourself."

"I am trying to avoid a separation so that I do not have to face them again with another problem," said Hon. Lamboi. "I want us to stay together and work on our problems."

"Misalie, you should realize that my mental condition is such that it is impossible for me to stay in this house with you," said Satta. "Staying in a place that I perceive as a torture chamber is not in my best interest. Going away will enable me to recover mentally. It is cruelty on your part to expect me to stay under conditions where I am likely to experience a mental breakdown in order to prevent you from facing your parents."

"I am sorry, Satta," said Misalie sadly.

"You are a selfish man that cares only for his own wellbeing," said Satta. "It is fine with me if you do to want to face your parents. I have already invited mine from the village. We shall settle without you. But being people who handle matters in the traditional way, they are going to insist on meeting with your parents. Since Rev. Matthew Lamboi is likely to agree to meet, the separation will be discussed in your absence. So you will be on your own without family backing and moral support. You will be regarded as an individual that does not subscribe to our custom."

Hon. Lamboi was quiet for a whole minute. He knew that isolating himself from his extended family was like going into exile. He knew of only one contemporary of his that did that rather than involve family members in a matter he regarded as personal. When his secret plans to solve his personal tragedy eventually failed making him to decide to go to them for moral support, he found himself facing a group of very angry relatives. It was only after a long and intense negotiation that they agreed to give him their moral support. This was the man that Misalie was thinking about during the minute he was quiet. Although this man was relatively wealthy, he learned the hard way that there are things money could not buy. These thoughts made him decide to yield.

"You can go ahead and make your complaints," he said sadly. "When I am summoned I will turn up."

CHAPTER THIRTEEN

The meeting about the issue of separation was scheduled for Saturday of that week. Expecting his parents to be reluctant about dealing with another complaint concerning him, Hon. Lamboi decided not to approach them directly by himself. On the Thursday before the scheduled date he asked his two brothers to help him convince them to participate in the hearing. But out of concern that his brothers, especially Michael who was the funniest in the family, would laugh at him, he decided not to brief them about the precise nature of the complaint.

Rev. Lamboi and his wife were at home when the three brothers arrived on Thursday evening. The conversation on the way was about the house that Michael had built for them. It was an impressive little house built in the neighborhood where Rev. Lamboi was a pastor for the fifteen years preceding his retirement. After vacating the parsonage in which he had lived while he was a pastor, he moved into a house that was badly in need of repairs. Since his retirement income was not enough to cover the cost of the repairs, he was not happy in it. What he did not know was that his son Michael was building a new house for him. It was small but attractive with modern amenities. After furnishing it he brought his parents and his brothers to show it to them. It was not until they had finished inspecting it that he announced unexpectedly that the house was a gift for his parents. The family who had thought that it was Michael's house was stunned. The father and the mother were so surprised and overjoyed that they did not know what to tell their kind son. After a while they thanked and blessed him and said a special prayer for him in the living room.

Rev. Matthew Lamboi who was lying in a hammock in the back verandah reading his Bible was in such a peaceful mood that Hon. Lamboi shuddered at the thought of bringing up a problem that could spoil that mood. On catching sight of his three children, he placed his Bible on the table that was next to him, sat up and greeted them politely with a broad smile. Their mother came from the kitchen to greet them and went inside to set the table. Although the children visited often, she enjoyed seeing them together. When they were raising them the father who was strict had accused her of trying the spoil them. He felt that she was pampering them. Traits of that treatment could still be seen in her. Not only did they eat well that day she also gave them some fruits and vegetables to take along. They were picked from a garden she still maintained in her village near Tilasa.

The most memorable clash over this idea of pampering the children occurred one year when they were going away to secondary school. The three of them were boarders. On examining their luggage the night before their departure while everybody was asleep, Rev Lamboi found in them more things than the school required. He took out all the extra clothes and shoes that the boys did not need and hid them. The couple had a sharp disagreement over the matter the following morning. Mrs. Lamboi's father who had come to visit them told her daughter that doing that would eventually spoil the boys.

After the three children had eaten, they sat in the back verandah and chatted with their father. When the mother joined them she commented that Hon. Lamboi did not look happy and asked what was bothering him. It was then that he started narrating the latest complaint that Satta was about to lodge against him. To earn some sympathy he left out many details but focussed mainly on Rosalyn's condition. The non-verbal reaction of the quiet and restrained relatives indicated that they were very much affected by the matter being put before them. The father who had been lying in his hammock, sat up suddenly at one time, clapped once and sat down. That was the time when Hon. Lamboi said that he had infected Rosalyn, the woman who was expecting his baby, with the virus. While the brothers gave deep sighs and made gestures that clearly reflected their frustration, the mother shed tears. However, no one talked although everyone was free to do so. The silence was due to the fact that the case was so difficult that Rev. Lamboi was the only one who was deemed qualified to deal with it. But the problem was that the latter was too angry to talk. Whenever he was that upset it took a while for him to properly articulate his thoughts. He would stutter if he talked making his rambling very difficult to follow. To avoid rambling he had to wait till he was better composed.

Hon. Lamboi's discomfort increased when his father refused to say anything about his horrible story. This silence made it clear that the man did not want to deal with another case involving his son's extra-marital affairs. Getting up suddenly and picking up his Bible, he tried to leave. But his wife got up and restrained him politely.

"Matthew, please sit down," she said. "We have to deal with this matter regardless of your feelings about it. If we don't, our son who started ruining himself years ago, will lose his mind. As all of us can see, he has not been able to escape the consequences of his sinful acts. The best we can do for him is to keep on advising him. Some day when it is all over we will not sit around regretting that we never tried to rehabilitate him."

Stephen and Michael then joined their mother in trying to persuade their father to participate in the meeting. The latter eventually agreed to go along with the rest of the family to meet with the Lansanas. But he said nothing other than "yes".

"As you can see, Misalie, your father has agreed to go but has refused to say anything to you about the complaint," said the wife. "In a sense this is good. He does not want to say anything that will embarrass you. You are an adult and you are regarded by the public as a big man. It is not good for him to vent his intense anger on you. There is no doubt that he is angry with you both for your promiscuous lifestyle and your childish behavior. I myself find it difficult to believe that you could keep such a diary. In any case, you will find out on Saturday what he thinks about this latest complaint."

It was on Friday night that Satta's relatives held a similar preliminary meeting in Judith's home. But the atmosphere there was very different. When the relatives who came from Palahun were briefed, a long and constructive conversation ensued. Instead of anger as in the case of Hon. Lamboi, what prevailed was sympathy for Satta who was given their complete moral support during her last visit to Palahun. What made possible such a calm atmosphere was the absence of Beimba, Satta's rash uncle, who had been deliberately left behind in the village. If he were present, he would have readily suggested a divorce as the best course of action to take. That would have led to disagreements. But although Musu and Abibu did not have such a measure in mind, they were resolved to take a firm action against Hon. Lamboi.

In general Beimba was feared because he was a fighter. Not being very patient and tactful he managed problems in a way that made family members either feel like fighting to the last man or making peace with everybody. He left no room for compromise. So when Musu was asked whether Beimba should come along for this case, she had this to say: "We should not take him with us at this time. It is when all peaceful alternatives have failed and conflict is unavoidable that he is best qualified to take over matters. But since the case has not yet reached such a dangerous stage, he should stay. Abibu is the right man to handle delicate matters. Although he also tends to be strict, he is nevertheless a good negotiator and knows how to take the other party to task when it comes to seeking the best interest of the family."

Satta knew well the differences in the way the important members of her family dealt with problems. She noticed the exclusion of Beimba but did not question its wisdom. She was satisfied with the two relatives that came. Abibu was expected to stand up to the Lambois while Musu, who had a calming influence on him, was expected to help him negotiate a reasonable and just settlement.

The meeting with the Lambois took place at the residence of Rev. Lamboi. Before it started, the pastor led them in prayer calling on God to bless the meeting and give them the wisdom needed to come up with a just settlement. When everybody had said "Amen" Satta was asked to make her complaint. Rev. Lamboi who was furious the other day on merely hearing a brief summary of the case, was stunned to hear the full complaint. Satta described in detail not only the deadly virus that Rosalyn had contracted but also how the latter's pregnancy was hurting her. This is the part of the complaint that the husband had focussed on during the preliminary meeting with his relatives. His wish was that Satta would also restrict herself to it. But unfortunately for him she went beyond that point explaining in detail the contents of the husband's dairy. The audience was shocked to hear about the large amount of money he had spent on his fifteen girlfriends. This part of the complaint, although serious enough to made all hearers angry, made Michael to chuckle a bit. What amused him were the nicknames which Hon. Lamboi had given his mistresses. He had said nothing about the diary when he approached them about his problem.

When she finished Rev. Lamboi remained calm. Unlike the day when he heard the summary of the story for the first time, his astonishment and indignation did not make him feel like refusing to participate in the settlement. He was in better control of himself.

"Misalie, is this what happened?" he asked quietly.

"That is exactly what happened," he replied. "Guilty as charged. So I am sorry and I request Satta's forgiveness. I want her to stay with me. If she does, she will help me get over my problems."

Everybody was amazed by Hon. Lamboi's decision not to defend himself in any way. All he was interested in was to have Satta back in the home. He felt that any attempt to defend himself would have led to arguments that would have wiped out the possibility of having his wife back.

"Satta, do you accept his apology?" asked Rev. Lamboi. "He says that he is very sorry. I also believe that he is."

"I believe too that he is," said Satta. "I however request a separation because that is what is good for me at this time. He is sorry but that feeling of his is not enough to make me maintain my sanity. You know the disappointing history of this marriage. This last crisis has affected me seriously. If I continue living with Misalie, I will get mentally sick. I need to stay away from his self-inflicted problems. Let him handle them by himself."

"Abibu, you have heard the case and the appeals of both Satta and Misalie," said Rev. Lamboi. "What is your reaction to what you have heard?"

"I believe that my niece's request for an informal separation should be granted," said Abibu. "Our concern had been that she would ask for a divorce. That would have been a much more difficult issue to deal with. It was in fact an issue that the couple had discussed but Judith had advised her daughter that in the short-run that would not be a good course of action. Those who want to get a divorce need more time to consider the consequences of their decision. To require only an informal separation for such a serious wrong looks like an easy way out of a big problem. Misalie should be happy that this all what his wife is requesting at this time. Things could have got much worse than this. A separation is thus a fair settlement. Musu, what do you think?"

"I also believe that a separation is the best course of action at this time," she said. "If my granddaughter stays in that house she will lose her mind. Misalie should understand this. What is good for him is not necessarily good for everyone. He has to realize that staying there is bad for my granddaughter. I will not allow him to use her in his struggle to recover from his disaster. Another thing we all have to realize is that staying in that house is not good for my niece's pride. Those who know her would wonder why she would live a slavish life. That's the kind of life people with no choice live. No matter what iniquities are inflicted on them they still stay around. My daughter is too intelligent to live under such conditions."

"I believe that Hon. Lamboi should find a way of dealing with the problems he causes," said Abibu, raising the sleeves of his traditional gown in order to be able to gesticulate freely. "A man who engages frequently in conflict should learn to seek solutions. Instead of taking this woman as hostage he should go an seek manly solutions."

"I believe that Satta should go and live with her mother for a while," said the Mrs. Dorothy Lamboi, Rev. Lamboi's wife. "Any woman will need time to recover from such a horrible treatment. I can say that my son is lucky that this woman is still married to him today. The kind of virus he has contracted can ruin a marriage. It can make many spouses to request a divorce. But hitherto Satta had not insisted on such a drastic measure. This makes her a very extraordinary wife to have. Despite all the scandals and marital infidelities she has stayed with him. She is a very strong woman who has helped him through some very difficult times. But in the human realm, unlike the spiritual, there are limits to what can be endured. She cannot endure the suffering that goes with this latest problem. She needs time to go and take care of herself. She is not leaving because of AIDS or the husband's marital infidelity. She had already endured all this. She is leaving because Misalie's problems never end. His life is a series of disasters. She has had her share of them to the limit that the strongest of people could endure. She is not leaving because of weakness. She is leaving because it is time to leave. She has to be applauded for her strength, her faithfulness, her devotion, her kindness and her love."

"I am in agreement with what my wife has said," said Rev. Lamboi. "My son was blessed with a good wife; but he failed to appreciate God's gift to him. He is paying the price today for his misconduct. Let Satta move in with her mother as she has requested. If both of them see it fit to get together again, that will be up to them to decide. But in the meantime, Misalie, it is in the best interest of this woman to move out. The request of her relatives is very fair."

"I want to thank all of you for this wise decision," said Judith. "I think that what has been decided here is in Satta's best interest. It is also in Misalie's best interest although he may not realize it. He is going home very convinced that he will be able to handle Satta if she continues living with him. But that is not just true. The problems associated with his failure in life are too much for Satta to withstand at this time. She needs to stay away until they are resolved. Misalie needs to learn to handle by himself the consequences of his past actions. It will be unfair for him to expect his wife to stay around and suffer unnecessarily along with him."

Satta finished moving in with Judith the following day. Michael offered a truck which was used to transport the remainder of her things. Musu and Abibu spent a week in Bassaya before returning to Palahun. Satta who had always needed people to share her experience enjoyed every minute of their stay. Everyday after work she would sit around and talk with them. Sometimes Alice came to join them. Musu who liked to entertain her granddaughter would tell stories and narrate the history of Palahun. Some of the episodes she narrated were so funny that Alice and Satta could not stop laughing. Sometimes Judith and Abibu would join the laughter. Most of her stories were about the vices of the former chiefs and great people of Palahun. One story that amused her audience very much was the one about one of the founders of the village.

"I was a girl when my grandmother told me about this great man," said Musu. "He was in those days reputed as the wealthy and revered chief who ended up becoming the poorest leader that ever lived. It was his love for women that made him live that life of degradation.

"One day this chief traveled to another village and saw there a girl that was said to be the most beautiful in the entire region. His immediate decision was to marry her. 'Give your daughter to the richest man in this region,' he urged the girl's parents. 'I promise that she will live in luxury.' The problem with his plan was that the girl was already engaged to be married to a man who lived in that village. But feeling that he would die if he did not marry the girl the great chief decided not to give up. In order to win her over, he offered all his wealth to her parents as bride-price. He gave them permission to go to his home and take possession of all his belongings. He was so much in love that he did not have second thoughts about the deal.

"The girl's father who loved money convinced his daughter that they should accept the offer. When the latter agreed they set out with ten men the following day and brought back with them all the chief's cows, sheep and goats and all the rice from his barns. They also brought back all his personal belongings leaving his house completely empty. After the marriage ceremony had ended, the chief set out for his village with his beautiful bride. On his way those who set eyes on her expressed their admiration of her beauty. He was so much in love that he did not care to mention that all his wealth had been moved to the home of the bride's parents before he was allowed to take her home. As more information about the girl's beauty spread, more people came to the main road to catch sight of her. The chief's face was glowing with pride by the time he reached his village where he was given a big welcome in the village barrie. But when he went into his house that evening, he found it completely empty. Since there was not even a bed on which to spend the night, he realized that he was now the poorest man in the village. The girl ran away saying that she would not spend her life with a poor man. 'You promised my parents that I would live in luxury,' she told him. 'Your failure to keep your promise annuls the marriage.' Little had he realized that he could not give away all his wealth and live in luxury at the same time. Unlike the in-laws, he did not foresee the contradiction in his promise. The chief was ruined by his vice."

This story amused the audience a lot. But it was the

following evening that Musu narrated a funnier one. Musu felt that this form of entertainment was good for her granddaughter. It helped take Satta's mind off her many problems. The second story was about the former Paramount Chief of one of the neighboring chiefdoms.

"This was one of the most revered chiefs that ever ruled that chiefdom," she said. "He was however one of the most feared. It was because of people's fear of him that all his sub-chiefs obeyed and frequently gave him presents. Their loyalty to him was absolute. But the chief's problem was that since everybody was afraid of him, he could not tell who his enemies were among them. The diviner told him that unless he knew his enemies, they would one day unexpectedly get rid of him. After spending a whole month thinking about this alarming information he came up with a plan.

"One day he lay in his bed pretending to be dead. Telling his wives to look sad as if they had lost a husband, he sent his eldest son to go and inform the sub-chiefs about his death. When they arrived they rejoiced making comments that they were relieved since their tyrant was dead. The foremost of the chiefs sent for a priest, an Irishman, because the chief was a Catholic. The latter was preparing for the mass when the chief stood up suddenly. Without doubt the dead had come alive among rejoicing sub-chiefs.

" 'My goodness! What is this celebration for?' he exclaimed. 'Each of you will pay a fine of one hundred British pounds.' Since those were colonial days, transactions could be readily done in that currency. 'You will pay this sum for rejoicing over my death. I had felt all along that I was revered but now I know that I am hated. Where is my clerk?'

"When the clerk stepped forward, he told him to make an official list of those paying the fine.

" 'You and the junior Clerk will be numbers one and two on the list,' he said. 'Put down your name first and that of the junior clerk and write the amount against both names. I heard both of you rejoicing. Then starting with the Senior Speaker write down the names of all the chiefs and ordinary people in this living room.'

" 'What about the Catholic priest?' asked the senior Clerk. 'He came to administer the final sacrament.'

" 'Write down his name and write one hundred pounds against it. I do not like the way he rushed here to have me buried. If I did not get up suddenly he would have said the *requiem* mass. You know that since I have more than one wife the Church has never liked me very much. He will pay one hundred pounds because I am convinced that he wishes me dead. The *Requiem* is for the repose of the souls of the dead. Today I will be a wealthy man. You have to know that I should be revered and feared even in death.' "

This story provoked lots of laughter. Those were some to the best times Satta had enjoyed in a long time. Judith was very pleased to see her daughter having a good time. She wished the relatives could stay around for a month. But since they had to attend their farms they could not stay for more than a week.

On Friday Satta drove Musu and Abibu back to Palahun. Judith went along with them. The carefree Satta traveled joyously with relatives that could give her all the comfort she needed to start her new life. The trip was very refreshing for her because it enabled her to get away from the city where she had had to endure the consequences of problems she had not caused.

When they got off the main road to enter the village Satta saw some things that reminded her again of the simplicity of village life. They drove past farmers returning from their farms. Some carried firewood on their heads. Others carried food and other items that they could sell in Tilasa when they had time. Just before they reached the first house Satta saw her cousin. The cousin stopped for a minute to greet her. She told her that the firewood on her boy's head was for her. The village story teller paused as he passed by. He promised to visit her later that evening to narrate some stories.

These incidents made her nostalgic. Although she now had to live in the city due to her education and job, she felt that life among the common folks was pleasant. It lacked all the corrupting influences of the western world. She felt that it was those influences that had contributed to the husband's bad treatment of her. What he did not know was that his girlfriends were after his money. They wanted to have the best that could be found in the big, modern shops - cosmetics, expensive clothes, jewelry - and also live a lifestyle of glamour and pleasure. But in the village there were many things the simple folks could enjoy for free. The story teller who had promised to provide entertainment for the evening charged no fees. He accepted whatever was given to him as a present. In his stories he extolled the virtues of his people and condemned the vices that corrupted society and the relationships between individuals. His stories contributed to societal stability.

Satta's mind was preoccupied with thoughts about the simple ways of life and the kind of happiness that they gave to the villagers when Pala came into view. Its size gave a feeling of awe. They passed by it and headed for their home. The sight of her car approaching their compound brought outside both adults and children. They were given a warm welcome. This made Satta feel that she was really at home.

The absence of Abibu and Musu for a week seemed to have left the compound without a leader. Although there were other elders residing there these two were the most important members. Abibu was the strong man that made things to work. So everyone came to him for advice. Musu also had the kind of caring attitude that made her win the admiration of the family. So when she too was away those who needed to be comforted missed her a lot. Beimba was around but nobody went to him for advice. His solutions were not welcome by most relatives. The absence of both Musu and Abibu created a vacuum in the compound.

After the new arrivals had eaten they sat down to relax on the verandah. Still many more visitors came from other houses and compounds to greet them. These were people who liked the Lansanas and missed the kindness and generosity of Abibu and Satta.

The only trouble that befell the compound while they were gone was the accident that Abibu's youngest son had. He had fallen from the tall pawpaw tree in the yard behind Musu's house. This accident happened on Monday. Beimba took him to the Government Hospital in Tilasa where he was admitted for two days. He did not incur any severe injury and was expected to fully recover in a week. The boy did not complain of much pain when his father questioned him that evening about his health. After Beimba had explained how he had helped save the boy's life, Abibu's senior wife made a complaint about him.

"When Beimba returned from the hospital, the first thing he did was to cut down that pawpaw tree," she said. "I appreciate his help but not his cutting down Musu's fruit tree. He was adamant and hasty about felling it."

"You mean that he cut down my tree?" asked Musu, getting up to go to see the fallen tree. She was followed by Abibu and Satta. Indeed the tree was lying across the yard with an axe lying by it. Beimba had started cutting the trunk in several pieces when it got dark. That had forced him to postpone the remainder of the task until the following day.

"Beimba, why did you cut down my tree?" asked Musu calmly when they had returned to the verandah.

"After my return to Tilasa, some children were still interested in climbing it," he replied. "The ripe fruits were so tempting that it would have been impossible for the adults to prevent them from climbing it. Since I did not have the time to keep on watching the tree, I solved the problem by cutting it down. Moreover, the tree was so tall that it would have eventually fallen on your kitchen."

"Beimba, you should have waited to ask Musu's permission before cutting that tree down," said Abibu.

"My goodness! I did not expect to get blamed for this," he said. "I thought that both of you would thank and praise me for taking the boy to the hospital and safely cutting down a tree that would have fallen on your kitchen thereby destroying your zinc roof. Satta, what do you make of this blame?"

Satta who had always felt that that pawpaw tree should be cut laughed. Beimba joined in. He laughed loud to his satisfaction.

"Grandmother, I have always had some concern about that tree," said Satta. "I felt that one of those ripe fruits would fall on somebody's head. . . ."

"That would have been instant death," interrupted Beimba, laughing loud again.

"Well, not really death," said Satta. "It would have incurred a serious injury.

"In any case I had no choice but to cut it down," said Beimba. "There is no middle ground when it comes to matters of life and death."

Satta's view made Musu to drop the matter. Since she very much valued her granddaughter's opinion on many matters, she too agreed that felling the tree was appropriate. So she changed the topic pretending to drop the matter of blaming Beimba.

"Beimba, has any animal fallen into your trap lately?" asked Musu. "It is quite some time since you last brought me some meat. I guess you have sold the catch in Tilasa without my knowledge."

"Oh no! I will not do that at all," said Beimba, trying to stop laughing. "If I catch something I will let you know."

"I know that you will," said Musu .

The matter ended there. Abibu's senior wife never got along with Beimba. She felt that the latter was too aggressive. She had expected to get Beimba into trouble with Musu but apparently her plan did not work.

Later that evening the story-teller who had earlier greeted Satta came to visit. When his presence in the compound was announced all the children came to the verandah expecting a story. Adults came too knowing that he had come to entertain Satta and Judith. Satta was delighted to see him. Although she knew this man very well and had listened to his stories when she was a child, she had never really taken time to assess his role in society. It was her disappointment with city life and her renewed interest in the simplicity and honesty of villagers that made her start perceiving him in a different light. She now felt that story tellers and oral historians should be accorded high praise because it is they who extolled those proven codes of behavior which over time had led to the stability of traditional societies. The lessons that children learned from their stories reflected the beliefs of the people.

Satta was not really interested in listening to a story that evening. She wanted the oral historian to tell her why the two other villages that were founded after Palahun did not prosper.

"Historically, Palahun occupied a unique place among the

earliest villages founded in this region," he said. "What makes her unique is Pala which stands at its center. The ground on which Pala stands is sacred because that is the spot on which our founding fathers were buried. From time immemorial people have come here to worship the ancestors through whom one could properly get access to the one Supreme God. As Palahun grew some residents moved out founding two other villages that prospered for a few years.

"At the beginning the two villages lived in peace with each other and with Palahun. But this peaceful coexistence ended when a diviner who claimed to have supernatural powers told the elders of the two villages that the reason why they were not as prosperous as Palahun was because it had the most sacred places. He insisted that their newly established holy places were inferior to hers. Believing that taking over Palahun's oracle would not only enable them to win the favor of the founding fathers, it would also enable them to prosper greatly.

"That same year the leaders of the two villages went in anger to Palahun and requested that some of the holiest shrines be moved to their villages. The diviners of Palahun told them that it was impossible to do that because it would desecrate the holy places and make the ancestors angry. A quarrel erupted and the visitors vowed that they would move some of the holy shrines by force. The diviner from Palahun then told them to go and reconsider their mission. On their return to their respective villages they prepared the spots where the shrines would be placed and got ready for a celebration. But the following day all these leaders drowned in a canoe accident on their way back to Palahun to get the shrines. On the day they died the cotton tree shed all its leaves. It was said that that was the way Pala purified itself after getting rid of the enemies of Palahun."

This explanation was followed by a song in praise of Pala

to which the story-teller referred as the protector of the village. After each verse the audience joined the chorus. It was really a familiar song but hitherto not many knew the history behind it. Knowing that history gave them a feeling of pride as they sang joyfully, clapping hands and swaying their bodies. Satta retired that night tired but obviously very relaxed. Not once did she think about Hon. Lamboi and his many problems.

On Saturday the family members held a meeting about Satta's case. Abibu Lansana, the head of the extended family, gave a full report about how they had handled her complaint and the decision at which they had arrived. Everyone including Beimba thought that the decision was a good one. The only thing that Beimba did not like was that the decision fell short of the demand for a divorce.

"I wish to thank Abibu and Musu for the good work they did in settling a difficult and complicated matter," said Abibu. "They went with the wisdom of the founding fathers and came with a settlement that has made our niece happy. She looks and feels better than the last time she was here. The only problem I have with the settlement is that it fell short of a divorce. Merely separating a couple whose marriage is plagued by scandal and anguish does not seem to be the best solution. All we are doing is prolonging the pain and suffering of our niece. Since a marriage in which a couple cannot share the same bed is worthless, our niece's anguish is likely to continue for a long time to come. When will she ever have children?"

"Beimba, divorce is one logical solution to the problems of our niece," said Abibu. "But we did not consider it at this time because separation is what Satta requested. According to her, it is what is good for her at this time. Expecting her to be too fragile to take a more drastic measure, we granted her wish by arranging a separation. The settlement fell short of a divorce, but divorce was never ruled out altogether; it remains a possibility."

"Beimba, you know that as a modern educated woman living in the city, Satta has a choice to deal with her marital problems the way she thinks fit," said Musu. "But she has decided to handle them traditionally by seeking the help of the extended family. That is why she came here some months ago to consult with us. She is here again to see us because she still believes in our wisdom and in our ability to deal with this latest crisis of her life. To encourage her to maintain communication with us we have to consider her wishes and her happiness. We do this not by forcing solutions on her but by finding out those wishes and advising her in light of them. That is why we did not move to the next step which is a divorce."

"Realize also, Beimba, that there are women who want to stay within our tradition no matter how pleasant city life is," said Ngele, Musu's brother. "Satta is one of them. That is why I like her very much. There are, however, women who handle matters the way they see fit. This is what happened to my friend's daughter who works in Bassaya. She got married without the consent of her extended family in the village. She did eventually present the husband to her extended family but that was long after the wedding. A year and a half later they divorced because the man started seeing another woman. The second time she went to visit her village she went with another man. The extended family was shocked to hear that that was her new husband."

"Are you talking about Tondo's daughter?" asked Bunduka, Abibu's eldest son.

"Yes, that's the lady," replied Ngele. "All of you know Tondo of Kemala. The latest I have heard is that she is having problems with the new husband."

"The problems with the second husband is not the latest

development at all," said Bunduka. "A friend of mine told me that she got married to a soldier after her second marriage. The latter, like in the previous two cases, was attracted to her beauty. But the relationship soon started to fall apart because she tried to dominate the man. Unlike the previous men who merely got rid of her, this soldier struck her on the mouth knocking out most of the front teeth."

"Tondo's daughter regards herself as a liberated, modern woman," said Jami, Satta's aunt. "She refused to consult with the extended family on the grounds that they are not educated. She fought all the battles with her former husbands by herself and lost them all."

"Yes, liberated but with no front teeth," interrupted Bunduka. Although he did not mean to be funny, this statement did provoke much laughter.

"I knew about the problems of Tondo's daughter but I did not know that they were that serious," said Beimba, still laughing. "Since handsome men love smiling front teeth, she is in big trouble. None of them will ever express interest in her."

"Unlike this woman, Satta does not regard her willingness to consult with us as a weakness," said Jami. "She is merely exercising prudence. That is why I suggest that we always consider her wishes when she comes to see us. I salute Abibu and Musu for not trying to force solutions on her. They did an excellent job."

"Well, let's see what a separation can lead to," said Beimba. "It is not a bad idea to wait and see."

The meeting broke on a good note. Satta thanked everyone present for their support and told them of her intention to keep on consulting them on matters that are important to her life. She returned to Bassaya with her mother the following day. On the way she thought a lot about the new life she was going to live.

CHAPTER FOURTEEN

While Satta was having a good time in Palahun, Hon Lamboi was lamenting their separation. Before leaving his office on Friday he telephoned her at Judith's place but was told that both mother and daughter had already left for their village. It was after he had hung up that it occurred to him that he was not supposed to have made that call. His action was in violation of the agreement they had reached exactly a week ago. But since he neither gave his name nor left a message with the girl that had answered the telephone, he hoped that no one would ever know that he had called. Giving a sigh of frustration, he walked slowly out of his office.

Although the driver took the usual direction to his ministerial residence, the minister was so preoccupied with Satta that he hardly noticed any of the familiar landmarks of the city. When the car stopped in front of the residence he put his hand into the pocket and took out some money for fuel. He thought that that was why the driver had stopped. On noticing that they had arrived home, he returned the money and waited patiently for the driver to open the car door for him.

The first thing that caught his attention on entering his bedroom was Satta's picture that was hanging above the dresser. He took a moment to examine it before turning away. "That is the woman that had loved me dearly," he said to himself. "What did I do to deserve such love? Why did she love a man that ended up making life miserable for her? Unfortunately I cannot recapture her heart again because there is nothing that a man threatened with a deadly disease can do for such a woman. I wish I had done for her the things that would make her value me today regardless of my medical condition. I am a worthless man."

Hon. Lamboi then walked around the house aimlessly for about five minutes before settling at the window that overlooked the town. Just below him the shrub-covered land dropped gradually for about two hundred yards before flattening out for about two miles. The landscape was dotted by beautiful well-maintained residential homes built during the colonial days for British administrators. They were now all occupied by Members of Parliament and top civil servants. Beyond this expanse of beautiful scenery was the city of Bassaya. On a clear evening like this the roofs of thousands of houses could be seen from that particular spot.

Hon. Lamboi wished that Satta were standing next to him at that moment. After remaining motionless for five minutes he imagined himself and Satta sitting in the well-maintained garden below enjoying the scenery provided by the variety of flowers she had planted about four months ago. In previous years Satta had taken time to sit in that garden to read in silence. It was during those times that he was busy visiting his girl friends and having a good time with them. He now wished that he had gone to sit by the woman who had made such a sacrifice on his behalf. He wished he could enjoy those quiet moments with her. "I wonder whether I can ever recapture those lost opportunities," he said to himself. On turning around to leave his eyes caught another picture of Satta. The tears flowed freely. He went to bed without having dinner.

Hon. Lamboi had a vivid dream about his beloved wife that

night. In his dream he saw himself sitting by her. They were at a cinema in Tilasa watching a movie they both liked. But this scene did not last at all. It gave way to a more memorable one. They were at the church in which they had exchanged their wedding vows some years ago. It seemed that they were going through the wedding ceremony again. As the skilled fingers of the professional organist struck the keys of the keyboard producing the most melodious and solemn of sounds he walked side by side with Satta toward the altar. He was moved by the sacred vows they took that day. But as soon as the words "I do" were pronounced by him, the huge chandelier in the center of the church dropped with such a crashing sound that Hon. Lamboi woke up. He wondered why he had such a terrible dream. Feeling remorseful for his past conduct, he lay there until he fell asleep again. But the second dream shook him as much as the first. He and Satta were cutting the wedding cake when a big pig entered the hall. It looked hungry. Taking a big mouthful of it, it dashed outside followed by many indignant people who felt that it should be punished for its mischief. When Hon. Lamboi woke up he decided not to go to sleep again. He was afraid that he may have another nightmare. As he lay on his back for over an hour trying not to close his eyes, he wondered whether a strange force was invading his body. At first he felt that the spirit of Satta was the one pursuing him. But since he could not figure out what that meant he came up with a more meaningful guess. He concluded that it was his imagination that was haunting him.

On Saturday evening his two brothers, Michael and Stephen, visited him. Both were at their parents' on Friday night where they prayed for him. The mother wept during the discussion about Hon. Lamboi's health. Similar prayer sessions were held every Friday evening thereafter. Their concern was about his developing AIDS. The father had never invited him to the sessions because they did not want him to start worrying about his future. Since he had remained relatively healthy so far, they wanted to portray an outward appearance that they had confidence in his health and in the treatment he was receiving from the clinic. They all decided to invite him to join them only when they felt it necessary to do so.

Hon. Lamboi was very pleased to see his two brothers. Their visit was a break in the loneliness he had lately been experiencing. As they moved to the backyard he asked the houseboy to serve them drinks.

"Have you heard anything from Satta yet?" asked Stephen.

"No, I have not," he replied. "Stephen, I do not expect Satta to call me anytime soon. I do think about her all the time but I doubt that she can take time to think about me."

"Thoughts about you may come to her mind although she may not consider seeing you for a while," said Stephen. "You should stay away from her for some time. That will allow her to rest her mind."

"I believe that she has all the time in the world for a good rest," said Hon. Lamboi. "I miss her so much. But the dreams that I had about her last night were not pleasant. They were terrible."

"Misalie, bad dreams should not bother you at this time," said Michael. "They do not mean anything."

"Misalie, you know that Michael does not believe in dreams," said Stephen. "That is why he is asking you to ignore your unpleasant dreams. But dreams can be correctly interpreted by those who are qualified to do so."

Hon. Lamboi who was anxious to narrate his dreams did so without getting involved in his brothers' debates over the importance of dreams. When he finished Stephen interpreted them.

"As you know, I have been interested in dreams since our childhood days," he said. "They say a lot about our lives. If we had not been raised in Christian homes we would have from time to time engaged the services of diviners to interpret our dreams. But notwithstanding my religious convictions, I still do interpret dreams, especially mine. Misalie's dreams are simple. An expert like a diviner is not needed to interpret them. The crash of the chandelier and the pig eating the cake simply symbolize Satta's unrequited love. These dreams are about his past. It is the dreams dealing with our future that are difficult to interpret. The reason is that we do not know our future. In our traditional societies people go to consult diviners for the interpretation of such dreams. But Misalie's dream points to the way he had lived his life."

"I accept that interpretation," said Michael. "But I do not think that the dream was caused by any outside agent such as a spirit, a devil or a witch. It was caused by Misalie himself. He got such a dream because he could not keep his mind off Satta and the wrong he had done her. These thoughts and his imagination of all the good and bad times had caused this dream. In fact all dreams are caused by the dreamer himself."

"The diviners will disagree with you," said Stephen. "They believe that dreams are caused by agents such as witches and mermaids. Witches normally threaten the dreamer, his property or a member of his family while mermaids make promises to the dreamer. It is said that one of the wealthy farmers in our village got his wealth from a mermaid."

"I have heard such stories before," said Michael. "But since I do not believe in divination, I would not consult diviners. The problem with them is that either they make conflicting predictions when you consult more than one of them about the same problem or they make incredible ones. I do not know,

Misalie, if you heard about the diviners that were consulted by Judith relative to whether Satta would have children."

"I am not aware of this," said Hon. Lamboi. "When was this done?"

"It was shortly after you were told that you had contracted HIV," said Michael. "During their first visit to Palahun a diviner there told them that Satta will raise a child in the near future. Since you cannot share the same bed with her, Judith and Satta found that interesting. When they returned to Bassaya they were introduced to another famous diviner by Saidu, Alice's father. The latter made the suggestion and I persuaded everyone to invite the diviner over. This second diviner told Satta the same thing. Both did not say that Satta would conceive; they only claimed that she would raise a child. Both predictions are incredible because Satta told us that she was determined to remain faithful to you till the very end. They are confusing because the condition of your health is such that she is not going to have a child with you. This reasoning made me to declare that we were dealing with two predictions that were identical but false. In a desperate attempt to make me believe, they invited over a third diviner. This man told them that no child is coming into Satta's life in the next twelve months. His prediction was disappointing but it was consistent with the facts of the matter at hand."

"If Satta remains faithful to me in the near future, there is no way the first two predictions can turn out to be true," said Hon. Lamboi. "The reputation of these two diviners is at stake. Did you tell them that Satta's husband has contracted the kind of virus that makes him to avoid having normal sexual relationship with his wife?"

"No, they were not told," replied Michael. "Since they have supernatural powers they are supposed to know all that. So,

Stephen, what do you think about this?"

"I am not going to pass judgment on these diviners at this time," said Stephen. "The time limit they have given is a year. So it is better to wait. I would have passed judgment if they did not have any time limit. But a year is not a long time."

"I am anxiously waiting for the expiration of the deadline date," said Michael. "These two diviners have a lot at stake. Their predictions will make or break their careers."

The conversation eventually shifted to Hon. Lamboi's health. He told them that he was feeling fine although the side effects of the medicine he was taking were at times painful. He however expressed lots of regret for the way he had lived. He was convinced that had he lived otherwise he would not have contracted the virus.

The following day, Veronica and Sefoi visited him. He was very pleased to receive them. This was another welcome visit for Hon. Lamboi because his interaction with friends and relatives did minimize his loneliness.

"So, Misalie, how are you doing?" greeted Sefoi as he advanced to hug his friend. Veronica also hugged him before taking a seat.

"Well, I am feeling alright," he replied. "The only thing is that Satta and I are now separated from each other."

"No kidding!" said Sefoi, altogether surprised. "But why did you not call to tell us?"

"Since I knew that you were coming here today, I decided to wait," replied Hon. Lamboi. "This was not the kind of issue I would have felt comfortable discussing over the telephone."

Hon. Lamboi then went on to describe the family meeting that was held and the reasons given for the separation.

"I am sad about the separation," he said in conclusion. "I get terrible dreams about Satta and I wish she would come back."

"I do not expect her to return soon," said Veronica. "It looks like she regards separation as a way of recovering. You have to come up with a way of coping without her. You do that by looking at the positive aspects of the measure she has decided to take. Misalie, if that woman stays here you will have a lot of problems. She cannot cope with life while you are around her. The information about the diaries and Rosalyn's child is too much for her to bear. So she needs to be away for a while."

"Misalie, I am in agreement with Veronica's view," said Sefoi. "Since she is not the cause of your problems, she will regard it as unfair to be bombarded by their unpleasant consequences. You may at present find it difficult to appreciate the advice we are giving to you; but in the long run you will find out that it is a good piece of advice. If she stays with you a divorce will eventually be the only logical consequence. That will be more painful than a separation. The advantage of a separation is that it gives both of you enough time to recover from your devastating experiences."

"This is what I was told at the meeting," said Hon. Lamboi. "But, as you know, staying away from all women is very difficult for a former womanizer. However, as you predict, I will get used to this life. My advice to you, Sefoi, is not to put yourself into the kind of situation in which I find myself today. This is a terrible life."

"I have terminated all my womanizing activities," said Sefoi. "In fact I finally decided to take the AIDS test. The three days I waited to receive the result were the most difficult in my life. I almost collapsed when Dr. Cole came into the room with the result. Fortunately it was negative. I have changed my ways completely. I would be the most stupid man in the world if I continue an activity that would eventually ruin me."

"In my case, I was warned but I refused to listen," said Hon. Lamboi. "Sefoi, you have always been a good listener. That is what has helped you."

"I am praying that you do not develop AIDS," said Veronica. "I also pray for Rosalyn all the time. So far she is not in any pain. The doctor says that her pregnancy is normal."

"Has she expressed any willingness to see me?" asked Hon. Lamboi.

"No, she has not," said Veronica. "In fact no one dares mention your name to her. Like Satta, she wants you to stay away. I believe that your doing that will be good for her mental health. It will be also good for yours. You do not want to get close to somebody whose reaction is going to make you feel bad. As things stand, you, Satta and Rosalyn should stay away from each other for quite some time."

"Veronica, what I want you to do for me is to keep on checking on Rosalyn. I want to know how the pregnancy is progressing. It is my hope that the baby will be alright. As you know, this is the only child I will ever have. So, I am very concerned about it. I am curious to set eyes on it."

After the two guests had left, Hon Lamboi returned to the living room to watch television. One of his favorite shows was on; but he could not sit up for long. Having spent the last three nights thinking and dreaming about his problems, he was exhausted to the point that he could not keep his eyes open. He turned off the set and went upstairs to his bedroom. Unlike the previous nights he did not have to wish that sleep would engulf him. Since both his mind and body were very ready to relax, it overtook his entire being as soon as he got into bed. It was a dreamless night.

The separation turned out to be a healing period for Satta. As the weeks and the months passed she abandoned her preoccupation with her failed marriage. The warm company of friends and relatives in Bassaya made her to recover from her mental anguish. Her monthly visits to Palahun enabled her to continue enjoying the simple ways of life that she had begun to genuinely appreciate. Although Hon. Lamboi was never completely forgotten, it came to a point when the mention of his name no longer triggered painful memories of a ruined relationship. She developed a positive outlook on life and nourished it to the extent that she could live on her own indefinitely. But since this recovery period was never used to make plans for a new relationship with men, she neither considered a divorce nor tried to get involved with another man. She told Judith and Alice that patience was the virtue that she admired most.

"When you are patient your mistakes are delayed," she said six months after the separation. "Patient people wait on difficult problems to start resolving themselves. The knots that complicate relationships are relaxed and untied as time goes on. When that happens the patient one moves in and takes advantage of the ease involved in resolving the entire problem. The impatient person, on the other hand, keeps on rushing at complicated problems like a senseless boxer in a fighting ring. He tries to deal with each problem without studying it well and assessing the consequences of a hasty resolution."

"Satta, I am glad that you are patient," said the mother. "It is not advisable to embark on any new relationship any time soon. If it fails while the old one is still unresolved, it will hurt you more than ever. My only question is how long your patience will last."

"Since I am young, I can afford to let it continue for a little longer," she replied. "After such wait I can decide on what is best for me."

Unlike Satta, Hon Lamboi was having a hard time adjusting to his new life. Veronica and Sefoi had advised him to exercise patience but he apparently could not. So his yearning to remain in contact with Satta did not subside even after six months. One day during work he went to see Satta unannounced but she was unwilling to see him. He was politely told to leave. He did so reluctantly. This ill-advised activity was repeated after two months. This time Satta was not too reluctant to see him but told him that he had to keep away so as not to disrupt her recovery. He went home in a sad mood. Three weeks after that he decided to visit Rosalyn hoping that she would be more receptive than Satta. He hoped that setting eyes on her would enable him to know how she was faring during her pregnancy. For him, physical appearance could be a good indicator of how well people performed healthwise. But he found out that Rosalyn was still very angry with him. On hearing that he was on the premises she locked herself up in her room and shouted out that he should leave her alone and go home. Memuna, her young cook, got out of the room and convinced him to go away so that her boss could rest.

"Miss Rosalyn is doing well," she said with a pleasant look on her face. "She is not sick but she does not want to see you. Anytime you try to see her she gets very angry and sick. I get very worried because Miss Rosalyn is a very kind woman. Since she is going to have a baby soon I do not want her to get sick. I am going to become her baby-sitter. It is going to be our baby. You, Miss and I are going to raise this baby. But first you have to go away so that Miss can have the baby in peace. If you insist on seeing Miss, she will get sick and something bad may happen to the baby. I get worried."

After giving Memuna some pocket money, he walked outside in a terrible mood. It dawned on him that Rosalyn was still in the depression stage of her grief while he was approaching the acceptance stage. At this stage she had no patience for the person that had inflicted this calamity on her. It would take a while for her to come to terms with her tragedy and accept it as part of living.

As he drove home he reflected a bit on Memuna's role in his ruined relationship with Rosalyn. She seemed to be the innocent one caught between warring factions. Although she was not a grown-up to be consulted by any of the parties involved in the conflict, she seemed to understand the problem very well. Because of this understanding she knew how to appeal to the people involved in the conflict. It was her gentle and innocent appeal that made him to abandon the attempt to talk to Rosalyn. He knew that it was also that appeal that brought back Alice to the living room on the evening Satta destroyed their dinner. What Hon. Lamboi admired about her was the convincing force behind her appeals.

A week after this painful encounter with Rosalyn, Alice came to see him in his office. Veronica who was just about to leave for the day told her that Hon. Lamboi had already gone home. The news she had brought concerned Rosalyn. She had delivered a baby boy. Thinking that this news was too important to wait the secretary suggested that they go at once to Hon. Lamboi's home to inform him about it.

"My heart leaps as two pretty women enter my household," said Hon. Lamboi jokingly as he offered seats to the two visitors.

"Well, we are pretty and available," said Veronica. "It's all up to you to make the first move."

"Of course, I know you very well, Veronica," said Hon. Lamboi. "You are only now extending that invitation because you know that I have retired from the business of chasing women."

The three of them laughed. Hon. Lamboi had the houseboy serve drinks to the ladies.

"I will take some wine," said Veronica. "It helps me relax after work."

"And you, Alice, what can you take?" asked Hon. Lamboi with a smile.

"I will take something soft," she replied.

"Please get us two cokes and get Veronica some wine," said Hon. Lamboi politely.

When the houseboy went to get the drinks, Alice wasted no time in breaking the exciting news to the new father.

"Rosalyn delivered a baby boy last night," she said quietly with a big smile.

This news made Hon. Lamboi stand up abruptly. It was as if he would abandon his guests and go to see his baby. The two ladies who were not too surprised at his reaction also stood up. The all hugged each other.

"Congratulations!"

"Thank you, Alice."

"Congratulations!"

"Thank you, Veronica. You kept to your promise by letting me know immediately about this baby. Alice, I appreciate your coming all the way here to see me. Thanks a lot."

"Well, Misalie, you have succeeded in joining the club for fathers," said Veronica sipping her wine. "It is an experience worth having. When you were struck by the virus, everyone thought that it was all over for you. But God has blessed you with a baby boy. Although it is not with Satta, I still share your joy."

"Everyone should share his joy because this is the only chance he has to experience fatherhood," said Alice. "As you know, my heart is with Satta who is my best friend. But at the same time, I should not feel bad that Hon. Lamboi is rejoicing. Being a man that has no other chance, he cannot help but dwell on this joyous moment."

As the conversation continued, Hon. Lamboi became sad. Both women noticed it. In order not to spoil their good mood he decided to make them aware of the cause of his sadness.

"I wonder what I am rejoicing for," said Hon. Lamboi. "I am not going to see the baby anyway. Rosalyn will not let me. When I tried to see her during her pregnancy she locked herself inside and refused to allow me to see her. Since she is still angry with me, there is no way she is going to allow me to see my baby."

"Misalie, let us take one thing at a time," said Alice. "Let us rejoice for now over the good news that a bouncing baby has been safely delivered. The second step, which is seeing the baby and holding him in our hands, can wait a bit. I will talk to Rosalyn about this."

"Please do," said Hon. Lamboi. "My desire to see my child is very strong. I find it hard to believe that satisfying that desire is going to be difficult."

"You have to exercise patience as you go about it," said Veronica. "We are going to help you with it but you have to cooperate with us. Rosalyn will reject your moves if you try to do it on your own. Wait until we talk to her about your wish."

That night Hon. Lamboi thought a lot about his child and how it looked like. He rolled over in his bed many times. He felt that it was disgraceful for him to have to struggle just to see his own child. In the morning he called the hospital but was told that Rosalyn was being discharged at that moment. He sped there but due to the traffic he could not make it. Rosalyn was gone with the baby before he got there. He was in a frustrated mood as he was being driven to the House of Parliament. As he got out of the car he felt it ironic that with all the power at his disposal he, the Minister of Health, could not see his own child. But he realized that the kind of power needed to make him see his child was not political power. It was the power of persuasion. But so far it had not worked.

Veronica and Alice tried unsuccessfully during the next four months to convince Rosalyn about the importance of inviting Hon. Lamboi over to see the child. She refused vehemently and threatened to send the child away to an unknown destination if he forced his way into the house to see it.

"He will never see this child," she told them angrily one evening. "This is his punishment for infecting me with the virus. Hopefully, he will not live long enough to see it."

When during the fifth month she received information from a reliable source that Hon. Lamboi was coming to see the child without her permission, she left Bassaya for Ndoba, her home town. While she was there she presented it to her relatives in a traditional ceremony. During her two weeks' absence Hon. Lamboi got very worried that Rosalyn would never return. He asked Veronica to investigate her whereabouts. When he finally found out that they were back in Bassaya, he decided to stay away out of concern that another attempt on his part might make Rosalyn decide to leave the country.

It was Christmas day. The country was in a festive mood and most people were celebrating one of the holiest days of the year. People danced in their houses and in the streets. The colorful African costumes and dresses made the atmosphere livelier than ever. Groups of traditional dancers went from street to street and house to house singing and dancing and accepting gifts and donations from friends, relatives and well-wishers.

Rosalyn who got up earlier that morning cooked together with Memuna and went to spend the joyous day at the home of her uncle, Henry Songa. They arrived there at noon.

Around four o'clock in the afternoon, a group of dancers and singers led by a masked dancer came to the home. They lightened the atmosphere with their beautiful costumes as they danced. Patricia and Henry who were in the holiday mood joined the dancing which took place in the living room. On hearing the singing, Rosalyn rushed downstairs with her child to join the jubilation. In a matter of minutes everyone was dancing in a circle. From time to time people stepped into the circle and danced. So it was that the masked dancer found himself face to face with Rosalyn dancing to the melodious music. When they got out of the circle and another couple entered it, the mask dancer took the child from Rosalyn and held it in his hands. As he wanted to take a break he sat down in the verandah for a while with the child on his lap. Other children came to him to be entertained. All the children were thrilled by the tricks he played. When the short celebration was over and the dancers were about to leave, Rosalyn and her uncle gave them a present. As they stepped out of the house the masked dancer gave the child a hug and returned him to Rosalyn. When it became quiet the Songas had Christmas dinner before continuing with the celebration.

The masked dancer did not really belong to the group of dancers that had just entertained Rosalyn and her relatives. He met them by chance in the neighborhood as they danced from house to house. The dancers accepted his proposal to lead them for a while because they knew that that would make their group more attractive. They also knew that their cooperation was also likely to lead to an increase in the amount of money they expected to earn that day. During the very brief discussion of the deal, the masked dancer thrilled the members by promising that all monies collected belonged to their group. So it was that they entered the residence of the Songas. When they left he gave them all the gifts they had collected and told them that they were now on their own.

Hon. Lamboi, who was the man behind the mask, had disguised himself so that he could see his child. Leaving home in the morning in a taxi for an unknown destination where he put on his costume and mask, he headed for the home of the Songas. By seeing his child, he satisfied a curiosity that had plagued him for months. Thence he set out for his parents' place where they had all planned to have Christmas dinner. On his arrival he headed straight for the dining room and took the seat opposite Michael. When his father asked who the stranger was he took off his mask. The laughter that erupted was uproarious. Michael almost fell off the chair. Before anyone could ask why he was in disguise he went into one of the bedrooms and changed. He had brought in an extra set of clothes a week earlier so that he could use it on Christmas day. After he had dressed up, he called his driver asking him to bring his car over before rejoining his parents and brothers at the dinner table.

"Michael, why were you in disguise?" asked the father with a smile.

"I went to see my son," he replied. "Since Rosalyn would not let me enter her home, this was the only way I could set eyes on a child I have never seen."

The father who was usually a serious man was the one that initiated this second round of laughter. Michael, as usual, was the loudest. He went into the living room and fell flat on the couch. His laughter was uncontrollable. He was still not quite composed when he returned to the table.

"So how was the child?" asked Mrs. Dorothy Lamboi anxiously.

"Mother, he looks exactly like me," he replied. "If you see that child you will think that it is me. We look like identical twins. That is my child."

Everyone was quiet as he narrated his entire adventure. No one among the relatives could believe that Hon. Lamboi could go to that extent in order to see the child.

"What is the child's name? asked the father.

"When I asked Rosalyn in a disguised voice, she told me that he is called Misalie Lamboi," he replied. "Father, that is my junior. He really is. Everybody in the house was referring to him as Misalie. I twice almost forgot that I was in a disguise and answered the call. Rosalyn was in such a great mood as she danced joyfully with me, his mortal enemy. She is a good dancer."

This comment made everyone to laugh. It seemed that the narration of the incident had become the entertainment of the day.

"Who would believe that a Minister of Health could do what you did?" asked Michael's wife.

"Nobody would readily believe this story," said Hon. Lamboi. "That is why I did not take off my costume and mask before I got here. This shows all of you that the passion involved in trying to meet one's offspring is very strong. It is innate and inexplicable."

"It made you to be that creative," said Michael. "I now strongly believe that creativity is the child of necessity."

Everyone laughed again. The incredible story had captured everybody's imagination.

"Yes, in cases of necessity people can be very creative," said Hon. Lamboi.

"I wonder what would have happened if someone had made known your identity as you danced in there," said Stephen.

"It would have been a disaster," said Hon. Lamboi. "I believe that Rosalyn would have hit me. I also suspect that she might have invited press reporters to the house so that they would put the story in the newspaper. But since I had prepared well for this day, the chances of my being caught were very slim."

"You have been the lost sheep of the family for a long time," said Rev. Lamboi. "Your past lifestyle has led you to get a child with a woman that is not your wife. Unfortunately you could not have a child with the woman with whom you were supposed to have one. This is a tragic and painful chapter in your past life. You have to pray to God and ask him for forgiveness."

Satta did not spend the Christmas in Bassaya. She went with her mother to Palahun. Hon. Lamboi wished he could share the good news with Satta but knew that that would only make her sadder.

On the day after Christmas he called Alice and told her that he had seen the child but did not explain how he succeeded in doing that. What he wanted to know was whether the child was free of HIV. When Alice told him that the child tested negative, he rejoiced. After he hung up he left for his parents' place to share the good news with them.

"I am glad that I have a healthy son that will inherit whatever I can leave for him," he said quietly. "Since he is not infected with the virus he is expected to live a full and normal life."

"Let us all pray," said Rev. Lamboi.

They all stood up and held hands. The prayer of the pastor was so moving that it brought tears to the eyes of Hon. Lamboi and his mother.

CHAPTER FIFTEEN

Five months later Rosalyn started to feel sick. After another thorough medical examination which included more blood tests, Dr. Cole told her that she had developed AIDS. Her symptoms which were mild at first soon started to get severe. Although she could move around and do many things on her own, she felt increasingly weaker as the weeks went by. The medication given to combat the virus had painful side effects. Since she could not cope with an active boy that could now walk and engage in wild play, Memuna and her aunt and uncle helped her with the child care.

This was a difficult time for Henry Songa who knew that very soon his niece would become incapacitated and die. Rosalyn too was aware of this possibility. Expecting to be hospitalized in the near future, she seriously started thinking about her son's future. One evening she went with Alice to her uncle's place for a discussion of this matter.

"Dr. Cole predicts that I would be dead in less than six months," she said. "But before I get to the point where I can no longer make a decision about my child I want to divulge my plans to you. For months now I have been very angry with myself, with the world and especially with Misalie who had infected me with HIV. I have struggled to the point of exhaustion. I still love life but I am tired of the struggle for survival. Indifferent now to all passions associated with living in this world - the love of material possessions, the joy of enjoying one's labor and the hatred of people like Misalie whose injurious act had ruined the future of an innocent victim - I am willing to depart in peace. I have at last stopped grieving over my pending death. In other words, I have accepted my death. The one unsettled matter is the future of my son. Once I settle that I will die peacefully and head for that unknown destination that had terrified me for so long.

"I am sure that if I leave my son Misalie in your hands you will take good care of him. This is in fact what I would have done if I were bitter and departing from this life in anger. But I am now free of the passions that I have mentioned. This freedom has enabled me to forgive Hon. Misalie Lamboi. I feel no more anger against him. Thus he can take our child. I would love to see him enjoy that child as much as I would have enjoyed him if I were to live a full life. As you all know, Misalie wants the child. He has suffered terribly because of my decision to stop him from seeing him. But since the passions of anger and hatred are now gone, I have no problem with his seeing him even at this moment. The biggest problem is that Misalie too is infected with the virus. I have heard lately that, like me, he would be pushed over very soon. Having ruled out myself and the child's father as possible guardians, I am left with you two relatives. Logically, the two of you are my choice. However, I have decided that I am going to leave him with someone else. I intend to leave Misalie, Jr. with Mrs. Satta Lamboi. If this plan does not work then you can take him. Uncle Henry and aunt Patricia, I am sorry for trying to leave this child to someone else before considering you. My decision is not due to any lack of confidence in your ability to do a good job in raising him. It is based on my desire to realize a certain goal."

This decision shocked the listeners. Since Rosalyn had expected that it would have such an impact she paused as if to allow them to adequately handle the blow. She would have entertained questions at that time but none was forthcoming. The uncle and the aunt wanted to allow the sick woman to give reasons for her decision.

"I am sure that Satta will be as shocked as you all are when she gets to know my decision," continued Rosalyn. "When Hon. Misalie Lamboi and I are dead and gone Satta can remarry and raise children of her own. But such possibility cannot stop me from making the offer to her. Since she is well-to-do some people may think that she does not need anything from anybody. I have also considered this point. They may also think that she may be too angry at Hon. Lamboi to accept his child. I have considered this point too. Without doubt my child is the result of one of the greatest wrongs that could be done to any spouse. But this reasoning should not make us overlook the kind of person Satta is. She possesses the kind of virtues that not only qualify her to raise my child, but also make it likely that she will accept him. First, she is very forgiving. That is why she is still married to the man who has done her so many wrongs. I have heard that they are separated now but I do not believe that a divorce is in the making. Satta could have divorced that worthless man a long time ago. Second, she is a very kind woman. She kept on comforting and giving moral support to Misalie long after he had contracted the virus. From what I know about their present relationship, Satta left not because of HIV but because she wanted to take a break from experiencing the consequences of the series of crises occasioned by her promiscuous husband. The last scandal embarrassed her to the point that she had no choice but to leave the home for a while. Third, she is a very patient woman. I have no problem understanding why she disrupted my dinner. It was a way of expressing her frustration. During all the years he had cheated on her, she never fought him and never did anything to ruin his political career. Her ability to keep out of the public eye shows the extent to which she can control herself. Finally, she is a very traditional woman. Her belief in our customs has made her not only to keep in contact with her relatives in the village but also take into consideration whatever advice they give her. She has also become very prudent as a result of her association with them.

"These are the qualities that I admire in Satta. They are noble and worth acquiring. From the fact that she possesses these qualities, it does not, of course, follow that she will accept my offer. She may have other good reasons for turning me down. It is, however, these qualities that have caused me to consider approaching her about raising my son. I have great admiration for her.

"There is also a personal reason for my making this offer. It has nothing to do with Satta's qualities. Since I have wronged her and feel very guilty about it I would like to give to her something by which she can remember the man she had dearly loved. Offering her Misalie Jr. is my way of showing how much I love her. I am going to see her tomorrow and ask her forgiveness. If she forgives me, I will initiate a friendship that will make her appreciate the serious guilt I feel for the wrong I have done her. It is through our association that she will hopefully accept my genuine offer. Both of us will raise the child together and give him all our love. When I pass away she will continue not only to shower the same love on him but also inculcate in his mind the very qualities I so much admire in her. So the adoption of my child is going to be based on friendship, love and mutual understanding between the two of us.

"I admire Satta a lot. If I had the kind of character and prudence that she has, I would not today be in the present circumstance in which I find myself."

This speech brought tears to all eyes including those of Rosalyn. Since her uncle was taken by surprise, he asked to be excused so that he could consult with his wife. As they moved into their bedroom they could hear Memuna and the child playing outside.

"So, Henry, what is your reaction to her request?" asked Patricia. She moved close to him so that they could hold hands as they talked.

"Since she is very convinced that this is what is best for her and the child, we should let her carry out her plan," he replied. "If Satta refuses the offer then we take the child. The success of her plan depends on Satta's forgiveness. If she forgives her they can initiate a friendship that may lead to the acceptance of the child. In any case, it is going to be a difficult task. Satta has to be extremely virtuous to accept the child of someone that ruined her marriage. But let us not try to discourage her from pursuing her goal. Let her try."

"I agree with your suggestion," said Patricia. "This woman is sick and discouraged. If Satta accepts her apology and adopts her child, the happiness that will ensue may be good for her mental health. It will sustain her till the end. If her plan fails then we shall look for other ways of making her feel happy and comfortable."

When they finished their discussion and returned to the living room, they told Rosalyn what they had agreed on.

"I wish to thank you very much for your cooperation," said Rosalyn with a smile. "Alice, I wish to thank you for coming. I am going to give you a note to take to Rev. Lamboi and his wife for me. I plan to request a meeting with his family on Saturday.

I will ask him to invite Judith and her daughter to our meeting."

Alice took the note to Rev. Lamboi the following day after work. After the pastor had consulted with his wife about Rosalyn's request to see him, both of them agreed to arrange the meeting. In his reply he told Rosalyn that although they did not know the exact purpose of her requesting the meeting, they would make sure that they invite all the people mentioned in her note.

Hon. Lamboi was the first to turn up on Saturday. He was in at a quarter to six. He was very happy because he expected to meet Rosalyn and their child under cordial conditions. He however did not know that Satta would be there. The pastor had decided not to tell him this because he felt that such knowledge would make him to decide against coming.

Most people arrived at six. Hon. Lamboi was very happy to see Rosalyn appear but was disappointed not to see her with the child. What, however, made him feel good was Rosalyn's politeness to him. That made him suspect that one of these days he may be allowed to see more of his son. But as he sat there talking happily with everyone he heard voices that made him very uneasy. They were the voices of Satta and Judith. "What in the world is happening here today," he asked himself. "Why did my father not tell me that both women would be here?" When he finally caught sight of them, the incident at the dinner came to mind. Feeling that Satta may decide to attack again, he got ready to dash forward to protect Rosalyn who was too weak to fight or quarrel with anyone. But he was relieved to see them take the two seats opposite Rosalyn and her relatives without expressing any hostility. Careful that nobody should notice how he felt he leaned back in his chair as if to let people know that he was completely relaxed.

By a quarter after six everybody invited to the meeting was

in the room. Stephen and Michael who were the last to arrive sat by Hon. Lamboi. They were shocked to see Satta and Rosalyn together in the same room. Rev. Lamboi had not given them information about who would be at the meeting. After a while Michael who normally sought the light side of even the most embarrassing of situations started to smile. He was amused by the serious look on Hon. Lamboi's face. But to avoid embarrassing him he did not look directly in his direction.

Although the guests were sitting in the same room, the division among them was obvious. Rosalyn and her two relatives who had sat together conversed in low voices while Rev. Lamboi and his wife seemed to be consulting with each other about something relative to the agenda ahead. Michael and Stephen were having a conversation to which Hon. Lamboi was listening. This apparent division of guests into groups made the atmosphere a bit tense. The setup could be likened to that of a public gathering of people with fundamentally diverse interests and backgrounds.

Just when Rev. Lamboi was about to declare the meeting open, some of the guests conscientiously took steps that relaxed the atmosphere a bit. The pastor's wife walked across and sat by Hon. Lamboi who was passively listening to the conversation between his brothers. She patted him on the back and held his hand trying to make him feel at ease. The warm physical contact was meant to assure him that everything would be alright. On sensing the purpose of that move, Rosalyn, who was sitting between her aunt and uncle, got up suddenly and walked to the chair standing next to the couch on which Judith and Satta were sitting. She greeted both of them warmly and sat down. They replied politely and continued with their conversation. The pastor's wife looked in their direction and gave a nod of assent. Everybody understood her as saying that it was appropriate for

Rosalyn to move to that seat. Rev. Lamboi then got up and positioned his rocking chair in such a way that he was in full view of everyone in the living room. These movements did not make all the guests engage each other in conversation but it considerably brightened the atmosphere. It gave Hon. Lamboi the confidence that another attack by Satta was not imminent. It also gave Satta the feeling that somebody was yearning to befriend her.

After soft drinks had been served and everyone had become attentive, Rev. Lamboi who felt that he knew the purpose of the meeting asked the audience to join him in prayer. It was a long passionate prayer in which he asked Jesus to touch everybody's heart so that peace could be achieved on that day. When he finished they responded in a chorus "Amen" and opened their eyes. Rosalyn was then asked why she had called the meeting.

Her voice was soft although it looked like she was exerting a slight force to utter the words. Hon. Lamboi who had admired that voice for years noticed that it was as melodious as it used to be. What came to everyone's attention as she spoke was her fading beauty. AIDS had dealt it a blow. Her face which was losing moisture as a result of a slight loss in weight did not glow as it used to. The mental anguish she had experienced for months had also left its mark. It looked sad. The overall look of her structure did not give Hon. Lamboi a good feeling. Rosalyn was no longer the vibrant person she used to be. In any case, she was calm and looked directly into people's eyes as she spoke.

"I am a dying woman who has come to ask Mrs. Satta Lamboi for forgiveness. I am not the only woman that has wronged her but I may be the only one to humble herself to the point of publicly apologizing to her. Before making this apology I am going to tell my own side of the story. Giving this account is in no way an attempt to assert that I am not guilty of anything.

It is intended to make Satta understand why I ruined her marriage so that she can have less difficulty in forgiving me if she wants to do so.

"My story begins from the day I lost my innocence. That was the day I met Hon. Lamboi. I had just graduated from secondary school with first-class grades that qualified me for any scholarship that I wanted. But during the one year I worked for the Ministry of Health before going for higher education, Hon. Lamboi pursued me so vigorously that I had no choice but to yield. He promised a naive girl everything she wanted and went all out to fulfill that promise. It was even through his help that I received a scholarship to study overseas. On my return I met a plush office waiting for me. In addition to this he provided me with comfortable living quarters and hired a houseboy and a maid to serve me. In short, he corrupted me. Somebody in this gathering would say that I had the choice to turn down his offers. But that is easier said than done. If you know the extent to which Hon. Lamboi pursues beautiful women you would not blame me for failing to turn him down. Since he was relentless, it came to a point when I concluded that if I refused I would never get the scholarship that I deserved. So, I started the affair with him.

"He also had affairs with many other women. Many of these may already be infected with HIV. It is not to make my affair with Misalie look harmless that I am mentioning these other affairs. I am doing so in order to help Satta understand that I am a victim of her husband's promiscuousness. She married a man who had an incredible passion for women. These women too are victims. At first I felt helpless and trapped but after a while I accepted the fact that life was like that. I no longer had the feeling that I was ruining Satta's marriage. I felt that getting something out of life is justified no matter what means are used to get it. Thus I became insensitive to the way Satta felt until the day that she destroyed the dinner I had made for her husband. What happened that evening made me realize that I had terribly hurt Satta. The big bangs carried the message that enough is enough. They made me realize that the truth can be concealed for a while but ultimately it will reveal itself.

"There is no way that a young girl from secondary school could have successfully controlled the situation I have just described. This explanation is not however intended to free me from blame. I accept full responsibility for my conduct. Ruining another's marriage is wrong no matter which way you look at it. So, Satta, I am sorry. Please forgive me. All of us who had wronged you will eventually pay a price. Mine is death. That's a big price.

"I now come to the second reason for calling this meeting. I want Satta to adopt my son."

This statement interrupted the intense concentration on Rosalyn's explanation. It shocked the Lambois to the extent that their sighs could have been heard by any outsider eavesdropping on the meeting. Hon. Lamboi could not believe that those words came from Rosalyn's mouth. Satta and Judith leant back in their sofa as if someone had pushed them back. This was the last thing they all expected from a woman who had wronged another so much. But Rosalyn was not surprised by their reaction. Since she had expected it, she decided to keep quiet for a minute to allow the Lambois to recover from their astonishment.

After that moment of silence Rosalyn resumed her explanation by giving the reasons she had given her uncle and aunt in the presence of Alice. She took her time to describe to the audience the virtues of forgiveness, kindness, patience, and love of tradition which she had found in Satta and which had led her to decide to give her child to her. She also added that the offer was a way of extending kindness and love to a person she had wronged.

"Satta, I first of all want you to forgive me. After that I want us to become friends. Both of us can then raise my child with mutual understanding. The love we shall show him will continue when I am gone. When he grows up both of you will remember me as the woman whom you had forgiven. Since he will be your son, I trust that you will teach him the qualities that I admire in you."

At this point Memuna who had just arrived by taxi entered the living room holding the boy by the hand. He was now almost 18 months old. The boy went straight to Rosalyn while Memuna headed for the backyard.

"This is the boy, Satta," said Rosalyn quietly. "You can readily see why I have named him Misalie. Fortunately he is free of the virus that may kill his father too. He has tested negative."

The admiration of the striking resemblance of the boy to his father left the audience speechless for about two minutes. He looked vibrant and attractive. For a while everyone tried to play with him. But being in a strange environment, he refused to accept them. He clung to his mother.

At that point Rosalyn took out a brand-new toy which she had bought for the occasion. As she was about to give it to him, the pastor's wife took it and handed it over to Satta. The boy rushed at her for it. Since he very much wanted the toy, he allowed himself to be held on her lap for a few minutes. This is something that Satta could not refuse to do. It brought cheers among the audience. But as soon as the boy had taken possession of the toy, he jumped off and ran away. Not comfortable in the company of strangers he went to the backyard to join Memuna to whom he was very attached.

Rosalyn's passionate appeal seemed to have had an impact

on the audience. It escalated the expectation for a peaceful resolution of the problem at hand. The presentation of the boy also enhanced the chances for forgiveness. His innocence and his uncertain fate after the death of both parents made everyone to hope that Satta would respond favorably. His presence also led to an appreciation of his mother's courage. The nods and smiles of Michael and Mrs. Dorothy Lamboi, a woman that was so easily moved to pity, were an indication that some individuals among the audience were getting ready to approve Rosalyn's request.

"Satta, we want to know your reaction to Rosalyn's apology and explanation of her conduct," said Rev. Lamboi. "We are all very surprised at her coming here to unexpectedly settle matters with you. We expect you in particular to be shocked by her request that you adopt her only child. Since this is a request that is very difficult to fulfill, it looks like you need time to think it over. In any case, we would like to hear from you."

"I thank you and your wife for bringing us together this evening," said Satta. "I am first going to consult with my mother before I tell you what I think of Rosalyn's apology and request. So, I ask all of you to excuse us."

When Satta and her mother went into the bedroom, it took a whole minute before they could say anything to each other. The mother who was prone to quick reaction was herself a bit hesitant to suggest anything.

"Mother, what do you think?" asked Satta, expecting the mother to give an immediate opinion as usual.

"My daughter, I do not have any thoughts about this matter," said the mother, trying not to influence her daughter's real desire. She had learned that reacting too quickly sometimes made her not to make her true feelings known. Being a prudent woman she wanted to know what the daughter felt before advising her.

"Mother, I have my own thoughts but I first want to know yours," she said.

"My daughter, I too have my own thoughts but I rather not influence your true feeling about such a important matter," replied the mother. "As you can see, I am as cautious as you are. If your uncles were here they may help us. But tonight I am alone. So, please tell me first what you feel about her apology and her request. I will know what to tell you after hearing your reaction."

"Thank you, mother," she replied with a smile. "Tonight you remind me of my grandmother Musu. Unlike my uncles who are quick to give their reaction on crucial matters, she tries to find out what I feel before advising me. That was the approach she employed when I first consulted with her in private about my husband's contracting AIDS."

"I am aware of her approach although I do not always use it," said Judith. "But tonight I better use it. So what do you think about Rosalyn's appeal?"

"To be honest with you, I am a bit confused," said Satta. "I would have wanted to wait a bit longer before making a decision. But time is of the essence because that lady is sick and can be incapacitated at any moment. Thus I would not want to delay her answer."

"My daughter, I expect you to be confused," said the mother. "This is a very sensitive request because the boy is the result of an affair that had caused you mental anguish for many years. Accepting him wholeheartedly requires a dramatic display of forgiveness and a genuine desire to love someone who has subjected you to terrible emotional suffering. This is the kind of decision that puts the entire human spirit to the greatest of tests.

Once you decide to accept the boy, you should never look back to consider your painful past. If you do, it would hurt your love for him. You should love him wholeheartedly like your own child. If by chance you ever happen to look back, ignore at once all negative thoughts about your painful experiences and try to see what good lessons can be learned from them. My daughter, if you cannot love this boy wholeheartedly, do not accept him. You have to be honest with yourself and with him. If you accept him, you have to do your best to make him happy."

"Thank you, mother," said Satta. "Your advice is excellent. I now realize that when it comes to the boy's future there should be no room for hesitation and second thoughts. Either I give him the best or turn down the request. I do not want to do anything that will make me feel guilty in the future."

"Now that both of us have come to an understanding about what is involved in accepting a child coming from such a background, let me probe deeply into your heart to determine your preparedness for adopting this child."

"Please do, mother," said Satta anxiously. "I prefer this approach to merely giving you my general reaction to Rosalyn's request."

"Now, tell me sincerely what you think of the boy you set eyes on a little while ago," asked Judith. "What was your first impression."

Satta's face glowed with a brilliant smile. She looked at the mother in the eyes and stood up. Her mother was struck by the sudden change in her countenance. She suspected that the question had thrilled her daughter but could not tell why.

"Mother, please get up and give me a warm hug," she said. "This is one of the happiest day of my life. So hold me, mother."

After they had hugged and sat down the mother looked in her eyes expectantly. She wanted to hear without further delay her daughter's reaction.

"Mother, I love that boy," said Satta with a laugh. "I want to have him."

"What do you like about him?" asked the mother.

"He is vibrant, charming and looks bright," replied Satta. "He is so lovable that anyone who can afford it will like to raise him."

"Is that all you like about him?" asked Judith.

"That is all, mother," said Satta. "In sum, he is attractive and has something about him that words cannot describe. You know what love is, mother."

"I know, of course, what love is," said the mother. "However, you have to tell me more about your love in addition to merely describing his good looks. Since, as you say, words cannot describe it well, let me make your task easier by asking you a specific question. Does he remind you of somebody or something you love dearly?"

"Mother, do you want me to compare my love for him with my love for something else or somebody else?"

"It looks like you know exactly what I want," said the mother with a smile. "The comparison will help me assess your love for him. Come on, Satta, probe deeper into your heart and tell me."

"He resembles Misalie whom I love very dearly," she said calmly with a smile. "Having him will also help me remember his father forever. I love both of them."

"You have now satisfactorily answered my question," said Judith. "I had suspected that that is how you felt when you set eyes on him. You were trying to keep this secret from me. But mothers know their daughters a lot more than people think."

This statement made both of them to laugh. Satta was surprised at the way her mother was handling the matter. She had not expected her to probe that deeply.

"How did it feel when you held the boy?" she asked.

"Mother, when I set eyes on the boy, I felt love for him," replied Satta. "My holding him make me feel good. I would have liked to hold him a bit longer. Mother, my husband is getting weaker. This is what Alice had told me. It looks like he will develop AIDS. Alice told me the other day that he himself is expecting the worst. I want this boy because he may be the only one I will ever have. The chances are that I will remarry if Misalie passes away, but in case I never get children I will be glad to raise this one. I will not want to turn down this unique opportunity and end up regretting it later. But even if I remarry and have many children I will still like to have this one. He will forever remind me of his father. They look strikingly alike. This is my decision. You can now tell me what you think."

"Satta, I would like you to adopt this boy," said Judith. "You have convinced me that you love him and that you will take care of him regardless of his connection with that gloomy past. I trust that you will sincerely give him your very best. Your ability to do this is due to the four qualities that Rosalyn admires in you. These same qualities have in the past enabled you to overcome many serious obstacles. Now, tell me what you think about her apology?"

"I forgive her with all my heart and all my soul" replied Satta.

"What made you decide to forgive her?" asked the mother.

"Mother, it is impossible to genuinely love that child and not forgive the mother that gave birth to him," replied Satta. "I realize that the child is a result of something the mother did to hurt me. If I am bitter toward the mother, the chances are that I will direct that feeling at the child. So forgiving the mother and adopting the child are two acts of mercy that go hand-in-hand.

The two acts have to be executed simultaneously."

"Will you feel comfortable raising the child together with her until such time when she can no longer perform that task?" asked the mother.

"Yes, I will," replied Satta. "I am going to have her as a friend. It is very important that we be friends as we raise him. He will grow up loving both of us. Our cooperation now will make the transition smooth when she passes away."

"My daughter, I have no further questions," said the mother. "I now have reason to believe that you are prepared to handle the task of adoption. You are very willing and are able to do the job. I am happy with your decision."

When mother and daughter returned to the meeting, they met Rev. Lamboi bombarding his audience with a favorite topic. He was narrating his adventures during the founding of their mission. But as soon as Satta and Judith stepped into the living room, all eyes turned toward them.

"What is your decision?" asked the pastor quietly.

"I have decided to forgive Rosalyn and adopt her child," said Satta with smile. "I am prepared to be her friend and raise the child with her until such time when she can no longer contribute to his welfare."

At this point Rosalyn got up and started moving in Satta's direction. She was so moved by the granting of her request that she wanted to fall at her feet and apologize. But Satta, on noticing it, prevented her from doing so.

"Rosalyn, a hug will do," she said.

"I apologize for ruining your marriage," said Rosalyn. "Please forgive me."

"Rosalyn, I forgive you wholeheartedly," said Satta. "Misalie, Jr. will be given the best that I can afford."

"Thanks for your forgiveness, Satta," said Rosalyn. "With

the resolution of this problem, I have reached the final stage of my struggles. At this stage there is no grief at all. It is all peace and joy. Yes, I will die in peace."

As they hugged and shook hands Hon. Lamboi got up and joined them. He hugged and apologized to Satta too.

"Please forgive me, Satta," he said. "I am sorry for letting you down and causing you so much harm. Misalie Jr. will give you the comfort that I failed to give you."

As the two ladies were about to go to their seats, Hon. Lamboi held back Rosalyn and drew her toward him. Both of them hugged.

"Rosalyn, I am sorry for ruining your life," he said. "Please forgive me for destroying your innocence and infecting you with a deadly disease."

"Misalie, I forgive you," said Rosalyn. "Both of us should now join Satta in her efforts to adjust to motherhood. She needs our moral support."

These hugs and apologies roused the whole gathering. Everyone got up to join in. After they had all sat down, Judith narrated what Satta had told her during the probing. Everybody was pleased with their discussion. It gave the assurance that Satta was ready to be a genuine mother. When she finished speaking, Rev. Lamboi addressed Satta, Misalie and Rosalyn.

"The three of you have to get together soon and start making arrangements about the child. Since all animosities have ended, this will not be difficult to do. I thank Satta for her courage and her appreciation of the problems that Rosalyn and Misalie are facing. All witnesses to this arrangement have learned a lesson about love, compassion and forgiveness. I believe that it was Jesus who brought the three of you together. He will give you the wisdom that you need to overcome any obstacles that may arise."

"In the next few days I will be moving in with Misalie again," said Satta. "Our being together will help us to do a better job in taking care of the child. Rosalyn is welcome to come over anytime she wants and we shall also be going often to her place. This is the only way the child will get to know us."

"I love this arrangement," said Mrs. Dorothy Lamboi. "The three of you should have to have open minds and clean hearts in order to succeed in your plan. We now want to hear from Rosalyn's relatives."

"After discussing this issue yesterday, we gave Rosalyn our approval," said Henry Songa. "So we are very glad with Satta's decision. We want her to know that we are always available for consultation about the child's future. But it is her child to raise. My wife and I thank her for her agreement to accept him."

"May God bless both of you and Rosalyn," said Dorothy Lamboi. "This is a great day in my life. Let us all now proceed to the dining room and eat."

Before everyone got up Rev. Lamboi made a few positive comments about the adoption and also gave his full approval. When they entered the dining room he asked everyone to remain standing for a special prayer for Rosalyn and her son. He also thanked God for the peaceful outcome of that evening's negotiation.

The following day Satta moved back into her husband's residence. Since it was the child that had reunited them so quickly, their entire conversation was centered around him. They discussed their impressions of the child and gave their assessment of its potential. They readily agreed that Rosalyn had done a good job raising him. It was during this conversation that Hon. Lamboi told his wife about his adventure at Rosalyn's house on Christmas day. The wife laughed uncontrollably on learning about the trick he had to play in order to see his child.

Despite her knowledge of her husband for years she would never have suspected that he would go to that extent to get what he wanted. Before they retired to their respective bedrooms for the night, they called Rosalyn to greet her and also tell her that they would come to see the child the following evening. She was happy to talk to both of them and told them that they were very welcome.

Hon. Lamboi did not sleep until after midnight. He was rejoicing over the right granted him to participate in raising his child. He felt like a new man, first, because his mental anguish had ended. The return of his wife and his ability to see his child put him in the best of moods. Second, he had been forgiven by both Rosalyn and Satta. Having infected the one with a deadly virus and caused the other much sadness, he had never expected them to forgive him wholeheartedly. Third, since all the people of consequence in his life had already discussed his tragic mistakes, he had nothing more to be ashamed of. He could face all of them at any time without any hesitation. "Yes, I am a new man," he said aloud to himself. He then clapped and rolled over several times joyfully. He could not believe that it was the same man that used to roll from side to side on that same bed in deep sadness. He gave a big sigh of relief and started singing religious hymns. After rejoicing like this for a while he did something that could be regarded as strange. He started singing nursery rhymes. Happy thoughts about his son made him to sing them. Since this activity was spontaneous, he did not seem to care if he was overheard even by outsiders. He had reason to be happy and wanted to enjoy every minute of it. Ahead of him lay a new life to be enjoyed in the company of his wife and child.

When Satta at first heard the singing, she could not believe that it was her husband expressing his joy that way. Getting up quietly, she walked on tiptoes to her husband's door to eavesdrop a bit. After confirming who the singer was, she returned to her room. Since she was herself in a similar mood, she felt good about her husband's reaction. After getting into bed she could not sleep either. But instead of singing and clapping, she shed tears of joy. She considered having the child a big blessing although she looked forward to having children of her own.

When Judith visited them the following day she found the house glowing with happiness and love. Satta and her husband did not look like people who had gone through a painful separation. She noticed at once that the boy was the bond that was now holding the marriage together. After they had eaten, they set out for Rosalyn's place. The latter received them joyfully and sat down to talk with them. It was a joyous meeting because nothing about the painful past was mentioned. The presents that the three visitors had brought for Misalie Jr. were presented. Rosalyn thanked them for their kindness. The boy did not receive the visitors well because he was not used to them. But they did not mind since that was the beginning of his exposure to his future family. Before leaving Satta extended an invitation to Rosalyn to come to her place. She told her to bring along her aunt and uncle. Rosalyn accepted and promised to leave the boy and Memuna behind after the visit. She assured them that with Memuna around the boy would be willing to stay with them for a few days.

CHAPTER SIXTEEN

Two months later Judith suggested to Satta that they go to Palahun to present the chil*'* to the extended family members. The daughter readily agreed and sent a message to Palahun about the visit. Since it was expected to be a big occasion, Satta and Judith bought lots of food to take along. Hon. Lamboi worked hand-in-hand with them on this project.

Rosalyn was more than willing to allow her son to be taken to Palahun. But since she was herself not strong enough to go, she asked her uncle and aunt to go and represent the family at the ceremony. The latter also bought food and drinks which they planned to present to Satta's extended family on arrival. Since the child was already sufficiently used to Satta and Hon. Lamboi, no one expected any problem during that brief separation from its mother. Besides, Memuna to whom he was very attached, went along to help take care of him. Some new toys were taken along to make the trip enjoyable for him.

The journey took place on a Friday. It was a happier trip for Satta compared with the last few trips. This time she was taking a joyful news to the extended family.

Abibu Lansana and other family members were informed about the adoption a month before the trip. At first there was confusion about the arrangement because the person that took the message was not knowledgeable about what led to the decision to adopt the child. But when two weeks later Abibu received a long letter from Satta explaining in detail what had happened, the picture became very clear to him. He then called a meeting to officially inform the relatives about the adoption and the preparations to be made for the presentation ceremony.

"I wonder why Satta would adopt the child of a woman that had inflicted so much pain on her," said Beimba. "With the woman almost on her way out of this world and Hon. Lamboi not too far behind her, I believe that Satta should have waited to remarry and raise her own family. Everything about this adoption looks very strange."

"The arrangement indeed looks strange," said Abibu. "According to Satta's letter, it was initiated by Rosalyn herself who felt that Satta was the woman with qualities best suited to raise her child. She approached Rev. Matthew Lamboi and his wife Dorothy who helped with the arrangement. The child is at present the main link in the bond of friendship that is holding together Rosalyn, Satta and Hon. Lamboi. The adoption which looks unusual to some of us here happened very quickly. Here is the photograph of the child."

The photograph was passed among the six members at this meeting. It was quiet while they viewed it.

"In effect the adoption instantly solved all the problems that we had wrestled with for months," said Jami, Satta's aunt.

"Yes it did," said Abibu. "It reunited the husband and wife at once. In fact she moved in the with him the following day. During that same week they went to Rosalyn's house with Judith. After that the son came to spend a week with Satta and her husband."

"I am really astonished at how quickly such a long-standing and complicated marital problem was resolved," said Jami. "The knots caused by family and marital problems are normally very difficult to deal with. But this one was publicly untied in less than two hours. It is genuine but it sounds like a fairy tale with a happy ending."

This statement made Beimba to laugh loud. Others joined in. He felt that the arrangement was bad for Satta but had not yet come up with the right words to adequately articulate what he wanted to say.

"I am in favor of the adoption," said Bunduka, Abibu's eldest son. "It is good for Satta. I came to this conclusion after carefully analyzing the situation and asking myself whether her interests were compromised in the adoption process. I believe that they were not at all. She gained tremendously from the arrangement. In the first place, she is in excellent health while those who had caused her much anguish have contracted a virus that would eventually destroy their lives. Secondly, she has gained a child from the mishap. Since she is herself childless, motherhood will comfort her and give her a new perspective about life. We all know that if Satta had never gone to school she would have had two or three children by now. Look at all our girls here who did not have the chance to go to school. They got married immediately after their initiation into the secret society for women. She is older than many of these girls although she is still childless. It is not her fault of course that she has no children. Her formal education caused the delay. But by the time she remarries and has children she will probably be in her mid-thirties. So it is not a bad idea for her to be raising a child while waiting to get some of her own."

"I agree with your view," said Ngele, Musu's brother. "Satta is the winner in this strange arrangement. "Let the lioness get her share."

Beimba laughed loud again. As always the others joined him. They were surprised that he was quiet and wondered whether he was going to argue against an adoption he had characterized as strange. At this time Musu, who was concerned about whatever opposition Beimba would raise later, decided to say something in favor of the way the complicated problem was resolved. She hoped that her support would make Beimba think twice before criticizing the arrangement.

"I readily agree that such sudden resolutions of difficult problems are rare," said Musu. "But once in a long while problems do resolve themselves that way. I know of a few delicate arrangements that have turned out to be permanent solutions. When they were made many thought that they would not last. The doubt was due to the explosive nature of the cases..."

Musu did not quite finish when Beimba interrupted her. She had wanted to give some examples of the kinds of rare arrangements that had worked out well; but a pause in her speech had given the impression that she had finished speaking.

"Such arrangements are rare indeed," said Beimba, now ready to criticize the deal. "The solution of this case reminds me of an unexpected solution of a very complicated conflict that occurred between two powerful brothers of a famous Kemala family ten years ago. To this day there are people that believe that that problem was satisfactorily solved. But the wiser people of Kemala do not think so. I side with the latter because the solution was so artificial that it did not address the complexities of that case. Likewise, the adoption of Misalie Jr. is an artificial solution to a long and complex marital problem. For those of you who do not recall the case of the two brothers of Kemala, I will first summarize it very briefly."

At this point he got up to get a drink of water. This only took a minute but it seemed to have lasted much longer than that. Everyone was very anxious to hear what he had to say.

Musu was worried because she felt that Beimba's criticism would be so convincing that it would win over some members at the gathering. The criticism came at a bad time because everyone was already leaning toward approval of the deal. In any case, all waited for him to finish expressing his concern.

"The conflict between the two powerful brothers was over the deceased father's wealth," continued Beimba, after settling down. "Each wanted all of it on the grounds that he was the one that took the best care of the father while he was sick. The problem with their claim was that neither of them was willing to consider the interests of other members of the extended family that had helped take care of their old and sick father. These stood at the sidelines in silence lamenting the fact that the warring brothers would neither give them the credit they deserved nor offer them a portion of the heritage. That conflict, however, ended one day when all of a sudden both of them were killed in a auto accident while on their way to submit their dispute for arbitration. Both had agreed to let the chief of the village hear their case. The wealth that was left behind was fairly and peacefully shared among the living relatives. There were some who claimed that death solved the complicated problem. But I do not share their view. It was never really solved. The warring brothers went to their graves with it. The solution looks effective and everlasting because the two brothers cannot return to rekindle the chaotic atmosphere they had created. I believe however that the solution, if it can be so called, is artificial because it does not address many of the complicated issues. For example, one of the houses the two brothers quarrelled over still stands unfinished. The father's ill health prevented him from finishing the project. The family members who divided up the heritage did not address the completion of this house. Its standing there unfinished is a testimony to the fact that the problem was not solved. The case would definitely have continued if one or both brothers had survived that crash. So, death did not solve the problem.

"Likewise, there is no way the adoption of Rosalyn's child can lead to the solution of the long-standing marital problems between Satta and Misalie. It may bring momentary happiness but I believe that after the excitement dies down, the old problems will resurface. Hon. Lamboi, as far as I know him, will continue spending money on other women. Then the same anguish that my niece had experienced in the past would be experienced again. Just as death never solved the problem of the two brothers, likewise adoption will not produce the solution to my niece's problems."

When Beimba finished there was some confusion as to who would respond. Some expected that Abibu would but it soon became apparent that he did not want to say anything. He too felt that there were problems with the adoption although he still favored it. His concern at that time was that criticizing the arrangement would strengthen Beimba's argument to the extent that others might withdraw their support. He kept quiet because despite the immediate problems, it would be to Satta's advantage in the long run to accept the child. "What if Satta loses this opportunity and ends up never getting a child of her own?" he asked himself.

Musu, Satta's grandmother, was not pleased with Beimba's criticism. She felt that it was disruptive of the adoption process. When Abibu failed to say anything it became clear to her that he too had some reservation about the matter. But since he was unwilling to voice it, she guessed that it was a problem that did not bother him. The fight then was with Beimba who felt strongly about his own reservation.

Musu's intimate knowledge of Abibu and Beimba enabled

her to guess with great accuracy how exactly they felt about the case at hand. Her decision was to address Beimba's opposition but not in a way that would make him to feel that his concern was worthless.

"I do remember the case of the two brothers that Beimba has used as an example in making his point," she said very calmly with a smile. "The way the complicated problem involving Satta, Rosalyn and Misalie was suddenly solved by the adoption of the child should not be compared to the way death ended that fraternal conflict. The adoption issue was dealt with in Bassaya in the presence of family members from both sides. After that they wrote us this letter respectfully requesting our input. If we leave here today without approving this adoption, Abibu will state our reasons when they come for the presentation ceremony. Our concerns will be addressed and negotiations will recommence and continue until we come to a solution that is satisfactory to all sides. This problem will not be solved like the way the conflict between the two hard-headed brothers in Kemala was suddenly resolved. There were no negotiations and there were no opinions expressed. The heritage was just distributed among the living relatives. Lingering problems were not addressed either. That is why the deceased father's house still stands uncompleted. Death ended the fraternal fight but did not resolve the case. In our case the adoption of the boy is not supposed to solve all problems. What it does is to encourage the different factions to cooperate in building a relationship that will grow indefinitely. It is part of a long process, not the end of the matter. It is a stage in the move toward the formation of a strong bond of friendship. We are not going to make the mistake that the extended family in Kemala made. Since we understand that adoption will not solve the problems, we are going to make sure that the three people that initiated the process - - Satta, Misalie and Rosalyn - - keep on working hand-in-hand until all the problems are solved. I will tell them that without such cooperation the arrangement will collapse and the child will suffer. Our task is to give our moral support and advice them on how to nourish the relationship. In fact Satta mentioned in her letter that Judith had already started advising them about how to build the kind of healthy relationship that will benefit the child.

"My own opinion, therefore, is that the adoption should be approved. We may be astonished by its instant approval by those who were at that meeting. But if we realize that forgiveness is one of the strongest and most revered virtues in the human realm, we should not be so surprised that Satta was able to give it that quickly. We all know that our daughter had forgiven Hon. Lamboi for many past wrongs. It is her ability to forgive that enabled her to be patient with him for years. Forgiveness is one of her natural gifts. She has no problem giving it in the appropriate context. We should appreciate her courageous effort to use it to solve a complicated problem that had caused her anguish. Since this is the first time that Satta is genuinely rejoicing in three or more years, we should rejoice with her. Let us not try to rekindle old problems. Let us not take her back to her gloomy past. Finally, if she had in the past used her natural gifts to make the husband happy, why should she not use them now to peacefully take possession of a child she loves dearly? Why should she not seize an opportunity that would make her happy for many years to come? I agree with my brother that the lioness should get her share."

The silence that followed Musu's appeal was profound. The smiles on Beimba's face was an indication that he was pleased with her reasoning.

"I want to thank Musu for carefully explaining the role of

adoption in the solution of this complex problem," he said. "She has made me understand that the adoption of the boy is only a part of the total healing process. Since matters have been clarified to me, I have no objection to the arrangement."

In the end everyone approved the adoption. After the meeting Abibu wrote a letter to Satta telling her of their decision. It was received a week before their travel to Palahun.

This discussion by family members helped prevent beforehand any unexpected problem that could have marred the joyous occasion. It enabled the visitors and those already in Palahun to better prepare themselves for the occasion. There was rejoicing when Abibu's reply was received. It was, therefore, in an elated mood that the Lambois set out with the Songas for Palahun taking with them the most precious gift that Satta had ever received.

On their arrival that evening many family members came to see them. The child was of course the center of attention. Many held him in their hands. Later in the evening Satta went to see Musu in her bedroom. Both talked a lot about the child and also about Satta herself. The grandmother wanted to find out how comfortable Satta was with the adoption. By the time their meeting broke she had no doubt in her mind that Satta had made the right decision.

Saturday was a busy day. The cooking started early. Two sheep were slaughtered and a bag of rice was cooked. Friends and relatives brought gourds of palm wine and raffia wine. Satta and her husband provided soft drinks, beer, wine and gin. The ceremony took place about four in the afternoon. A friend of the family prayed for the child asking God and the ancestors to shower their blessings on him. He held the child's hand as he said the prayer and invoked the names of many ancestors. When he finished the pastor of the small village church also prayed for the child. He called on Jesus Christ to guide and protect it as well as all those gathered in the compound. After that the feast began. There was enough food to eat and drink. The dancing continued till late into the night.

The following day the family members gathered at noon. It was Hon. Lamboi who had summoned them to that meeting. He informed them of his apology to Satta in private and in public for his misconduct and marital infidelity. He then told them that he had invited them to the short meeting so that he could thank them for their moral support and their contribution to the feast. He also made mention of their letter of approval which had made him and his wife very happy.

When he finished Abibu spoke on behalf of the family. He told Hon. Lamboi that all of them appreciated his courage to publicly admit his wrongdoing and apologize to his wife for it. He also expressed their concern about his health. He expressed the wish that the medicines he was taking would cure him. He ended by thanking the Songas for their cooperation in the adoption process and their contribution to the feast.

Later during the day Musu invited her diviner to do some divining for her. She wanted to know something about the future of the adoption. This time Satta and Judith did not take interest in what she wanted to know. They were however not surprised by her desire to inquire. Musu was the kind of person that felt that living safely consists in knowing the outcome of all enterprises that one undertook.

When the diviner arrived he did not have any idea that his prediction about the child had come to pass. It was during the discussion about the future of the adoption that he learnt about it. Naturally, he was excited but did not show it. He first wanted to do the divining.

After carefully listening to Musu's request, he took out his divining materials, set them up and meditated on the task for about two minutes. Then he started the investigation. Musu watched quietly but a bit anxiously. Now that this man had successfully predicted that Satta would have a child, everybody would take seriously any prediction he made. So she wondered what would happen if some bad news emerged. The ensuing sadness would end the pleasant weekend on a bad note. In any case, she remained quiet as she watched. When the man finished and looked up, she anxiously inquired the outcome.

"So what did you find out?"

"The prediction is good," he said with a broad smile.

"Then please do not continue your explanation," said Musu. "I want my daughter to share the result with me. Please sit in the living room and wait for me. One of my grandchildren will serve you some food and the kind of drink you want."

As the diviner packed his things to move to the living room, Musu left the house hastily. She walked over to Abibu's house to invite him over to her place for a short but important meeting. Beimba was there drinking palm wine with him. She invited him too and then went into Satta's house. They were finishing lunch when she entered. She waited impatiently for them to finish before asking them to go to her place.

The meeting was brief but lively. The diviner was asked what he had found out about the future of the adoption. At first Satta was worried about what he would say but when he started saying favorable things she relaxed and listened attentively with smiles.

"The last time you were here I predicted that Satta will have a child. The prediction has come to pass. I did not of course tell you that she would conceive and give birth to a child. All I told you was that she would have a child in the near future. That is what I saw during my divination. Now she has the child. Musu called me today to predict the future of the adoption. After probing twice I found out that it has an excellent future. This child will grow up and become a great man. He will ever remain grateful and devoted to Satta. I wish to congratulate Satta on her good fortune."

This news brightened the room. Everyone was very pleased. Beimba was pleased too but he definitely had something to say to the diviner. He had promised to double the grand total of whatever amount was paid by the relatives as his fee if things happened as predicted. So, as the fees were being placed on the center table in front of the diviner he felt very uncomfortable. As if to increase his discomfort, Satta and her husband who were overjoyed by the prediction, gave a big sum. Beimba watched quietly and attentively as the diviner counted his small fortune.

"That is not all," said Abibu, getting up. "I am going to ask the other relatives who are not in this room to contribute something. Bunduka, Jami and Ngele are still around. So, I will be right back."

When he stepped out to get the monies, Beimba gave a sigh and stretched back in him arm-chair. Since he could not match the grand total, he knew that he was in big trouble and was sad about it. But he sat up quickly trying not to show any anxiety. Having always projected a strong image of himself, he did not want news to go around that he had expressed some weakness in the face of adversity.

Abibu soon arrived with some more contributions. He announced the names of those who had contributed and how much each had given. The diviner recounted the money and announced the grand total.

"Beimba, you promised that you will double this grand total," said the diviner with a smile. "You of course did not have to do that but you obviously never expected my prediction to come to pass. So, you became more generous than expected."

This statement made everyone, including Beimba, to laugh. All eyes were now turned towards him. The diviner wanted his money so that he could leave.

"Come here at the end of the month and collect your money," said Beimba. "I will pay you then."

"Thank you, Beimba. If I do not come please send it with one of your children. I will put it to some good use at that time. You know that money never rots. That is why our people have said that it brings joy wherever and whenever it is employed. So this amount will always come handy. At the time it becomes available, the bride-price for my fourth wife will have been due. It will help me get a brand-new woman."

This statement made everyone laugh. The amount was not much; however, the diviner felt that Beimba should pay it. But as he stood up to leave, Hon Lamboi decided to pay what Beimba owed. That set Beimba free instantly. He thanked his in-law and leaned back to relax. When the diviner left he explained why he was penniless at that time.

"Satta, as I told you when you were here the last time, I did take my contractor to court," he said. "It has been an expensive litigation because my houses in Tilasa are still unfinished while he is working on other people's houses. Our next appearance in court is at the end of next month. I am going to make sure that he ends up in jail."

The visitors left for Bassaya at around six o'clock that evening. On their arrival they called Rosalyn to tell her about their return. They told her that they would see her over the weekend.

Just before Satta went to sleep she called Alice who had been expecting her call. Alice had some interesting news to share with her. But they first embarked on the news about Palahun.

"So how was the trip?" asked Alice.

"It went well, very well," said Satta. "Everybody was happy to see the child. We were given a big welcome. On Saturday we had the traditional ceremony followed by a feast. My uncles Abibu and Beimba sent something for you. I will bring it over tomorrow."

"Great! I can hardly wait to see it," said Alice. "How are they doing?"

"They are doing fine," said Satta. "By the way Uncle Beimba got into trouble while we were there."

"With whom did he get into trouble this time?" asked Alice.

"With the diviner, of course," replied Satta. "He could not pay him his money. This was the diviner I told you about at the time we visited your home. He too had predicted that I will have a child. Beimba had told him that if that ever happened he would double the grand total of the amount my family members would give him as his fee. Well, the diviner was invited again this morning to predict the future of the adoption. His prediction made all of us very happy. But when it came to paying him Beimba was the only one that became unhappy. He had promised to double the grand total."

Both women laughed. Alice knew Beimba very well and his rash ways. She was not surprised to hear of his challenge.

"Did he pay the amount?" asked Alice.

"No, he could not," replied Satta. "He was too broke to pay it."

The two women laughed again. Alice seemed interested in the story.

"Fortunately, my husband paid on his behalf. The diviner said that he would use the money to get a fourth wife."

The laugher continued. Alice had expected some interesting things to happen but she did not suspect that Beimba, a farmer with some means, would be broke at this time. Satta forgot to say why he was broke.

"So how was your weekend?" she asked.

"It was exciting," replied Alice. "You cannot guess whom I went out with."

"You mean some gentleman took you out?" asked Satta. "What a surprise! Then something interesting did really happen while I was away in Palahun. Who is the lucky man?"

"Ali Saffa, the journalist," replied Alice.

"Well, that's a real surprise," said Satta. "He is one of the most eligible bachelors. Where did he take you to?"

"To the Golden Complex," replied Alice. "We had a delicious dinner and then danced all evening. I enjoyed his company thoroughly. Saturday was a great day."

"Well, Alice, that's really a gentleman," said Satta. "Gentlemen take women out to the best places in town."

"Do you like him?" asked Satta.

"Yes, I do," replied Alice.

"I do not know Ali very much," said Satta. "I liked the articles he used to write on AIDS. I have heard that he is a good and serious man. One thing we can rule out is that he is not like Hon. Lamboi or his friend Sefoi. I doubt that any man in this city will surpass these two in the pursuit of women. Do you think that he is interested in you?"

"I think that he is," replied Alice. "He called today and told me that he would like to go out with me again next Saturday."

"Alice, it looks like things are looking up for you," said Satta. "Be open-minded and hope that he turns out to be actually nice."

On Saturday Satta and her husband went to visit Rosalyn. They took the child with them so that he could spend some time with his mother. Rev. Lamboi and his wife Dorothy were there when they got there. The day before, Henry, Rosalyn's uncle, had visited the pastor with regard to Rosalyn's request for a prayer session. She was so sick that she wanted the pastor to conduct the session. The prayers were just about to begin when Satta and her group entered. They all joined hands and took turns to pray for the sick woman.

After the prayers, Rosalyn, who looked thin and weak told them about her health and the side effects of her medicines. She told them that in less than two months she would be dead. This brought tears to the eyes of both Satta and her husband. The child who was sitting on his mother's lap kept on bothering her for something she had in her hands. Being too young to understand the great calamity that had befallen his mother, he kept on struggling for the items until they were given to him. They were his mother's keys. Once he gained possession of them he shook them and danced to the noise they made. From time to time he would go to Satta and play with her. The two had already become close enough for him to feel free around her. But when the time came for the visitors to leave it became clear who the real mother was. The child rushed to Rosalyn and sat on her lap thinking that he may be taken away again.

That night Rosalyn's illness became serious. The fever and the pain had become so unbearable that Henry sent one of his children to inform Alice about it. The latter was still out with Ali but on receiving the message later, she rushed to Rosalyn's residence. Finding her in such a miserable state she called Dr. Cole who told her to tell the uncle to take her to the hospital. When the doctor in charge told the relatives that he was going to admit her for a few days, they suspected that it was all over for Rosalyn. Alice confirmed that suspicion by telling them that any AIDS patient in such a terrible state was likely to stay in the hospital until her death. This made the two grieving relatives weep for a while.

The following day Hon. Lamboi and Satta visited Alice in the evening. On their way they passed by Judith's house and asked her to go with them. It was Alice who had requested that they bring Judith along. The conversation first centered on Rosalyn's condition but after a while the topic of Alice's new love came up.

"Judith, Alice is in love these days," said Satta.

"Is this a joke?" asked Judith. "I am surprised that you had not told me this news."

"I thought you already knew about it," said Satta.

"No, I do not," said Judith. "What a surprise! Alice, can we know the lucky man?"

Everybody turned toward Alice with smiles that made her laugh. What they did not know was that Alice had invited Ali Saffa over so that they could all meet. That is why she had asked that Judith be brought along. She was just about to answer Judith's question about the identity of the lucky man when Ali Saffa and Michael Lamboi entered. Her hesitation to talk at that time made everyone to suspect that it must be Ali Saffa. Michael was ruled out at once because it was known that he was married.

Hon. Lamboi's question about the identity of the new man was overheard by the two close friends as they entered the house. They knew at once that the subject of the conversation was Ali. So as soon as they entered the living room, Michael tried to create some fun by answering Hon. Lamboi's question in an indirect way.

"Misalie, I am not that lucky man at all," said Michael.

This statement brought lots of laughter. The question as to who was the lucky man was still unanswered but there was some pressure on either Alice or Ali to say who it was.

"Who then is the lucky man?" asked Hon. Lamboi.

"Please ask Ali," said Michael. "He dashed over to my home this afternoon singing a love song. When he finished he asked me accompany him here."

This comment caused much laughter. Ali knew that his friend was a funny man but he did not expect that joke. To prevent further guesses he himself jokingly revealed the person's identity.

"I am the lucky man," he said.

The laughter continued for a while. Those who were learning about this for the first time were surprised but felt that Alice had made a good choice. Being a journalist, Ali was a public figure whose writings and opinions were known on any topic imaginable. But one thing that was clear to all was that he had never been personally involved in anything scandalous. Michael who had been his friend for years had already confirmed this in a private conversation with Alice.

"So, Alice, you are the lucky woman," said Michael.

"Perhaps I am," said Alice. "It takes time to find out."

"When are you going to tie the knot, Ali?" asked Judith.

"This affair has only been going on for two weeks," said Ali. "It is yet too early to say."

"You are right," said Judith. "I thought that you have been at it for a long time. Time is an important factor because it allows you to know each other. But a bit of luck is also helpful. You look like a good pair."

As they were talking Saidu Lavalie, Alice's father, entered the house. He was coming from his neighbor's place. He had gone there to express his sympathy for the latter who had had a misfortune lately. On entering the living room and greeting the entire company, he congratulated Satta on her courage to adopt Misalie, Jr. He expressed an interest in seeing the child in the near future. But as he walked to the backyard where his children had hung up a hammock for him, it came to his mind that the diviner that had predicted that Satta would have a child should be paid at that time. Fortunately the man was in town. His friend had brought him back from the village so that he could do some divining about his misfortune. Summoning one of his children, he asked him to go and ask the diviner to come over.

The company was at its best when Saidu and the diviner suddenly entered. With the exception of Ali who was not there at the time the divining was done, everybody knew at once why they had come.

"Michael, your friend is here," said Saidu. "Do you know that his prediction turned out to be true?"

"Yes, I have seen and held the child in my hands," replied Michael. "I congratulate him on the accuracy of his prediction. It is now time for him to get his reward."

"Thanks for your cooperation, Michael," said Saidu. "As you may recall, one diviner made a prediction that contradicted the one made by both this man and the diviner in Palahun. I want you to know that one contradiction does not affect my belief in divination. Since Satta actually got a child, I believe that the next diviner would have also predicted it. Unfortunately, Satta had declined my request to invite him over. You encouraged her not to insist on knowing her future because you have a different way of dealing with life's problems. Since I come from a traditional African society and do not have a western education, I do not arrive at the truth the way you do. When I am faced with problems that I cannot handle I go to my diviner. Your way works but our belief in ours is still strong. Any time you have a problem that you cannot handle, please come and tell me. I will get help for you. Do not be bothered by the possibility that once in a while some diviner may make a contrary prediction. Since the ones I employ are among the very best, what they predict will normally come true."

As he talked Michael placed the diviner's fees on the table. He gave much more than was expected of him. Satta and Judith added something to it. Saidu picked up the money and gave it to the diviner. He had not expected the extra money. After thanking them, both men left."

No sooner had they stepped out when everyone turned their eyes in Michael's direction. They wanted to know why he merely congratulated the diviner and made no attempt to discuss problems with divination with him.

"Well, if I had discussed such problems with this diviner, he would probably have claimed that his prediction came true because he is a better diviner. In any case, it would make no sense arguing with him since what he predicted happened. He even deserves praise for predicting that Satta will get the child without conceiving and giving birth. I will not however consult with a diviner on any problem. Since I am not used to doing that it will not bother me if I don't. It is really a matter of attitudes. Alice's father is used to consulting with diviners and medicine men. So as soon as he runs into some problem he goes to see them. He lives by what they tell him. Since I live differently, consulting them never comes to mind. I feel comfortable with the methods and means that I use to solve my problems."

"I gather from what you say that there is nothing wrong in consulting diviners," said Judith. "Am I right?"

"Yes, you are," replied Michael with a smile. "As we have seen, it works for those who believe in it. Likewise my methods work for me. So it is alright for those that believe in divination to consult people who perform them. Truth is not at stake here; it is a matter of attitudes."

Rosalyn remained hospitalized until her death two months later. During that period relatives and friends including the Lambois visited often. When the photographs taken during the presentation ceremony were ready, Satta showed them to her. Although she did not say much, her facial expressions revealed her pleasure to see her son in the midst of the festivities. The photographs served as a further assurance that her child would be well taken care of.

The day after her death Henry Songa made arrangements for her burial in Ndoba. The Lambois with whom she had formed a strong bond of friendship felt as much sadness over her death as her relatives. Both Satta and her husband wept. They attended the burial ceremony together with Alice.

CHAPTER SEVENTEEN

According to the agreement between the Lambois and the Songas, Misalie Jr. was to be taken away to his new home a week after the fortieth day burial ceremony of his mother. On the day that Hon. Lamboi and Satta went to get the child, they met Memuna in tears. The bad news that had caused this sad reaction was the announcement that the family that had adopted Misalie, Jr. was ready to take him away. That meant not only that Memuna would be separated from him but also that she would lose her job. The Songas had notified her about the changes that were about to take place in her life two days before the Lambois came to get the child.

"Memuna, we want to remind you that Hon. Lamboi and his wife, the adoptive parents of Misalie, Jr., are coming to get him the day after tomorrow," said Henry quietly. "Our plan is to recommend you to a nice family for the job of a maid. We are sorry that things have turned out this way."

"But why don't you hire me as a maid?" asked Memuna.

"First of all, Memuna, we would like to hire you if we can afford it," said Henry. "But we cannot. We do not have a servant because we cannot afford one either. You are welcome to live with us but you need a job because you have to take care of your needs and also help your mother financially. Your financial assistance to her lessens considerably the financial burden of your younger brothers and sisters. So, you need to go and work somewhere."

"And remember that you are welcome to come and visit us at any time," said Patricia somewhat hastily.

"Why don't you ask Mrs. Lamboi to hire me?" asked Memuna.

"I would love to do that," replied Henry. "But the problem is that the Lambois already have a cook and a maid. I doubt that they want to hire another maid."

This news struck Memuna so hard that she did not remain seated. Falling on the ground, she cried aloud as if death had occurred in her family. She called on Rosalyn for help but of course no response was expected. Her wish was that someone as nice as her former employer would hire her on the spot. It was a desperate wish. She referred to Rosalyn's death as a stoke of bad luck.

Memuna had reason to cry that loud. She had enjoyed a lot while working for her deceased boss. Coming from a poor home where none of the children went to school due to the lack of school fees, she had regarded her job as a great opportunity. Rosalyn had trusted her a lot and had taken good care of her. Besides paying her monthly wages, she had fed her and had provided her with clothes and most of her needs. This had enabled her to give most of her earnings to her mother who lived in a poor section of the city. Other privileges she had enjoyed included going out with Rosalyn whenever she had to take the baby somewhere. Thus she had the chance to visit many places of interest and also eat in nice restaurants. Since she was attractive and bright, Rosalyn had no problem taking her to public places. In appreciation for such kindness, Memuna had worked hard in the home and taken excellent care of Rosalyn's child.

It was over the loss of these privileges that Memuna was weeping. Those who understood her situation and the way she had lived would easily have appreciated her conduct. Misalie Jr. who was attached to her was so affected by her wailing that he too started to cry. Since the Songas found it impossible to stop them, they waited until fatigue naturally ended the emotional outburst an hour later.

This was how matters stood when the Lambois came to get the child two days later. They were surprised to learn of the extent to which the two children had cried. On asking Memuna the reason for her behavior she went upstairs and fell on her bed. She was too moved to explain. The child followed her. Satta then told the Songas that she had no intention of leaving Memuna behind. Hon. Lamboi informed them at once that she would get her full pay and most of the privileges that she had enjoyed in the past. The Lambois had no problem making this decision because they had had the chance to observe Memuna during the weekends she had spent at their place together with the child. She had proved to be a good baby-sitter. But it was actually during the full week that Memuna and the child spent with the Lambois that she proved beyond doubt that she could manage domestic matters by herself. Since the house maid happened to be sick that week, she demonstrated her skills by cooking a variety of delicious dishes and cleaning the house thoroughly. This had earned her the admiration of both Satta and her husband.

Satta's announcement that Memuna would be retained as maid was a welcome news for the Songas. Patricia rushed upstairs to get her. The miserable look on her face as she was being led downstairs showed the extent to which she had been affected by her predicament.

"Memuna, have you packed your things and those of

Misalie, Jr.?" asked Satta.

"I have packed Misalie's things," she answered. "Let me go and bring them."

When she returned with the things Satta smiled and told her the decision she had made.

"Now, go and pack your own things, bathe and get dressed so that we can go," she said.

"How long am I going to stay this time?" asked Memuna.

"Memuna, we are going to hire you as our junior maid. You will take care of small Misalie and also help the senior maid. You will be paid a little more than what Rosalyn paid you. In addition, we are going to send you to school. You will have a better future if you go to school."

Memuna thanked them and went to bathe. As she was getting dressed, she was heard singing nursery rhymes. The child was doing his best to imitate her. Since she had never gone to school she did not sing them well but she did the best she could.

The Songas were very relieved when the Lambois left taking Memuna with them. They had agonized over her fate the entire week. As soon as the car took off, they burst out laughing. They felt that although Memuna deserved sympathy, the way she had behaved was childish enough to warrant some laughter. They were joyful that everything ended well.

"Misalie, did you identify with Memuna's singing when she was getting ready this morning?" asked Satta later that evening.

"Not at all," replied the husband.

"Do you want to tell me that you don't sing that way at all?" asked Satta.

"I don't sing like that now but I did so when I was a child," said Hon. Lamboi. "Memuna and Misalie, Jr. behaved that way only because they are children. They were only doing what all children do."

"But don't adults sometimes also sing that way when they are as overjoyed as a girl like Memuna?" asked Satta.

At this time the husband suspected something. It came to mind that he did sing nursery rhymes on the night the case was settled between him and both Satta and Rosalyn. Suspecting very strongly that his wife had overheard him, he laughed and fell back in his chair.

"Oh no, darling, please do not tell me that you overheard me the other night," he said.

"Oh yes, I did," she said. "At first I could not believe it was you singing. But to confirm my suspicion I tiptoed to your door and listened for a while. Among the songs you sang were "London bridge is burning down", "Row, row your boat", "Hey diddle diddle", and "Twinkle, twinkle little star." But the funniest was "Old Macdonald". The way you were imitating farm animals was thrilling. "I almost burst out laughing when you imitated the cows saying "*Moo moo* here and *moo moo* there".

Both husband and wife laughed hilariously. They got up, hugged joyfully and went to look at the boy as he slept. When they returned to the living room, Satta continued to narrate her observation.

"Darling, it was appropriate for you to sing that way," said the wife. "You were celebrating your recovery from your disaster. Your shattered life was being put back on the right track. Likewise Memuna, who had wept for a week over the loss of her job, was celebrating her employment this morning. Her life is now on the right track. The same thing has happened to me. I no longer consider myself to be childless because I have young Misalie that I can refer to as my own. My life is on track. On the night I moved back in with you, I did not sing nursery rhymes but I did shed tears of joy."

The following months were joyous for Satta. After two

years her child came to know and accept her as his mother. She kept in contact with the Songas whom they visited from time to time. Alice got married to Ali Saffa after a year of dating. A year and a half after their wedding she gave birth to a baby girl.

Hon. Lamboi started to feel sick at the end of the his son's second year with them. After a physical examination and a diagnosis of his illness, Dr. Cole confirmed that he had indeed developed AIDS. Although this long-awaited news came as no surprise, it devastated the family to see the husband losing weight uncontrollably. The months that followed were very stressful. The painful side effects of his medication together with the fevers and persistent cough made him to give up his seat in Parliament and retire from politics. He also gave up the ministerial quarters and moved to a comfortable home which he had bought two years earlier. These changes in his social condition brought a lot of unhappiness in the home. On the eve he was to be taken to the hospital for constant care he told his wife that he did not have much time to live.

"Darling, I thank you for your moral support during the last two years," he said. "As you know I did fight to have you back although I knew that I could not do for you what a faithful and healthy husband could do for his wife. Nevertheless, knowing you to be a kind person I expected you to help me and be by my side when this moment came. My prediction was correct. You did stay by my side. Thank you for making me feel happy during these couple of years. I am sorry that I could not give you a child but I am pleased that the one I got out of wedlock is now yours. That is your own small fortune and joy. You are young and will still be able to remarry and have children of your own. But no matter what happens, Misalie Jr. will be the bond that will forever hold us together. Again, thanks for your love. God will bless you for your kindness to me and other people."

"Misalie, is it goodbye that you are now saying to me?" asked Satta in tears.

"I am afraid that it is," replied her husband quietly. "You know that once I get into that hospital I will not come back alive. It is a journey of no return."

Satta telephoned Rev. Lamboi and Judith and explained to them what her husband had said. Within the next hour all the Lambois and Judith were with them. Alice and the Songas also came. Sefoi and Veronica were the last to arrive. After Satta had explained what she had been told, Misalie Lamboi confirmed it.

"I know that we have all had good and bad times together," he said. "Fortunately, despite the tragedy of dying young my life ended on a good note. I am dying in peace after settling all my earthly problems and winning forgiveness from the people that I had hurt. I am not happy that I am dying but I do have peace of mind. I accept the inevitable because, as we all know, in life all things do come to an end. So is this new life which I have thoroughly enjoyed for two years before my departure.

"When I first contracted the virus I was shocked and lamented the tragic fate that lay ahead of me. I was overwhelmed by the fact that a successful soccer player who had become a successful politician was about to face death. But when the medicines I was taking seemed to work I tried to assume that I would be spared. This assumption grew stronger when Misalie Jr. moved in with us. The reprieve which lasted two years was mostly joyous. But when I finally developed the disease my frustration returned. It was, however, no longer a frustration over my shattered life because I had succeeded in putting my life together. It was a frustration over the fact that I was leaving behind a son who will grow up without the love and guidance of a father. It was a frustration over the fact that I was leaving behind a loving wife and parents who had helped me put my life together. But when my pain and suffering increased dramatically all my frustration disappeared. I abandoned that mental struggle to stay longer and continue enjoying what this life has to offer. I accepted my death. This is what happens to man in the aging process. As he ages, there are certain pleasures he gives up, some voluntarily but others involuntarily. Nature prepares him for death. But it is not nature alone that enabled me to accept my death. Other factors contributed to the resolution of my grief. The first was the birth of Misalie, Jr. His coming into this world helped me resolve my grief just as it helped Rosalyn resolve hers. I too will die knowing that I gave a precious gift to someone I have wronged. The other factors are my faith in God and the love of my family. I am leaving with the knowledge that my extended family will work hand-in-hand with Satta in raising my child. My thanks to all of you for your love, friendship and kindness. I have already personally thanked Satta. May God bless you all."

Satta and Judith were in tears. The others sat in sadness not knowing how to react. But soon Rev. Lamboi took over.

"Let us stand up and pray," he said quietly.

They all held hands while the pastor prayed for about ten minutes. When he finished, others prayed too. The pastor then read some Bible verses and interpreted them. Distributing the hymnals he had brought with him, they all sang some songs. The meeting ended with a benediction.

The following day, Satta did not go to work. She accompanied her husband to the hospital where he was admitted. He died three months later. Immediately after the husband's death Judith suggested that Satta go through the purification ceremony for women who lose their first husbands.

"Satta, since Misalie was your first husband you should be cleansed in accordance with our custom," she said. "This cleansing will set you free and make it proper for you to remarry later. When you were experiencing marital problems, you could not get the help you needed in the city. You yourself told me that the corrupt life of the city made it impossible for you to solve your problems and experience peaceful life. You were virtually driven crazy by all the information you received about your husband's many girlfriends. It was your decision to return to your village to identify with your people and share their simple and unsophisticated way of life that helped you to experience peace. From that time on you continued to consult with relatives in Palahun about your marital problems and problems related to your childlessness and your husband's disease. As time went on matters improved. When you got the child, you went to the village so that relatives could share your joy. It is now proper and fitting for you to complete the process of reconciliation with your people by undergoing our traditional purification ceremony. This ceremony is common but in your particular case it is a way of demonstrating your willingness to continue participating in the simple ways of life that you had always yearned for."

"Mother, I want to go through this ceremony and also continue communicating with my people," said Satta. "What happens in the city is vital to my professional future; but the link with my people is vital to my mental health."

When Satta arrived in Tilasa where her husband's body was laid for public viewing, she was handed over to three elderly women and confined to a particular room where she stayed until the cleansing ceremony. She left the room only when she had to and avoided staying outside any longer than was necessary. It was there that she received all her visitors. The only exception was the day the husband was buried. She had to leave the room to attend the burial and meet the guests that came to attend it.

These included the president of the country, politicians and many important people. It was a very busy day since food and drinks were served to all the guests. After the departure of the guests Satta returned to her room.

The third and seventh day ceremonies were both big occasions. It was on the eve of the seventh day ceremony that Satta's cleansing ceremony took place. Musu was present during the performance of this rite.

Early the following morning she was taken to a stream for one more important rite - confession of whatever wrongs she had done to her husband while he was alive. She then bathed and put on a white dress. After the prayers and the expression of many good wishes she returned to the town in the company of the women in charge of the ceremony. She was now completely cleansed and could remarry whenever she wanted to.

The fortieth day ceremony on behalf of the deceased husband was one of the biggest ever to be held in the town. It included traditional dances as well as a formal, western-style reception. After all the outpouring of grief it was appropriate at this time to celebrate life.

The months that followed were not very easy for Satta. She missed her husband and wept from time to time. Alice and Judith visited often to comfort her. Her greatest joy was still her child who was growing up well. Since Memuna was now enrolled in a special program for older children, the senior maid took care of him during the day. In the mornings this lady would take him to the day-care center and pick him up at noon. Memuna took over after school.

About a year and a half after the husband's death, Judith received one of the distinguished service awards from her department. This award came as a surprise. The ceremony which was held in the town hall was attended by important people including politicians. The following day, Satta, who felt that that was the best time to do something special for her mother, took her to the Golden Complex for an evening of entertainment. It was a way of thanking her for her help and devotion.

They set out for the Complex at about four in the afternoon. They were talking about the award and the mother's plan to retire in a few years when a big billboard with the message "Welcome to the Golden Complex" appeared. The motto of the complex, "Excellence in Tourism", was written under the welcome message. On the opposite side of the street was another billboard with several portraits. One was a very colorful picture of the Complex and the kinds of entertainment it offered to its guests. For Satta these signboards did bring some memories of her husband but she did not dwell on them. She drove through the main gate and headed for the parking lot. Although this was not the first time that both women were visiting the place it looked different than when they were there for its inauguration. The Complex had since then been expanded.

It was during their delicious dinner that the mother brought up a topic that she had hitherto hesitated to discuss with her daughter.

"Satta, I did admire your devotion to your husband when he was alive," she said. "Many women would have easily abandoned him because of his illness and his conduct. But you did not. You proved to be a decent and loving wife. I am curious however as to whether you ever plan to remarry? This is something you have never said anything about."

"Yes, mother, I intend to marry again some day," she replied. "I am however just a bit cautious because the men I have met so far seem to be more interested in themselves."

"Are you currently in a relationship that I am unaware of?"

"No, I am not," replied Satta. "However, I am willing to go

out with any suitable gentleman that interests me. This is for me a period of observation. In any case, I definitely plan to remarry."

"I am glad to hear from your own lips that you are willing to remarry," said the mother, patting the daughter on the back. "That is all I wanted to know. I was under the impression that you had decided to remain single for the rest of your life. Such a decision would have broken my heart. It's a great feeling to learn that Misalie Jr. will likely have some playmates."

"Mother, thank you for your concern," said Satta with a smile. "I promise you that I will definitely remarry when the opportunity arises."